PRAISE FOR

"Garmadon... is an exciting new foray into the expansive world of LEGO® NINJAGO®, exploring new facets of the world, and its rich tapestry of characters."
-JAY'S BRICK BLOG

"Tri Vuong's writing and art make this new addition to the Ninjago universe fun and compelling. Longtime LEGO fans and new readers will both get a kick out of this exciting adventure."
-CBR

"Vuong uses everything that has come before effectively and in a way that's not overwhelming for new readers. It's very new reader friendly in fact... The comic feels visually perfect for its audience no matter their age."
-GRAPHIC POLICY

"The highlight of Vuong's work on this comic is easily the art. It's reminiscent of Stan Sakai with patient storytelling, and it also features multiple references to Kurosawa. Simply put, this is a story that plays well visually."
-COMICS BOOKCASE

"For NINJAGO fans it really is an essential read, adding to the already rich history of the much loved LEGO theme."
-BRICKS FANZ

"Writer/artist Tri Vuong truly is a master builder, expanding upon the foundation of the Ninjago TV series and adding new layers to one of its most complex characters."

-GEEK'D OUT

"Tri Vuong has done an impeccable job of capturing the ever-evolving animation of LEGO NINJAGO with backgrounds and artwork, representing the action and beauty of the original LEGO theme's animated show and sets well."

-BRICK FANATICS

"An all-ages adventure that's exciting, approachable, and fun to read."

-LOTUSLAND COMICS

"I fell in love with this after the first two pages... We get to continue the canon story in a way that's different from the TV and media that we usually get to see... I absolutely loved it."

-MASTERS OF BRICKJITZU

"Fantastic! I can't believe how much fun this was."

-COMIC BOOK CLUB

"LEGO NINJAGO GARMADON... retains the Ninjago franchise's charm with action and worldbuilding."

-MONKEYS FIGHTING ROBOTS

Dedicated to Dad
for getting me my first LEGO set.

TRI VUONG

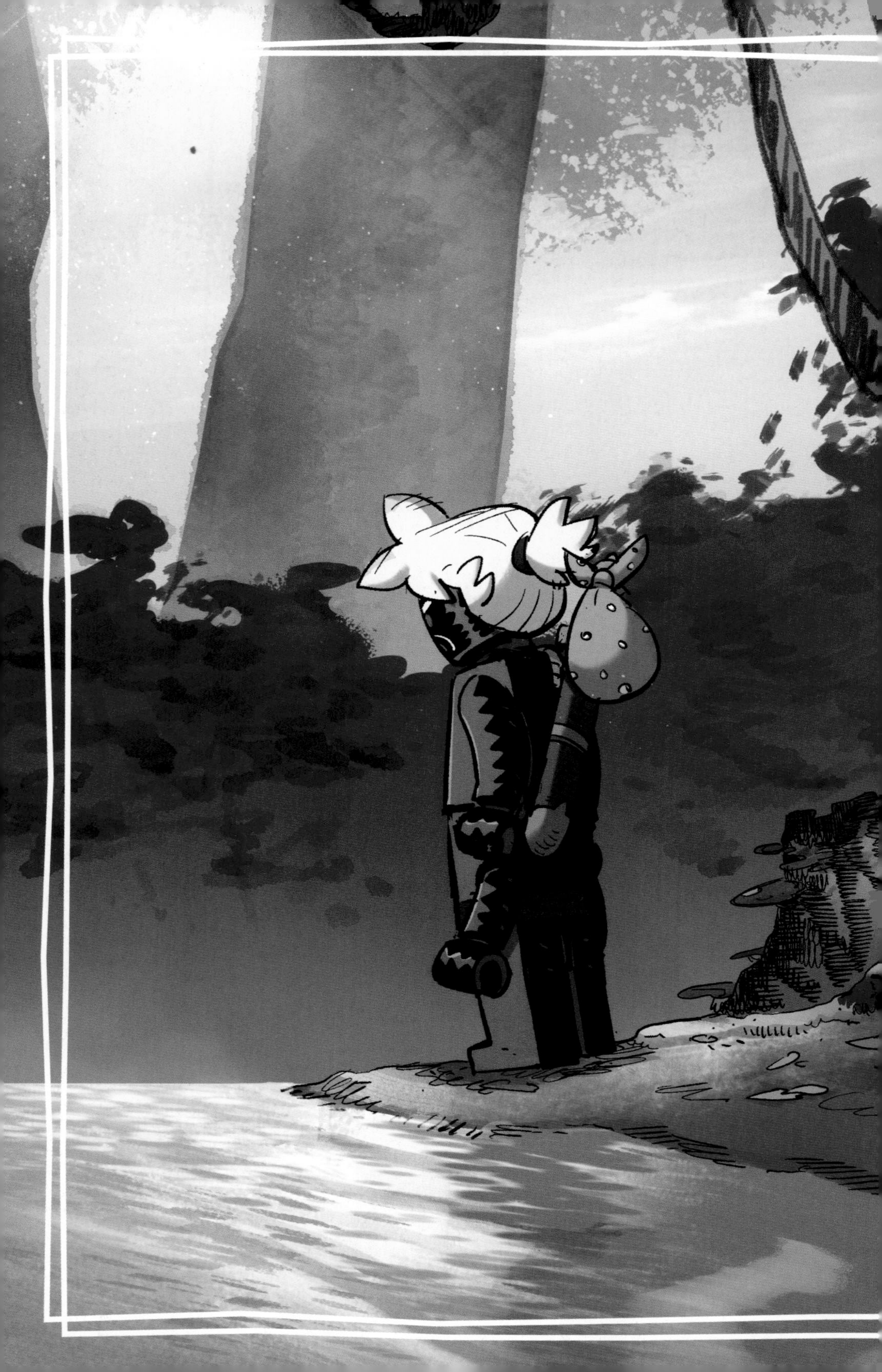

LEGO NINJAGO

GARMADON

TRI VUONG
WRITER, ARTIST

ANNALISA LEONI
COLORIST

RUS WOOTON
LETTERER

™

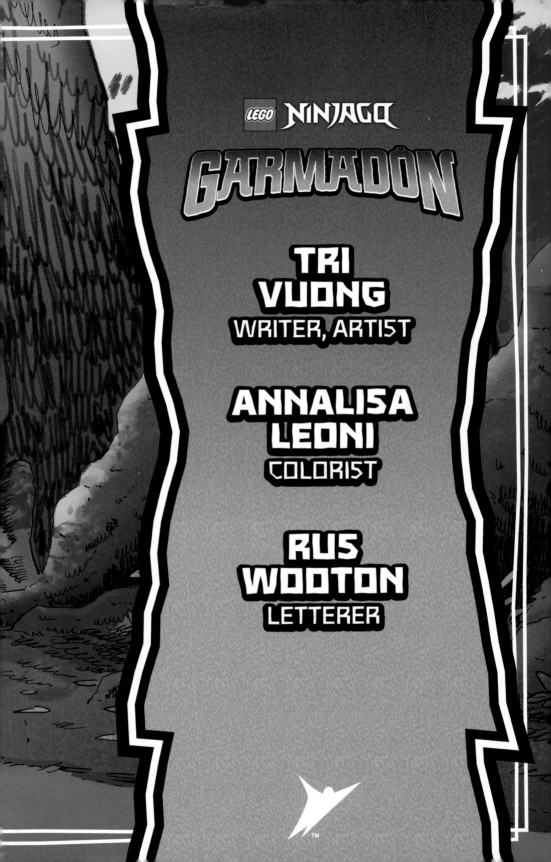

CHAPTER 1
TWO MOON VILLAGE

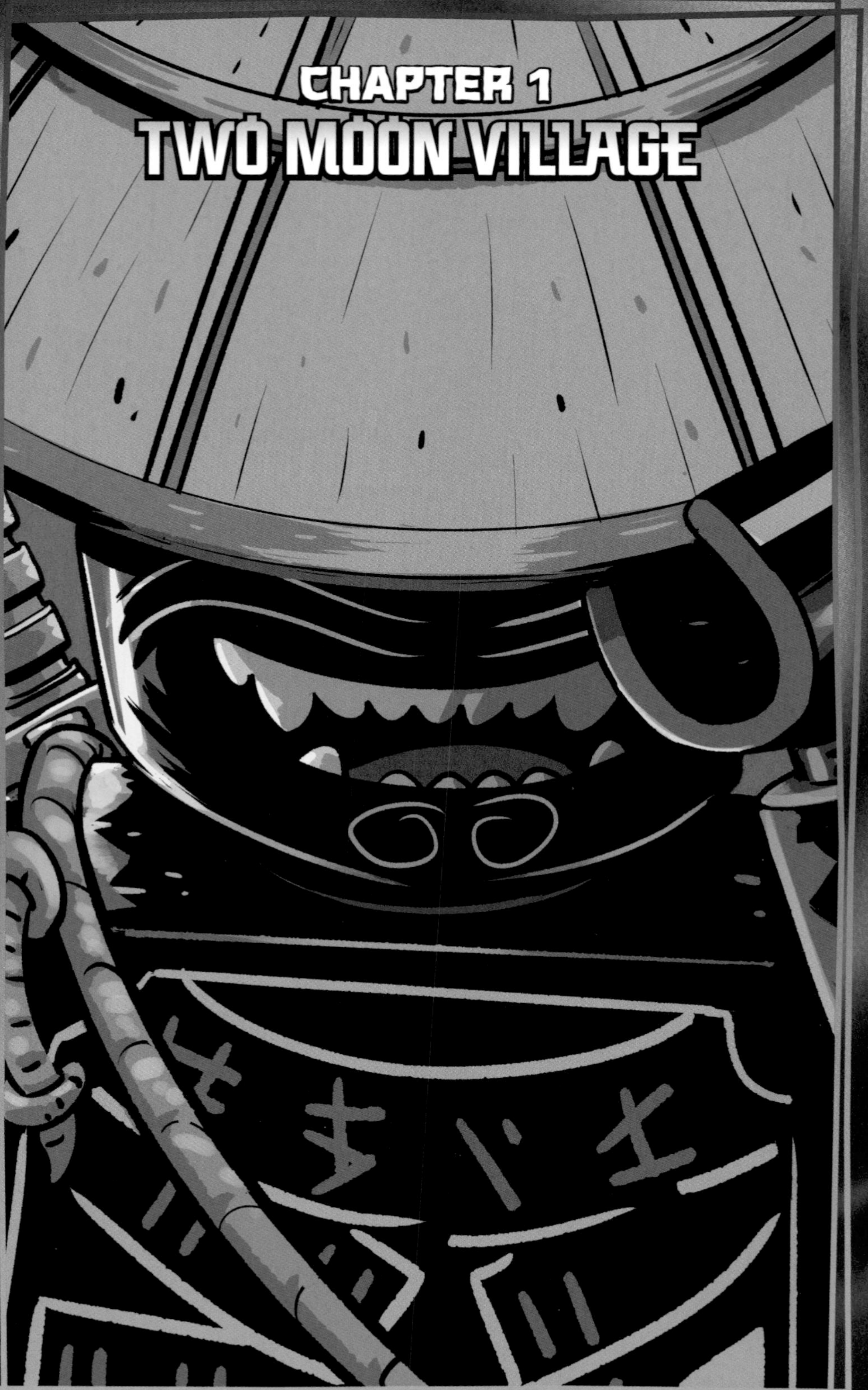

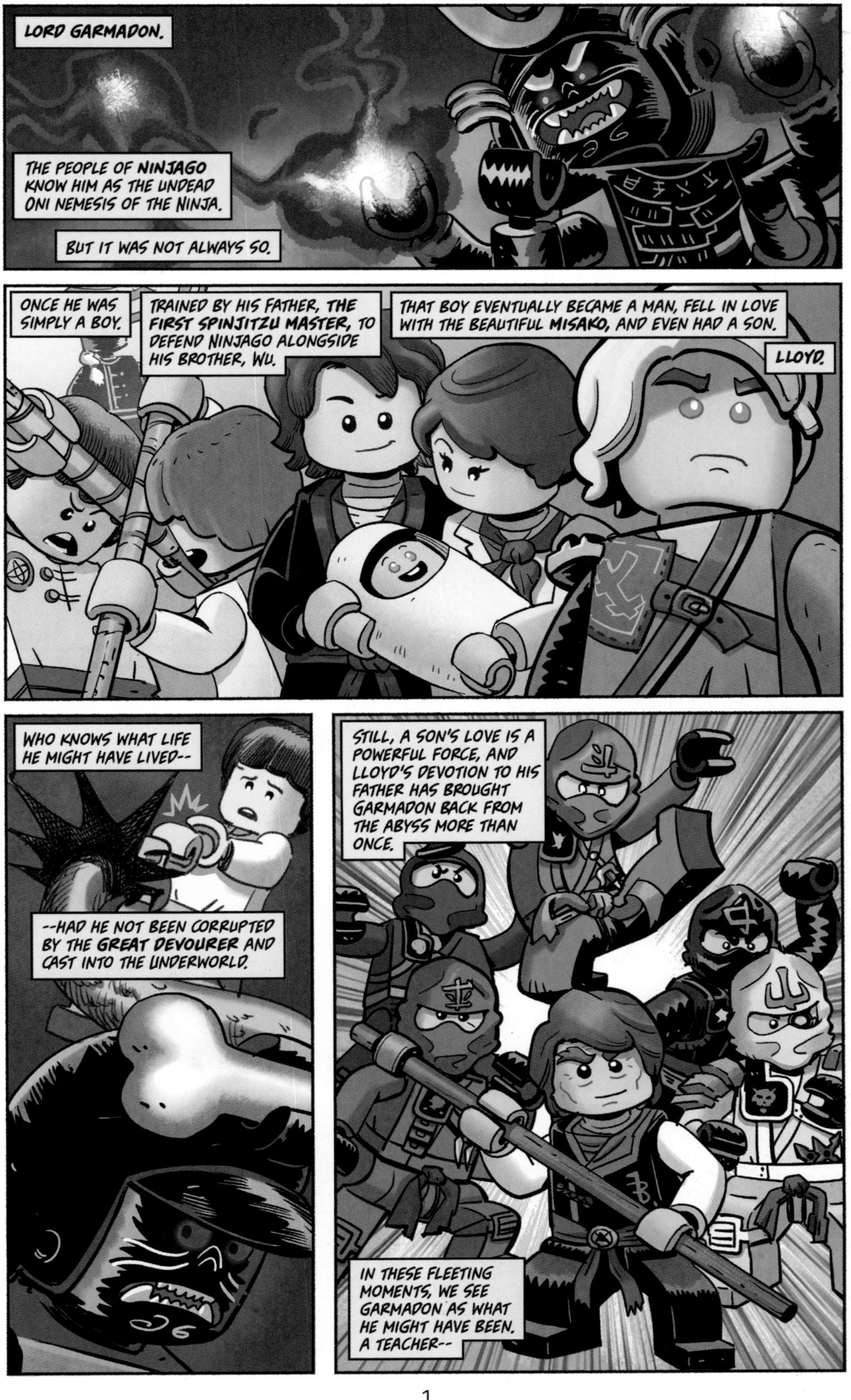

LORD GARMADON.
THE PEOPLE OF NINJAGO KNOW HIM AS THE UNDEAD ONI NEMESIS OF THE NINJA.
BUT IT WAS NOT ALWAYS SO.
ONCE HE WAS SIMPLY A BOY.
TRAINED BY HIS FATHER, THE FIRST SPINJITZU MASTER, TO DEFEND NINJAGO ALONGSIDE HIS BROTHER, WU.
THAT BOY EVENTUALLY BECAME A MAN, FELL IN LOVE WITH THE BEAUTIFUL MISAKO, AND EVEN HAD A SON.
LLOYD.
WHO KNOWS WHAT LIFE HE MIGHT HAVE LIVED--
--HAD HE NOT BEEN CORRUPTED BY THE GREAT DEVOURER AND CAST INTO THE UNDERWORLD.
STILL, A SON'S LOVE IS A POWERFUL FORCE, AND LLOYD'S DEVOTION TO HIS FATHER HAS BROUGHT GARMADON BACK FROM THE ABYSS MORE THAN ONCE.
IN THESE FLEETING MOMENTS, WE SEE GARMADON AS WHAT HE MIGHT HAVE BEEN. A TEACHER--

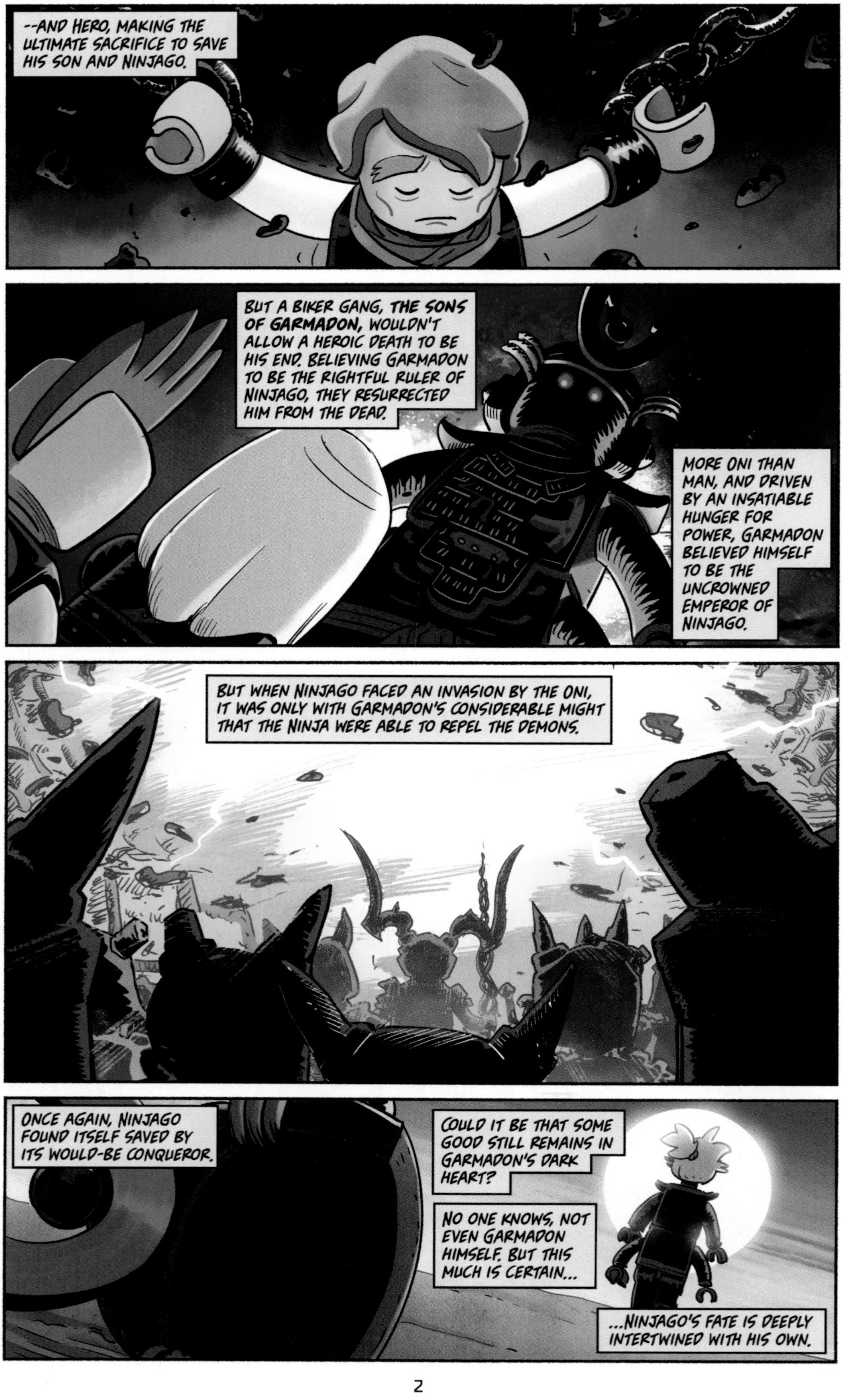
--AND HERO, MAKING THE ULTIMATE SACRIFICE TO SAVE HIS SON AND NINJAGO.
BUT A BIKER GANG, **THE SONS OF GARMADON,** WOULDN'T ALLOW A HEROIC DEATH TO BE HIS END. BELIEVING GARMADON TO BE THE RIGHTFUL RULER OF NINJAGO, THEY RESURRECTED HIM FROM THE DEAD.
MORE ONI THAN MAN, AND DRIVEN BY AN INSATIABLE HUNGER FOR POWER, GARMADON BELIEVED HIMSELF TO BE THE UNCROWNED EMPEROR OF NINJAGO.
BUT WHEN NINJAGO FACED AN INVASION BY THE ONI, IT WAS ONLY WITH GARMADON'S CONSIDERABLE MIGHT THAT THE NINJA WERE ABLE TO REPEL THE DEMONS.
ONCE AGAIN, NINJAGO FOUND ITSELF SAVED BY ITS WOULD-BE CONQUEROR.
COULD IT BE THAT SOME GOOD STILL REMAINS IN GARMADON'S DARK HEART?
NO ONE KNOWS, NOT EVEN GARMADON HIMSELF. BUT THIS MUCH IS CERTAIN...
...NINJAGO'S FATE IS DEEPLY INTERTWINED WITH HIS OWN.

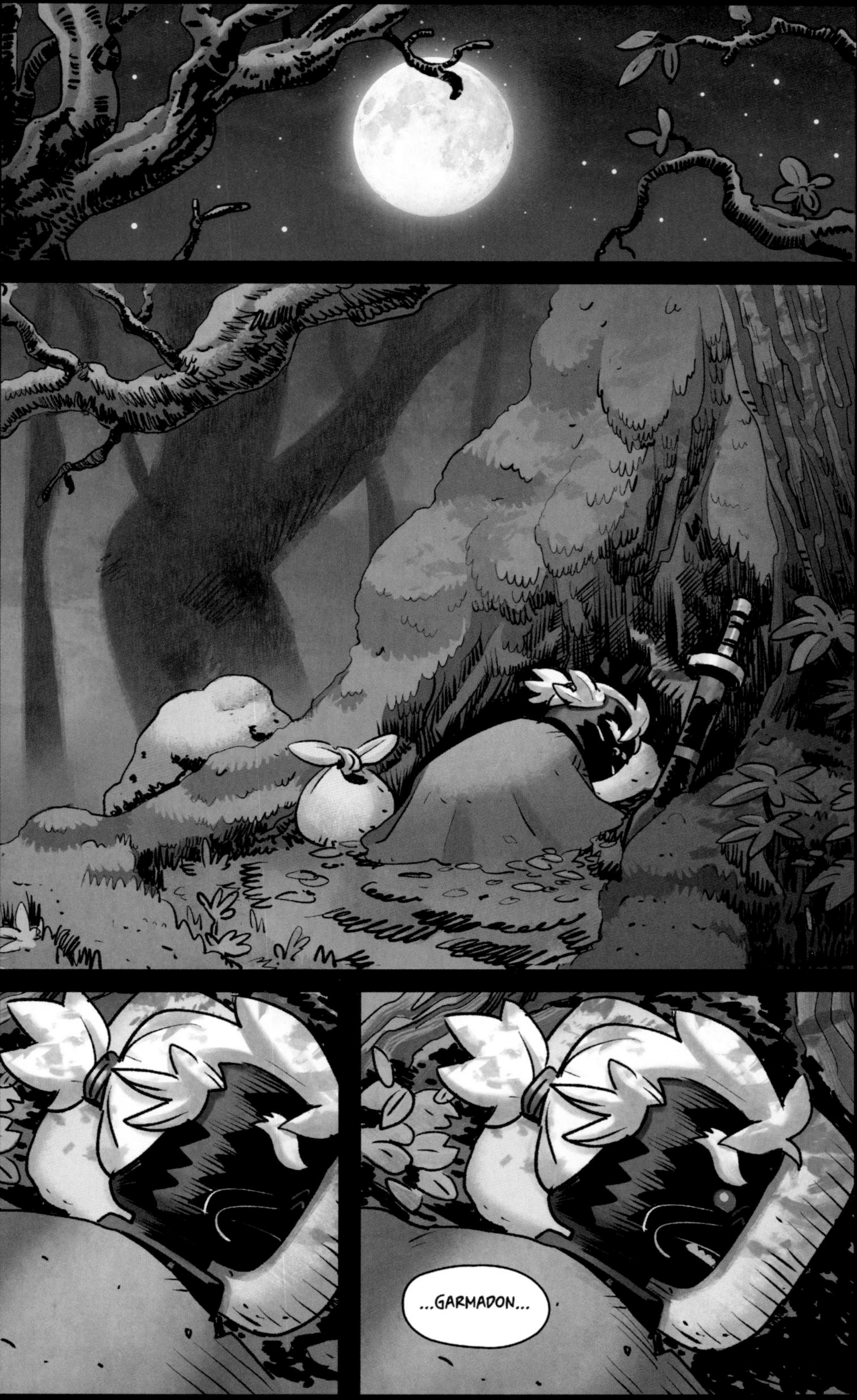
...GARMADON...

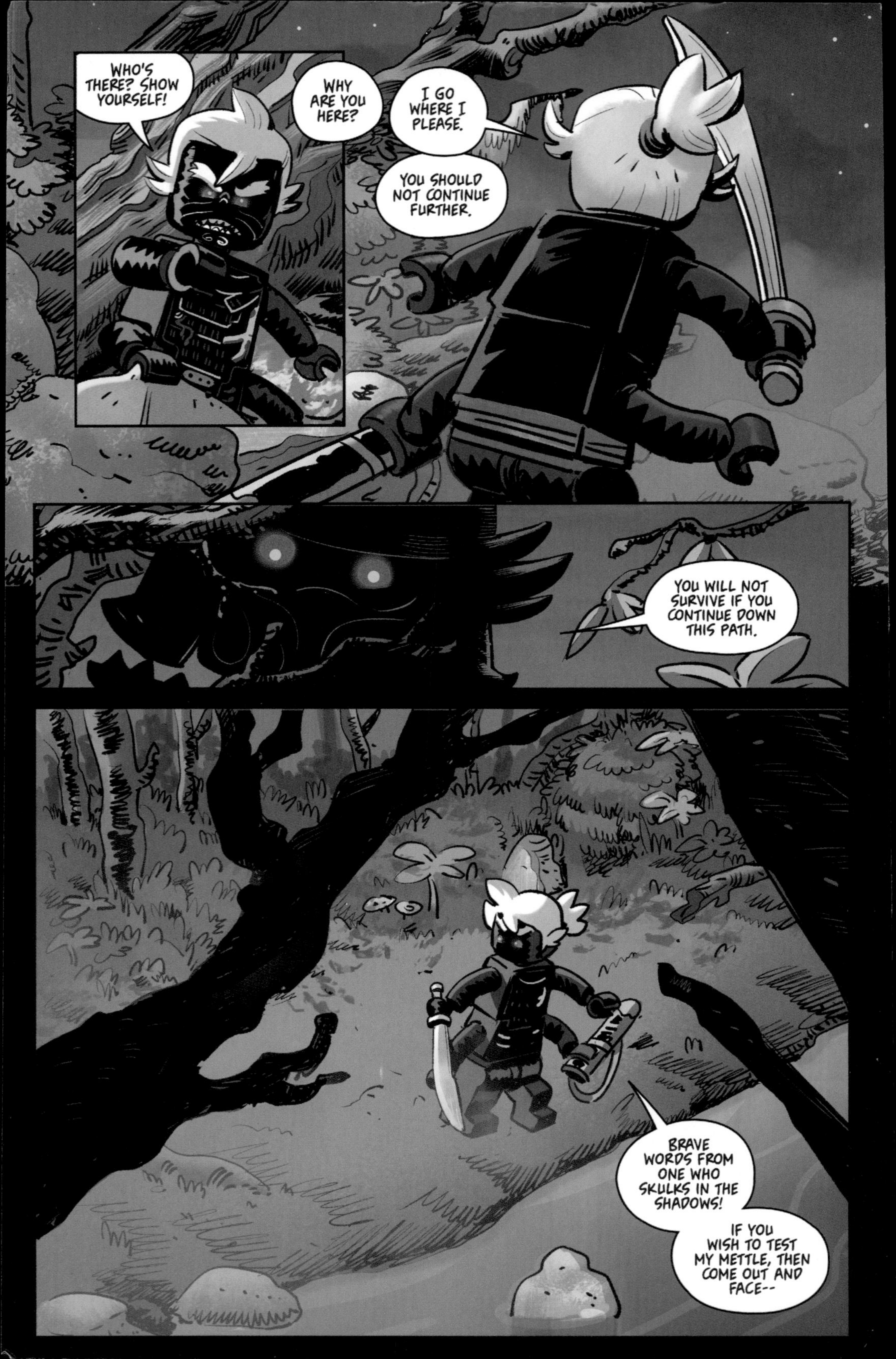
WHO'S THERE? SHOW YOURSELF!
WHY ARE YOU HERE?
I GO WHERE I PLEASE.
YOU SHOULD NOT CONTINUE FURTHER.
YOU WILL NOT SURVIVE IF YOU CONTINUE DOWN THIS PATH.
BRAVE WORDS FROM ONE WHO SKULKS IN THE SHADOWS!
IF YOU WISH TO TEST MY METTLE, THEN COME OUT AND FACE--

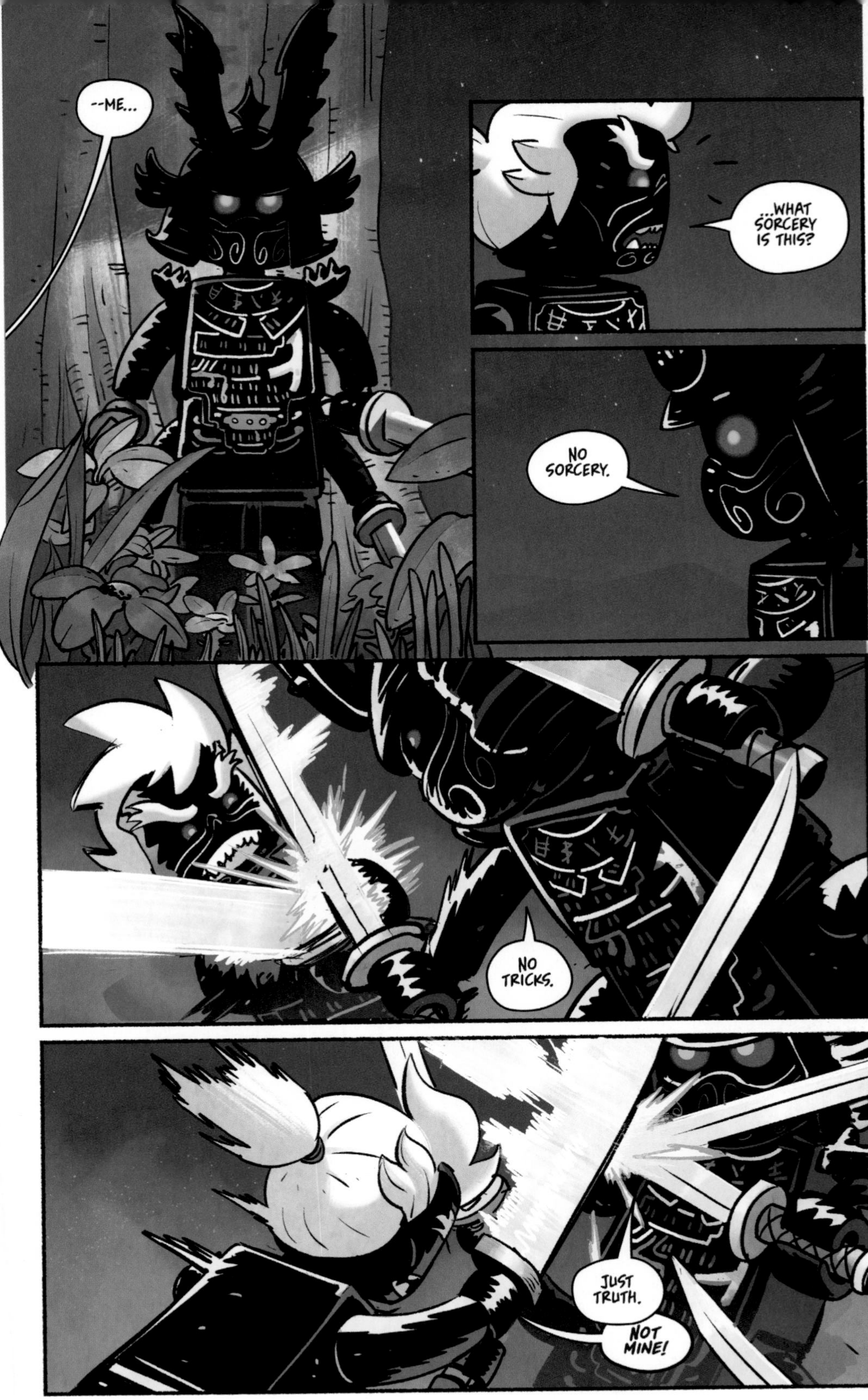
--ME...
...WHAT SORCERY IS THIS?
NO SORCERY.
NO TRICKS.
JUST TRUTH.
NOT MINE!

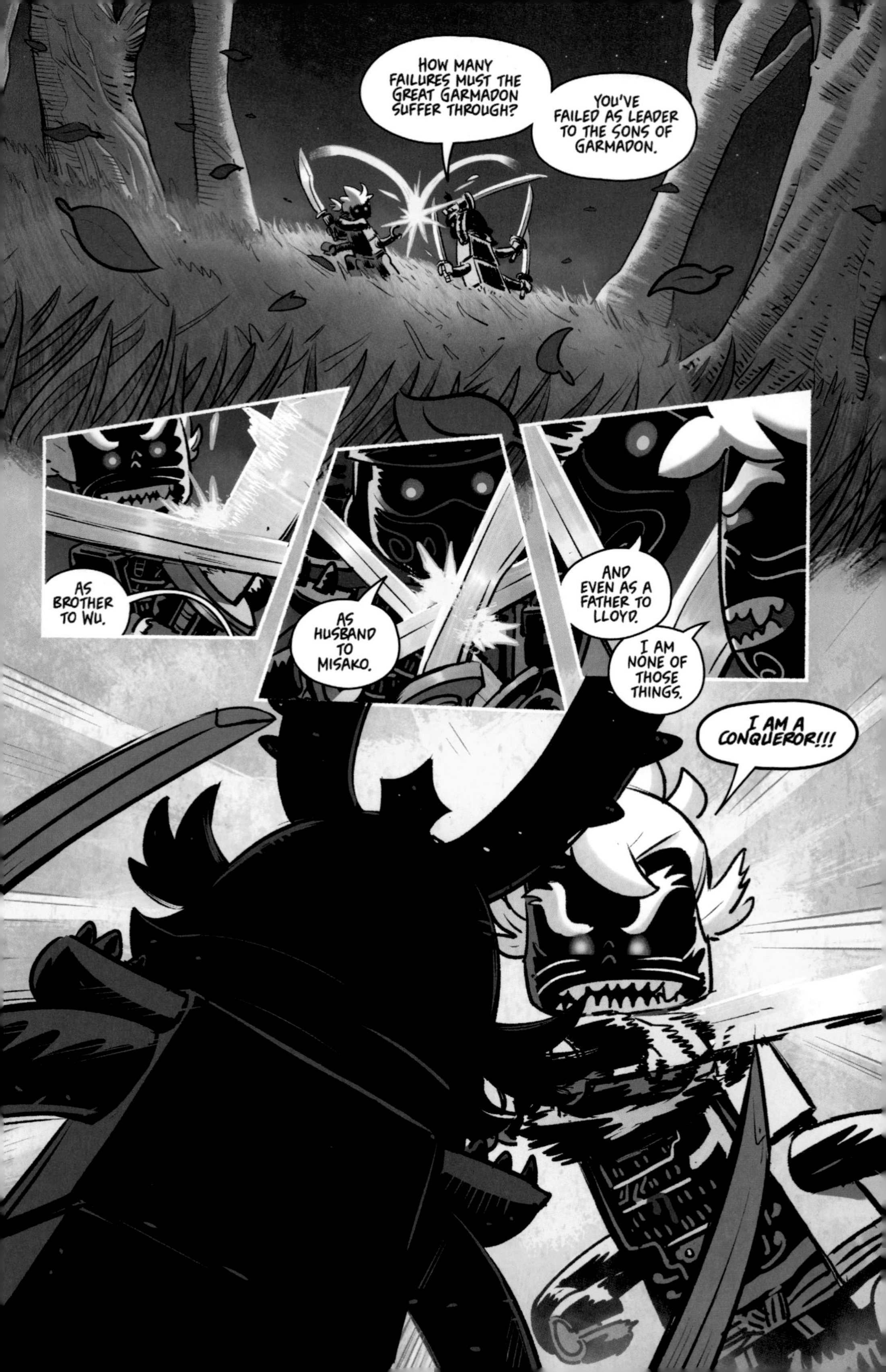
HOW MANY FAILURES MUST THE GREAT GARMADON SUFFER THROUGH?
YOU'VE FAILED AS LEADER TO THE SONS OF GARMADON.
AS BROTHER TO WU.
AS HUSBAND TO MISAKO.
AND EVEN AS A FATHER TO LLOYD.
I AM NONE OF THOSE THINGS.
I AM A CONQUEROR!!!

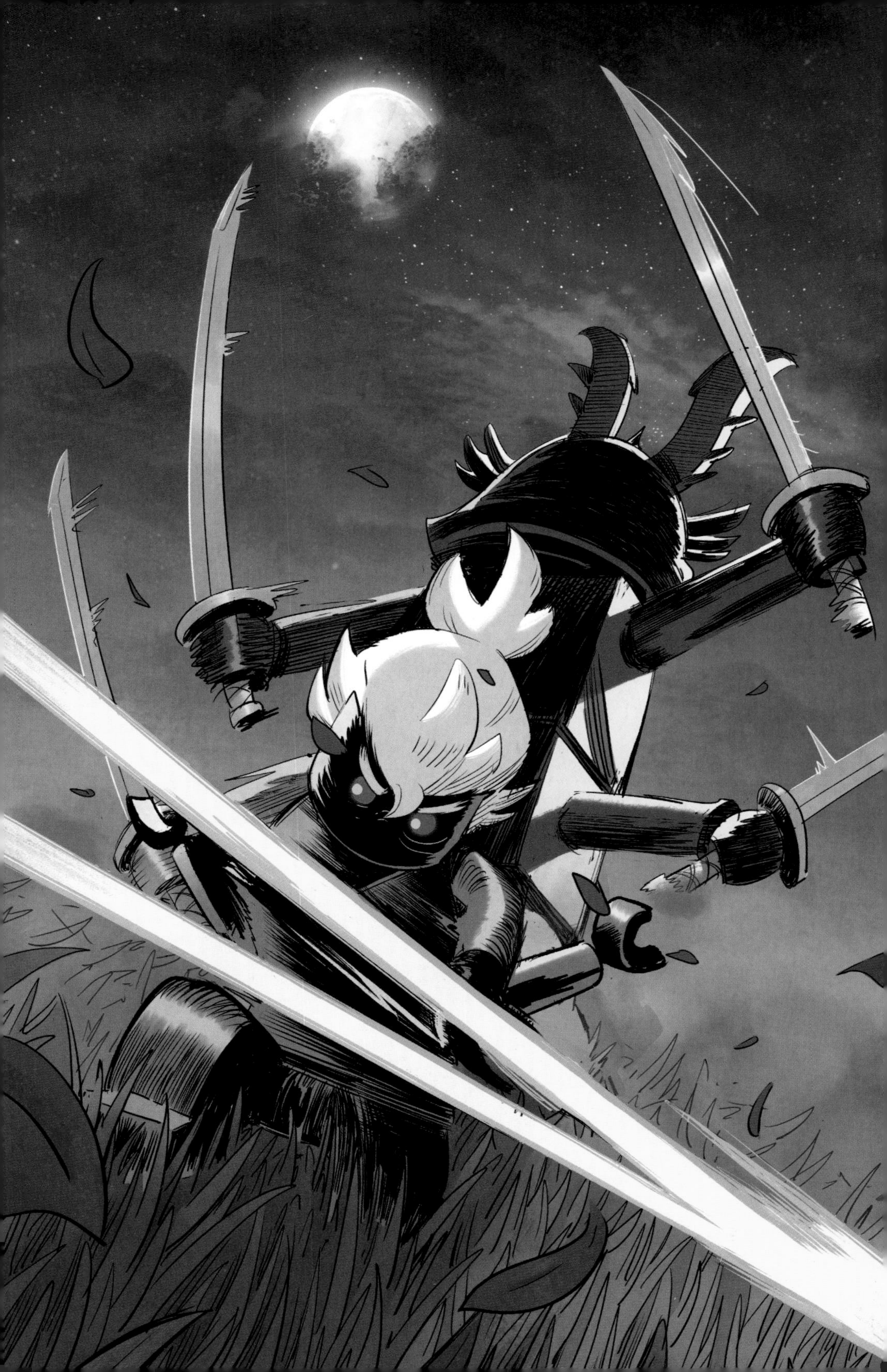

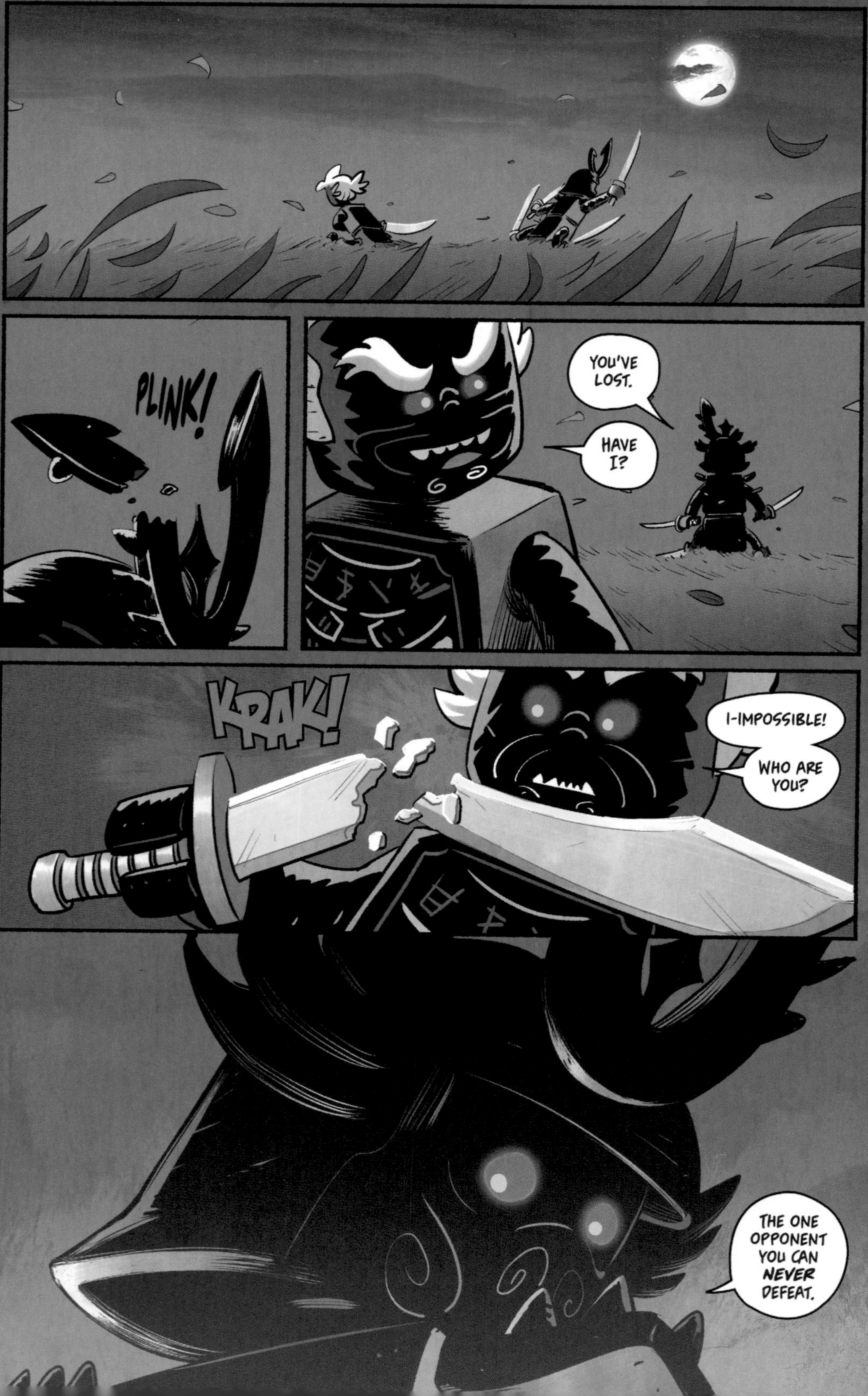
PLINK!
YOU'VE LOST.
HAVE I?
KRAK!
I-IMPOSSIBLE!
WHO ARE YOU?
THE ONE OPPONENT YOU CAN NEVER DEFEAT.

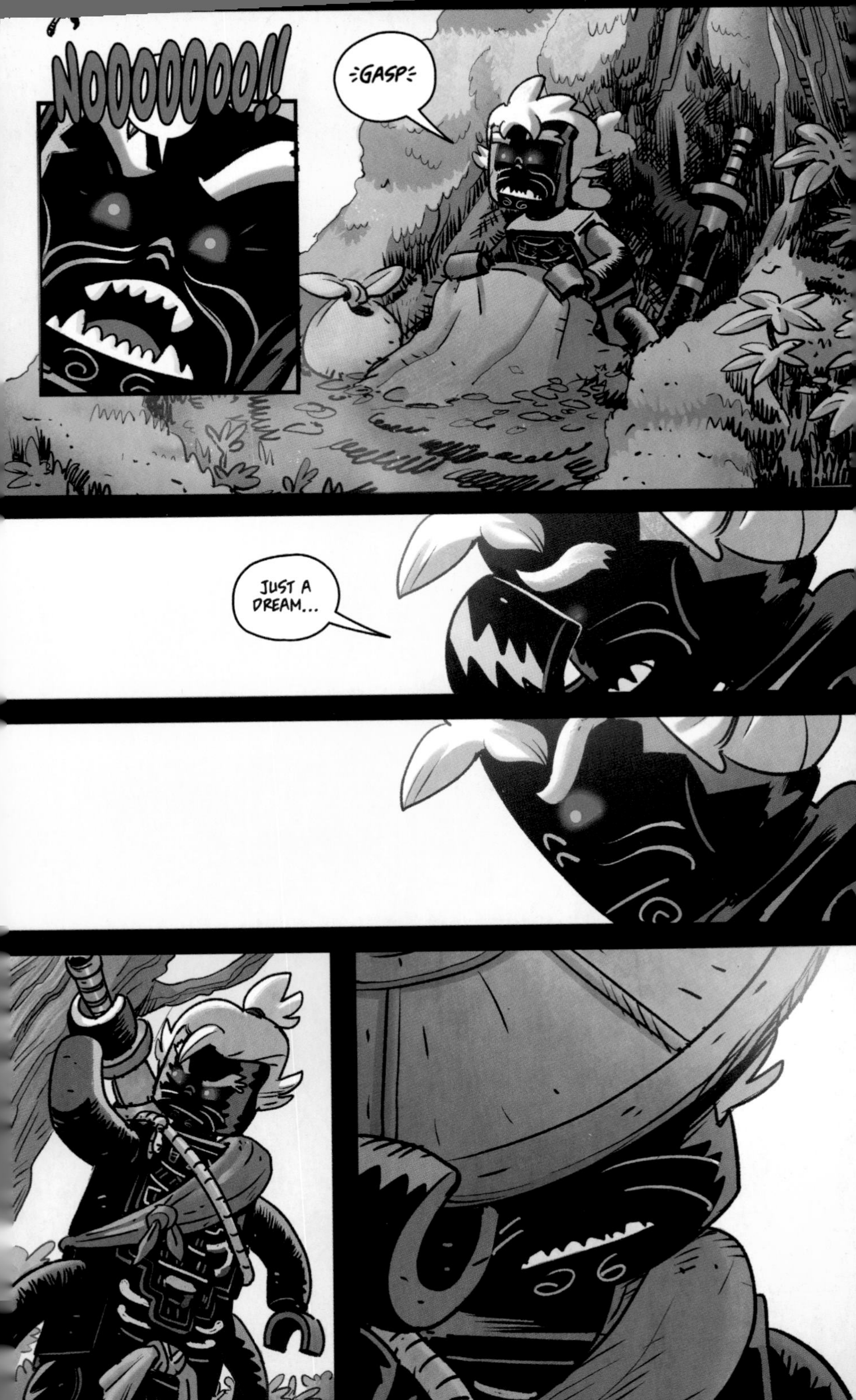
NOOOOOOO!!
GASP
JUST A DREAM...

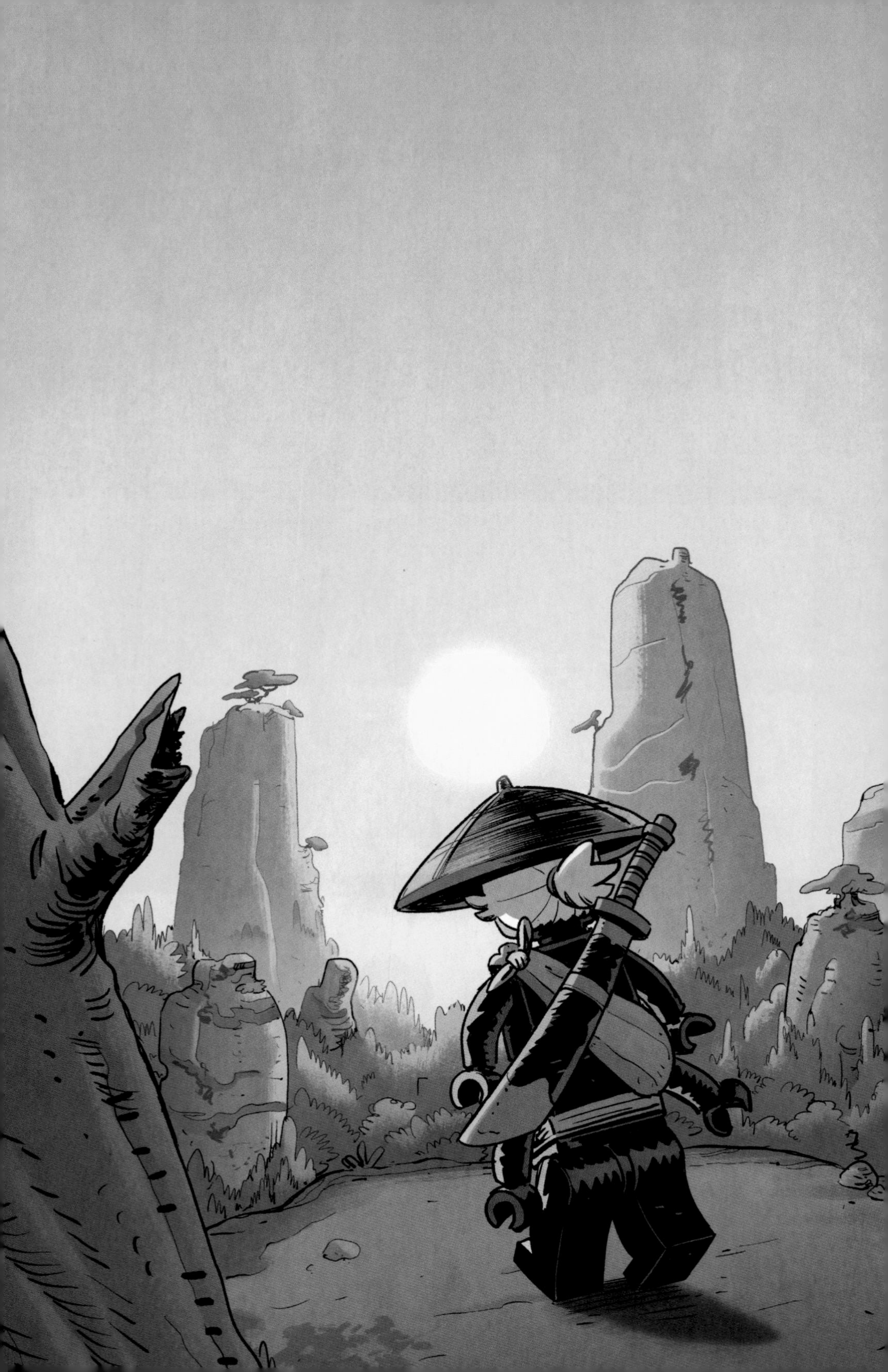

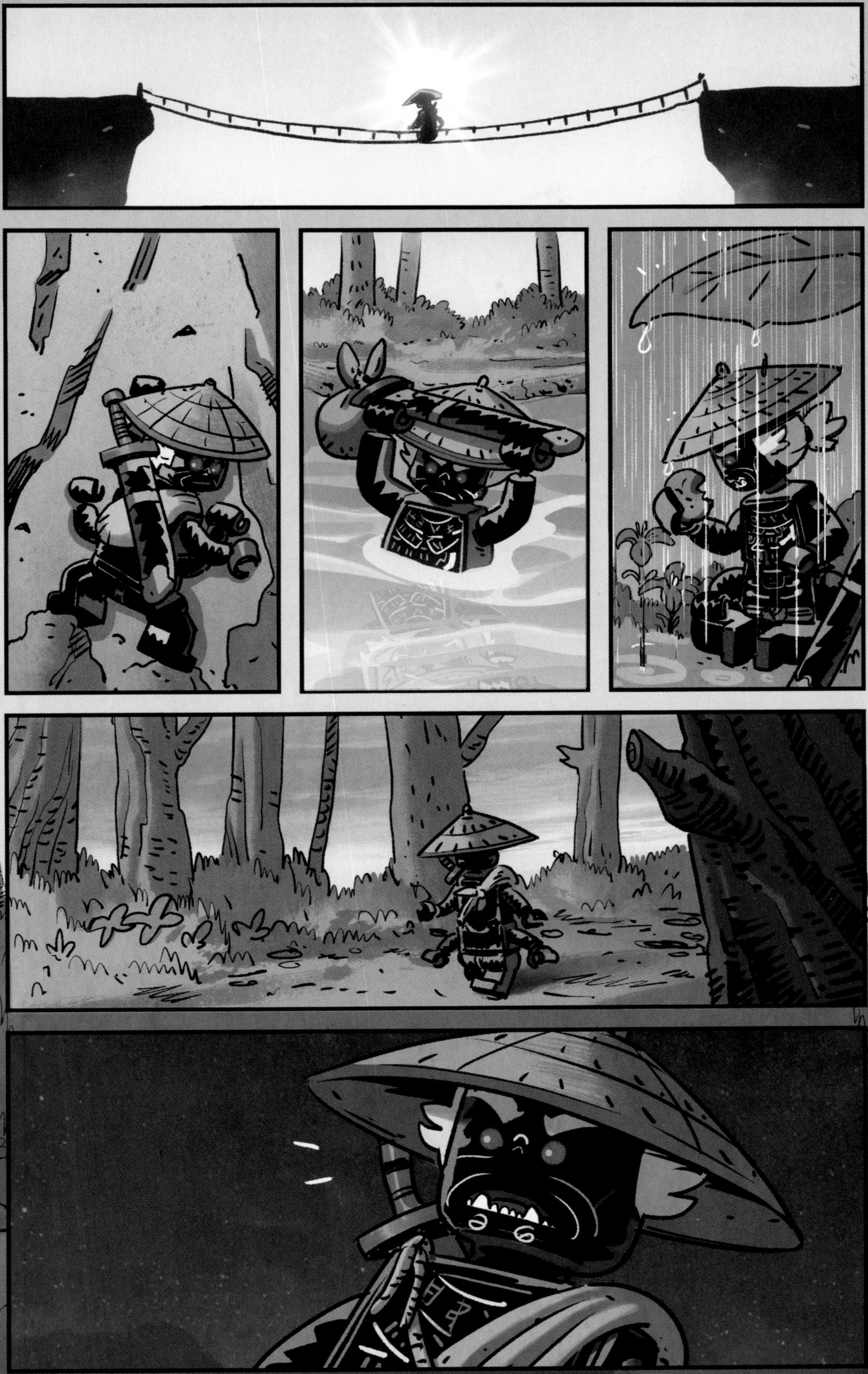

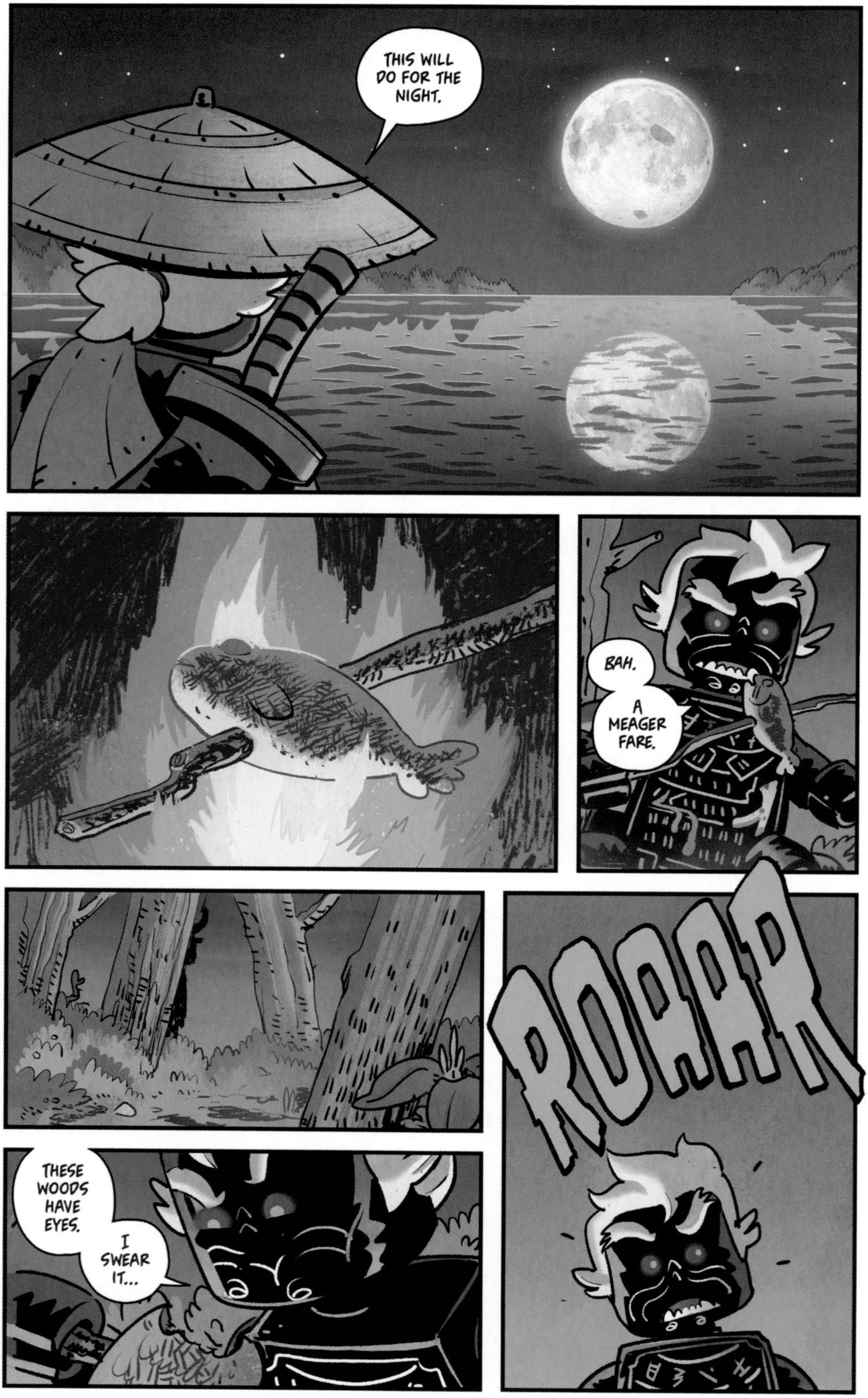

THIS WILL DO FOR THE NIGHT.
BAH.
A MEAGER FARE.
ROOAAR
THESE WOODS HAVE EYES.
I SWEAR IT...

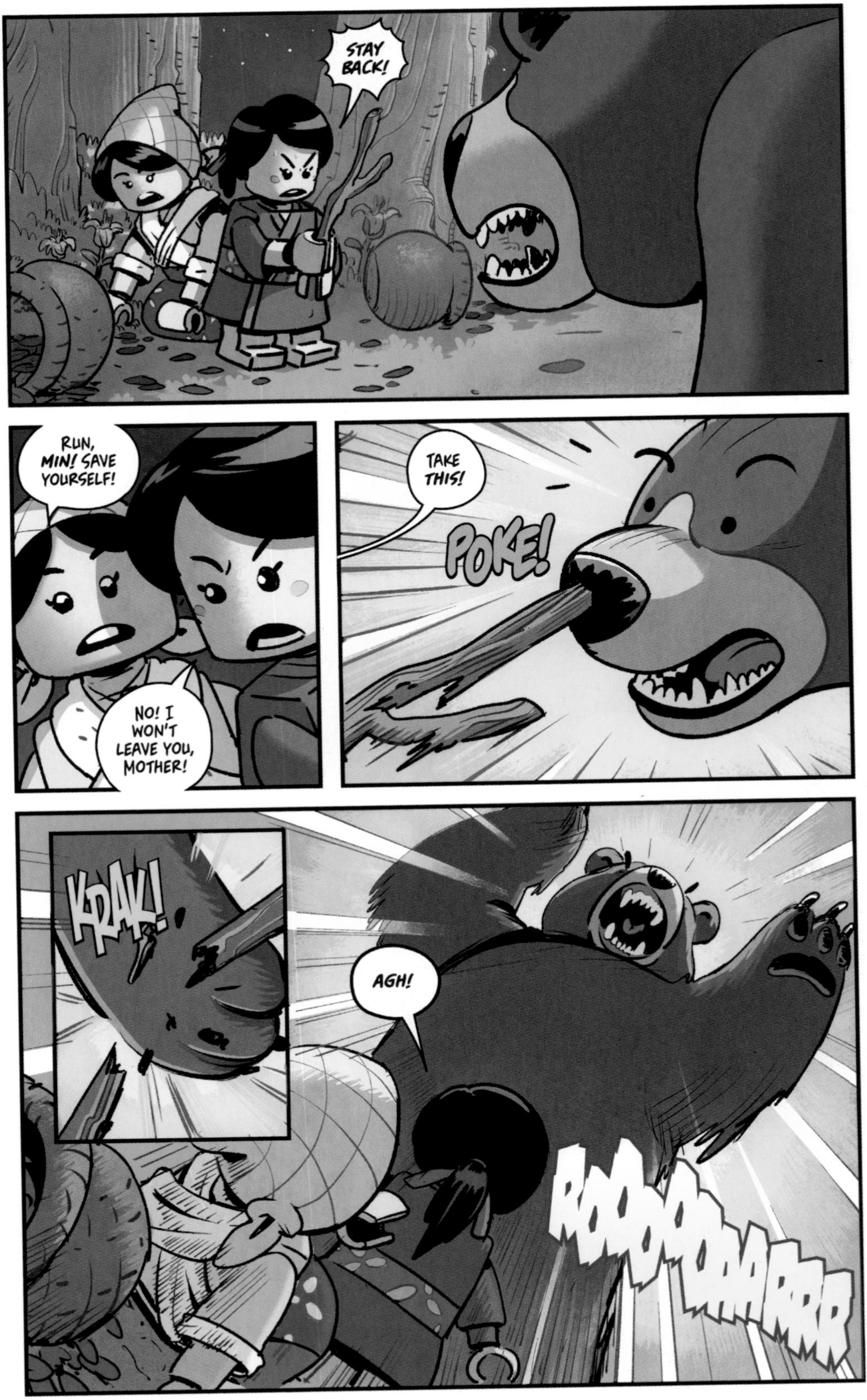
STAY BACK!
RUN, MIN! SAVE YOURSELF!
NO! I WON'T LEAVE YOU, MOTHER!
TAKE THIS!
POKE!
KRAK!
AGH!
ROOOOOAARRRR

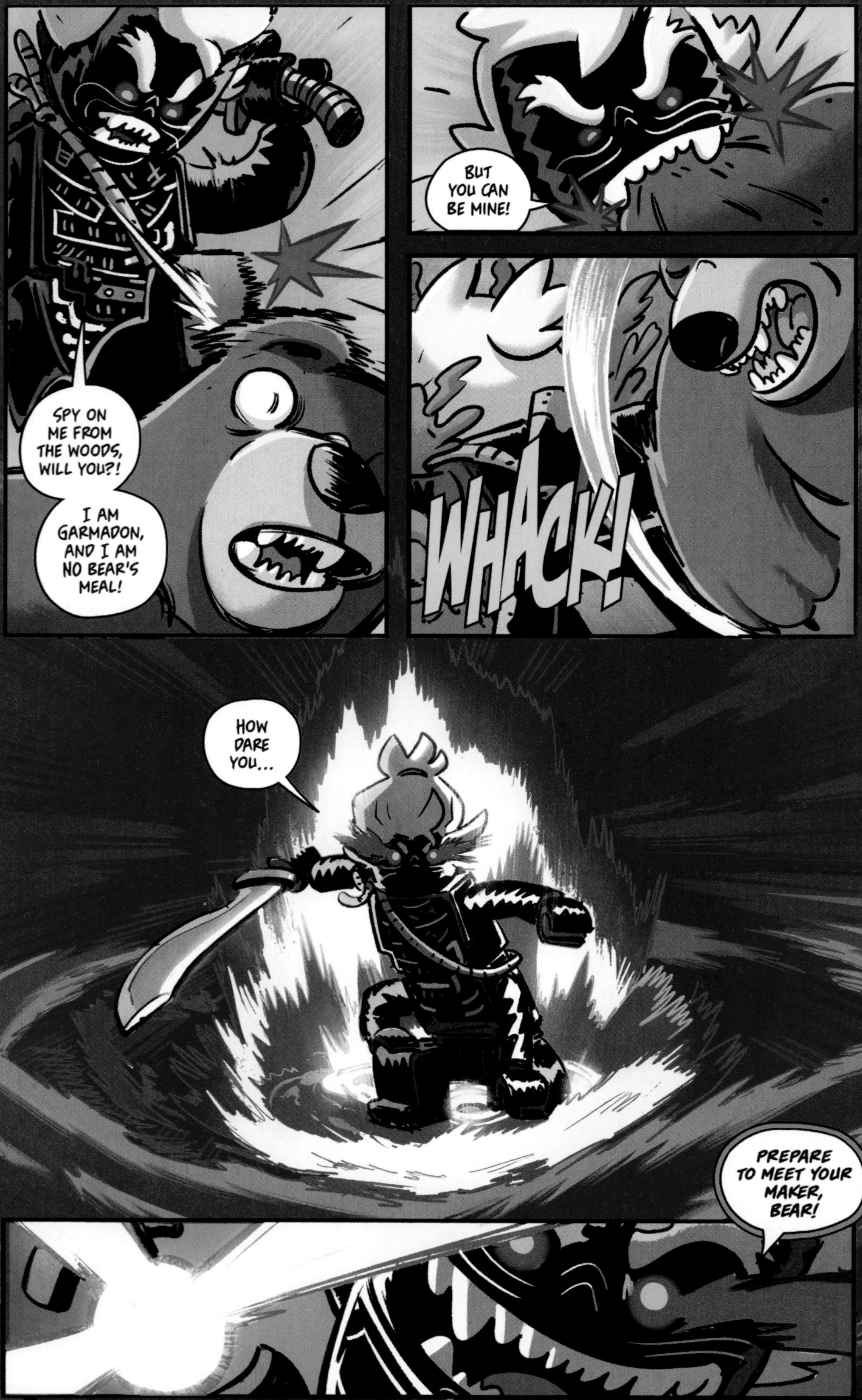

SPY ON ME FROM THE WOODS, WILL YOU?!
I AM GARMADON, AND I AM NO BEAR'S MEAL!
BUT YOU CAN BE MINE!
WHACK!
HOW DARE YOU...
PREPARE TO MEET YOUR MAKER, BEAR!

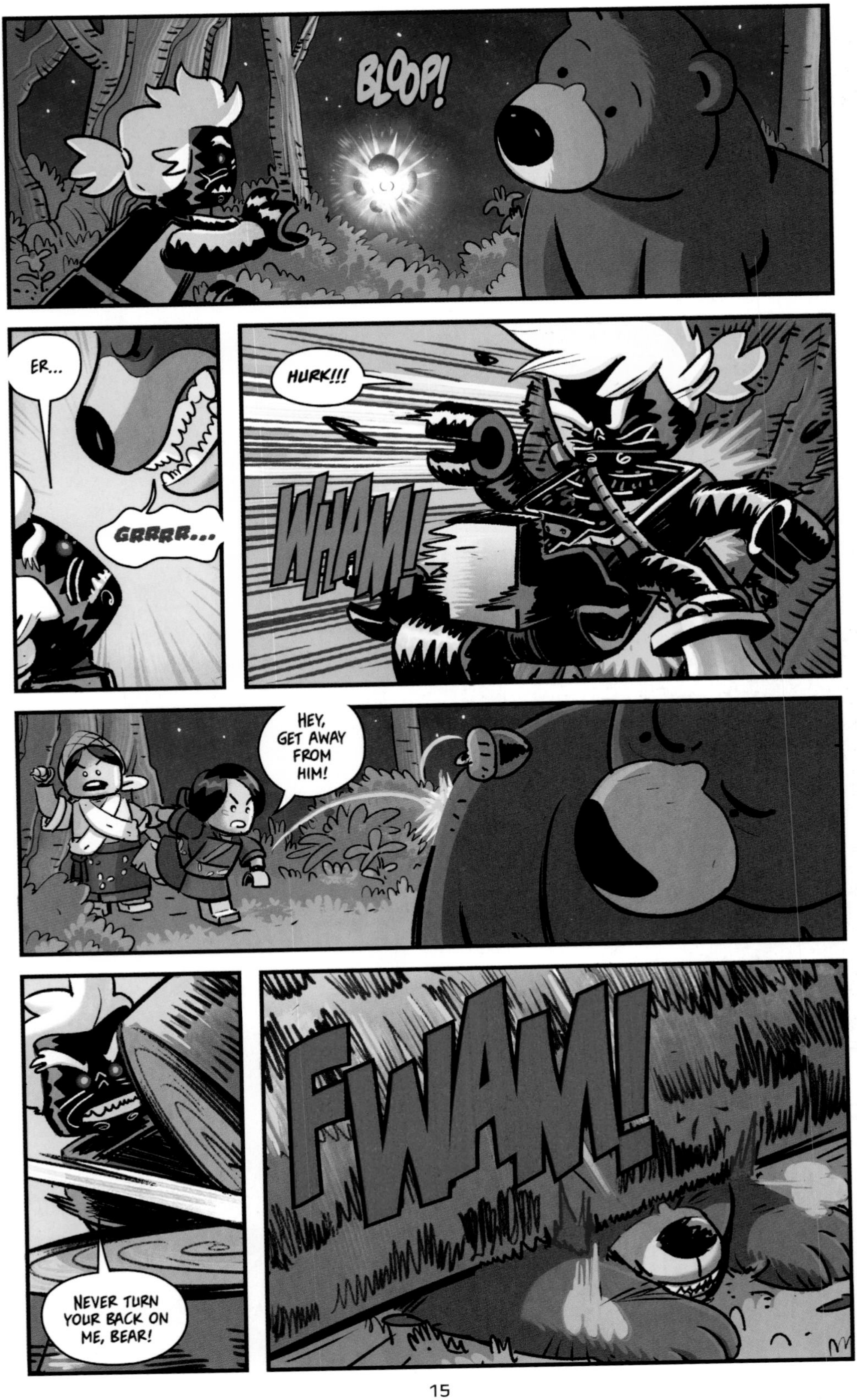
BLOOP!
ER...
GRRRR...
HURK!!!
WHAM!
HEY, GET AWAY FROM HIM!
NEVER TURN YOUR BACK ON ME, BEAR!
FWAM!

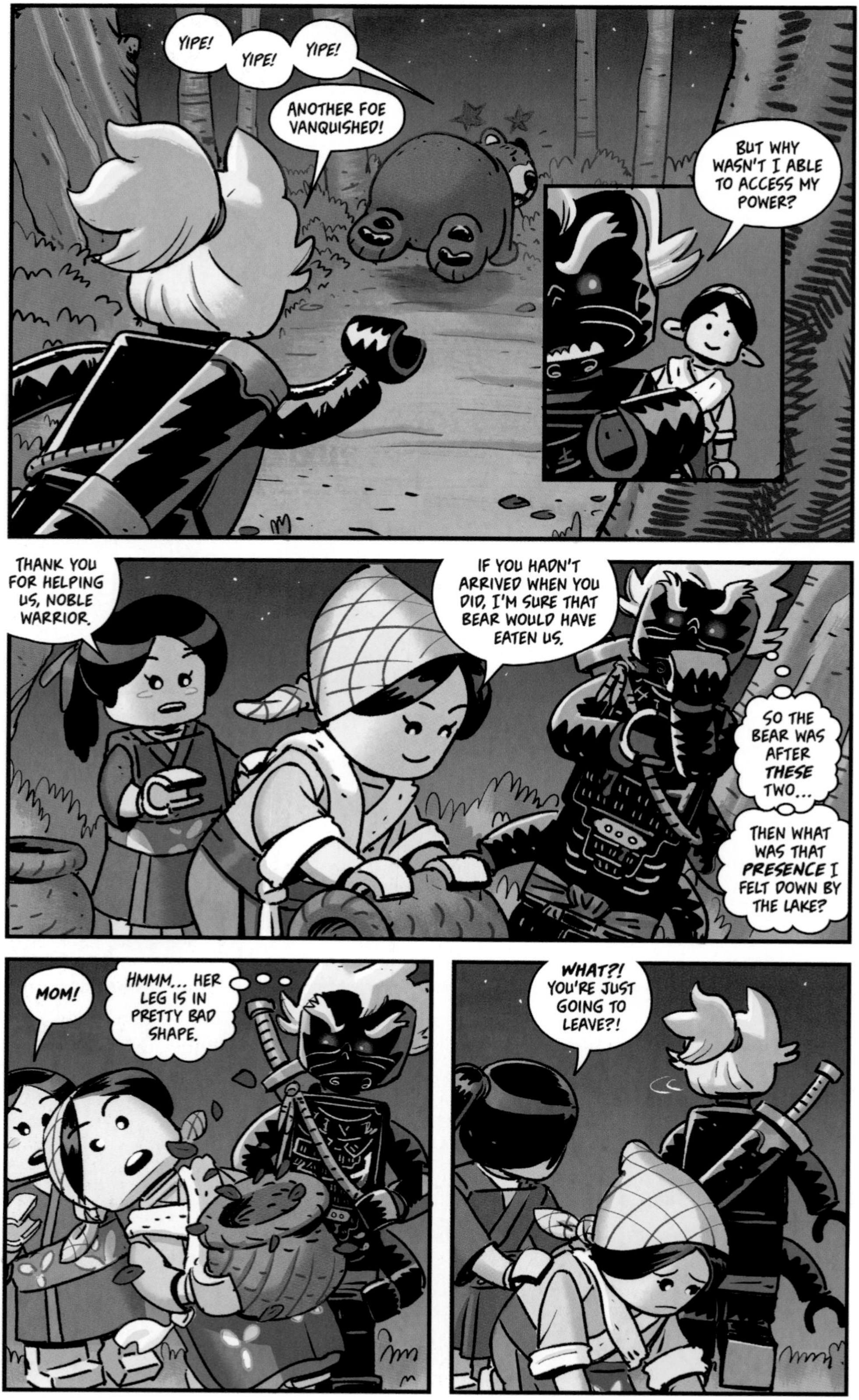
YIPE!
YIPE!
YIPE!
ANOTHER FOE VANQUISHED!
BUT WHY WASN'T I ABLE TO ACCESS MY POWER?
THANK YOU FOR HELPING US, NOBLE WARRIOR.
IF YOU HADN'T ARRIVED WHEN YOU DID, I'M SURE THAT BEAR WOULD HAVE EATEN US.
SO THE BEAR WAS AFTER ***THESE*** TWO...
THEN WHAT WAS THAT ***PRESENCE*** I FELT DOWN BY THE LAKE?
MOM!
HMMM... HER LEG IS IN PRETTY BAD SHAPE.
WHAT?! YOU'RE JUST GOING TO LEAVE?!

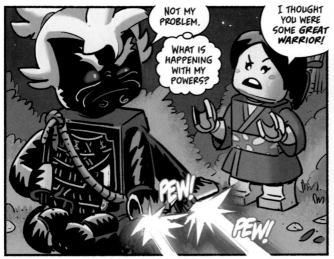

NOT MY PROBLEM.

WHAT IS HAPPENING WITH MY POWERS?

I THOUGHT YOU WERE SOME *GREAT* WARRIOR!

I AM *LORD GARMADON*, SON OF THE FIRST SPINJITZU MASTER.

NOT SON OF THE FIRST *MULE*.

PEW!

PEW!

LORD GARMADON! WE'VE HEARD TALES OF YOUR STRENGTH!

YOUR *LEGEND* PRECEDES YOU, EVEN THIS FAR FROM *NINJAGO CITY!*

MMF--

OH, REALLY?

PLEASE, I ASK YOUR HELP IN CARRYING NOT MYSELF--

--BUT THESE BASKETS OF *GLIMWILLOW LILIES.*

EH... I'M KIND OF IN THE MIDDLE OF MY OWN PROBLEM HERE.

BLOOP! BLOOP!

--AND HOLD A MAGNIFICENT *FEAST* IN YOUR HONOR!

IF YOU WOULD AID US, I'M SURE THE ENTIRE VILLAGE WOULD GIVE YOU A *HERO'S* WELCOME--

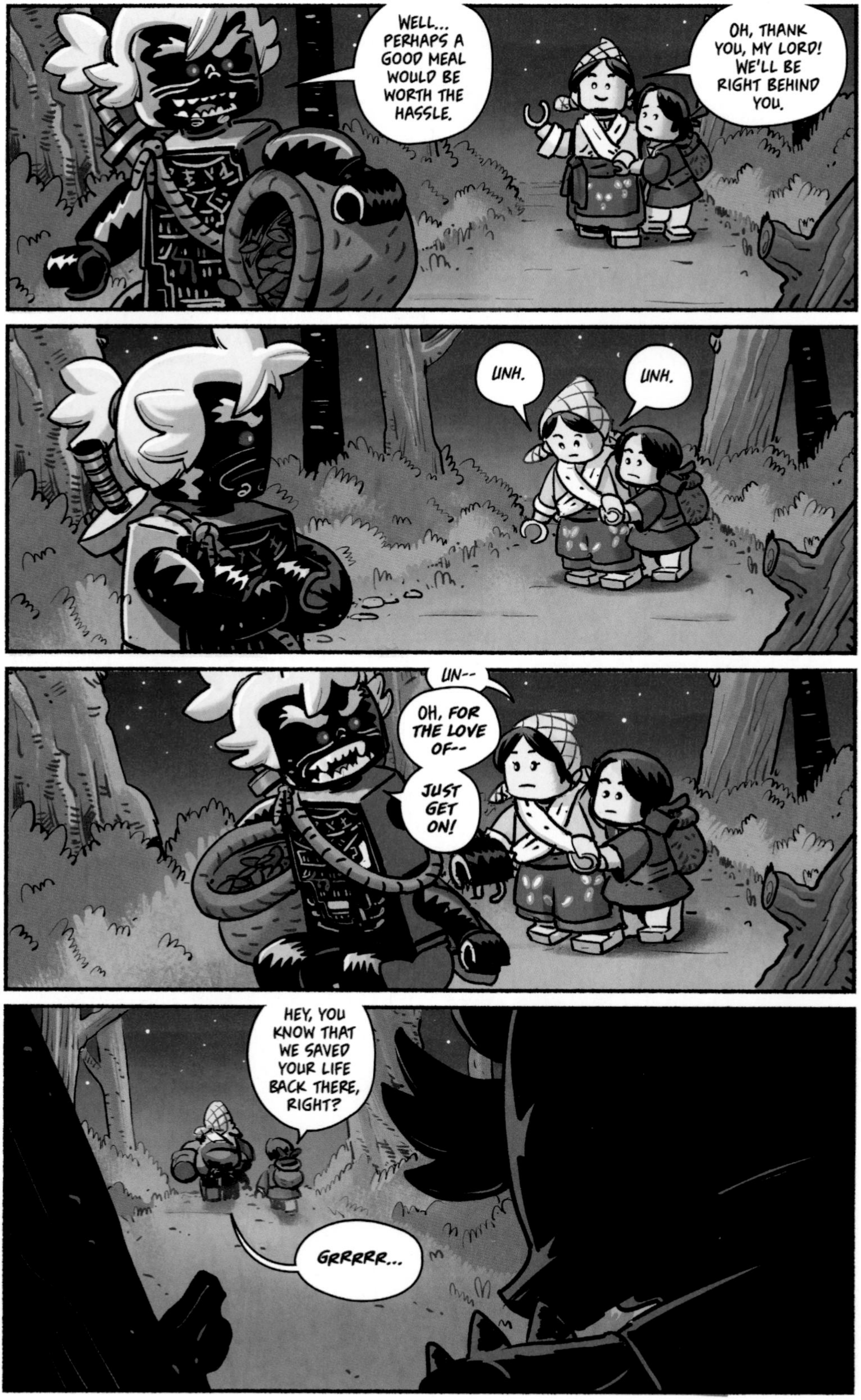
WELL... PERHAPS A GOOD MEAL WOULD BE WORTH THE HASSLE.
OH, THANK YOU, MY LORD! WE'LL BE RIGHT BEHIND YOU.
UNH.
UNH.
UN--
OH, FOR THE LOVE OF--
JUST GET ON!
HEY, YOU KNOW THAT WE SAVED YOUR LIFE BACK THERE, RIGHT?
GRRRRR...

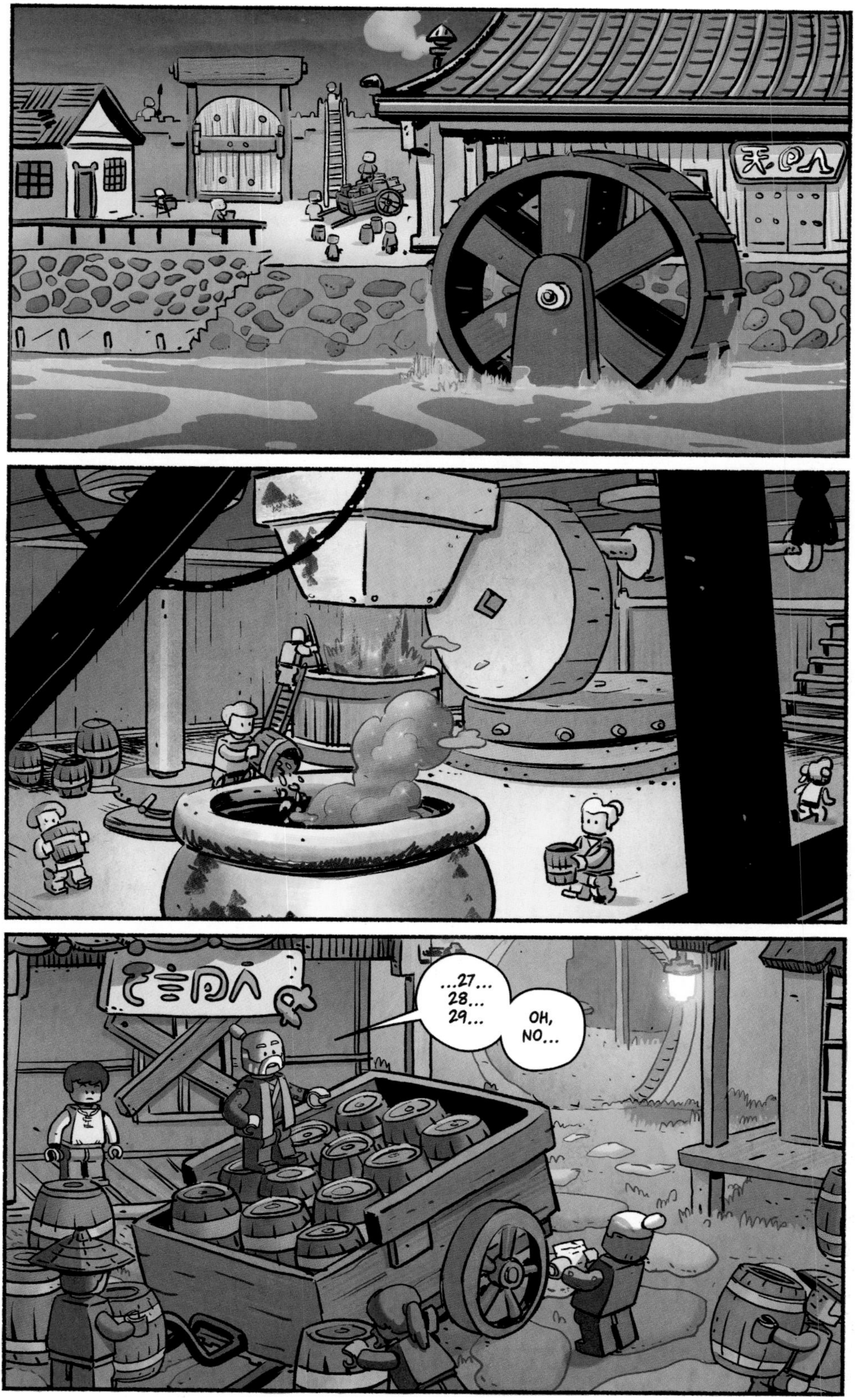
...27...
28...
29...
OH,
NO...

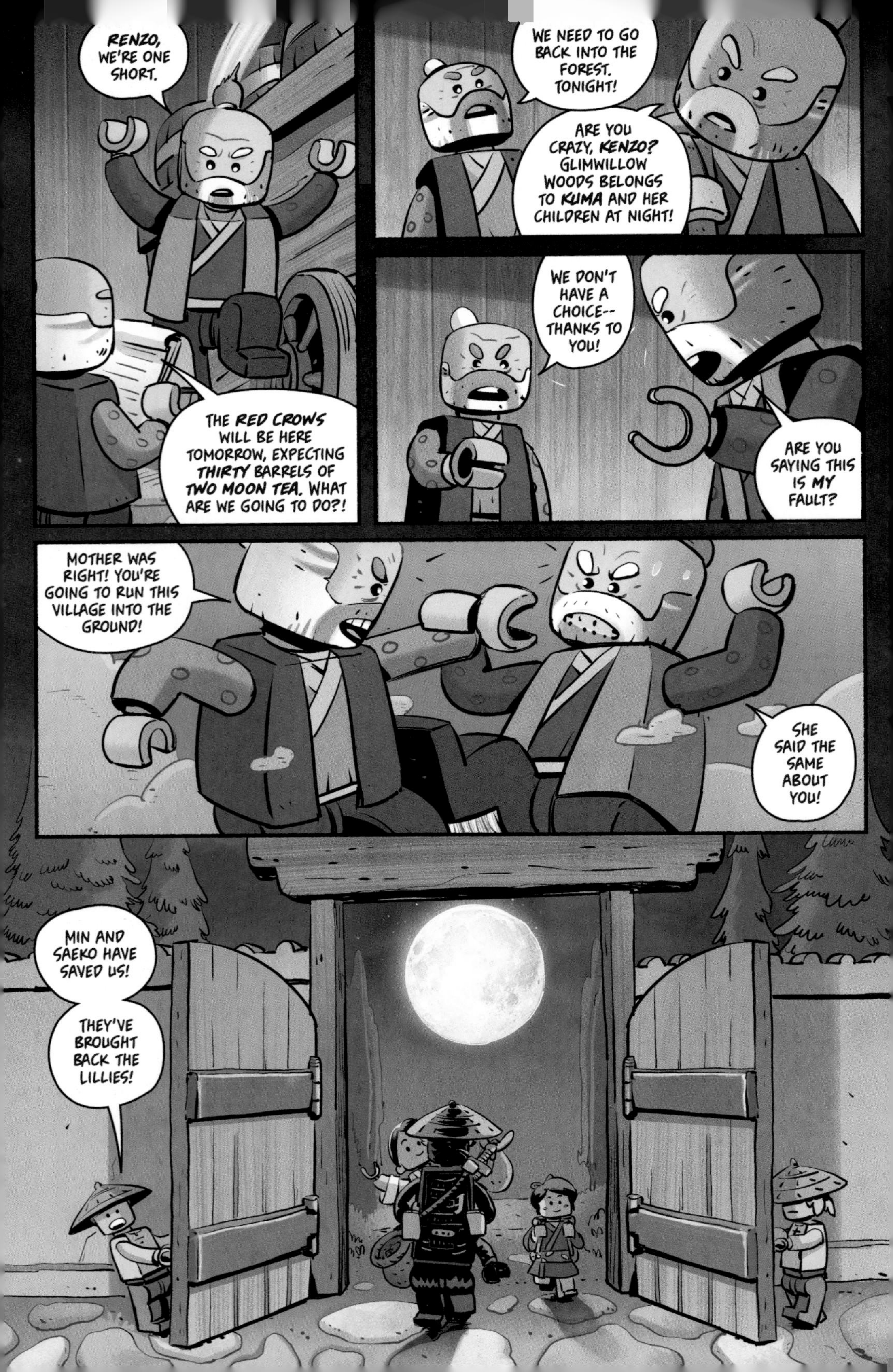
RENZO, WE'RE ONE SHORT.
THE RED CROWS WILL BE HERE TOMORROW, EXPECTING THIRTY BARRELS OF TWO MOON TEA. WHAT ARE WE GOING TO DO?!
WE NEED TO GO BACK INTO THE FOREST. TONIGHT!
ARE YOU CRAZY, KENZO? GLIMWILLOW WOODS BELONGS TO KUMA AND HER CHILDREN AT NIGHT!
WE DON'T HAVE A CHOICE-- THANKS TO YOU!
ARE YOU SAYING THIS IS MY FAULT?
MOTHER WAS RIGHT! YOU'RE GOING TO RUN THIS VILLAGE INTO THE GROUND!
SHE SAID THE SAME ABOUT YOU!
MIN AND SAEKO HAVE SAVED US!
THEY'VE BROUGHT BACK THE LILLIES!

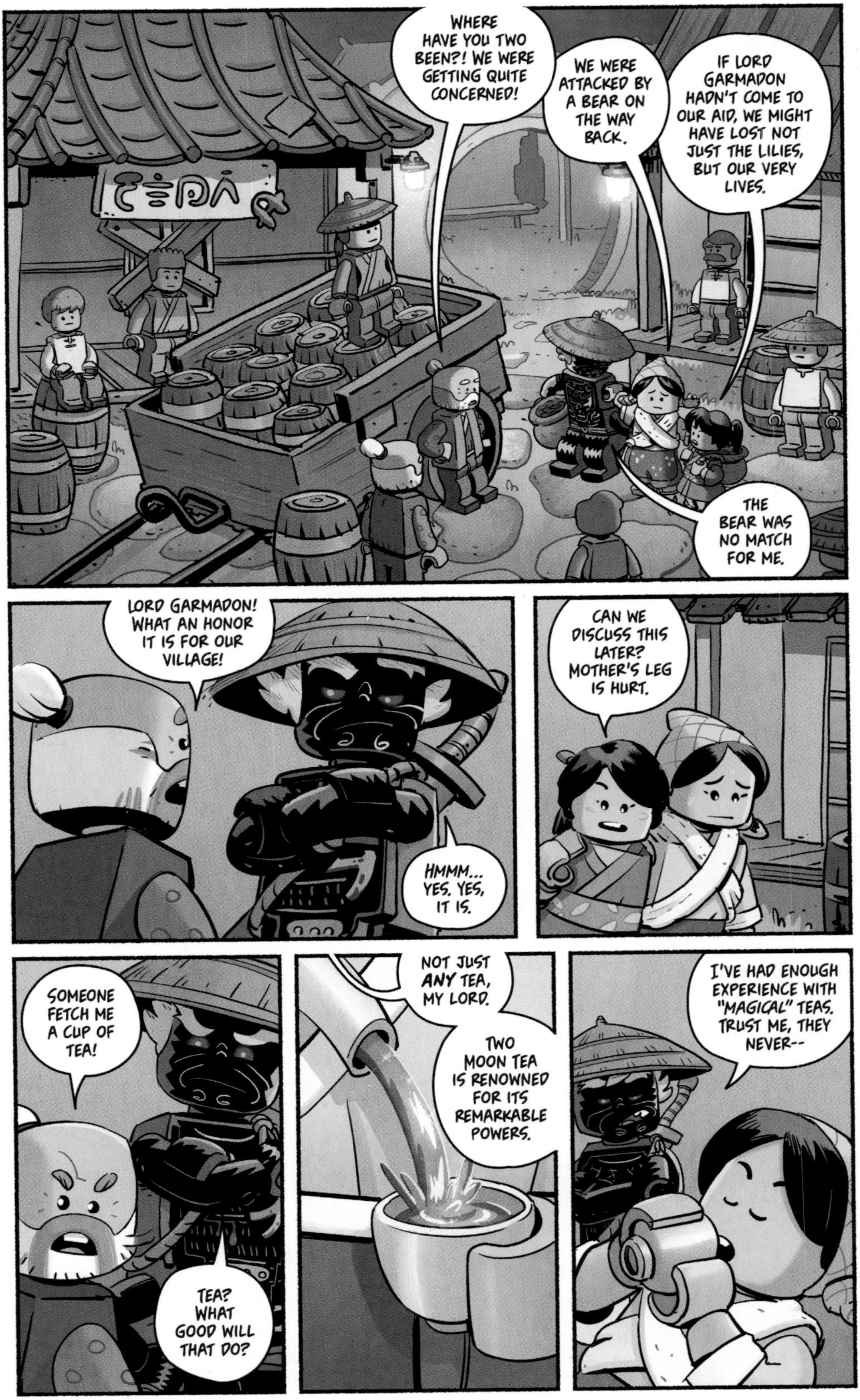
WHERE HAVE YOU TWO BEEN?! WE WERE GETTING QUITE CONCERNED!
WE WERE ATTACKED BY A BEAR ON THE WAY BACK.
IF LORD GARMADON HADN'T COME TO OUR AID, WE MIGHT HAVE LOST NOT JUST THE LILIES, BUT OUR VERY LIVES.
THE BEAR WAS NO MATCH FOR ME.
LORD GARMADON! WHAT AN HONOR IT IS FOR OUR VILLAGE!
HMMM... YES. YES, IT IS.
CAN WE DISCUSS THIS LATER? MOTHER'S LEG IS HURT.
SOMEONE FETCH ME A CUP OF TEA!
TEA? WHAT GOOD WILL THAT DO?
NOT JUST ANY TEA, MY LORD.
TWO MOON TEA IS RENOWNED FOR ITS REMARKABLE POWERS.
I'VE HAD ENOUGH EXPERIENCE WITH "MAGICAL" TEAS. TRUST ME, THEY NEVER--

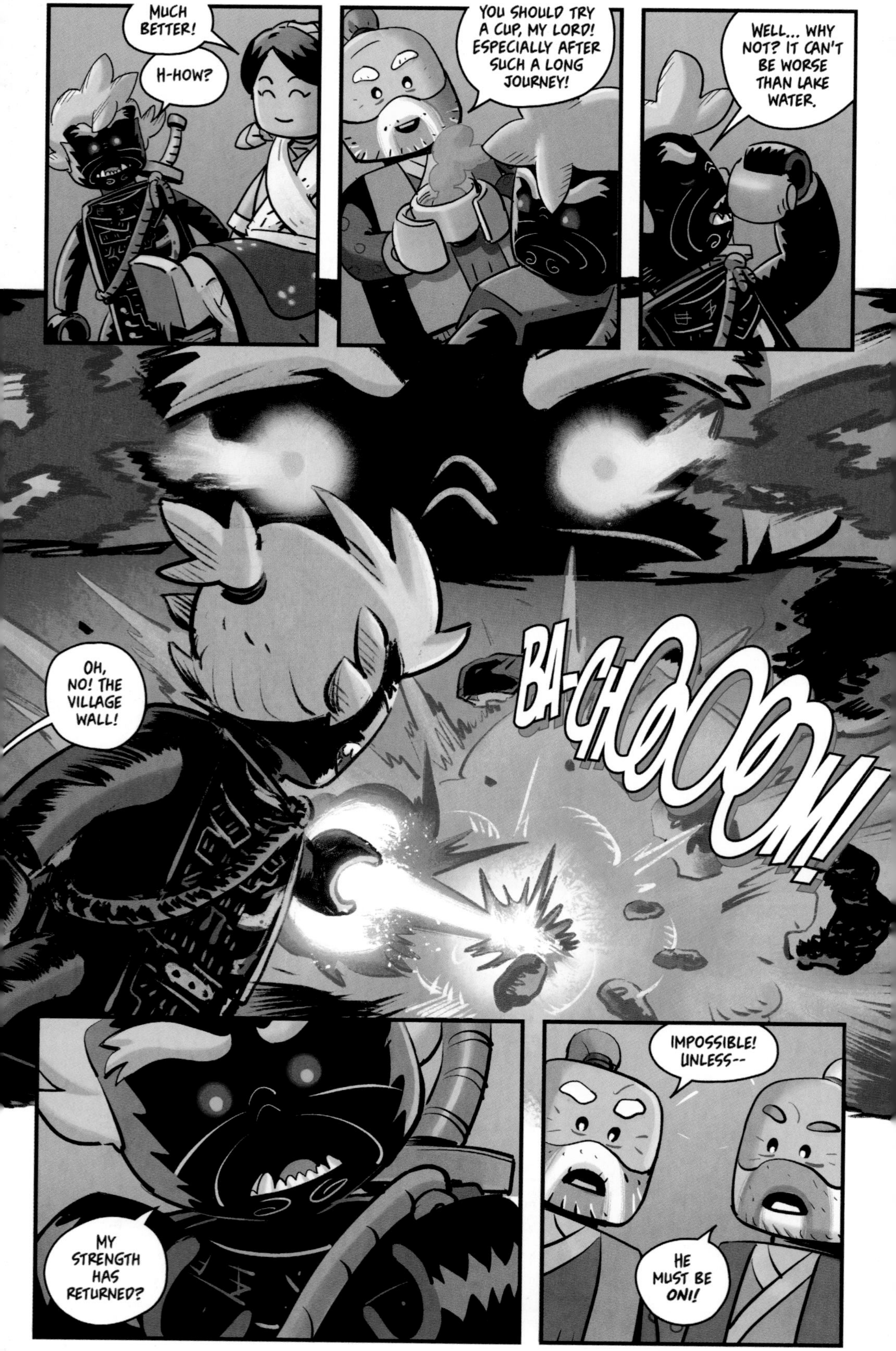
MUCH BETTER!
H-HOW?
YOU SHOULD TRY A CUP, MY LORD! ESPECIALLY AFTER SUCH A LONG JOURNEY!
WELL... WHY NOT? IT CAN'T BE WORSE THAN LAKE WATER.
OH, NO! THE VILLAGE WALL!
BA-CHOOOOM!
MY STRENGTH HAS RETURNED?
IMPOSSIBLE! UNLESS--
HE MUST BE ONI!

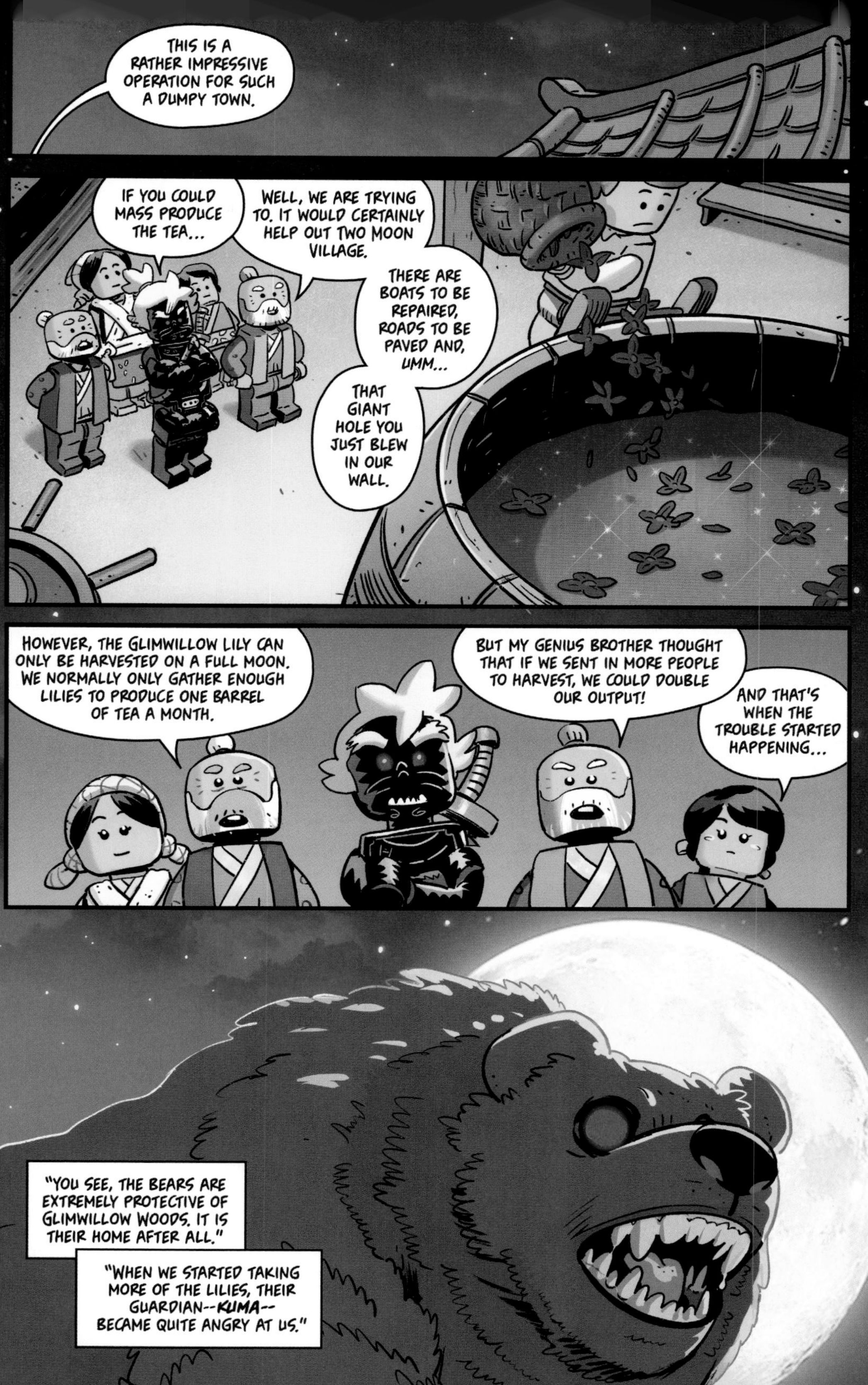
THIS IS A RATHER IMPRESSIVE OPERATION FOR SUCH A DUMPY TOWN.
IF YOU COULD MASS PRODUCE THE TEA...
WELL, WE ARE TRYING TO. IT WOULD CERTAINLY HELP OUT TWO MOON VILLAGE.
THERE ARE BOATS TO BE REPAIRED, ROADS TO BE PAVED AND, UMM...
THAT GIANT HOLE YOU JUST BLEW IN OUR WALL.
HOWEVER, THE GLIMWILLOW LILY CAN ONLY BE HARVESTED ON A FULL MOON. WE NORMALLY ONLY GATHER ENOUGH LILIES TO PRODUCE ONE BARREL OF TEA A MONTH.
BUT MY GENIUS BROTHER THOUGHT THAT IF WE SENT IN MORE PEOPLE TO HARVEST, WE COULD DOUBLE OUR OUTPUT!
AND THAT'S WHEN THE TROUBLE STARTED HAPPENING...
"YOU SEE, THE BEARS ARE EXTREMELY PROTECTIVE OF GLIMWILLOW WOODS. IT IS THEIR HOME AFTER ALL."
"WHEN WE STARTED TAKING MORE OF THE LILIES, THEIR GUARDIAN--KUMA--BECAME QUITE ANGRY AT US."

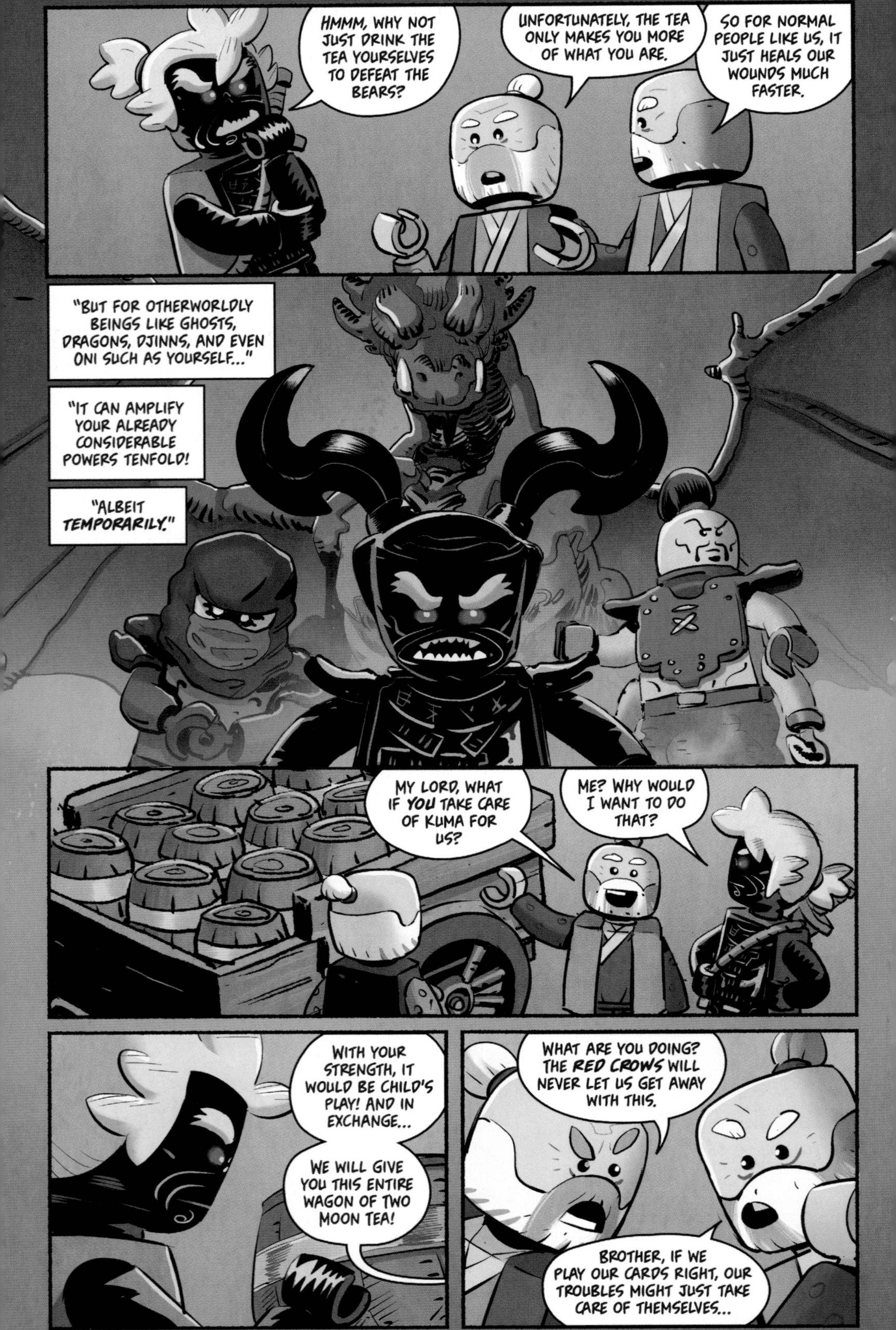
HMMM, WHY NOT JUST DRINK THE TEA YOURSELVES TO DEFEAT THE BEARS?
UNFORTUNATELY, THE TEA ONLY MAKES YOU MORE OF WHAT YOU ARE.
SO FOR NORMAL PEOPLE LIKE US, IT JUST HEALS OUR WOUNDS MUCH FASTER.
"BUT FOR OTHERWORLDLY BEINGS LIKE GHOSTS, DRAGONS, DJINNS, AND EVEN ONI SUCH AS YOURSELF..."
"IT CAN AMPLIFY YOUR ALREADY CONSIDERABLE POWERS TENFOLD!
"ALBEIT TEMPORARILY."
MY LORD, WHAT IF YOU TAKE CARE OF KUMA FOR US?
ME? WHY WOULD I WANT TO DO THAT?
WITH YOUR STRENGTH, IT WOULD BE CHILD'S PLAY! AND IN EXCHANGE...
WE WILL GIVE YOU THIS ENTIRE WAGON OF TWO MOON TEA!
WHAT ARE YOU DOING? THE RED CROWS WILL NEVER LET US GET AWAY WITH THIS.
BROTHER, IF WE PLAY OUR CARDS RIGHT, OUR TROUBLES MIGHT JUST TAKE CARE OF THEMSELVES...

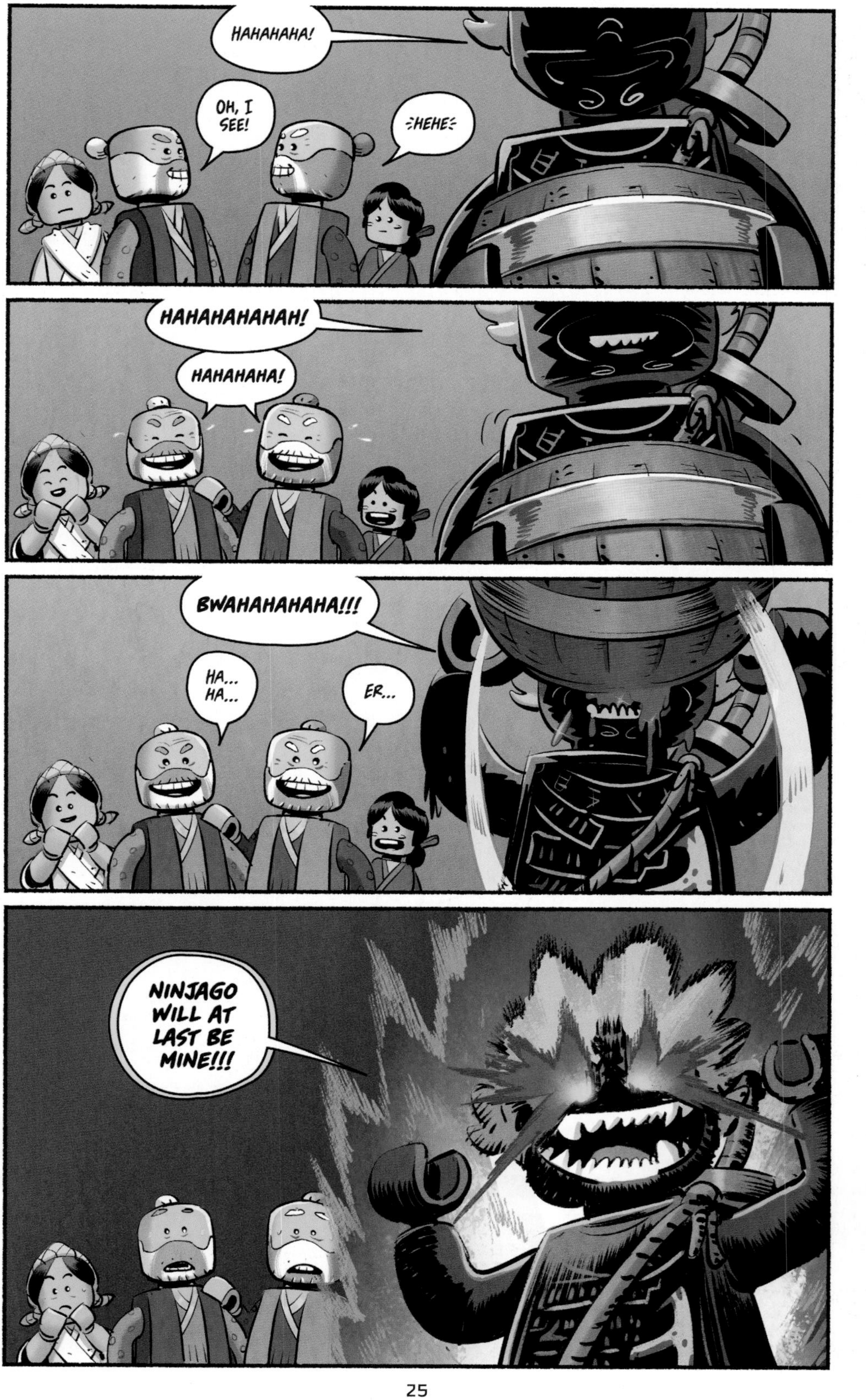
HAHAHAHA!
OH, I SEE!
HEHE
HAHAHAHAHAH!
HAHAHAHA!
BWAHAHAHAHA!!!
HA... HA...
ER...
NINJAGO WILL AT LAST BE MINE!!!

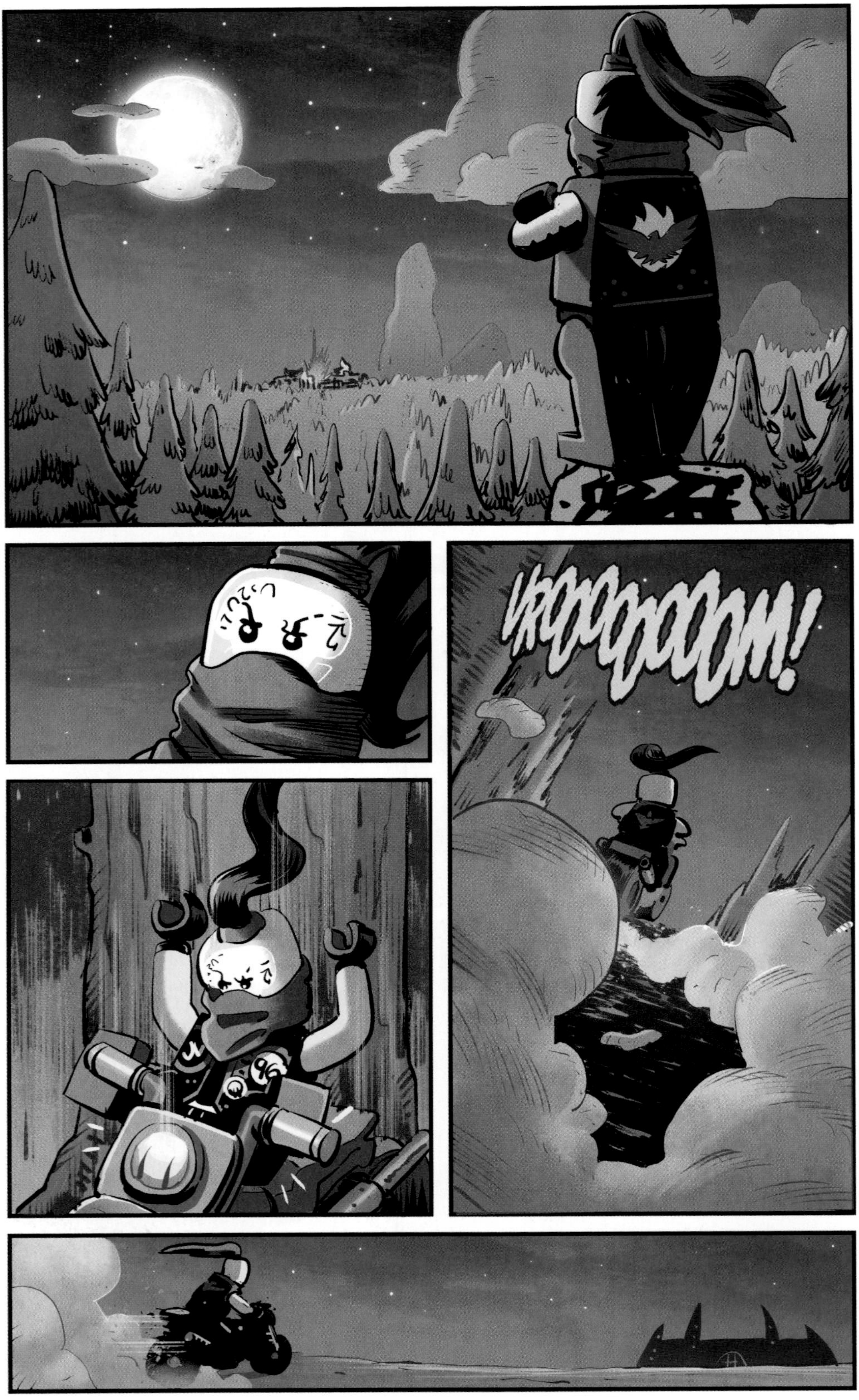
VROOOOOOOM!

LORD MOGRA! GARMADON HAS RETURNED!

HAS HE NOW?

AND DOES THAT COMPLICATE YOUR LOYALTIES, *ULTRA VIOLET*, NOW THAT YOUR FORMER MASTER HAS RESURFACED?

IT DOES NOT.

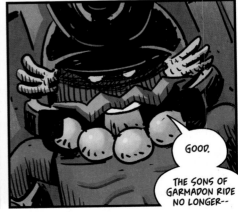

GOOD.

THE SONS OF GARMADON RIDE NO LONGER--

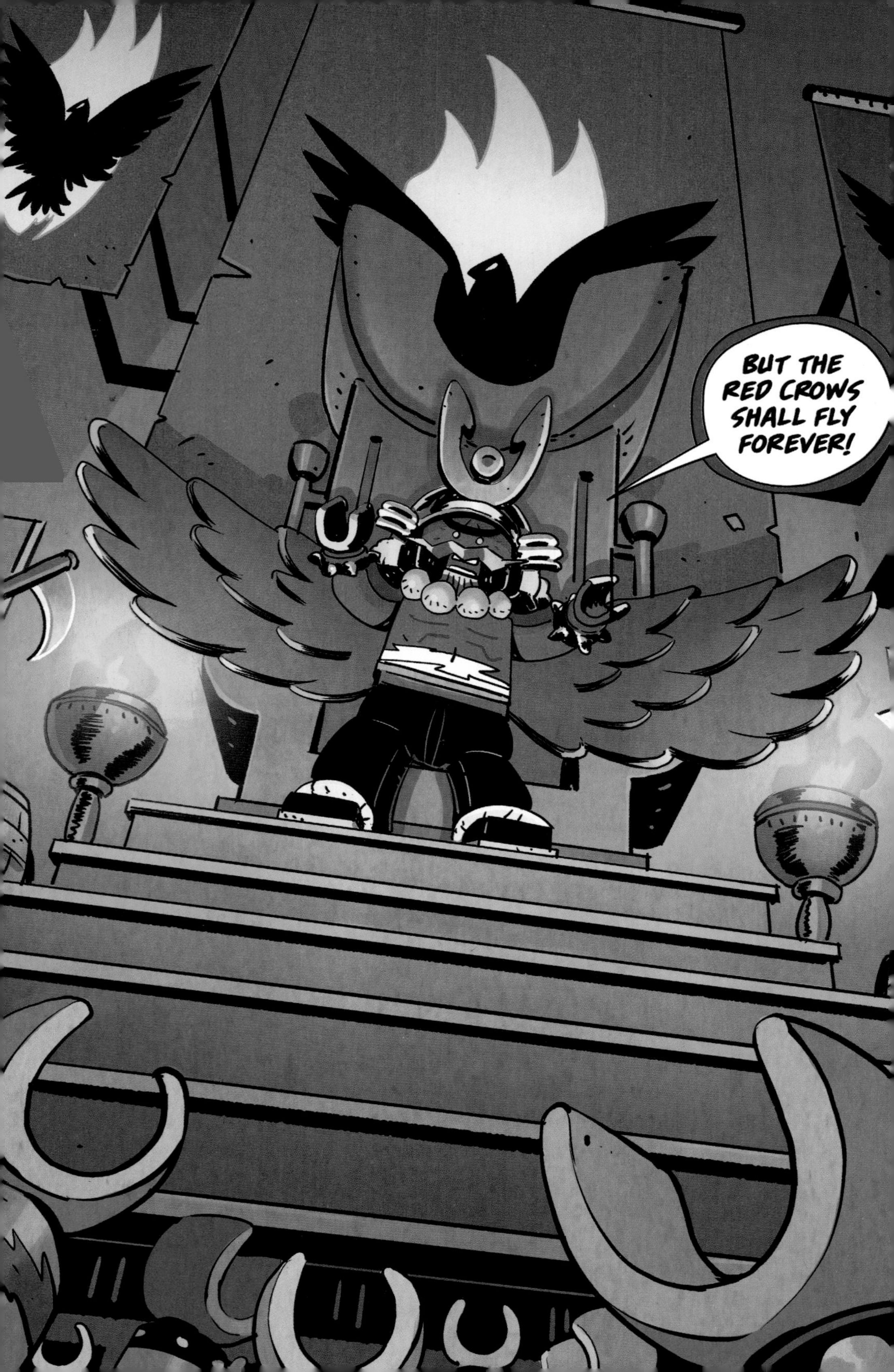
BUT THE RED CROWS SHALL FLY FOREVER!

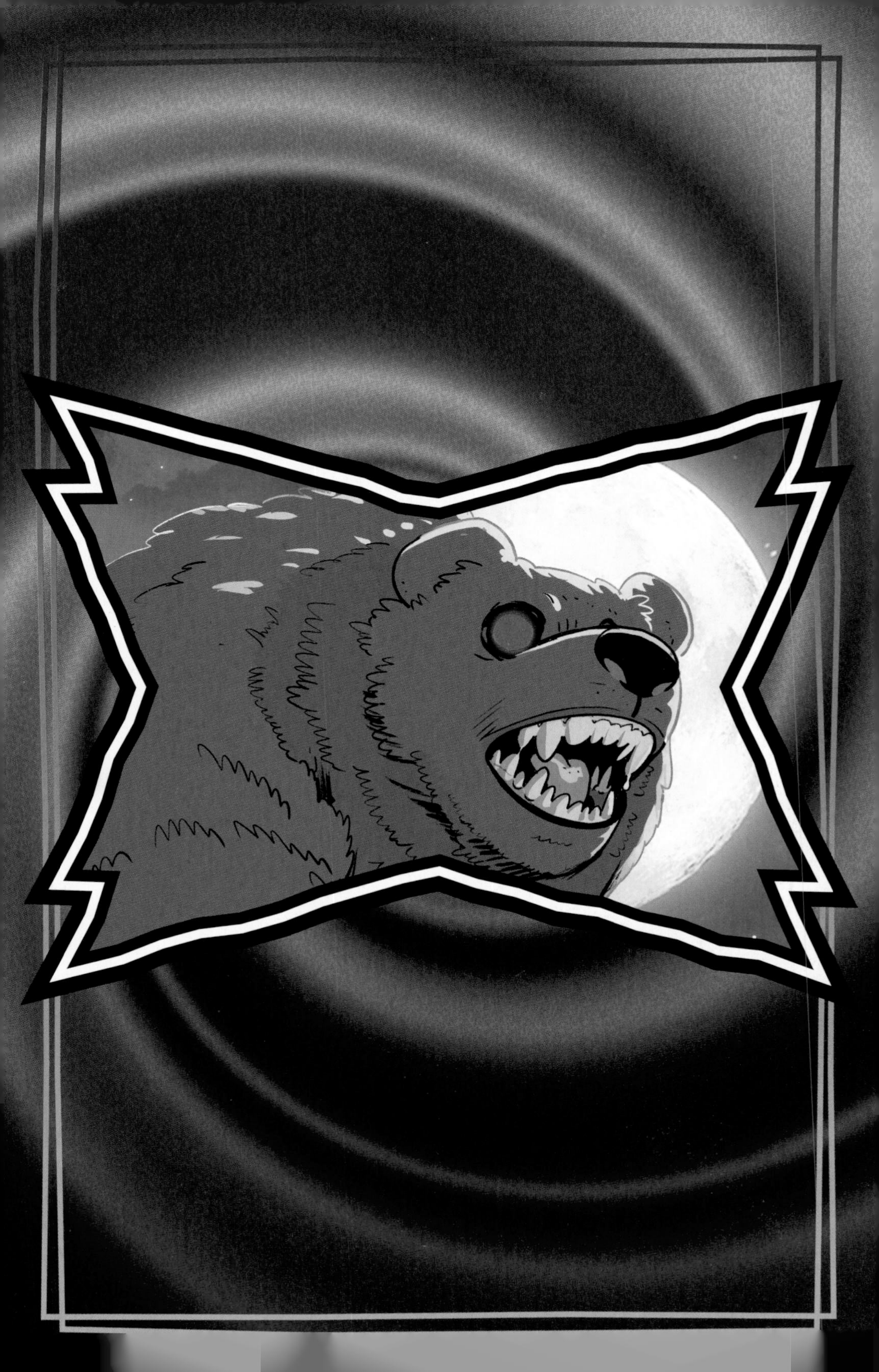

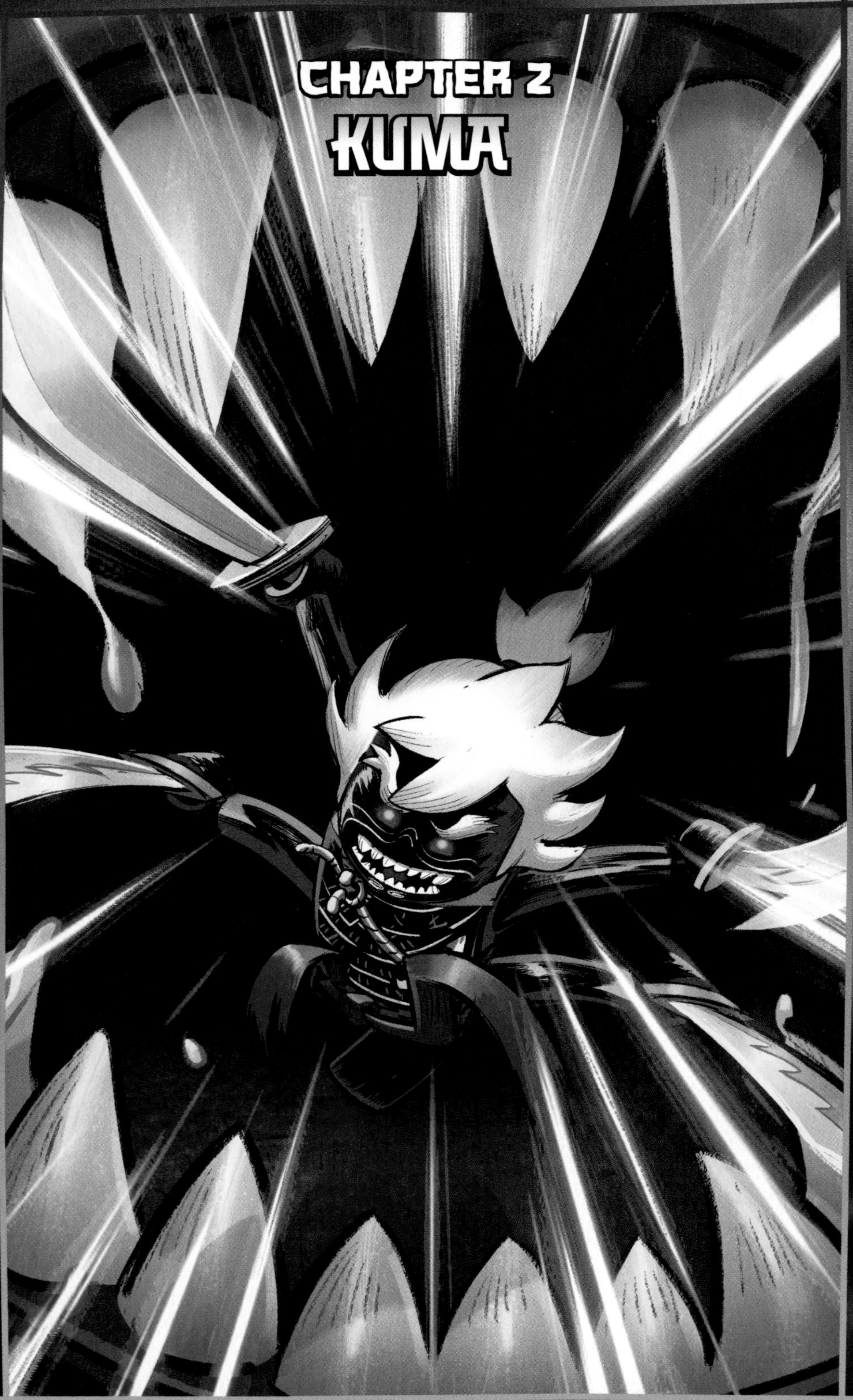
CHAPTER 2
KUMA

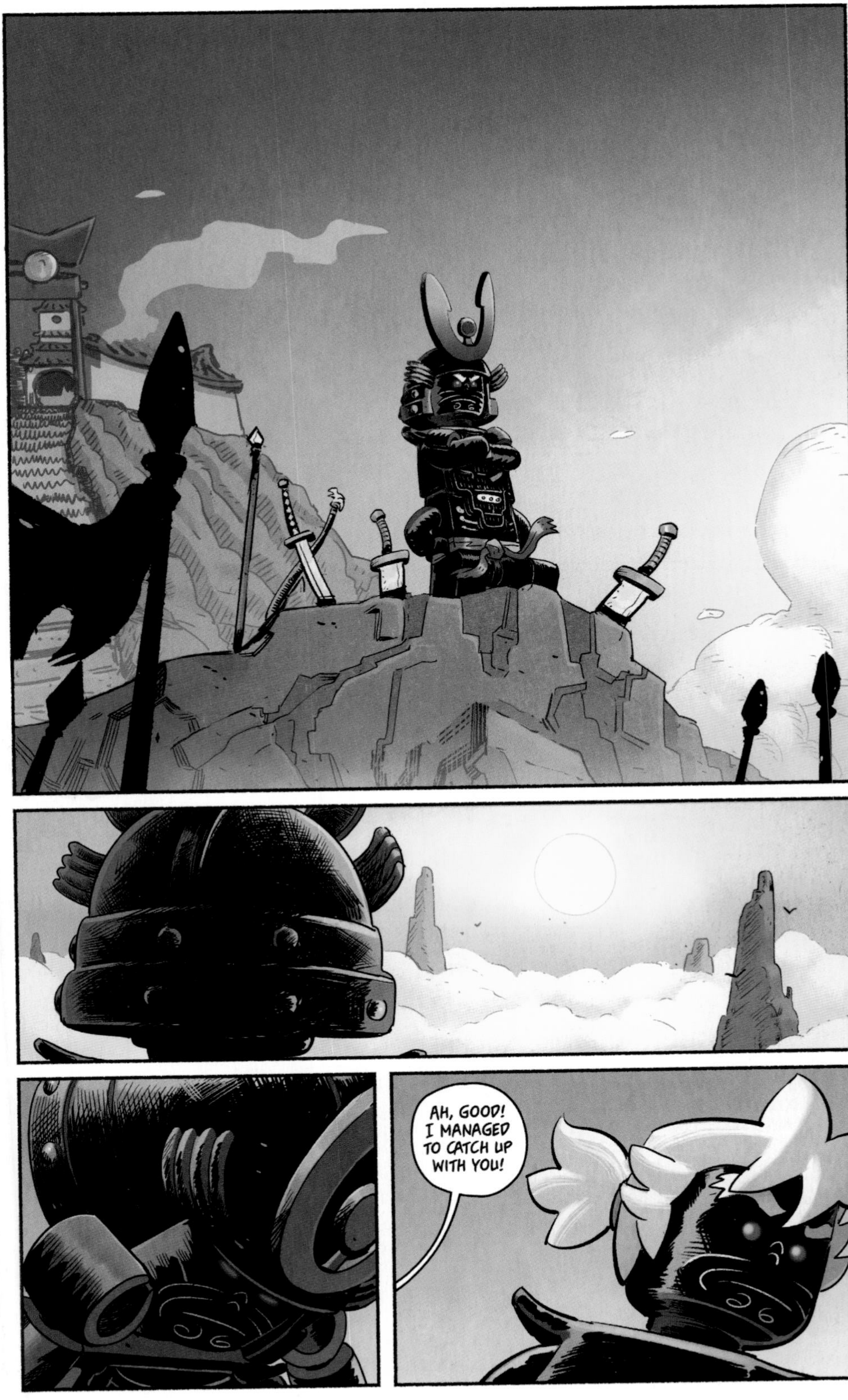
AH, GOOD! I MANAGED TO CATCH UP WITH YOU!

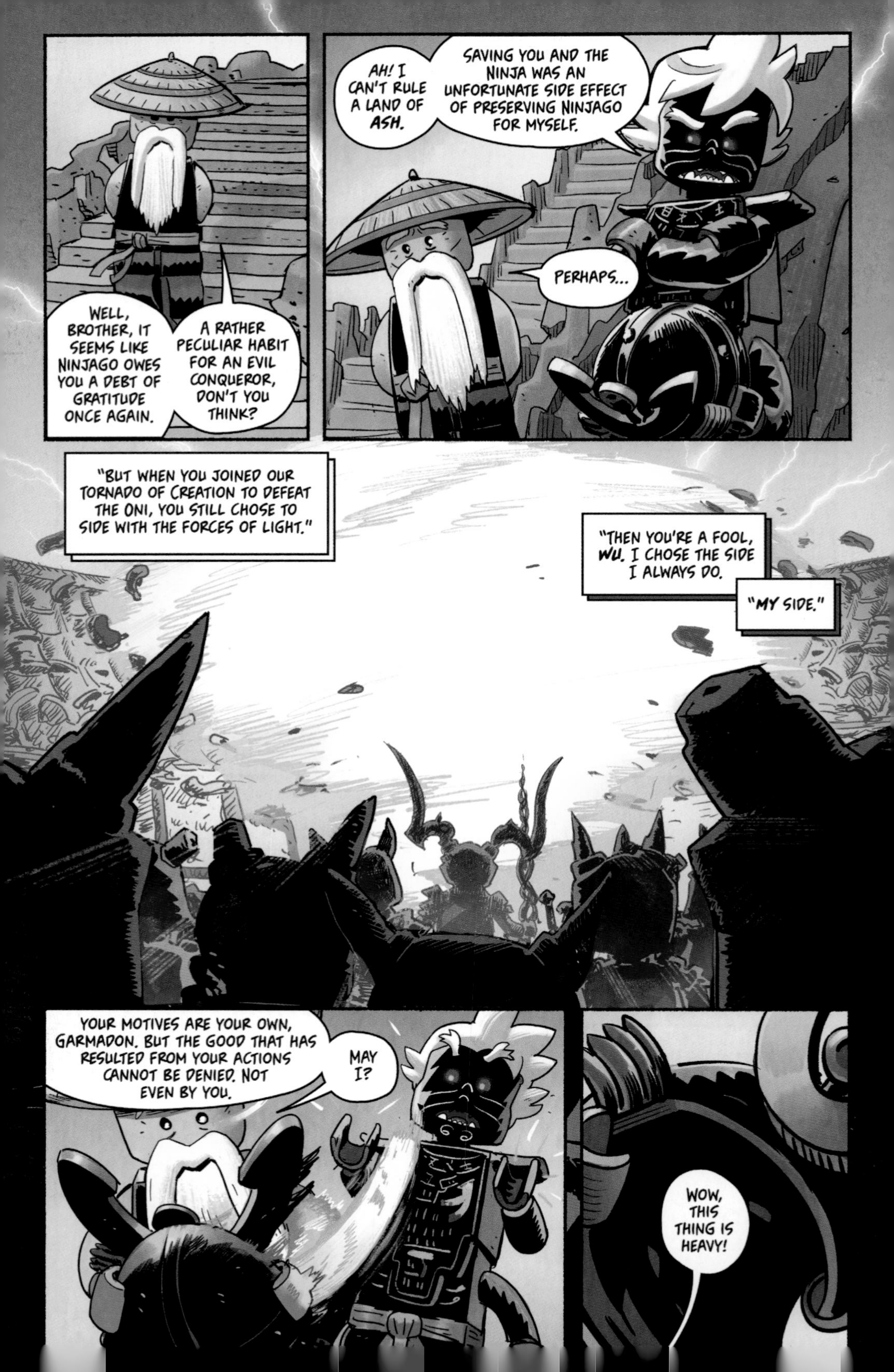
WELL, BROTHER, IT SEEMS LIKE NINJAGO OWES YOU A DEBT OF GRATITUDE ONCE AGAIN.
A RATHER PECULIAR HABIT FOR AN EVIL CONQUEROR, DON'T YOU THINK?
AH! I CAN'T RULE A LAND OF ASH.
SAVING YOU AND THE NINJA WAS AN UNFORTUNATE SIDE EFFECT OF PRESERVING NINJAGO FOR MYSELF.
PERHAPS...
"BUT WHEN YOU JOINED OUR TORNADO OF CREATION TO DEFEAT THE ONI, YOU STILL CHOSE TO SIDE WITH THE FORCES OF LIGHT."
"THEN YOU'RE A FOOL, WU. I CHOSE THE SIDE I ALWAYS DO.
"MY SIDE."
YOUR MOTIVES ARE YOUR OWN, GARMADON. BUT THE GOOD THAT HAS RESULTED FROM YOUR ACTIONS CANNOT BE DENIED. NOT EVEN BY YOU.
MAY I?
WOW, THIS THING IS HEAVY!

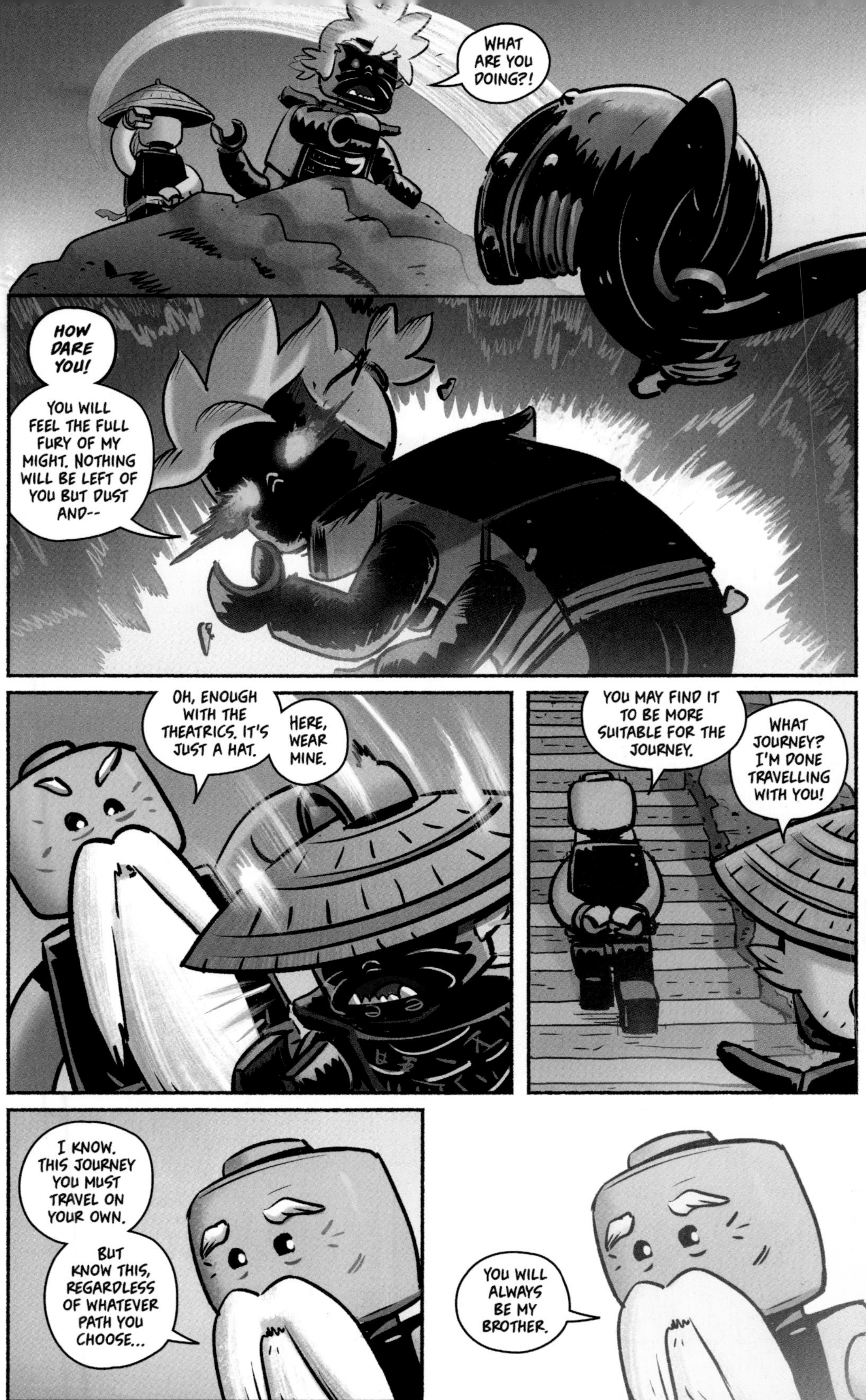
WHAT ARE YOU DOING?!
HOW DARE YOU!
YOU WILL FEEL THE FULL FURY OF MY MIGHT. NOTHING WILL BE LEFT OF YOU BUT DUST AND--
OH, ENOUGH WITH THE THEATRICS. IT'S JUST A HAT.
HERE, WEAR MINE.
YOU MAY FIND IT TO BE MORE SUITABLE FOR THE JOURNEY.
WHAT JOURNEY? I'M DONE TRAVELLING WITH YOU!
I KNOW. THIS JOURNEY YOU MUST TRAVEL ON YOUR OWN.
BUT KNOW THIS, REGARDLESS OF WHATEVER PATH YOU CHOOSE...
YOU WILL ALWAYS BE MY BROTHER.

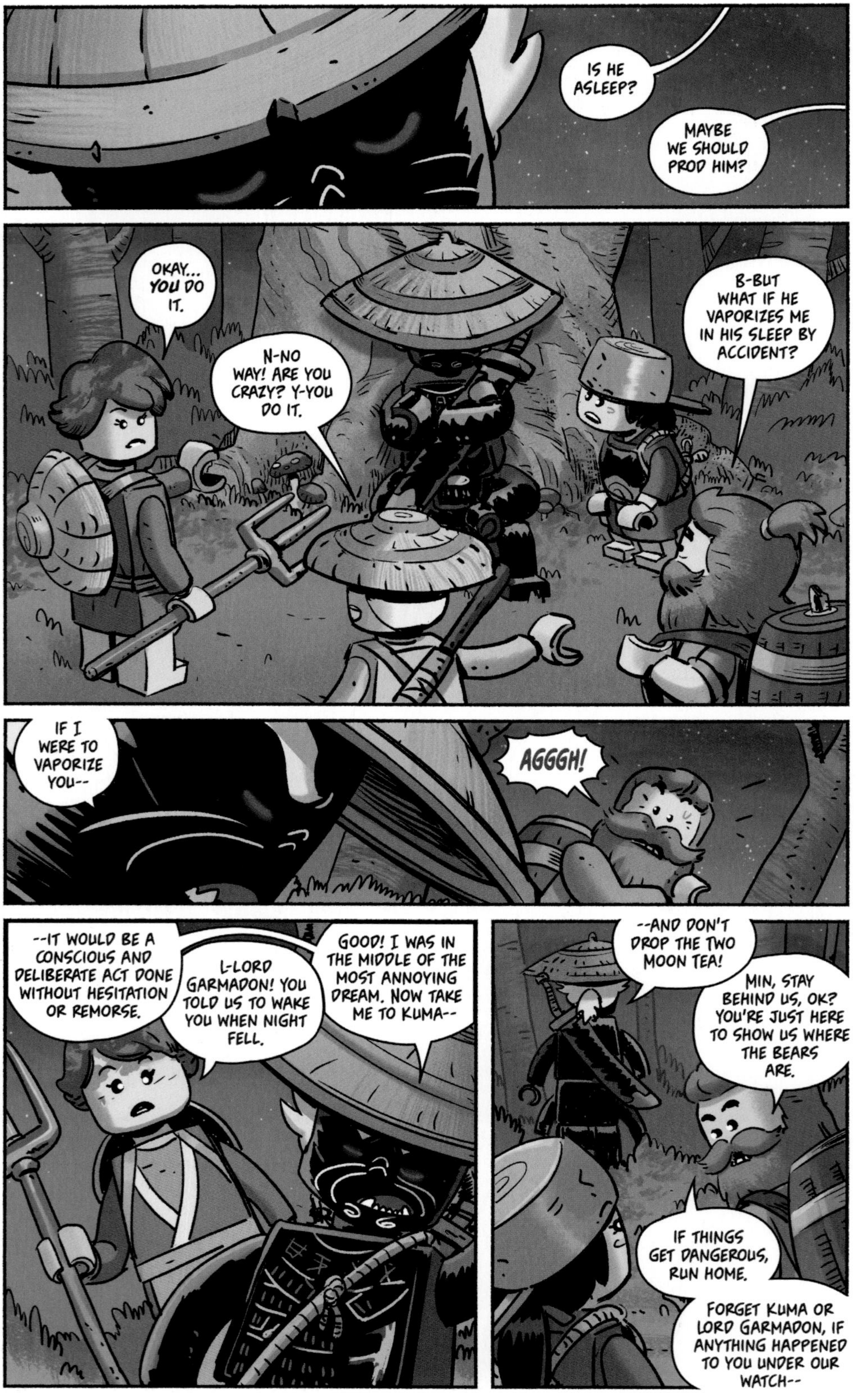
IS HE ASLEEP?
MAYBE WE SHOULD PROD HIM?
OKAY... YOU DO IT.
N-NO WAY! ARE YOU CRAZY? Y-YOU DO IT.
B-BUT WHAT IF HE VAPORIZES ME IN HIS SLEEP BY ACCIDENT?
IF I WERE TO VAPORIZE YOU--
AGGGH!
--IT WOULD BE A CONSCIOUS AND DELIBERATE ACT DONE WITHOUT HESITATION OR REMORSE.
L-LORD GARMADON! YOU TOLD US TO WAKE YOU WHEN NIGHT FELL.
GOOD! I WAS IN THE MIDDLE OF THE MOST ANNOYING DREAM. NOW TAKE ME TO KUMA--
--AND DON'T DROP THE TWO MOON TEA!
MIN, STAY BEHIND US, OK? YOU'RE JUST HERE TO SHOW US WHERE THE BEARS ARE.
IF THINGS GET DANGEROUS, RUN HOME.
FORGET KUMA OR LORD GARMADON, IF ANYTHING HAPPENED TO YOU UNDER OUR WATCH--

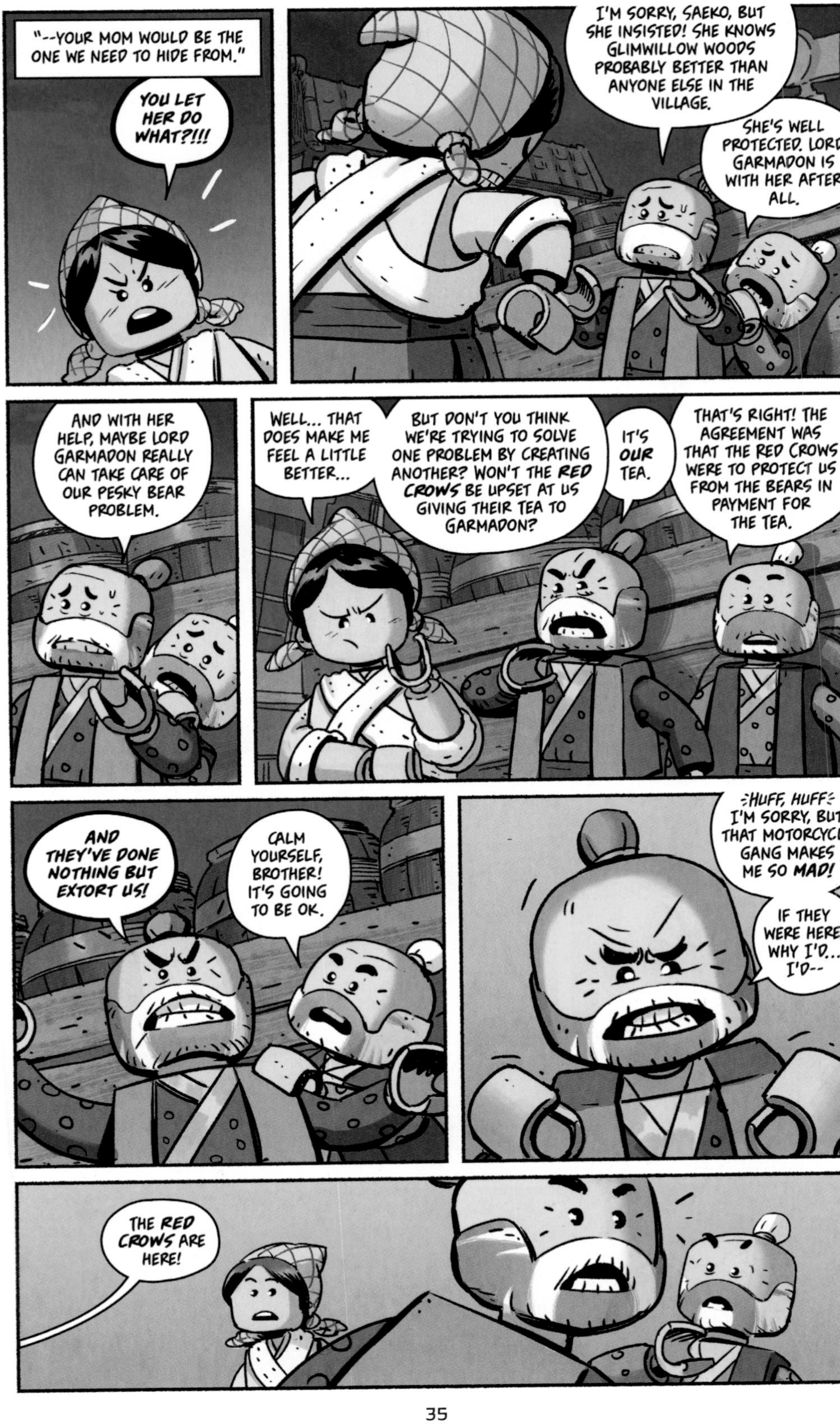
"--YOUR MOM WOULD BE THE ONE WE NEED TO HIDE FROM."
YOU LET HER DO WHAT?!!!
I'M SORRY, SAEKO, BUT SHE INSISTED! SHE KNOWS GLIMWILLOW WOODS PROBABLY BETTER THAN ANYONE ELSE IN THE VILLAGE.
SHE'S WELL PROTECTED. LORD GARMADON IS WITH HER AFTER ALL.
AND WITH HER HELP, MAYBE LORD GARMADON REALLY CAN TAKE CARE OF OUR PESKY BEAR PROBLEM.
WELL... THAT DOES MAKE ME FEEL A LITTLE BETTER...
BUT DON'T YOU THINK WE'RE TRYING TO SOLVE ONE PROBLEM BY CREATING ANOTHER? WON'T THE RED CROWS BE UPSET AT US GIVING THEIR TEA TO GARMADON?
IT'S OUR TEA.
THAT'S RIGHT! THE AGREEMENT WAS THAT THE RED CROWS WERE TO PROTECT US FROM THE BEARS IN PAYMENT FOR THE TEA.
AND THEY'VE DONE NOTHING BUT EXTORT US!
CALM YOURSELF, BROTHER! IT'S GOING TO BE OK.
HUFF, HUFF
I'M SORRY, BUT THAT MOTORCYCLE GANG MAKES ME SO MAD!
IF THEY WERE HERE, WHY I'D... I'D--
THE RED CROWS ARE HERE!

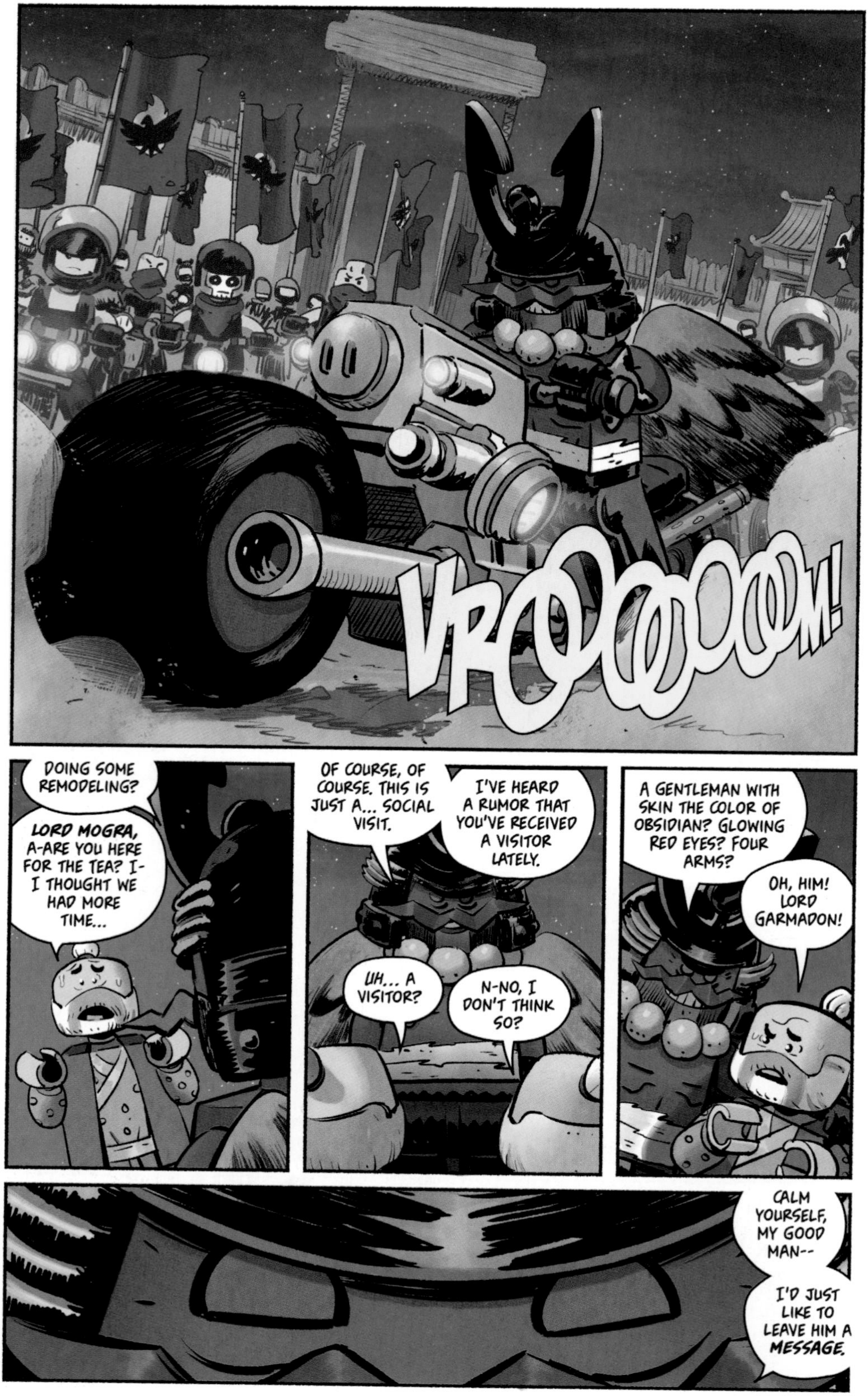
VROOOOOOM!
DOING SOME REMODELING?
LORD MOGRA, A-ARE YOU HERE FOR THE TEA? I- I THOUGHT WE HAD MORE TIME...
OF COURSE, OF COURSE. THIS IS JUST A... SOCIAL VISIT.
I'VE HEARD A RUMOR THAT YOU'VE RECEIVED A VISITOR LATELY.
UH... A VISITOR?
N-NO, I DON'T THINK SO?
A GENTLEMAN WITH SKIN THE COLOR OF OBSIDIAN? GLOWING RED EYES? FOUR ARMS?
OH, HIM! LORD GARMADON!
CALM YOURSELF, MY GOOD MAN--
I'D JUST LIKE TO LEAVE HIM A MESSAGE.

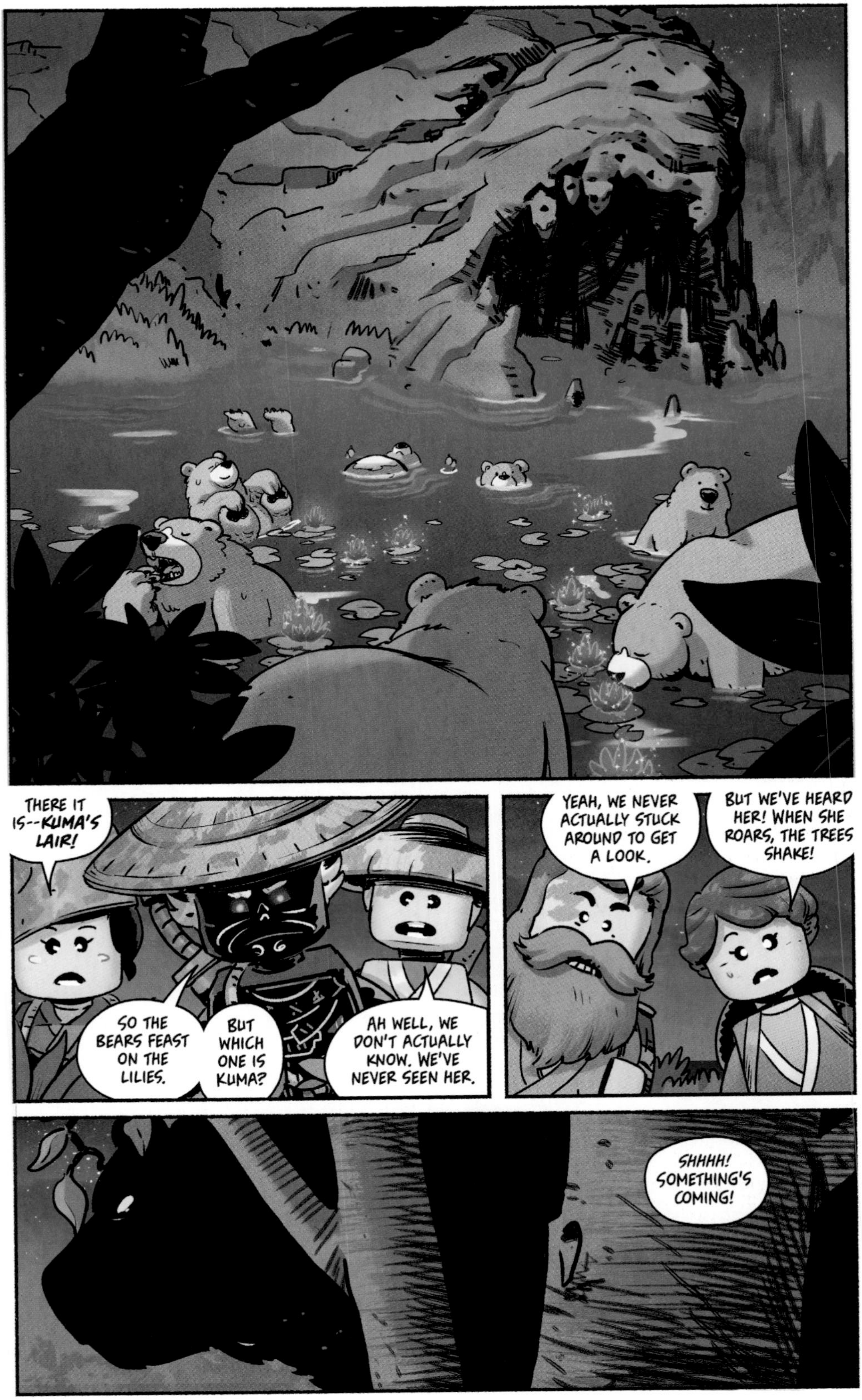
THERE IT IS--KUMA'S LAIR!
SO THE BEARS FEAST ON THE LILIES.
BUT WHICH ONE IS KUMA?
AH WELL, WE DON'T ACTUALLY KNOW. WE'VE NEVER SEEN HER.
YEAH, WE NEVER ACTUALLY STUCK AROUND TO GET A LOOK.
BUT WE'VE HEARD HER! WHEN SHE ROARS, THE TREES SHAKE!
SHHHH! SOMETHING'S COMING!

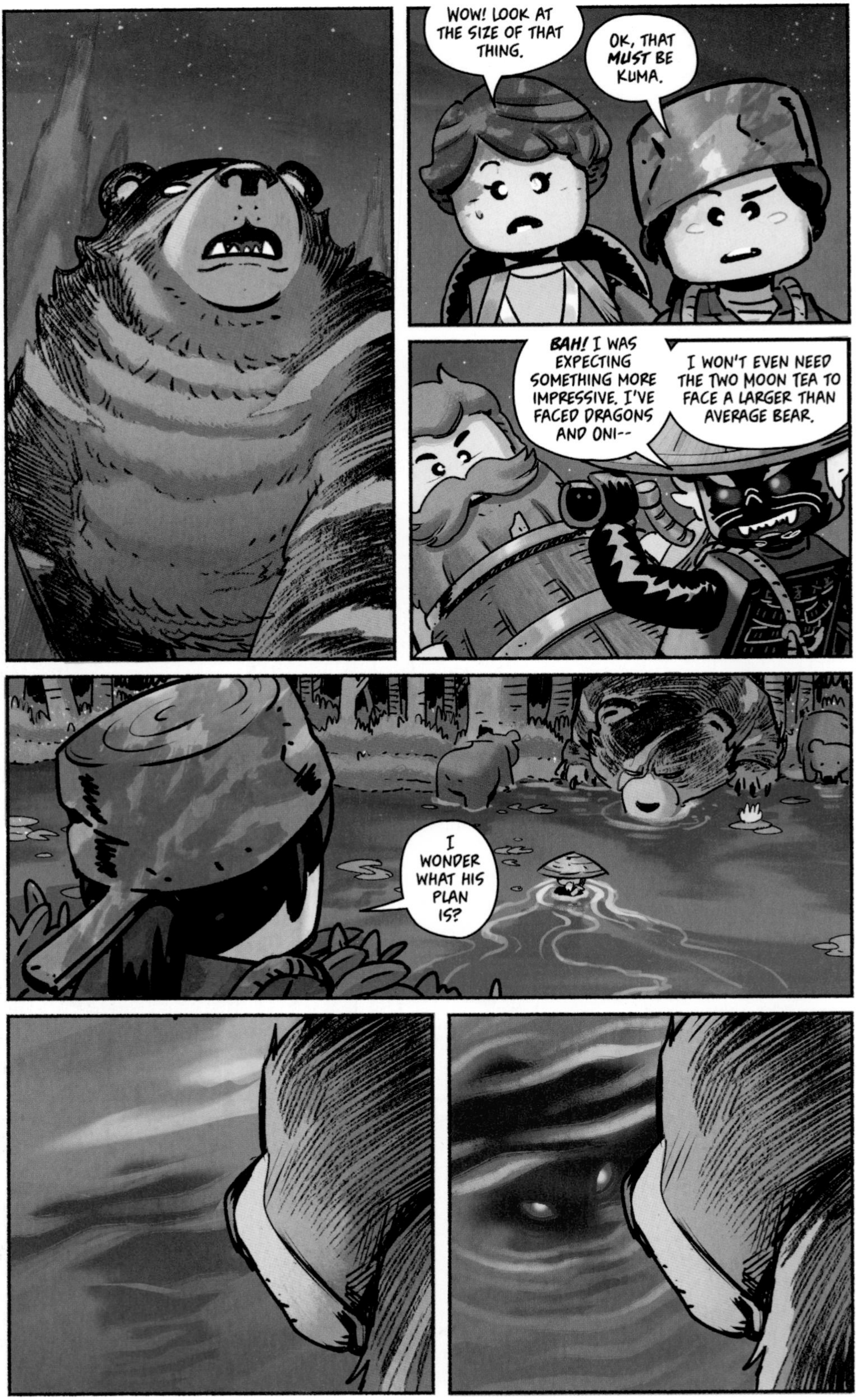
WOW! LOOK AT THE SIZE OF THAT THING.
OK, THAT *MUST* BE KUMA.
BAH! I WAS EXPECTING SOMETHING MORE IMPRESSIVE. I'VE FACED DRAGONS AND ONI--
I WON'T EVEN NEED THE TWO MOON TEA TO FACE A LARGER THAN AVERAGE BEAR.
I WONDER WHAT HIS PLAN IS?

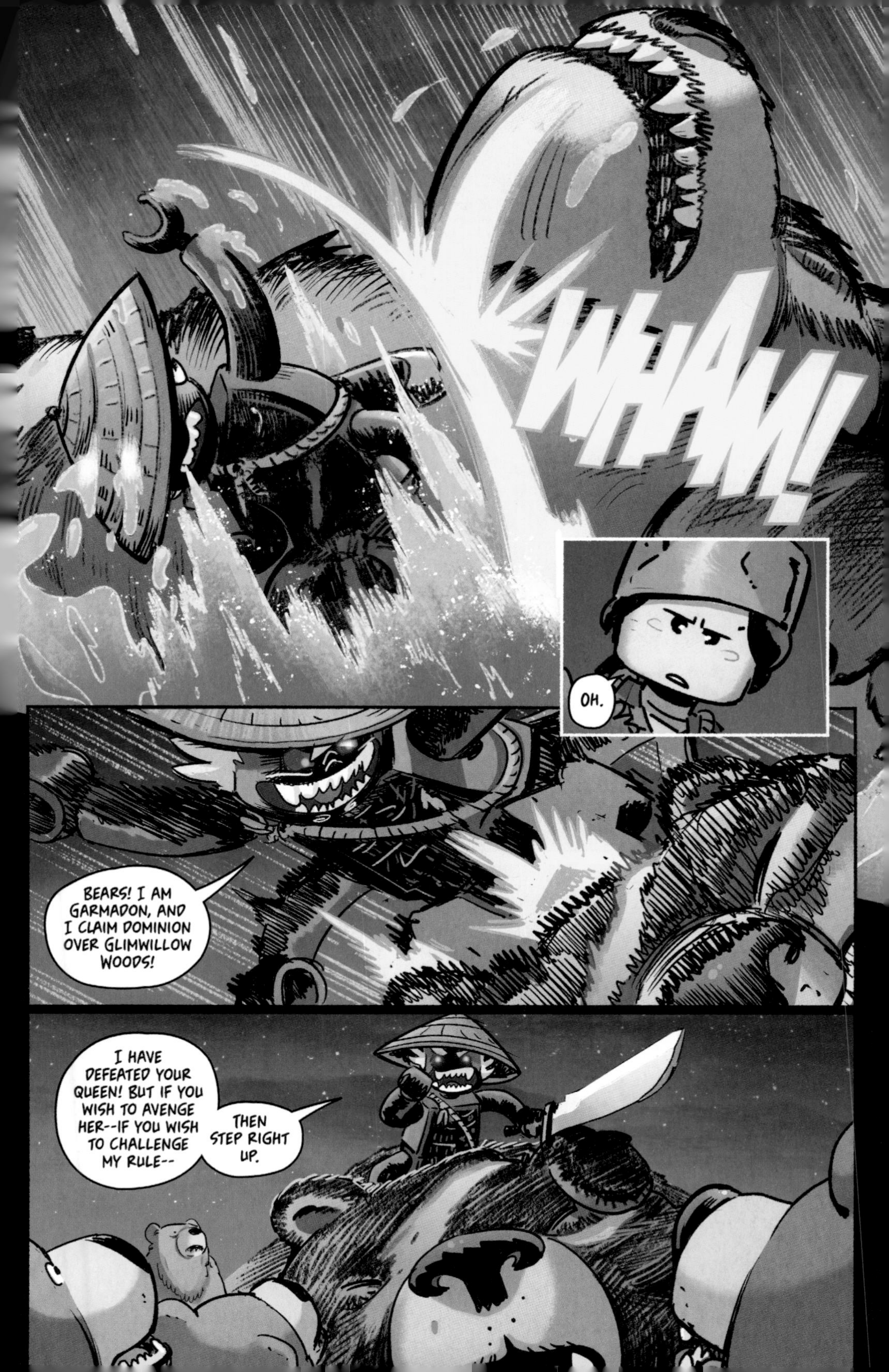
WHAM!
OH.
BEARS! I AM GARMADON, AND I CLAIM DOMINION OVER GLIMWILLOW WOODS!
I HAVE DEFEATED YOUR QUEEN! BUT IF YOU WISH TO AVENGE HER--IF YOU WISH TO CHALLENGE MY RULE--
THEN STEP RIGHT UP.

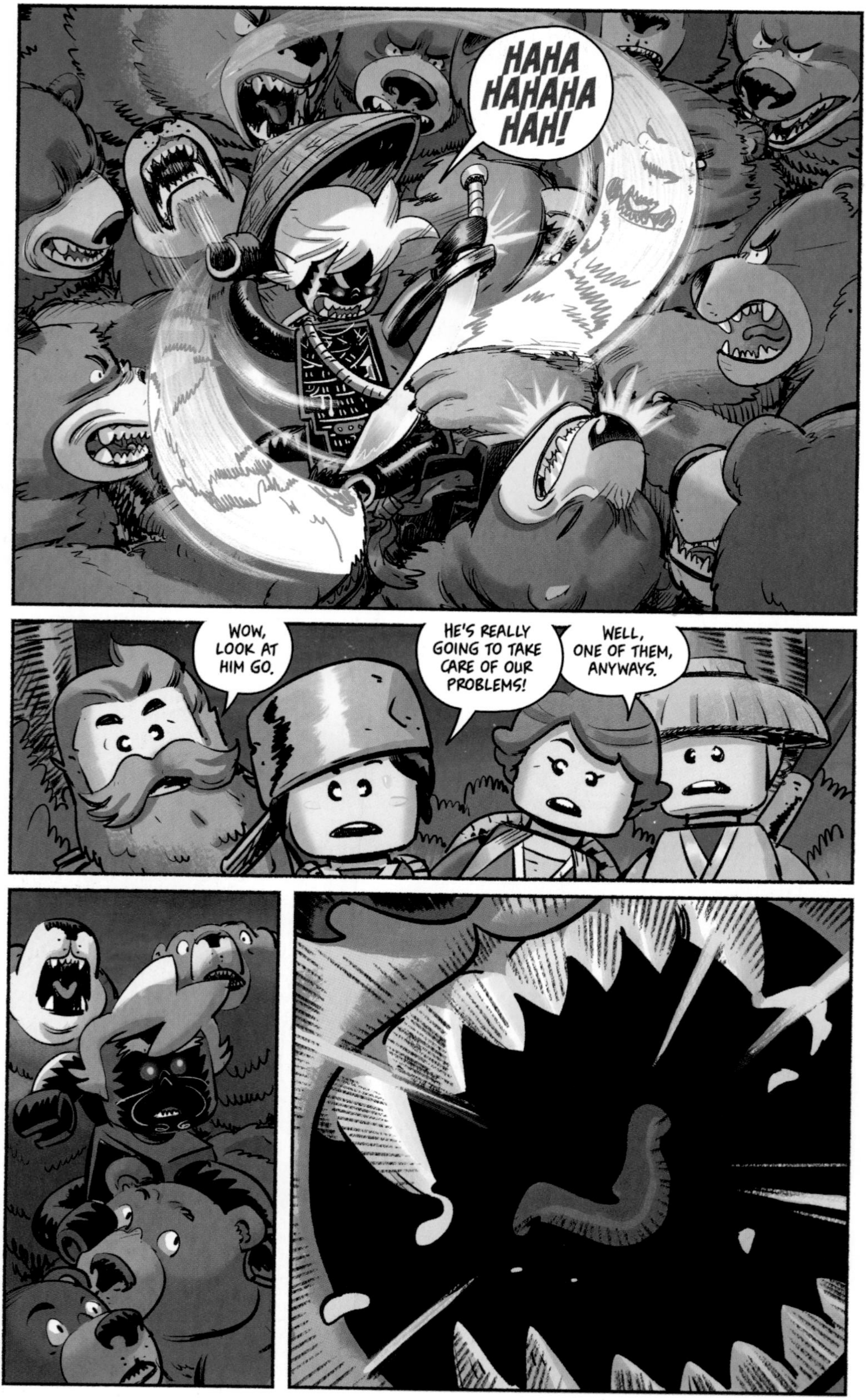
HAHA HAHAHA HAH!
WOW, LOOK AT HIM GO.
HE'S REALLY GOING TO TAKE CARE OF OUR PROBLEMS!
WELL, ONE OF THEM, ANYWAYS.

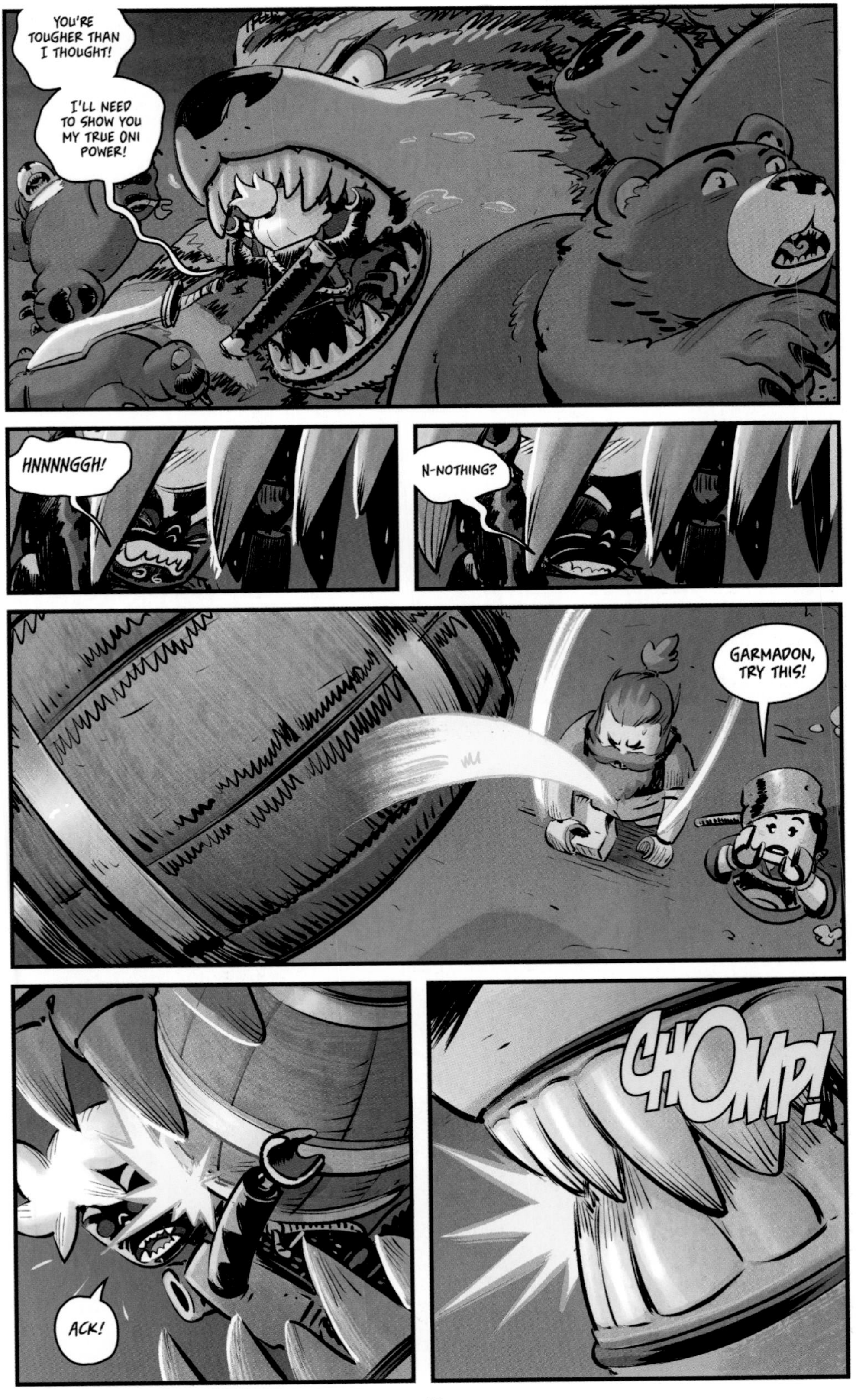
YOU'RE TOUGHER THAN I THOUGHT!
I'LL NEED TO SHOW YOU MY TRUE ONI POWER!
HNNNNGGH!
N-NOTHING?
GARMADON, TRY THIS!
ACK!
CHOMP!

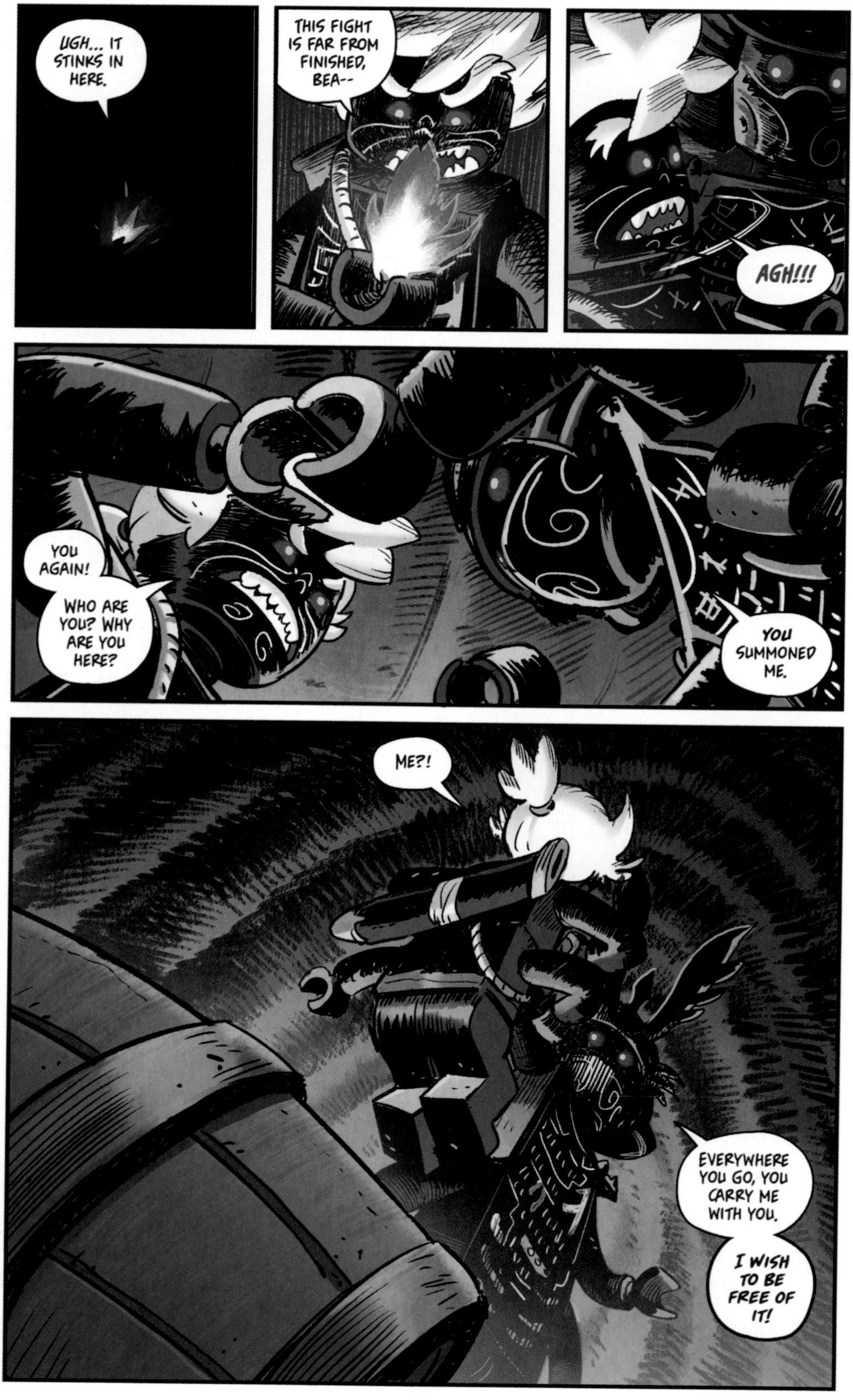
UGH... IT STINKS IN HERE.
THIS FIGHT IS FAR FROM FINISHED, BEA--
AGH!!!
YOU AGAIN!
WHO ARE YOU? WHY ARE YOU HERE?
YOU SUMMONED ME.
ME?!
EVERYWHERE YOU GO, YOU CARRY ME WITH YOU.
I WISH TO BE FREE OF IT!

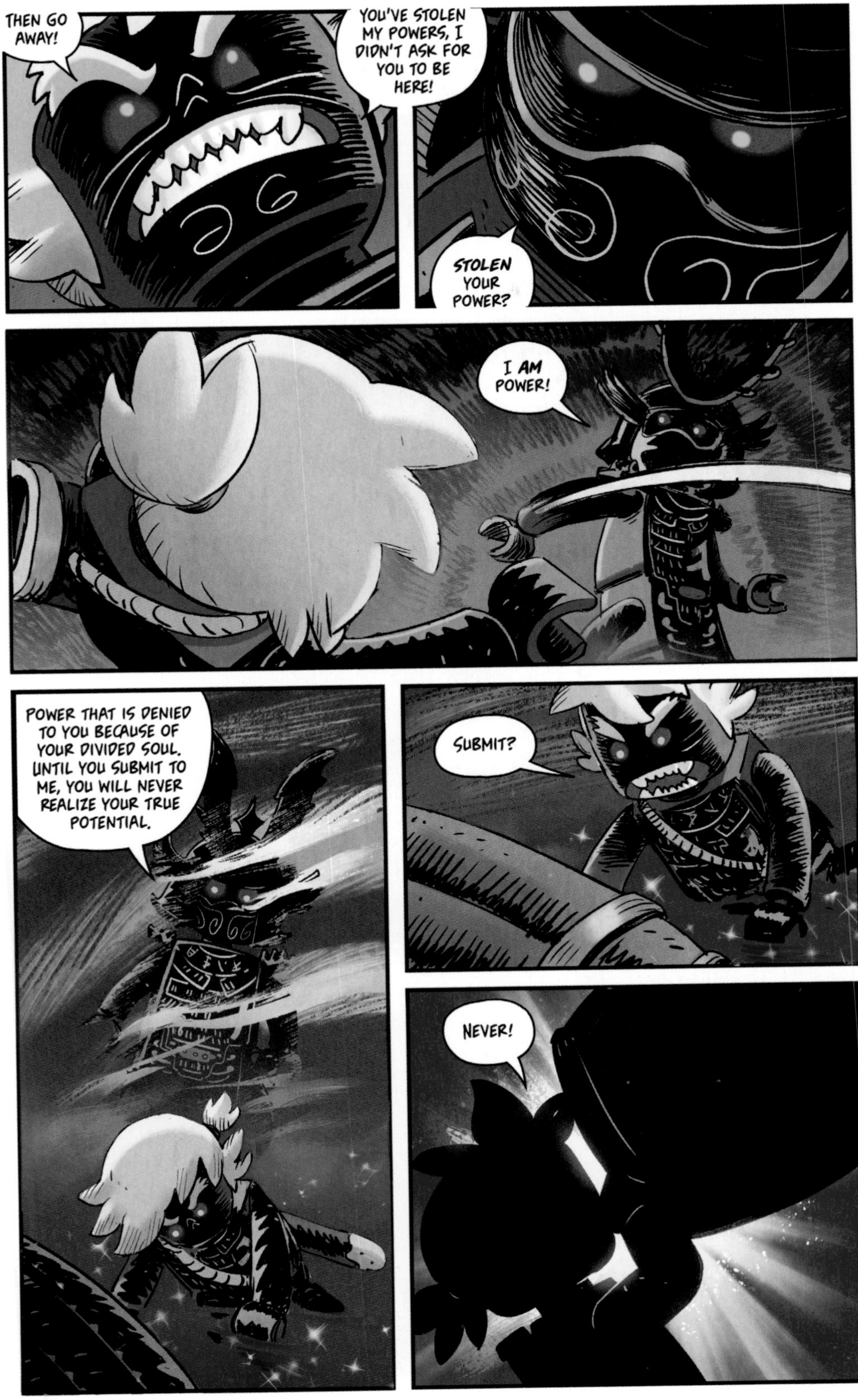
THEN GO AWAY!
YOU'VE STOLEN MY POWERS, I DIDN'T ASK FOR YOU TO BE HERE!
STOLEN YOUR POWER?
I AM POWER!
POWER THAT IS DENIED TO YOU BECAUSE OF YOUR DIVIDED SOUL. UNTIL YOU SUBMIT TO ME, YOU WILL NEVER REALIZE YOUR TRUE POTENTIAL.
SUBMIT?
NEVER!

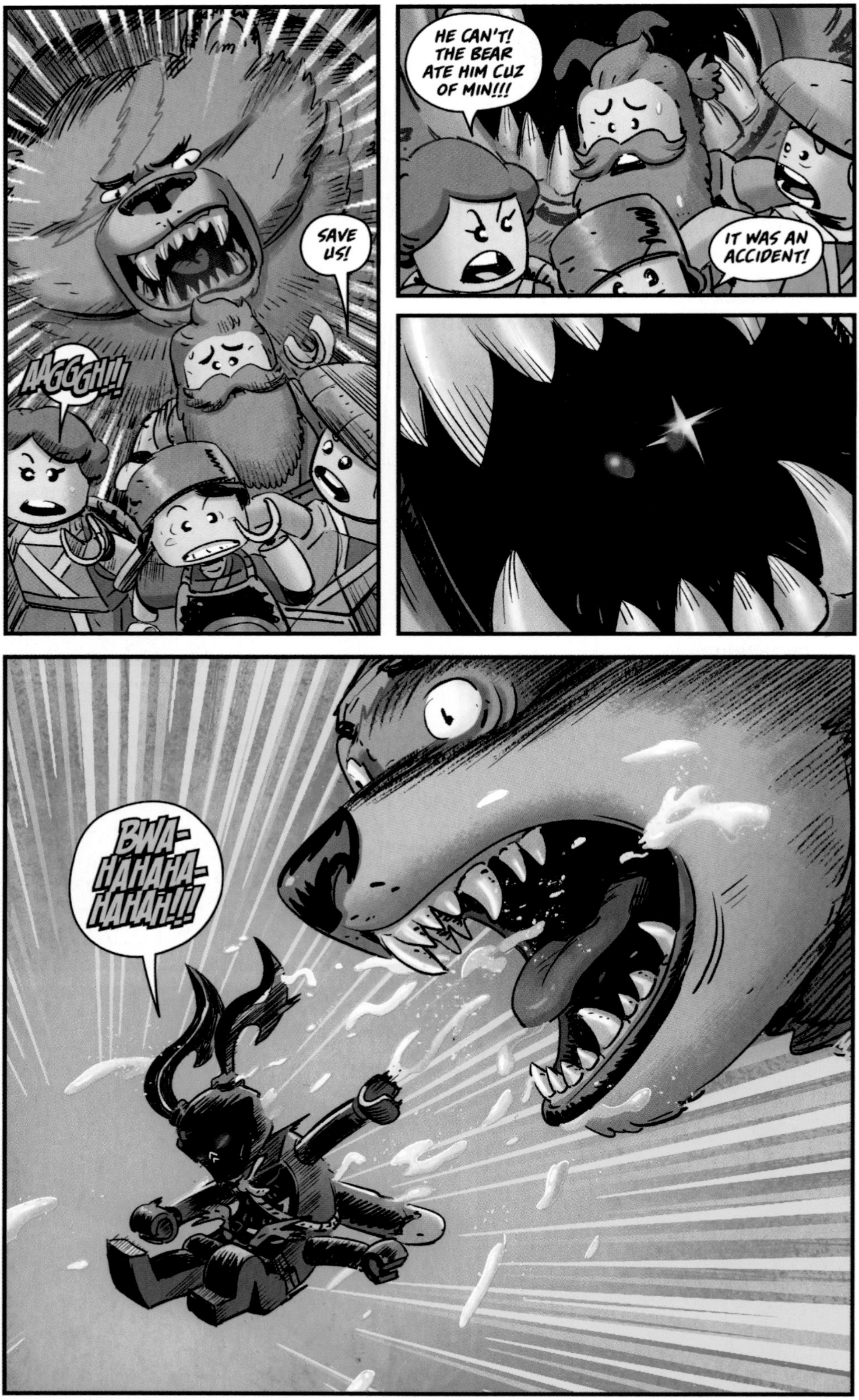
AAGGGH!!!
SAVE US!
HE CAN'T! THE BEAR ATE HIM CUZ OF MIN!!!
IT WAS AN ACCIDENT!
BWA-HAHAHA-HAHAH!!!

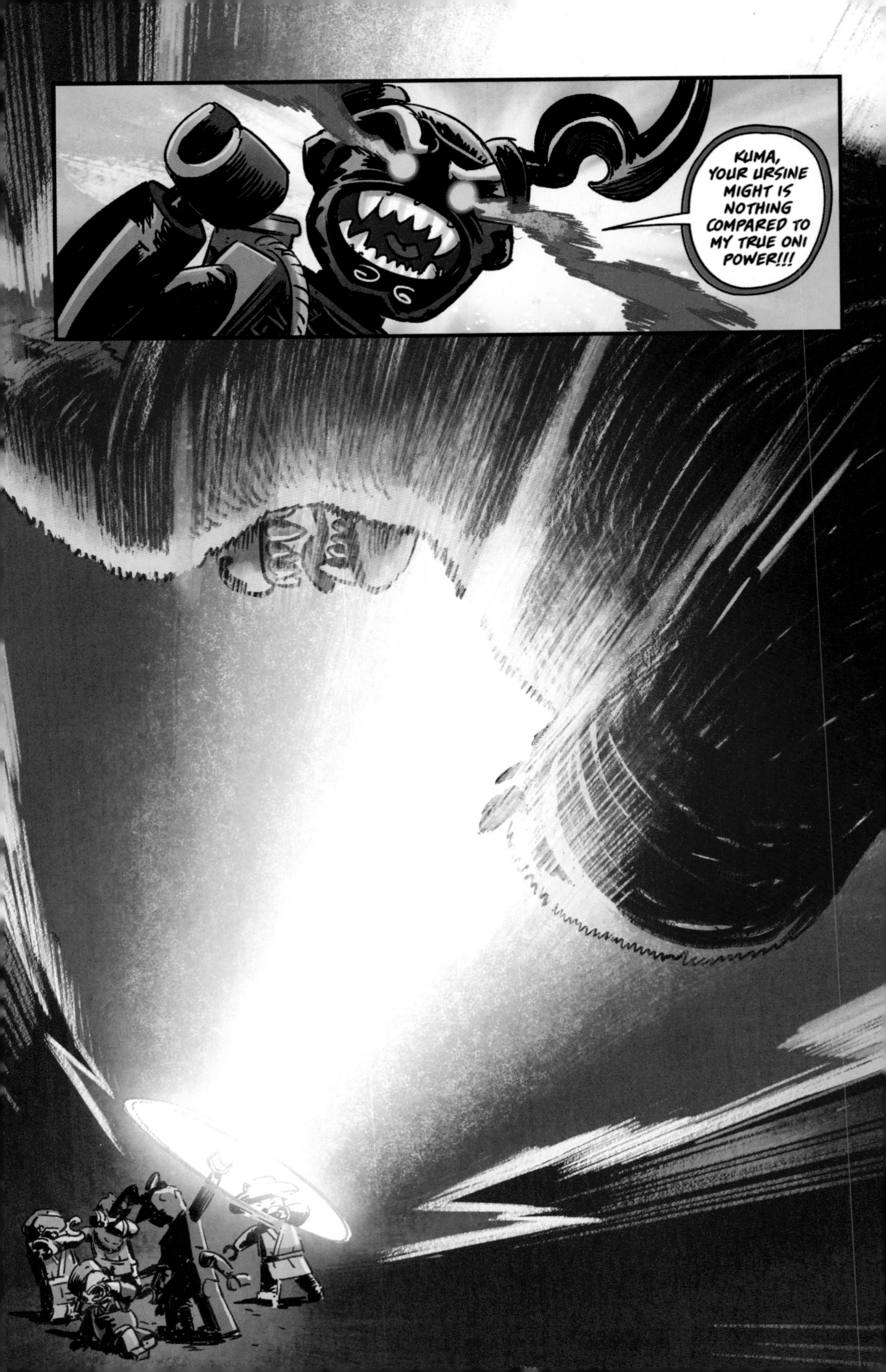
KUMA, YOUR URSINE MIGHT IS NOTHING COMPARED TO MY TRUE ONI POWER!!!

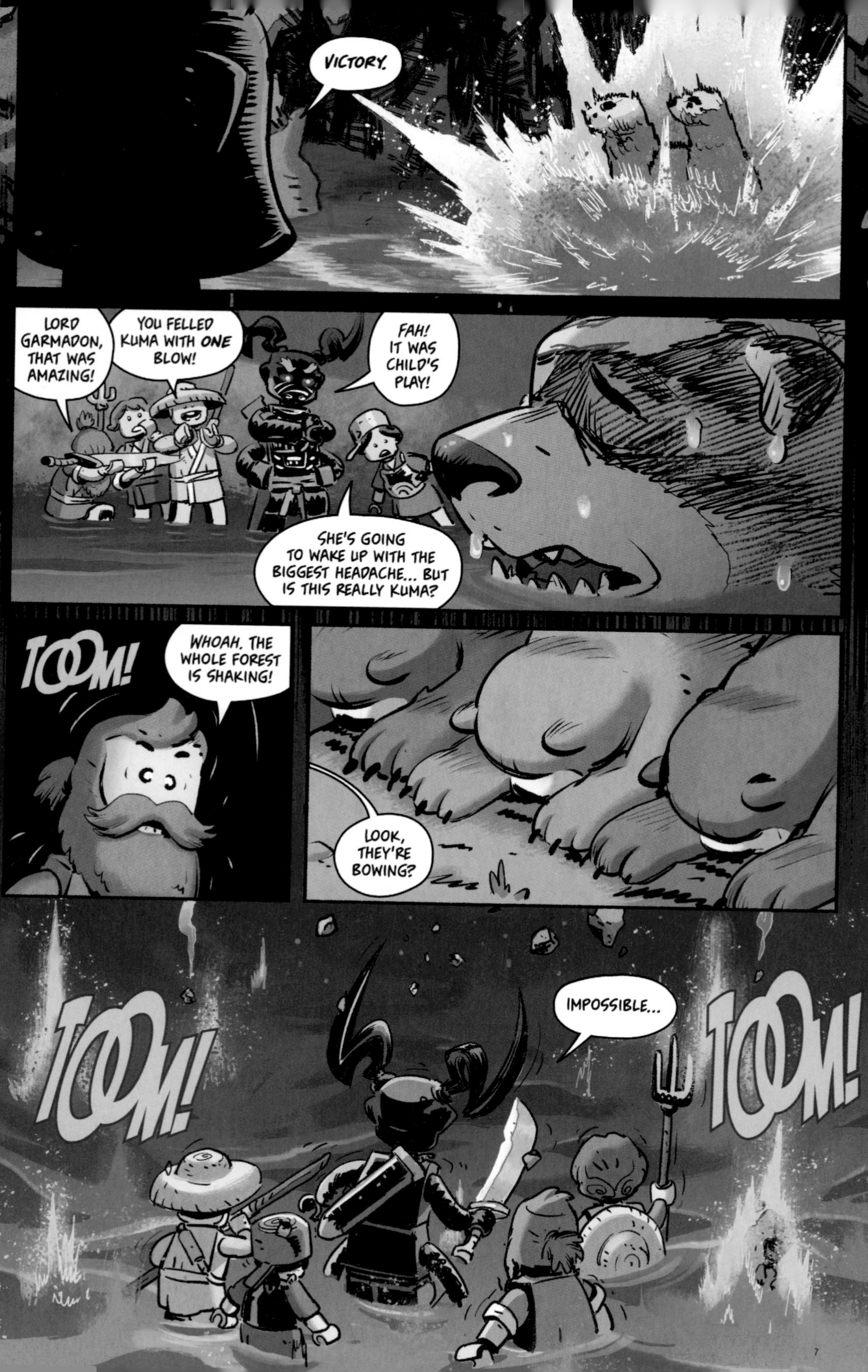

VICTORY.
LORD GARMADON, THAT WAS AMAZING!
YOU FELLED KUMA WITH ONE BLOW!
FAH! IT WAS CHILD'S PLAY!
SHE'S GOING TO WAKE UP WITH THE BIGGEST HEADACHE... BUT IS THIS REALLY KUMA?
TOOM!
WHOAH. THE WHOLE FOREST IS SHAKING!
LOOK, THEY'RE BOWING?
TOOM!
IMPOSSIBLE...
TOOM!

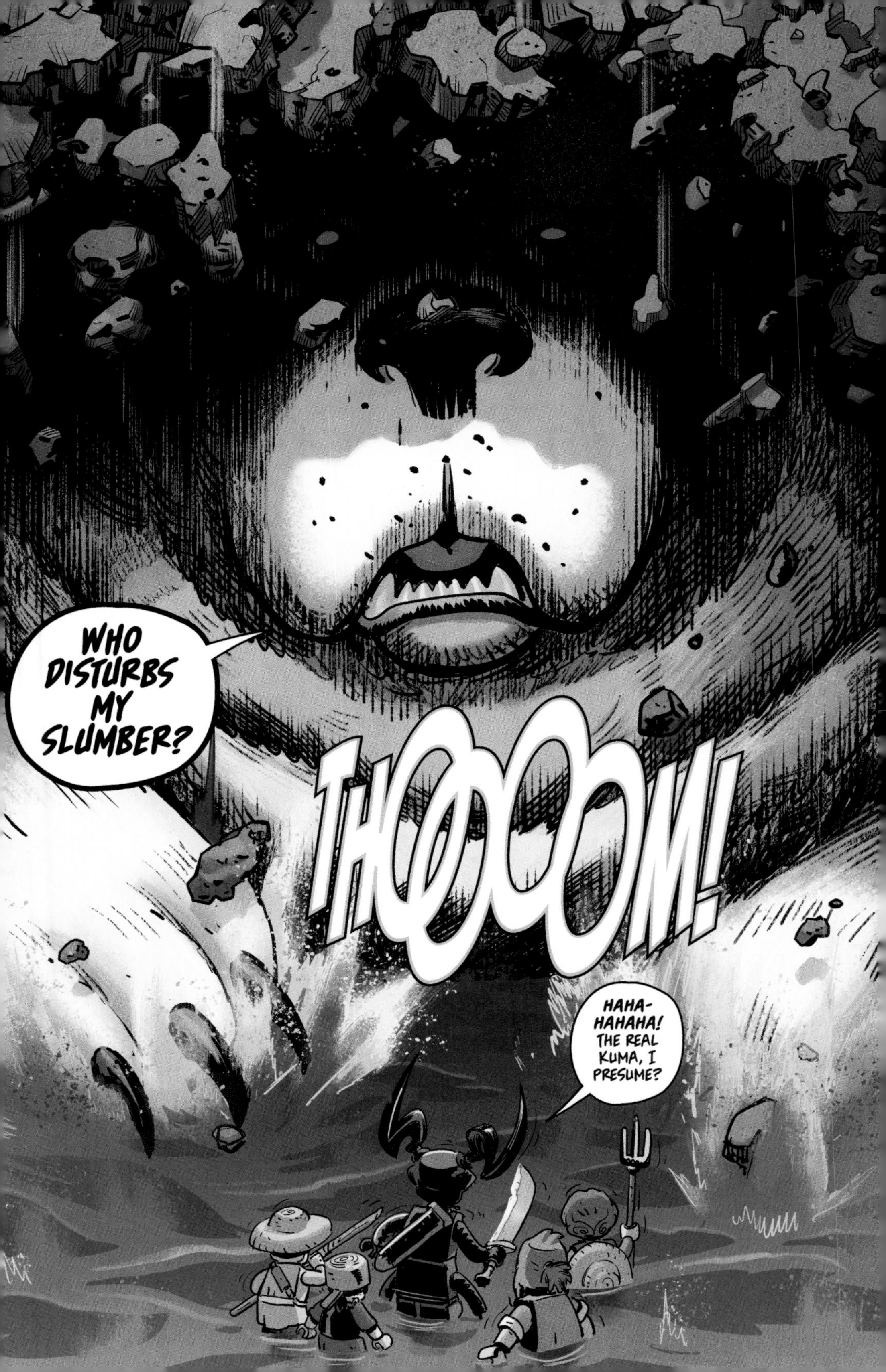
WHO DISTURBS MY SLUMBER?
THOOOOM!
HAHA-HAHAHA! THE REAL KUMA, I PRESUME?

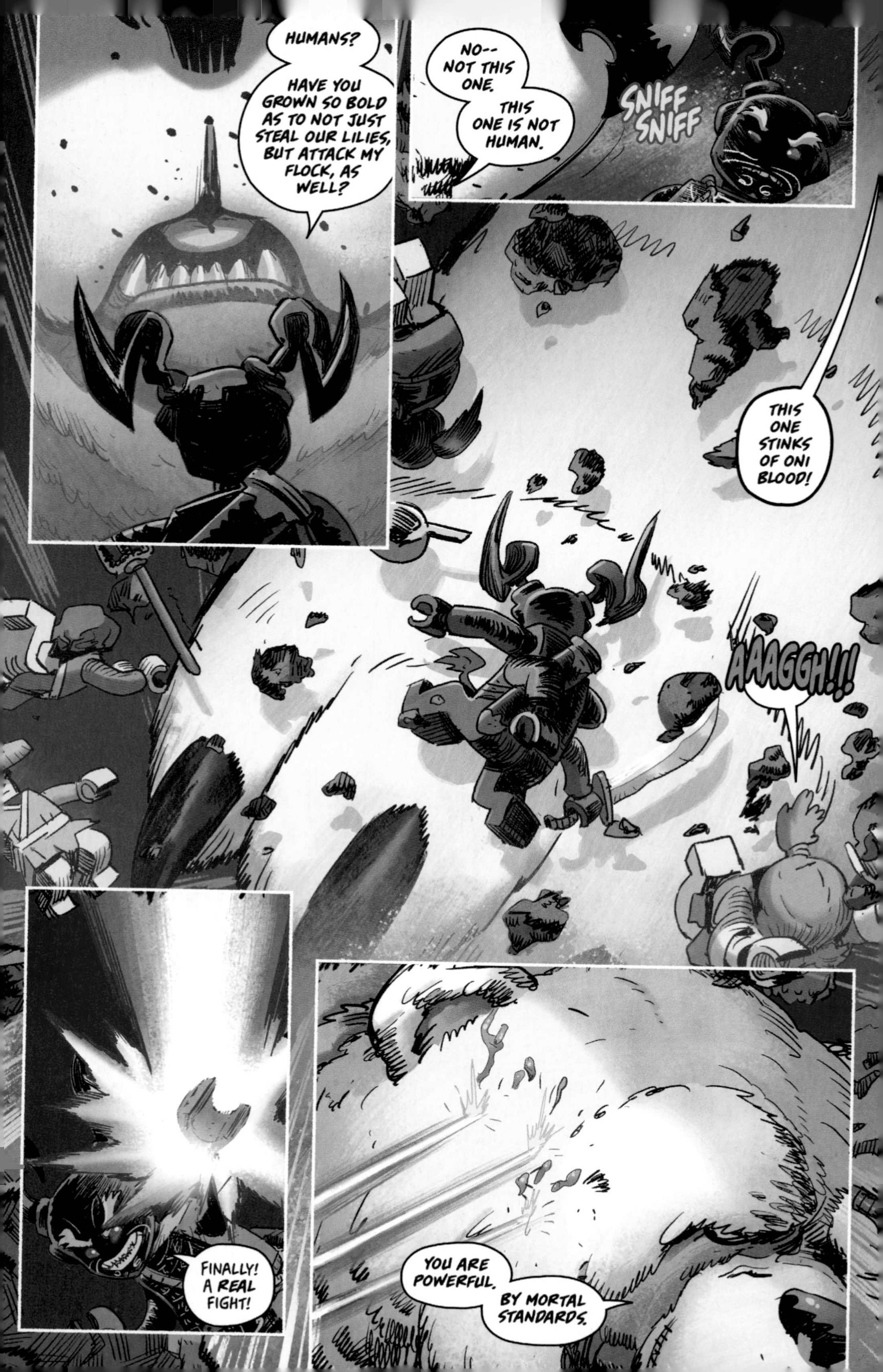
HUMANS?
HAVE YOU GROWN SO BOLD AS TO NOT JUST STEAL OUR LILIES, BUT ATTACK MY FLOCK, AS WELL?
NO-- NOT THIS ONE.
THIS ONE IS NOT HUMAN.
SNIFF SNIFF
THIS ONE STINKS OF ONI BLOOD!
AAAGGH!!!
FINALLY! A REAL FIGHT!
YOU ARE POWERFUL.
BY MORTAL STANDARDS.

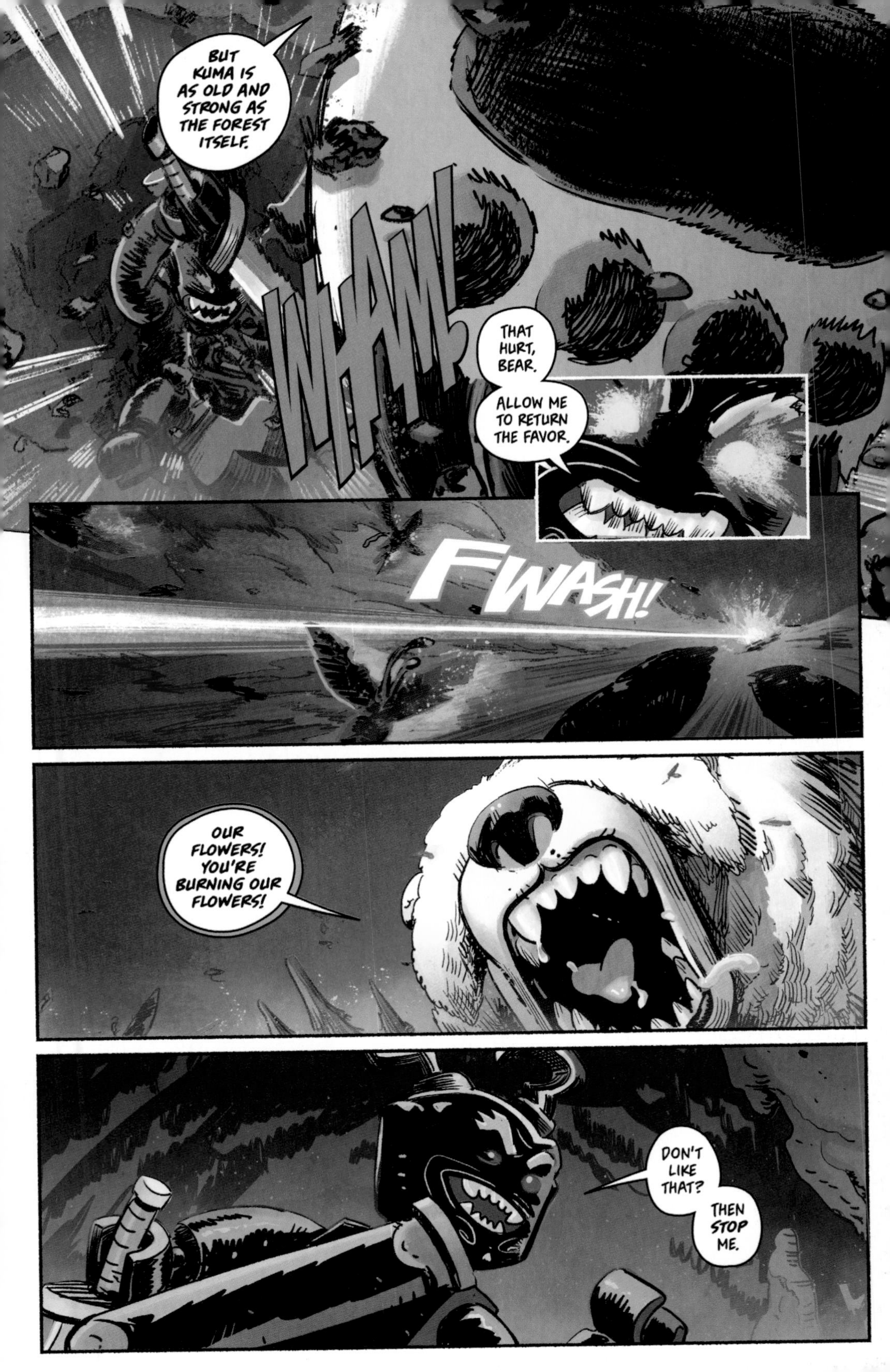
BUT KUMA IS AS OLD AND STRONG AS THE FOREST ITSELF.
WHAM!
THAT HURT, BEAR.
ALLOW ME TO RETURN THE FAVOR.
FWASH!
OUR FLOWERS! YOU'RE BURNING OUR FLOWERS!
DON'T LIKE THAT?
THEN STOP ME.

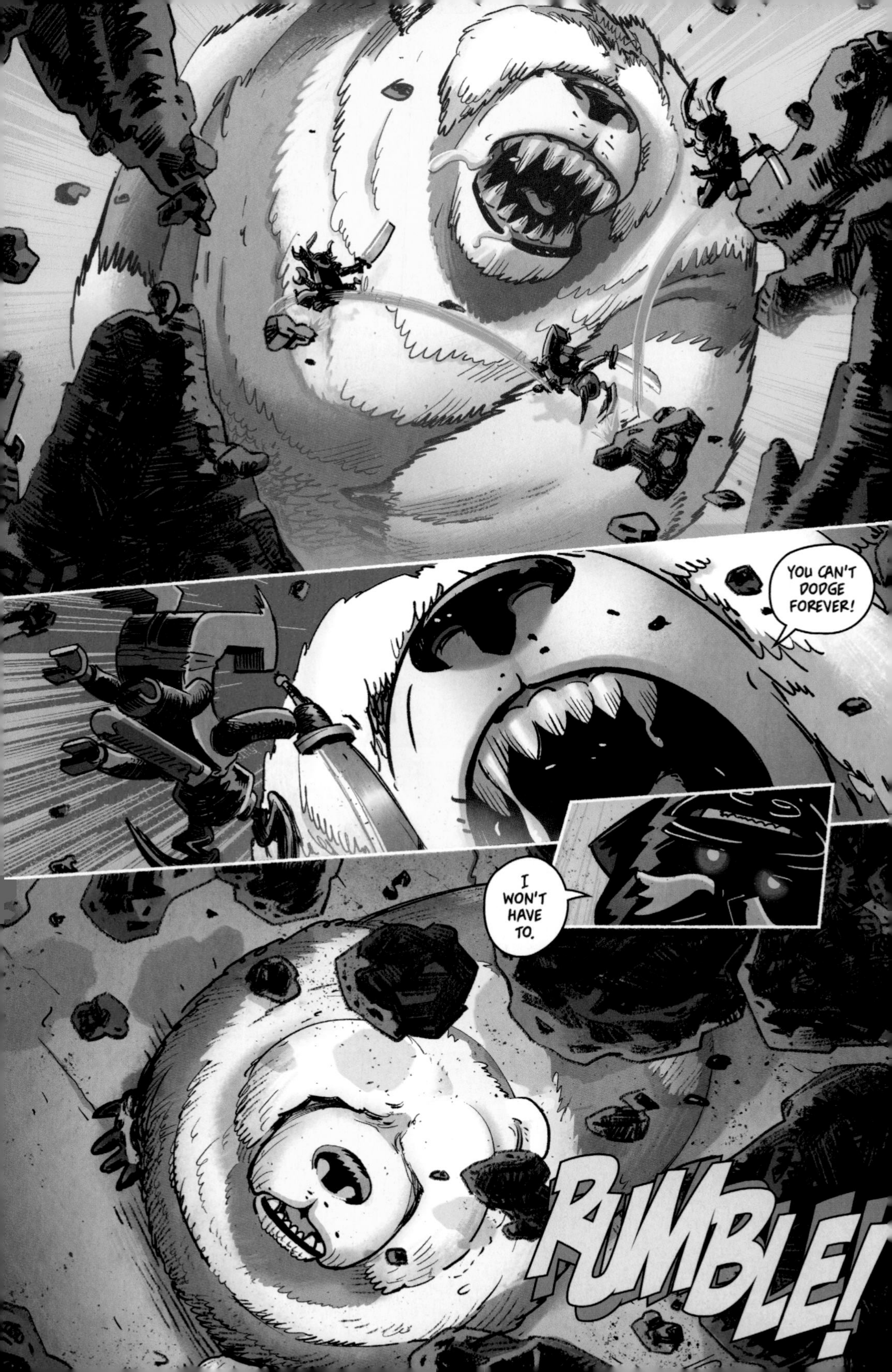
YOU CAN'T DODGE FOREVER!
I WON'T HAVE TO.
RUMBLE!

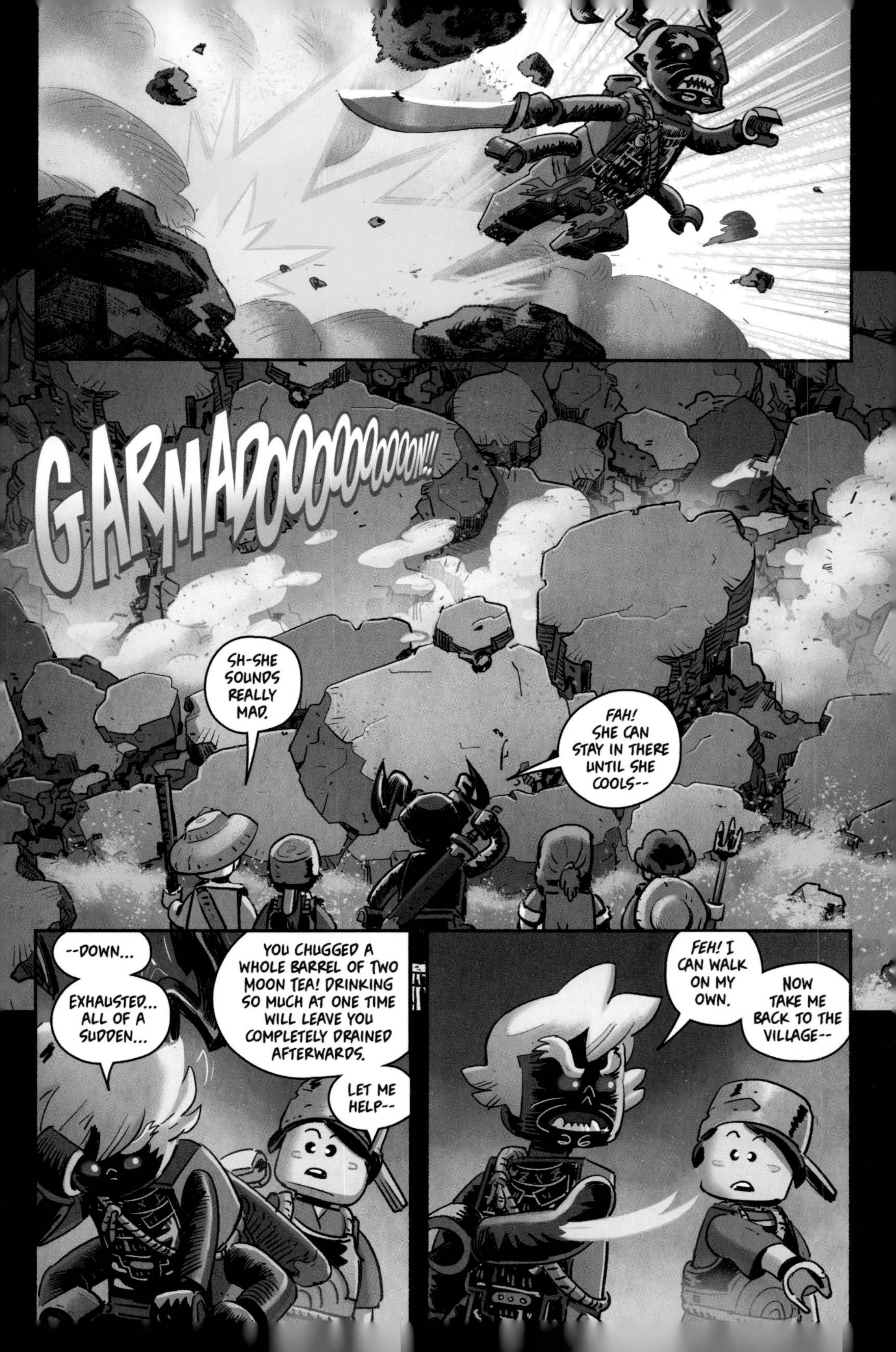
GARMADOOOOOOOOOON!!
SH-SHE SOUNDS REALLY MAD.
FAH! SHE CAN STAY IN THERE UNTIL SHE COOLS--
--DOWN...
EXHAUSTED... ALL OF A SUDDEN...
YOU CHUGGED A WHOLE BARREL OF TWO MOON TEA! DRINKING SO MUCH AT ONE TIME WILL LEAVE YOU COMPLETELY DRAINED AFTERWARDS.
LET ME HELP--
FEH! I CAN WALK ON MY OWN.
NOW TAKE ME BACK TO THE VILLAGE--

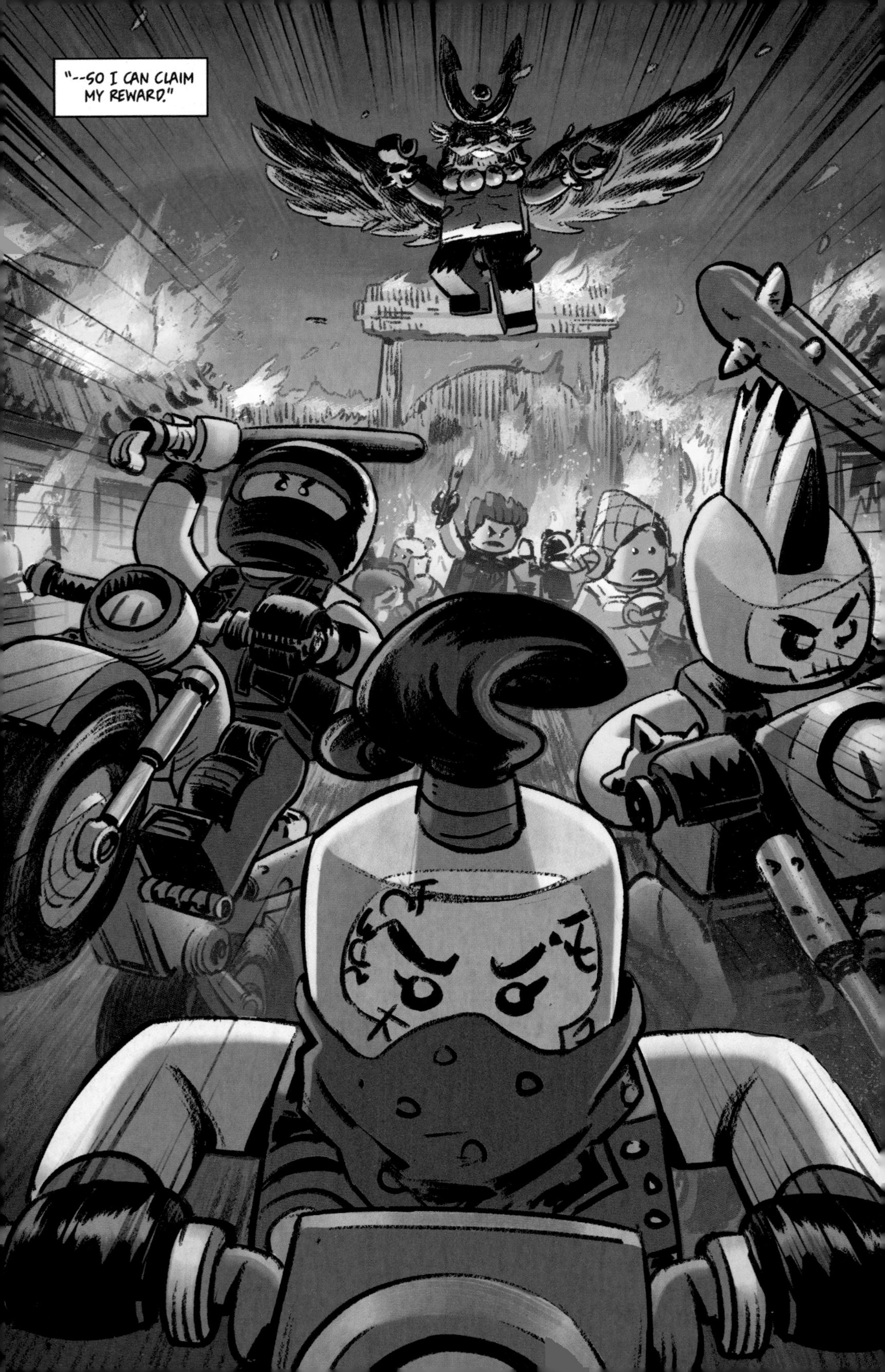
"--SO I CAN CLAIM MY REWARD."

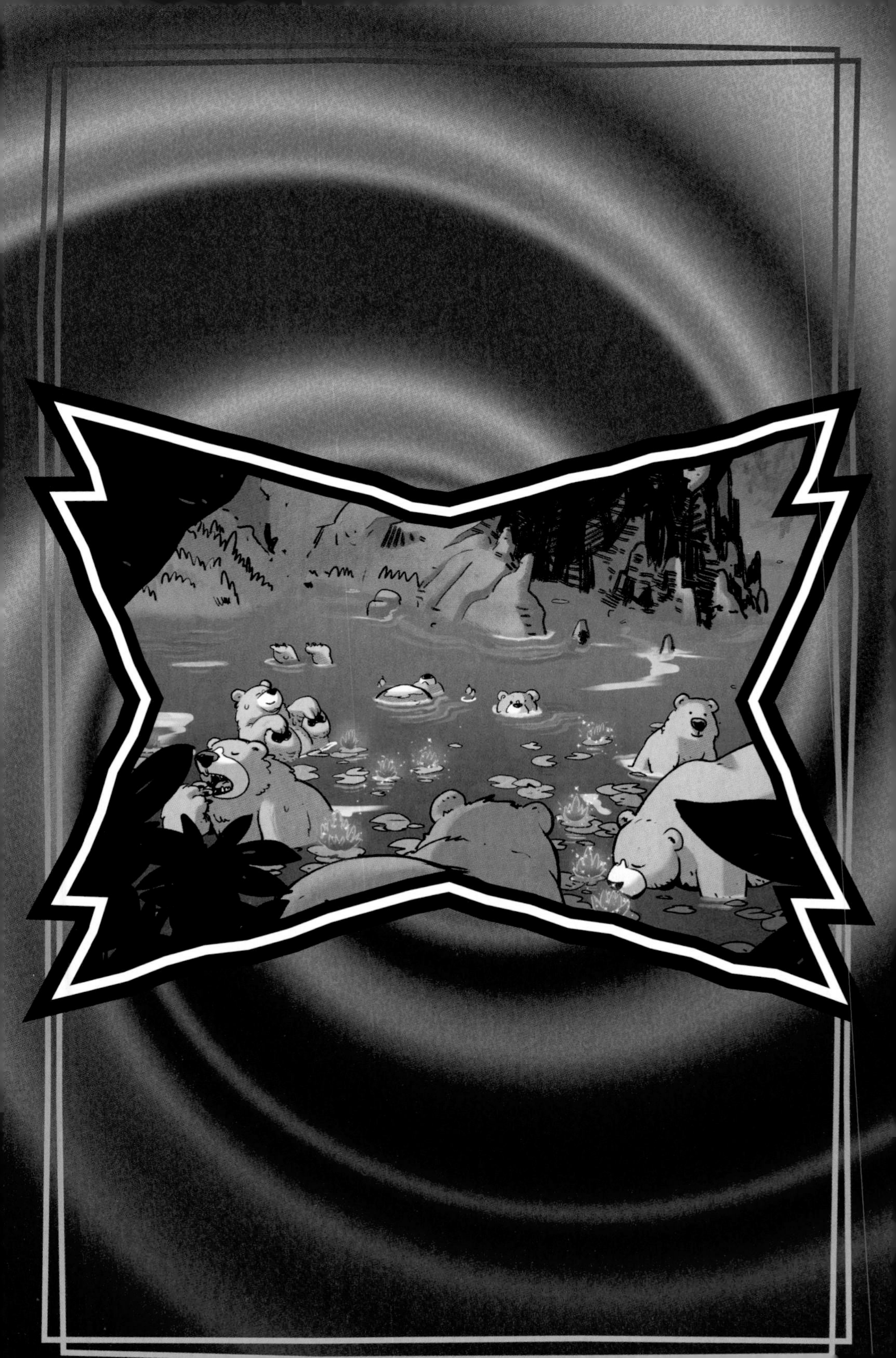

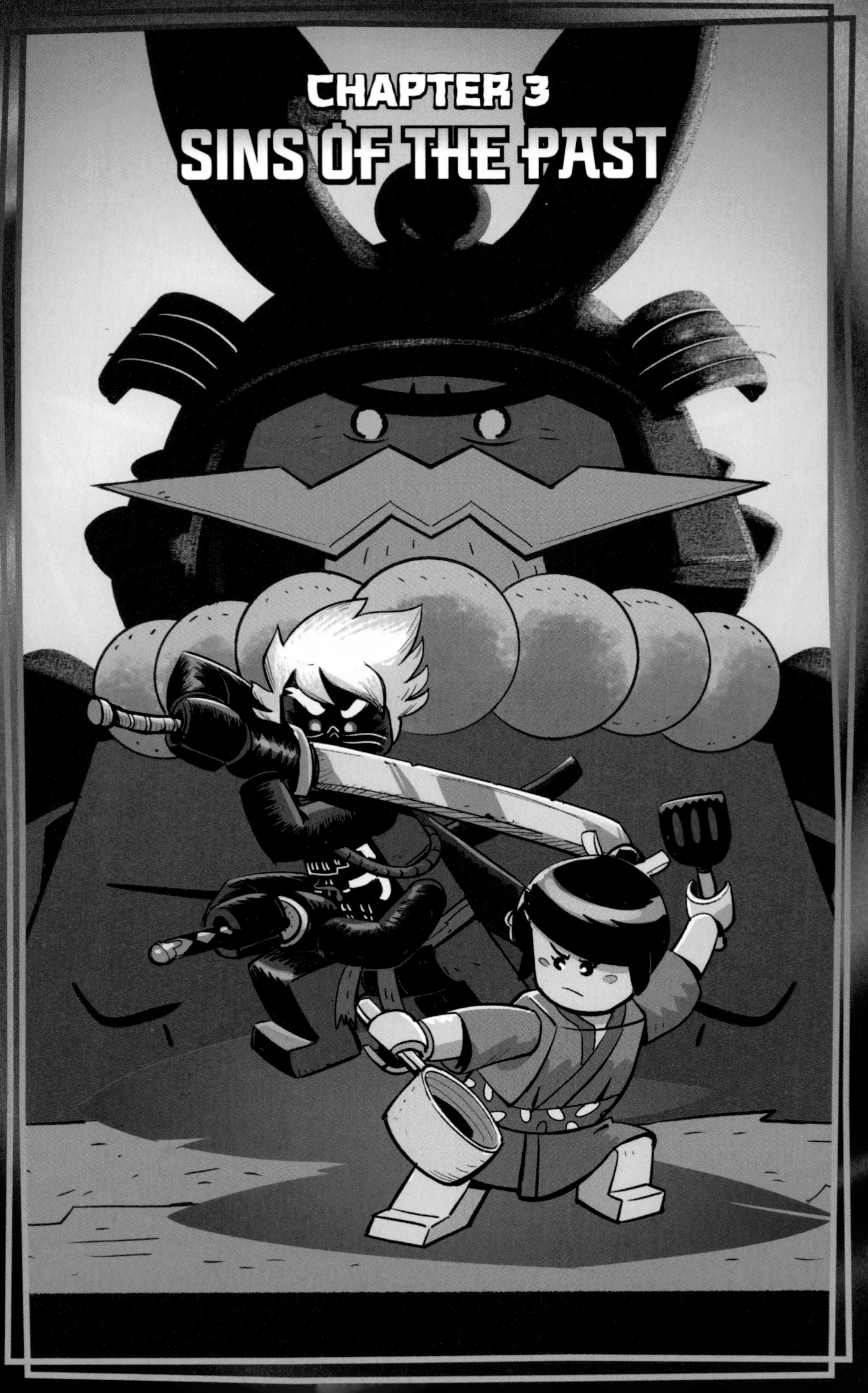
CHAPTER 3
SINS OF THE PAST

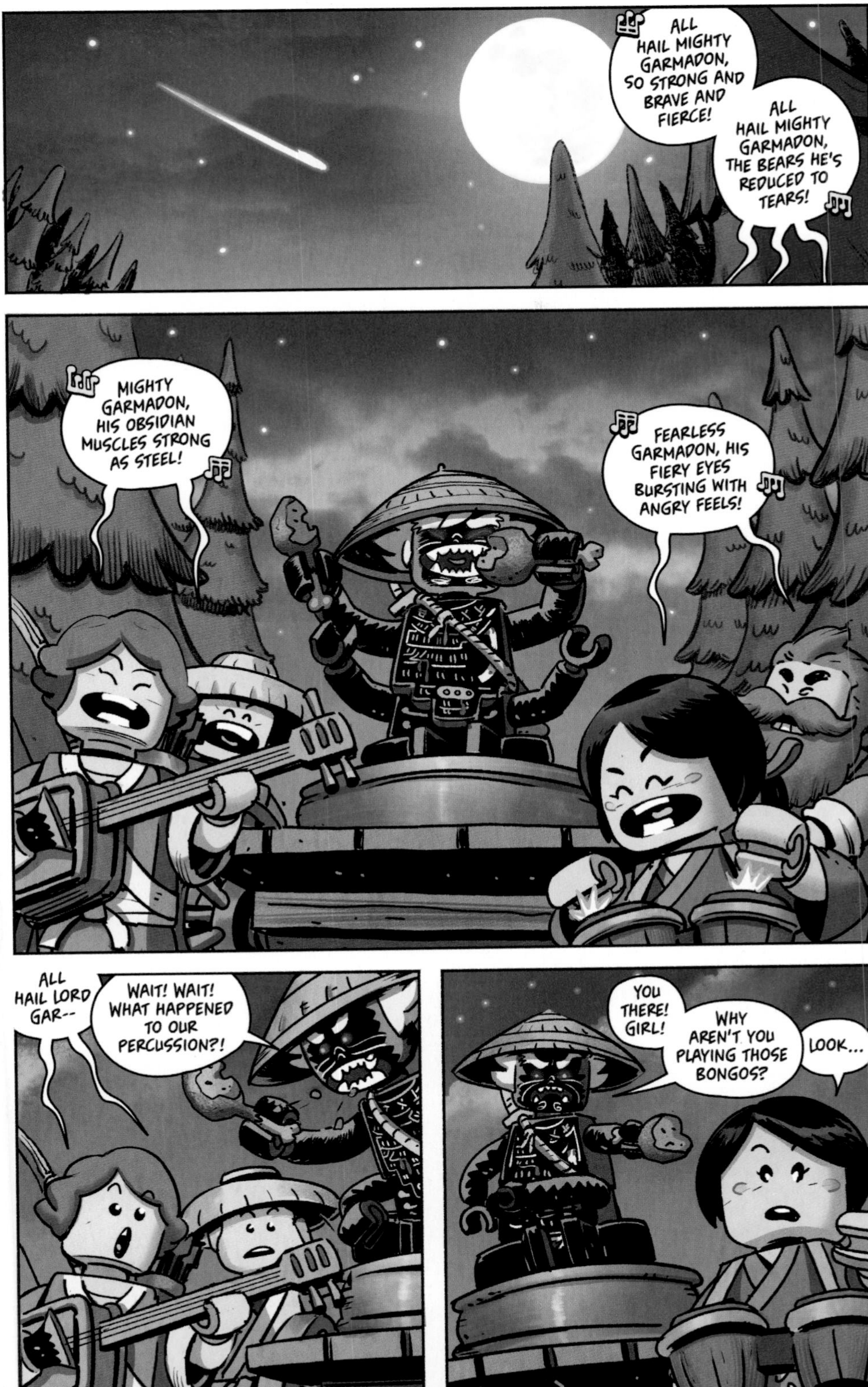

ALL HAIL MIGHTY GARMADON, SO STRONG AND BRAVE AND FIERCE!
ALL HAIL MIGHTY GARMADON, THE BEARS HE'S REDUCED TO TEARS!
MIGHTY GARMADON, HIS OBSIDIAN MUSCLES STRONG AS STEEL!
FEARLESS GARMADON, HIS FIERY EYES BURSTING WITH ANGRY FEELS!
ALL HAIL LORD GAR--
WAIT! WAIT! WHAT HAPPENED TO OUR PERCUSSION?!
YOU THERE! GIRL!
WHY AREN'T YOU PLAYING THOSE BONGOS?
LOOK...

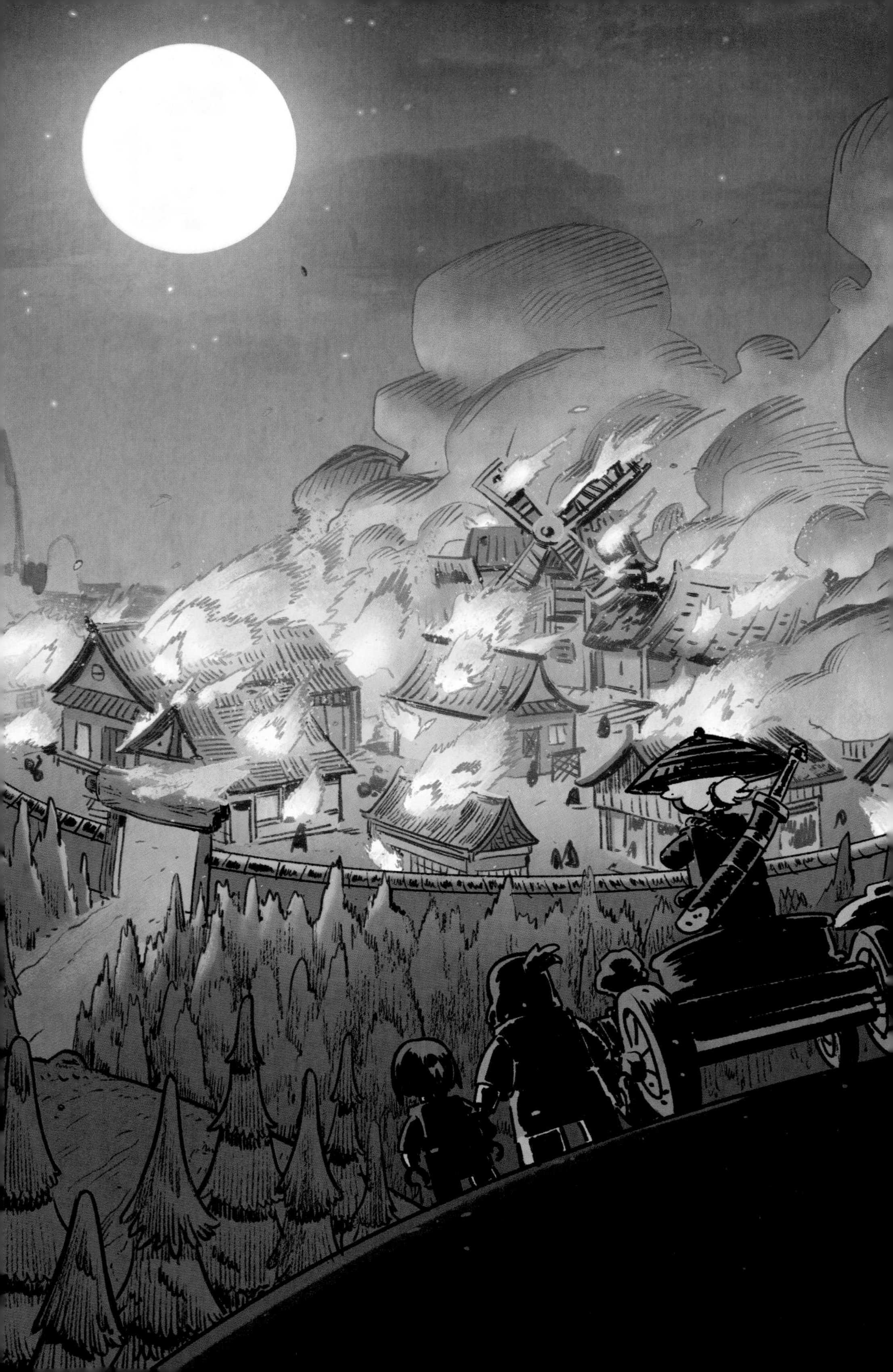

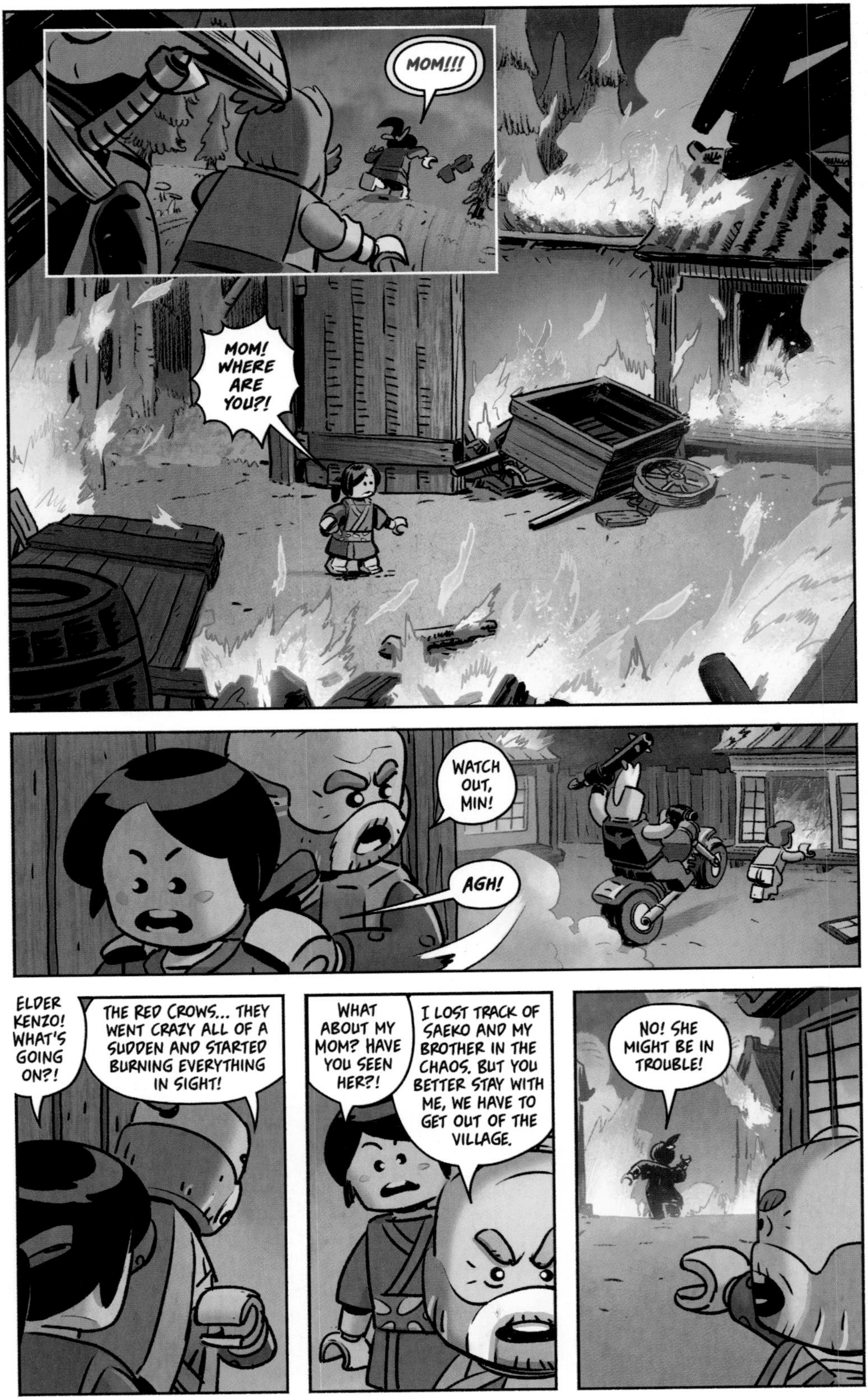
MOM!!!
MOM! WHERE ARE YOU?!
WATCH OUT, MIN!
AGH!
ELDER KENZO! WHAT'S GOING ON?!
THE RED CROWS... THEY WENT CRAZY ALL OF A SUDDEN AND STARTED BURNING EVERYTHING IN SIGHT!
WHAT ABOUT MY MOM? HAVE YOU SEEN HER?!
I LOST TRACK OF SAEKO AND MY BROTHER IN THE CHAOS. BUT YOU BETTER STAY WITH ME, WE HAVE TO GET OUT OF THE VILLAGE.
NO! SHE MIGHT BE IN TROUBLE!

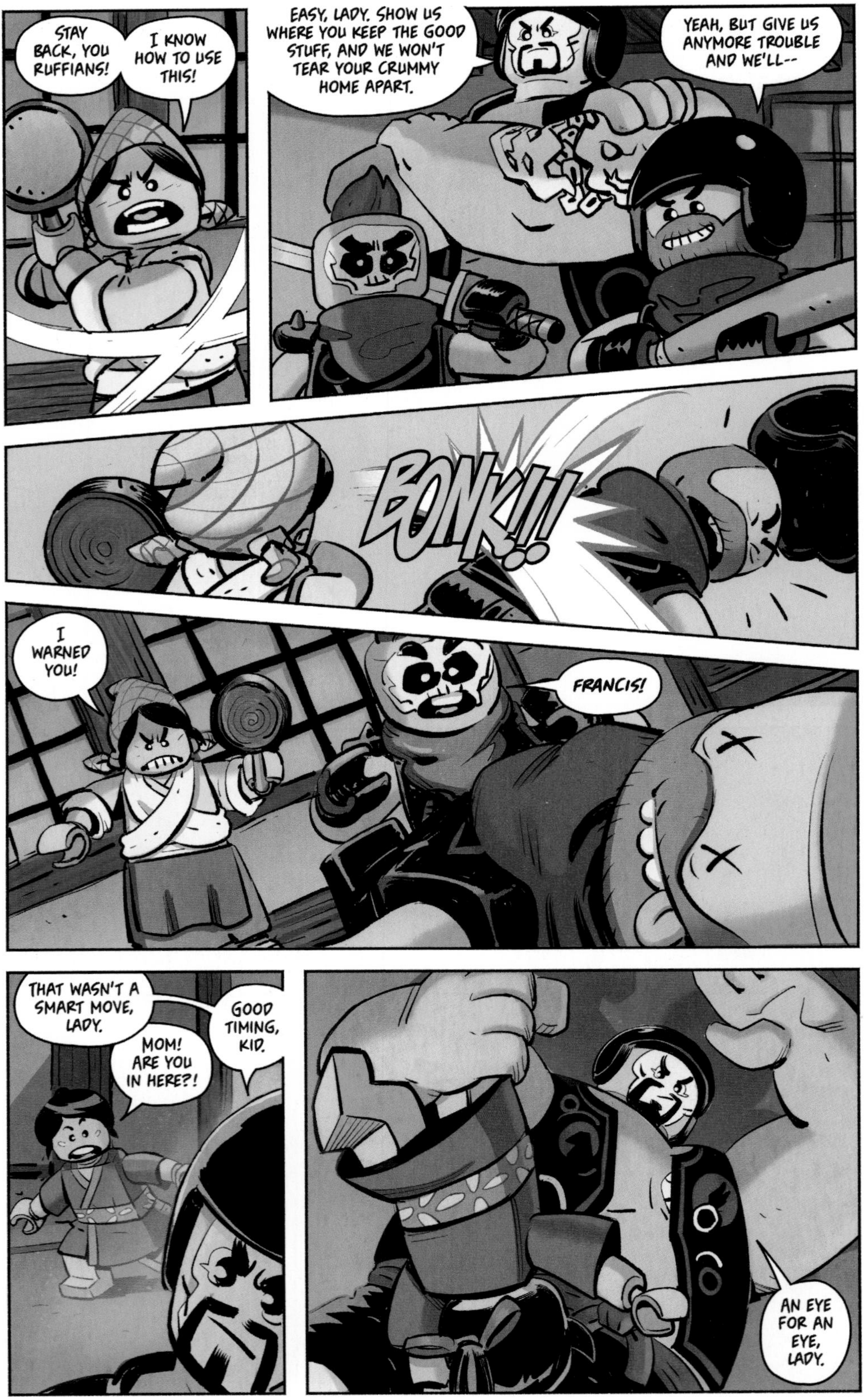
STAY BACK, YOU RUFFIANS!
I KNOW HOW TO USE THIS!
EASY, LADY. SHOW US WHERE YOU KEEP THE GOOD STUFF, AND WE WON'T TEAR YOUR CRUMMY HOME APART.
YEAH, BUT GIVE US ANYMORE TROUBLE AND WE'LL--
BONK!!!
I WARNED YOU!
FRANCIS!
THAT WASN'T A SMART MOVE, LADY.
MOM! ARE YOU IN HERE?!
GOOD TIMING, KID.
AN EYE FOR AN EYE, LADY.

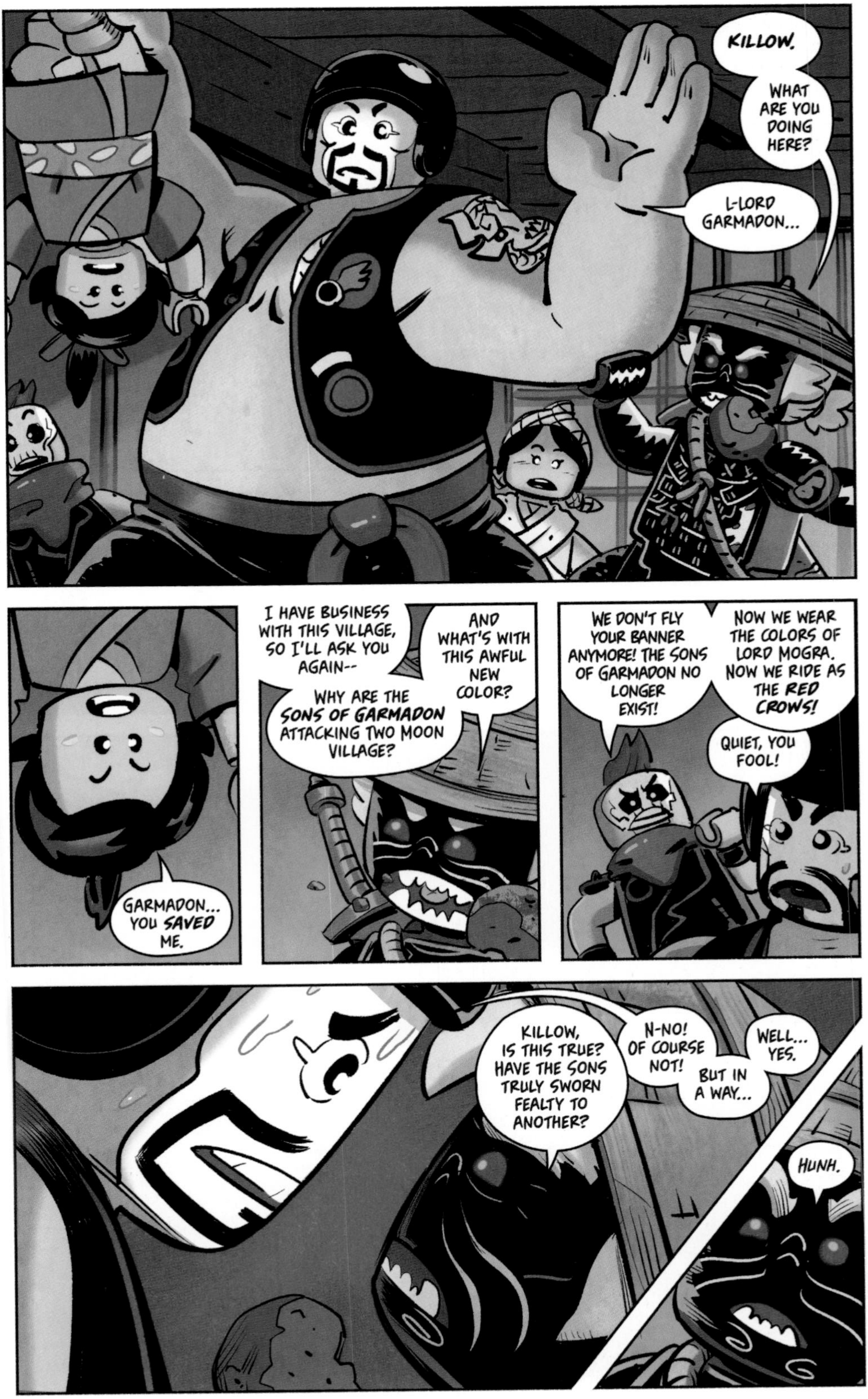
KILLOW.
WHAT ARE YOU DOING HERE?
L-LORD GARMADON...
GARMADON... YOU SAVED ME.
I HAVE BUSINESS WITH THIS VILLAGE, SO I'LL ASK YOU AGAIN--
WHY ARE THE SONS OF GARMADON ATTACKING TWO MOON VILLAGE?
AND WHAT'S WITH THIS AWFUL NEW COLOR?
WE DON'T FLY YOUR BANNER ANYMORE! THE SONS OF GARMADON NO LONGER EXIST!
NOW WE WEAR THE COLORS OF LORD MOGRA. NOW WE RIDE AS THE RED CROWS!
QUIET, YOU FOOL!
KILLOW, IS THIS TRUE? HAVE THE SONS TRULY SWORN FEALTY TO ANOTHER?
N-NO! OF COURSE NOT!
BUT IN A WAY...
WELL... YES.
HUNH.

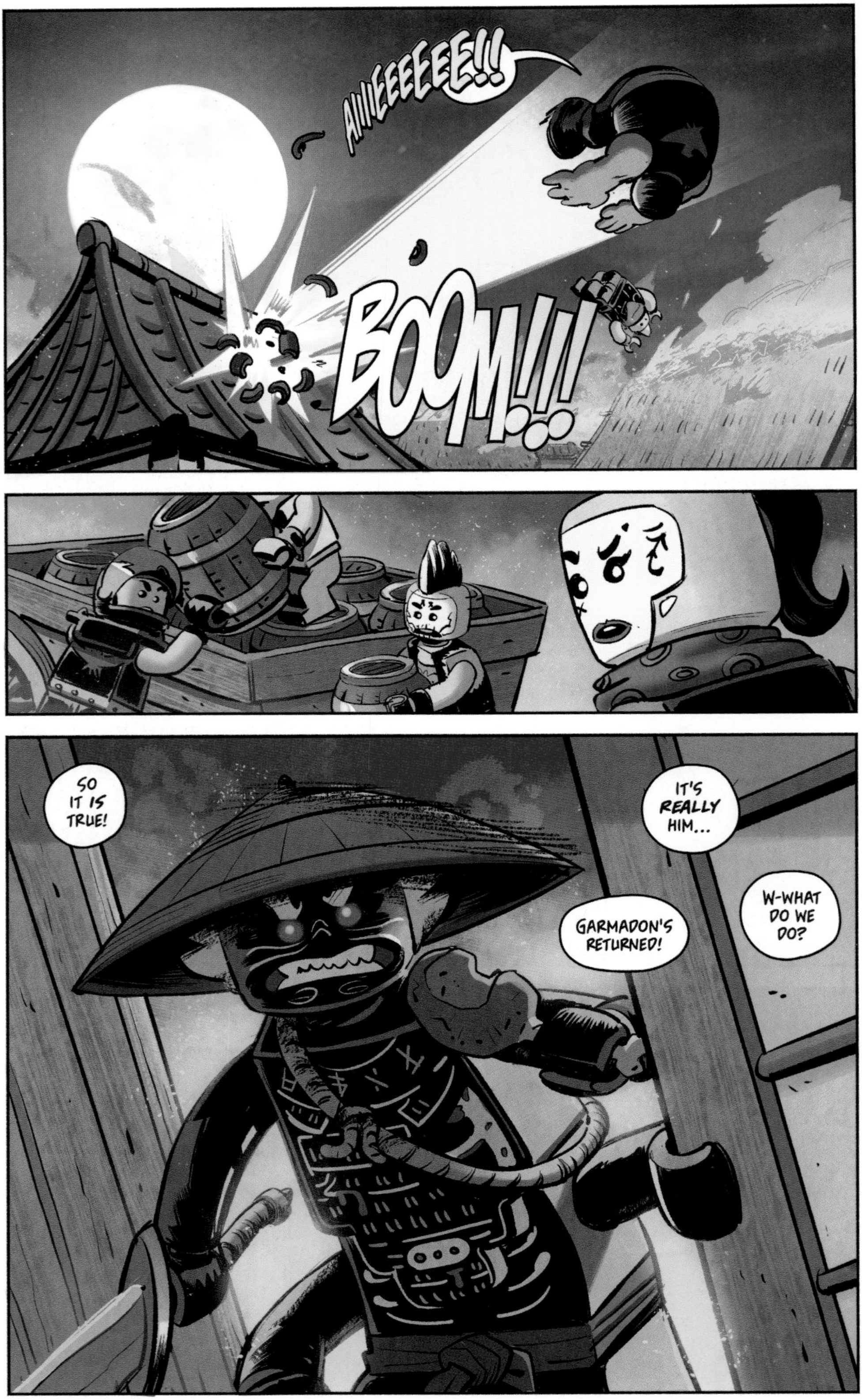
AIIIEEEEEE!!!
BOOM!!!
SO IT IS TRUE!
IT'S REALLY HIM...
GARMADON'S RETURNED!
W-WHAT DO WE DO?

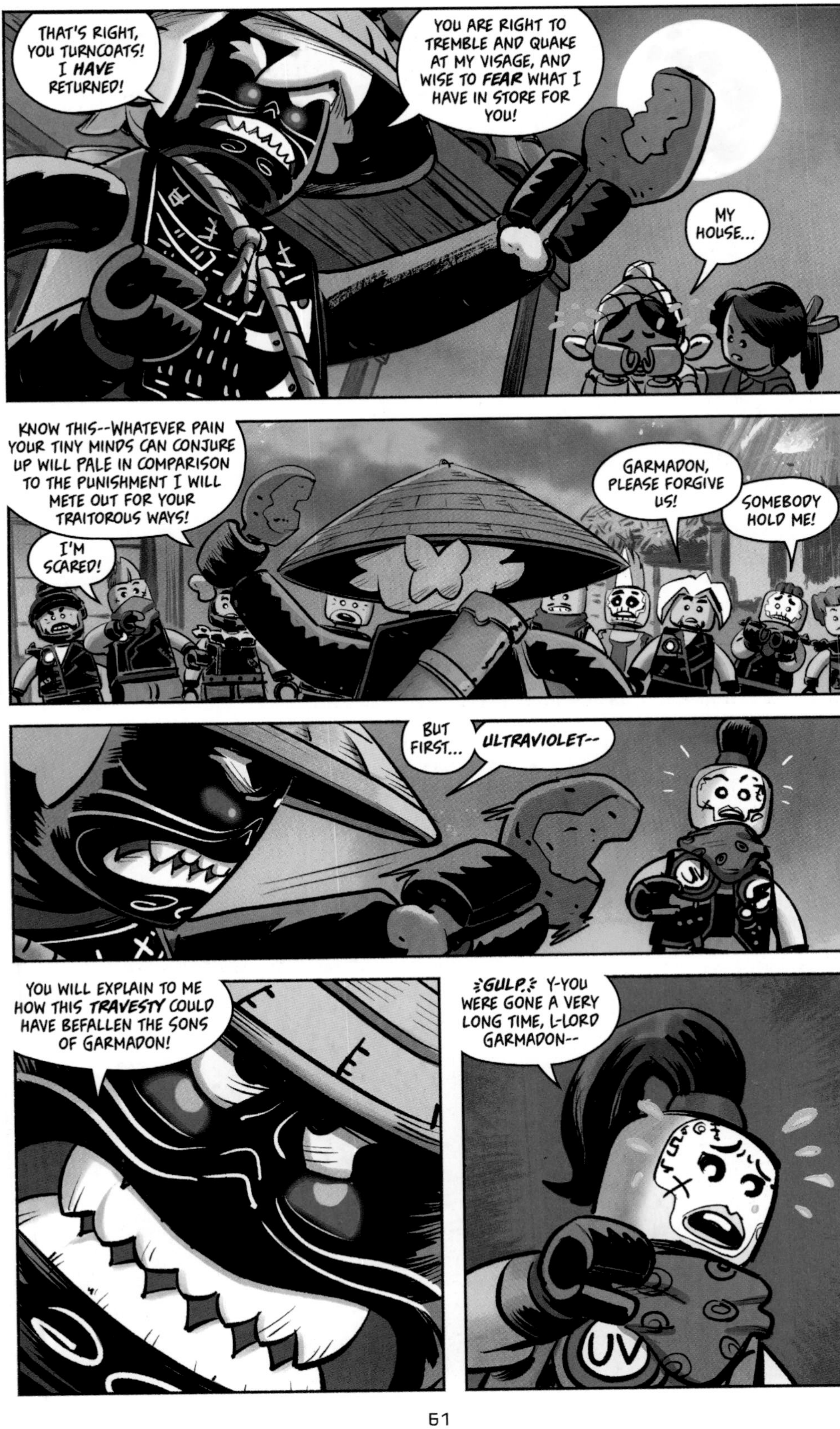
THAT'S RIGHT, YOU TURNCOATS! I **HAVE** RETURNED!
YOU ARE RIGHT TO TREMBLE AND QUAKE AT MY VISAGE, AND WISE TO **FEAR** WHAT I HAVE IN STORE FOR YOU!
MY HOUSE...
KNOW THIS--WHATEVER PAIN YOUR TINY MINDS CAN CONJURE UP WILL PALE IN COMPARISON TO THE PUNISHMENT I WILL METE OUT FOR YOUR TRAITOROUS WAYS!
I'M SCARED!
GARMADON, PLEASE FORGIVE US!
SOMEBODY HOLD ME!
BUT FIRST...
ULTRAVIOLET--
UV
YOU WILL EXPLAIN TO ME HOW THIS **TRAVESTY** COULD HAVE BEFALLEN THE SONS OF GARMADON!
GULP. Y-YOU WERE GONE A VERY LONG TIME, L-LORD GARMADON--
UV

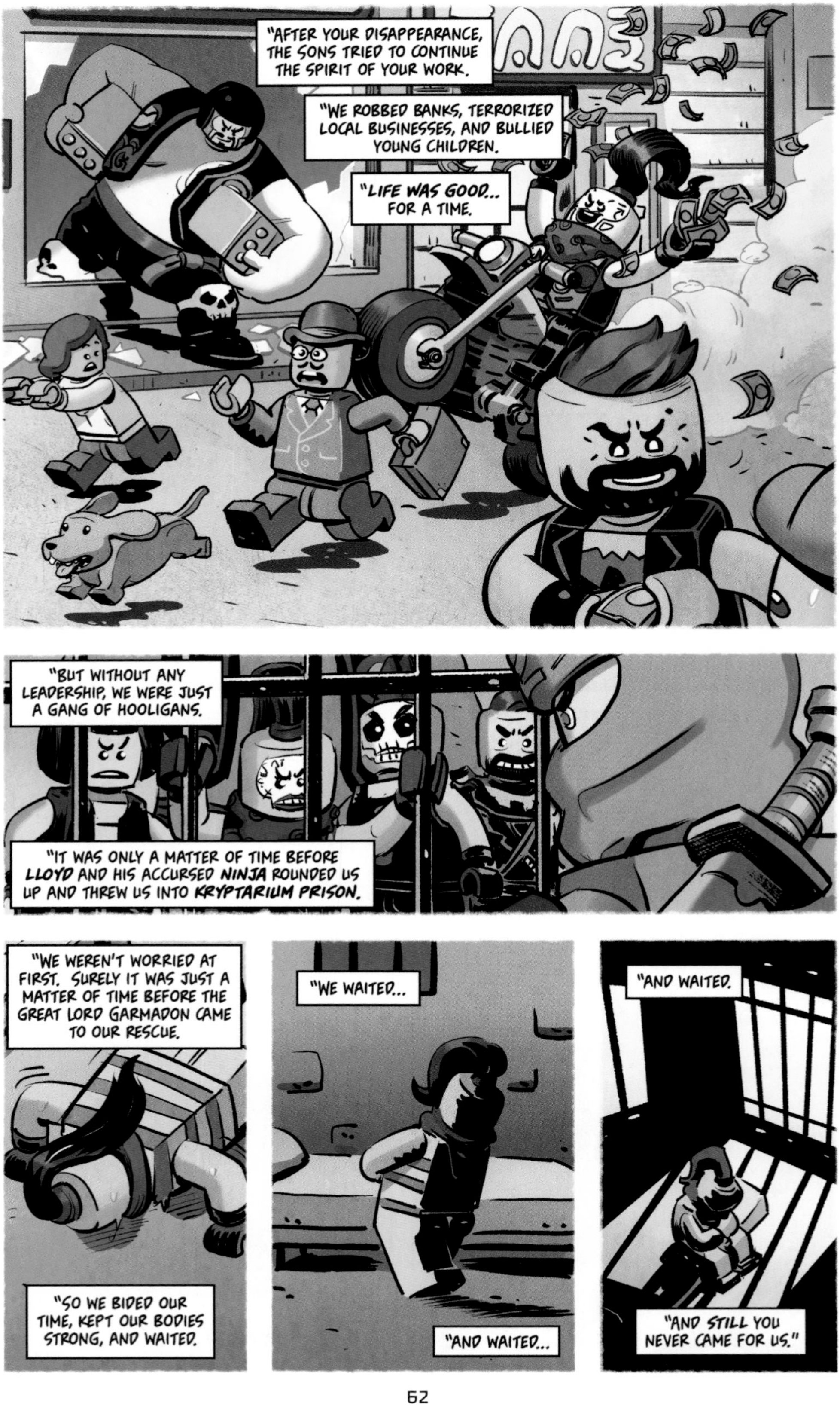
"AFTER YOUR DISAPPEARANCE, THE SONS TRIED TO CONTINUE THE SPIRIT OF YOUR WORK.
"WE ROBBED BANKS, TERRORIZED LOCAL BUSINESSES, AND BULLIED YOUNG CHILDREN.
"LIFE WAS GOOD... FOR A TIME.
"BUT WITHOUT ANY LEADERSHIP, WE WERE JUST A GANG OF HOOLIGANS.
"IT WAS ONLY A MATTER OF TIME BEFORE LLOYD AND HIS ACCURSED NINJA ROUNDED US UP AND THREW US INTO KRYPTARIUM PRISON.
"WE WEREN'T WORRIED AT FIRST. SURELY IT WAS JUST A MATTER OF TIME BEFORE THE GREAT LORD GARMADON CAME TO OUR RESCUE.
"SO WE BIDED OUR TIME, KEPT OUR BODIES STRONG, AND WAITED.
"WE WAITED...
"AND WAITED...
"AND WAITED.
"AND STILL YOU NEVER CAME FOR US."

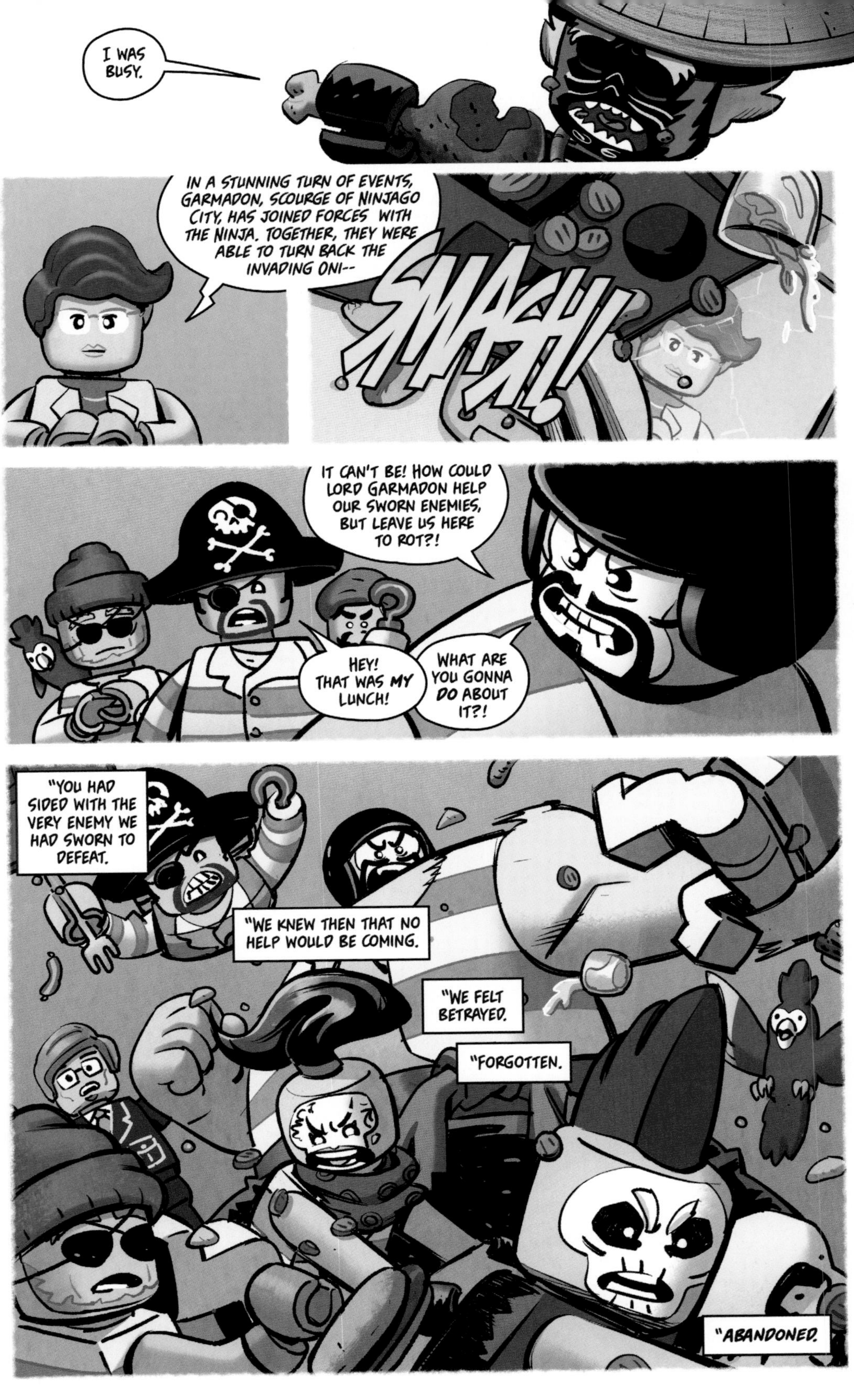
I WAS BUSY.
IN A STUNNING TURN OF EVENTS, GARMADON, SCOURGE OF NINJAGO CITY, HAS JOINED FORCES WITH THE NINJA. TOGETHER, THEY WERE ABLE TO TURN BACK THE INVADING ONI--
SMASH!
IT CAN'T BE! HOW COULD LORD GARMADON HELP OUR SWORN ENEMIES, BUT LEAVE US HERE TO ROT?!
HEY! THAT WAS MY LUNCH!
WHAT ARE YOU GONNA DO ABOUT IT?!
"YOU HAD SIDED WITH THE VERY ENEMY WE HAD SWORN TO DEFEAT.
"WE KNEW THEN THAT NO HELP WOULD BE COMING.
"WE FELT BETRAYED.
"FORGOTTEN.
"ABANDONED.

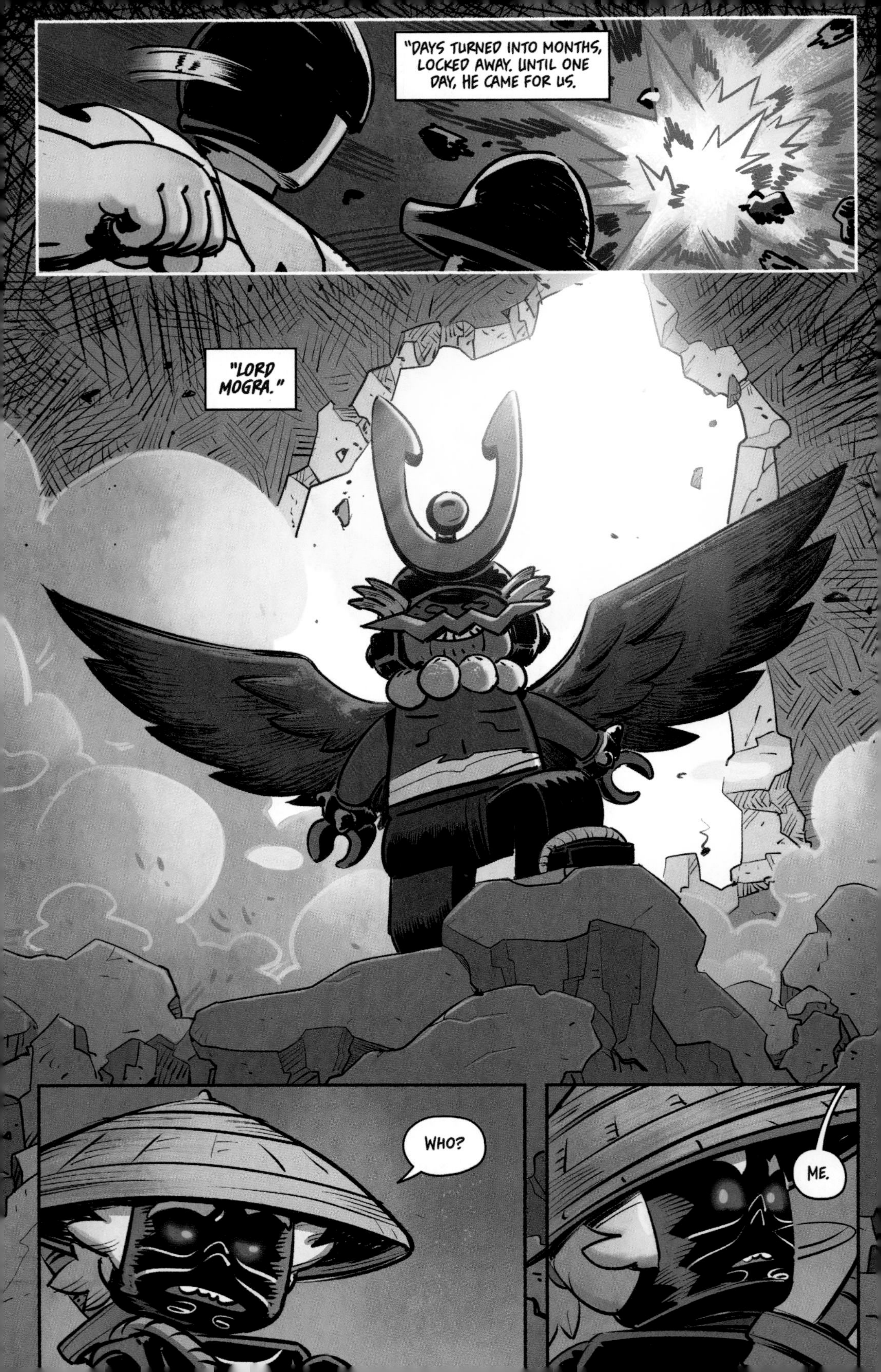
"DAYS TURNED INTO MONTHS, LOCKED AWAY. UNTIL ONE DAY, HE CAME FOR US.
"LORD MOGRA."
WHO?
ME.

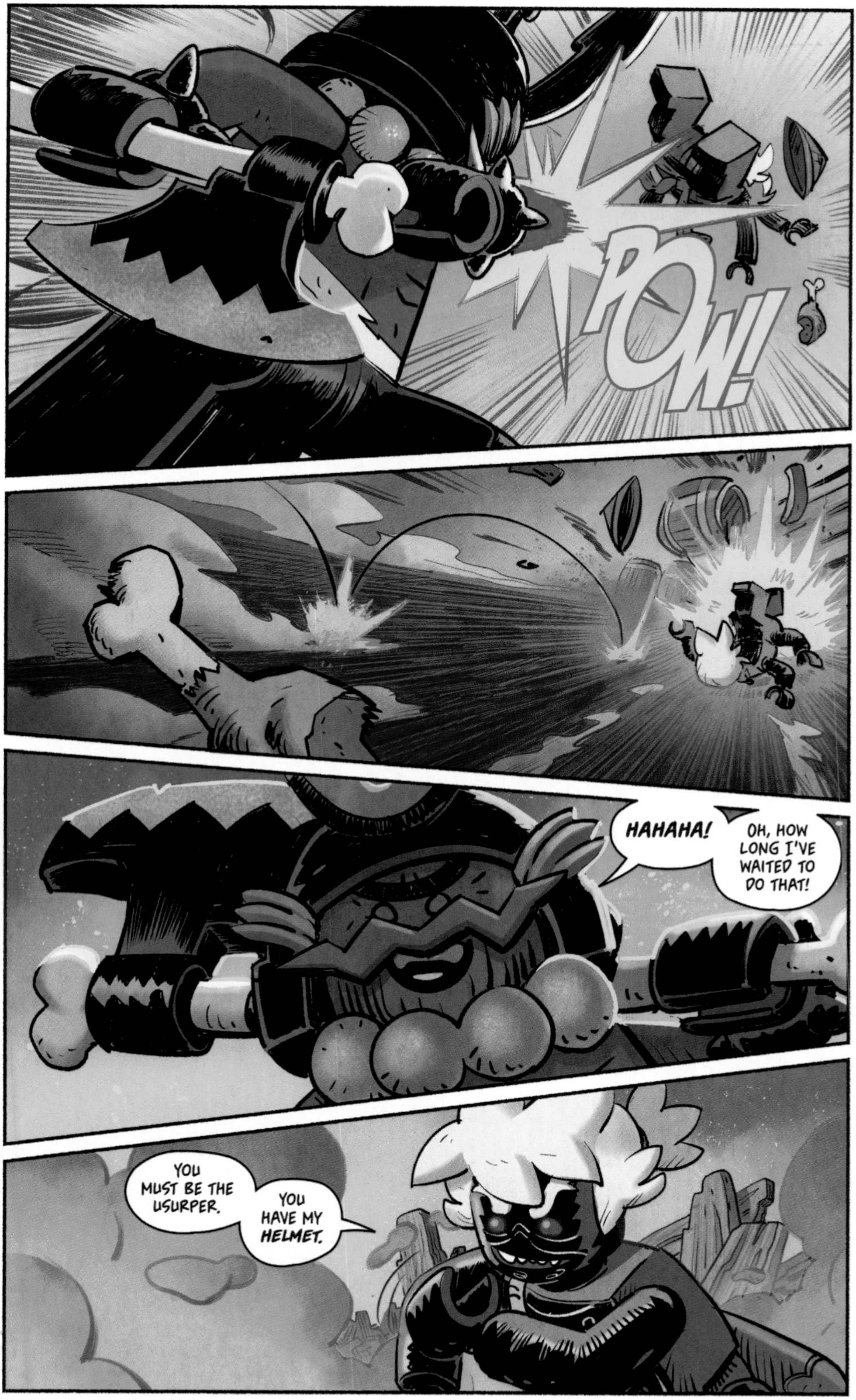
POW!
HAHAHA!
OH, HOW LONG I'VE WAITED TO DO THAT!
YOU MUST BE THE USURPER.
YOU HAVE MY *HELMET.*

AMONG OTHER THINGS.
ULTRAVIOLET. FINISH LOADING THAT WAGON OF TWO MOON TEA.
Y-YES, LORD MOGRA!
ULTRAVIOLET. LEAVE THE WAGON HERE.
THEN FIND MY DRUMSTICK. I DROPPED IT SOME-WHERE.
HAS ANYBODY SEEN LORD GARMADON'S DRUMSTICK?!
I DON'T SEE IT.
ANYBODY SEE IT?
I HAVE A BURGER. YOU THINK HE'LL WANT IT?
WHAT ARE YOU IDIOTS DOING?! I'M YOUR LEADER NOW!

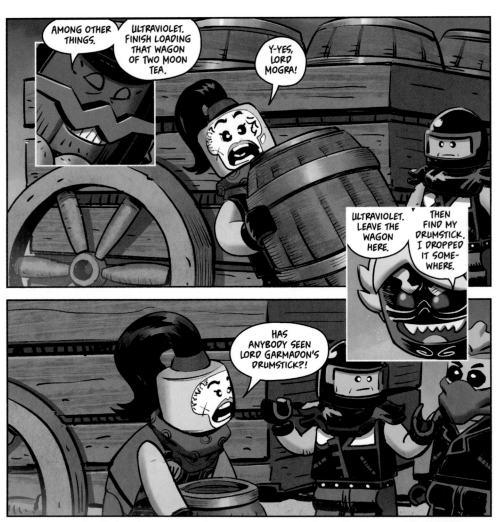

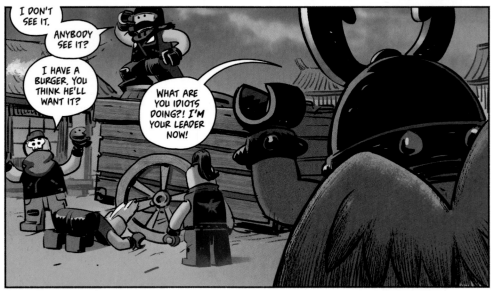

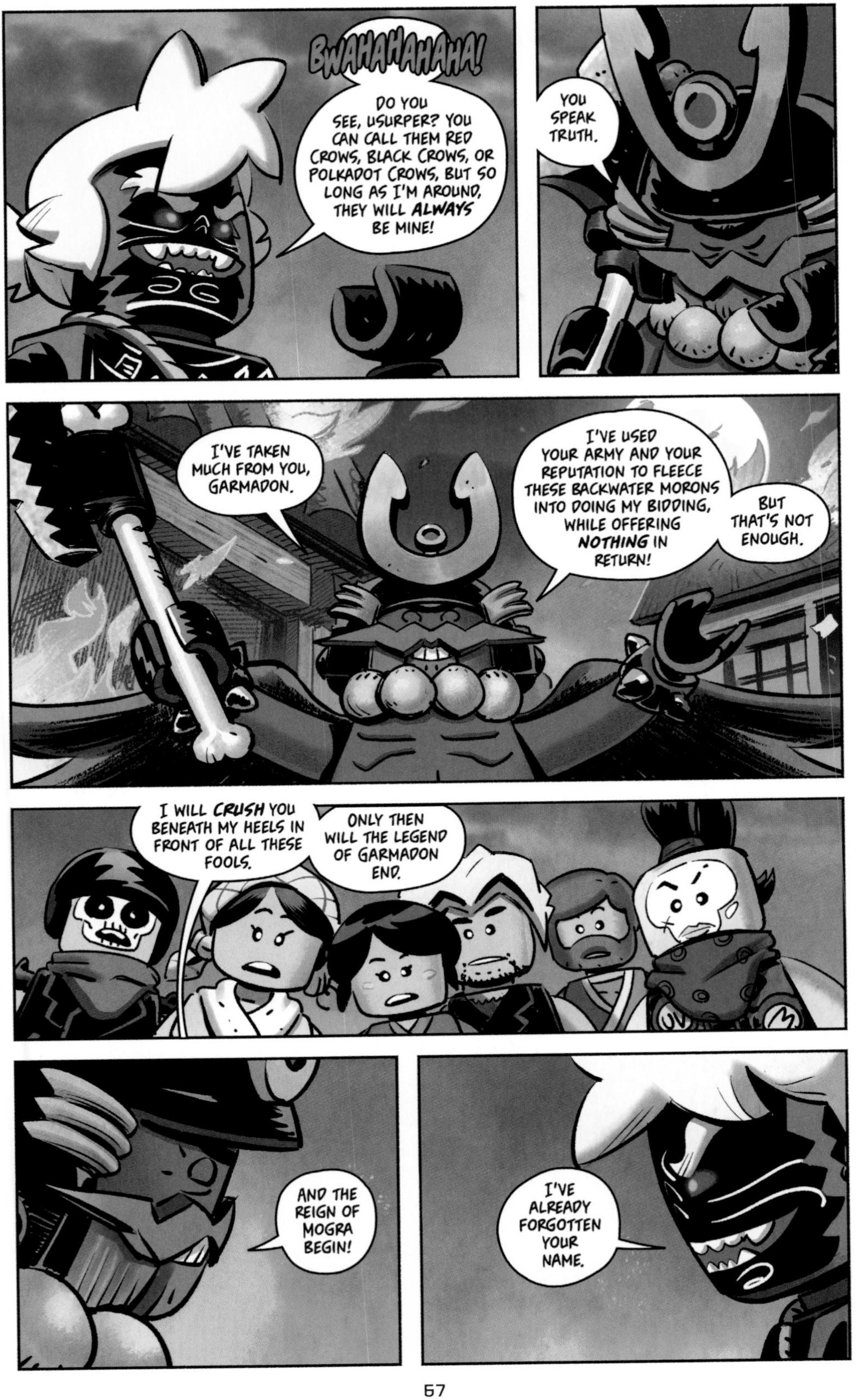
BWAHAHAHAHA!
DO YOU SEE, USURPER? YOU CAN CALL THEM RED CROWS, BLACK CROWS, OR POLKADOT CROWS, BUT SO LONG AS I'M AROUND, THEY WILL ALWAYS BE MINE!
YOU SPEAK TRUTH.
I'VE TAKEN MUCH FROM YOU, GARMADON.
I'VE USED YOUR ARMY AND YOUR REPUTATION TO FLEECE THESE BACKWATER MORONS INTO DOING MY BIDDING, WHILE OFFERING NOTHING IN RETURN!
BUT THAT'S NOT ENOUGH.
I WILL CRUSH YOU BENEATH MY HEELS IN FRONT OF ALL THESE FOOLS.
ONLY THEN WILL THE LEGEND OF GARMADON END.
AND THE REIGN OF MOGRA BEGIN!
I'VE ALREADY FORGOTTEN YOUR NAME.

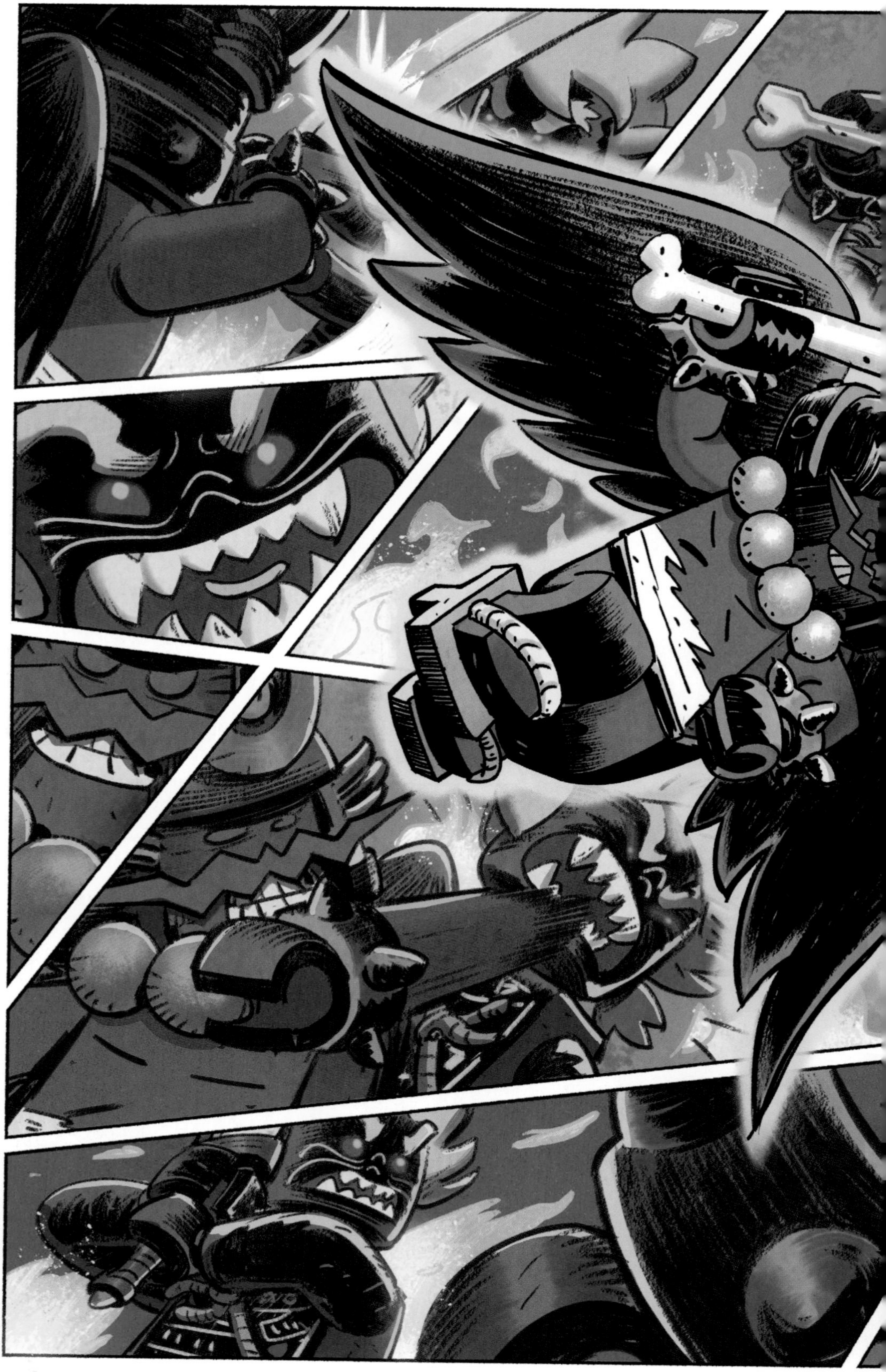

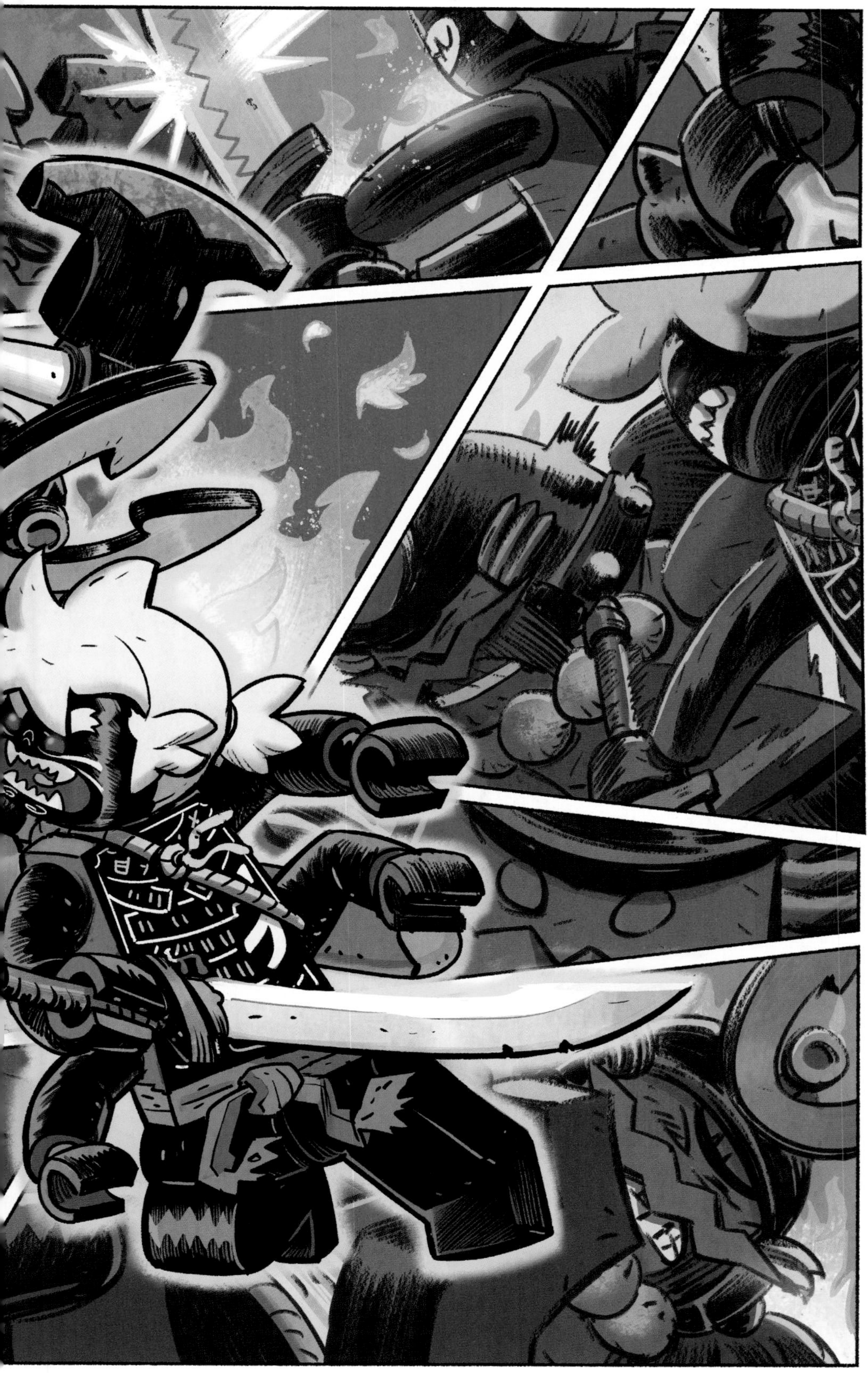

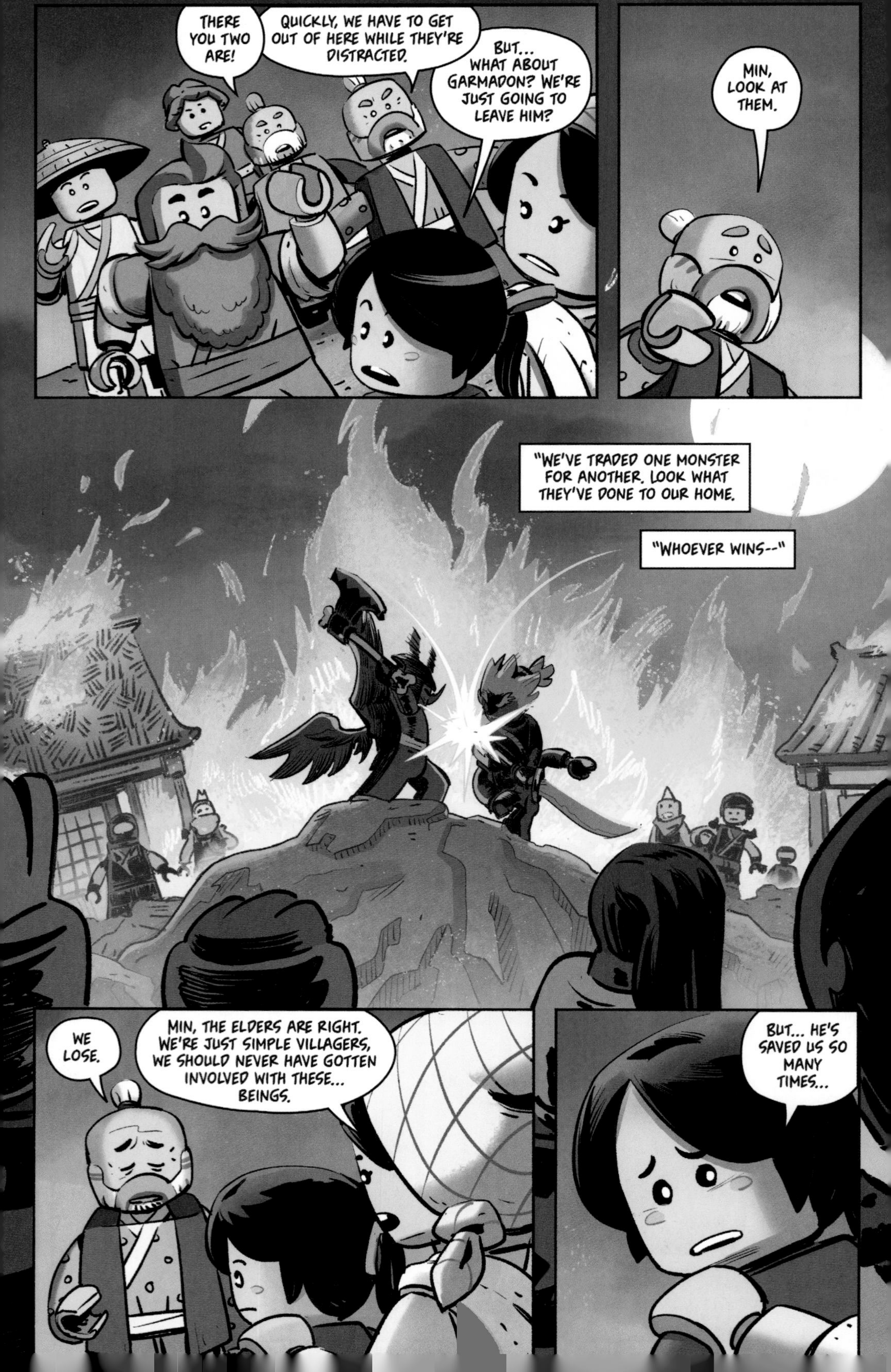
THERE YOU TWO ARE!
QUICKLY, WE HAVE TO GET OUT OF HERE WHILE THEY'RE DISTRACTED.
BUT... WHAT ABOUT GARMADON? WE'RE JUST GOING TO LEAVE HIM?
MIN, LOOK AT THEM.
"WE'VE TRADED ONE MONSTER FOR ANOTHER. LOOK WHAT THEY'VE DONE TO OUR HOME.
"WHOEVER WINS--"
WE LOSE.
MIN, THE ELDERS ARE RIGHT. WE'RE JUST SIMPLE VILLAGERS, WE SHOULD NEVER HAVE GOTTEN INVOLVED WITH THESE... BEINGS.
BUT... HE'S SAVED US SO MANY TIMES...

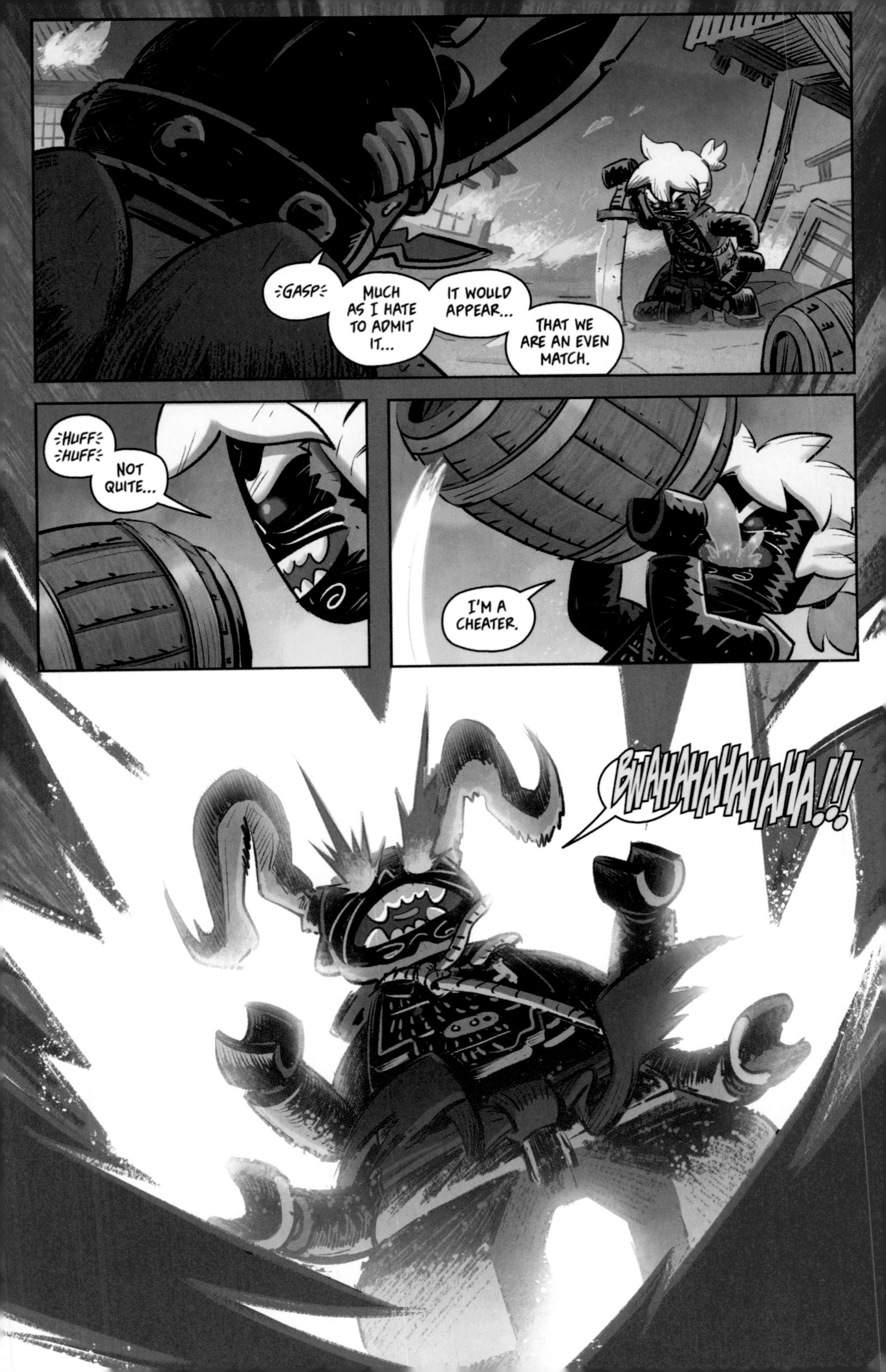

GASP
MUCH AS I HATE TO ADMIT IT...
IT WOULD APPEAR...
THAT WE ARE AN EVEN MATCH.
HUFF HUFF
NOT QUITE...
I'M A CHEATER.
BWAHAHAHAHAHA!!!

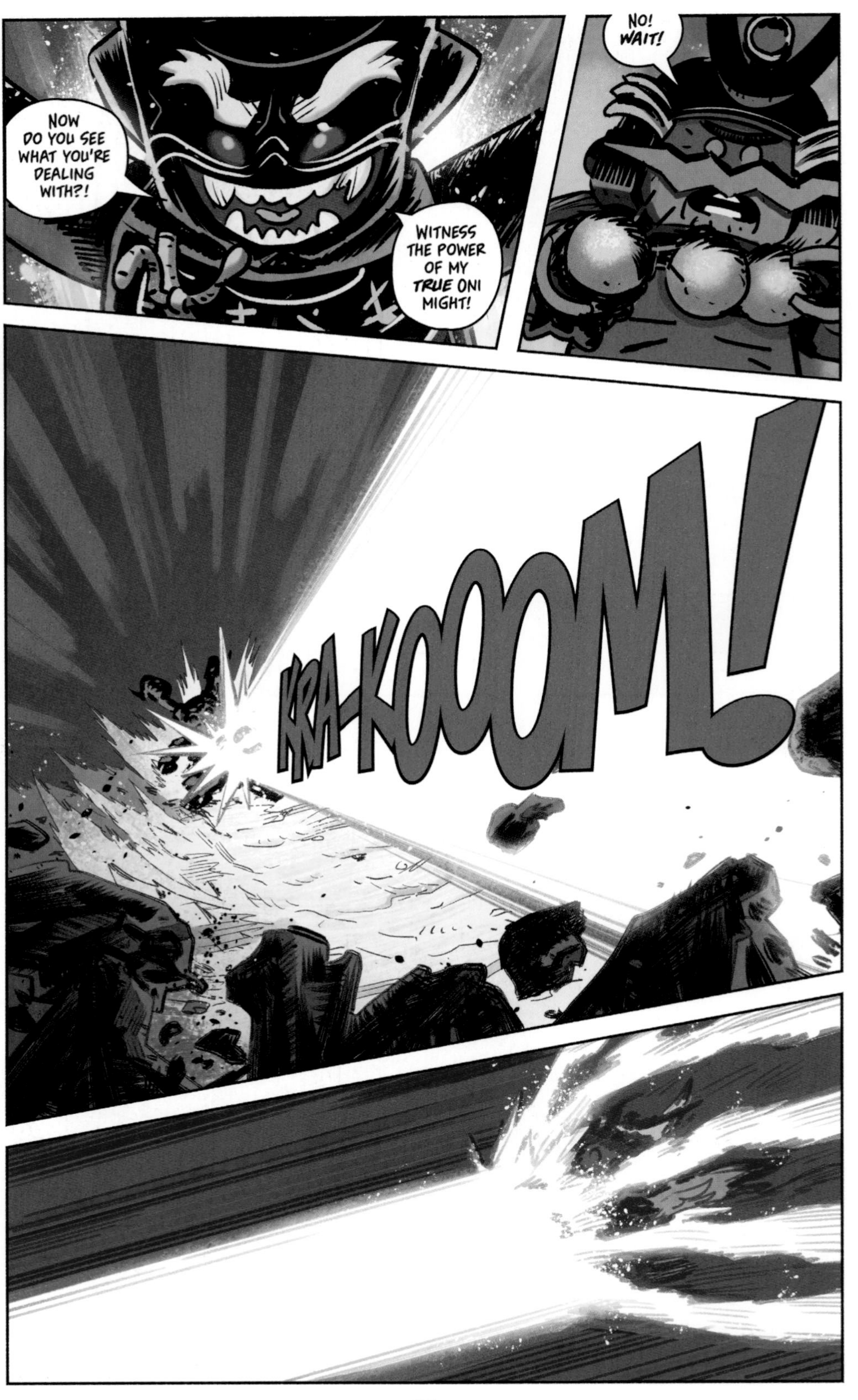

NOW DO YOU SEE WHAT YOU'RE DEALING WITH?!
WITNESS THE POWER OF MY *TRUE* ONI MIGHT!
NO! WAIT!
KRA-KOOOM!

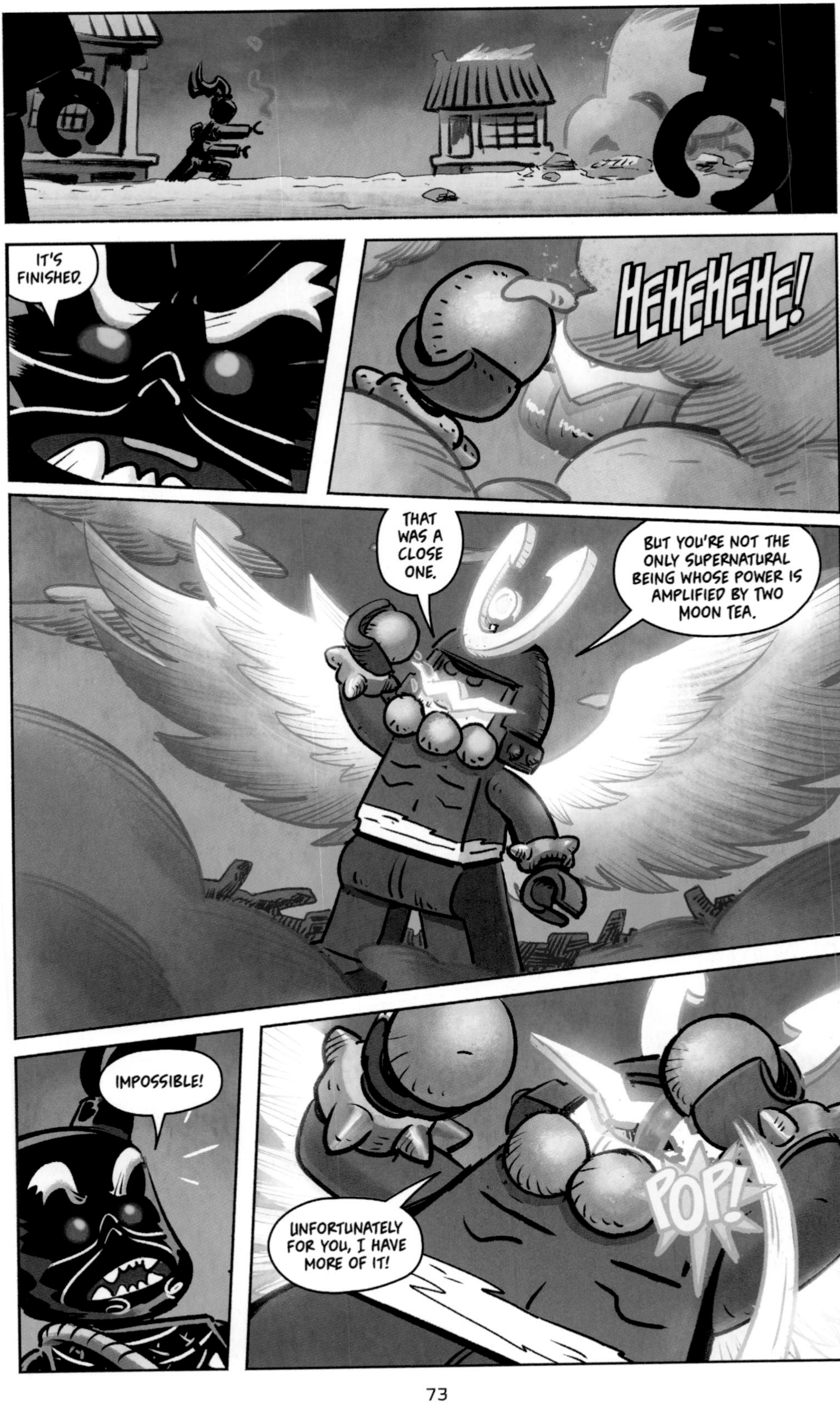
IT'S FINISHED.
HEHEHEHE!
THAT WAS A CLOSE ONE.
BUT YOU'RE NOT THE ONLY SUPERNATURAL BEING WHOSE POWER IS AMPLIFIED BY TWO MOON TEA.
IMPOSSIBLE!
UNFORTUNATELY FOR YOU, I HAVE MORE OF IT!
POP!

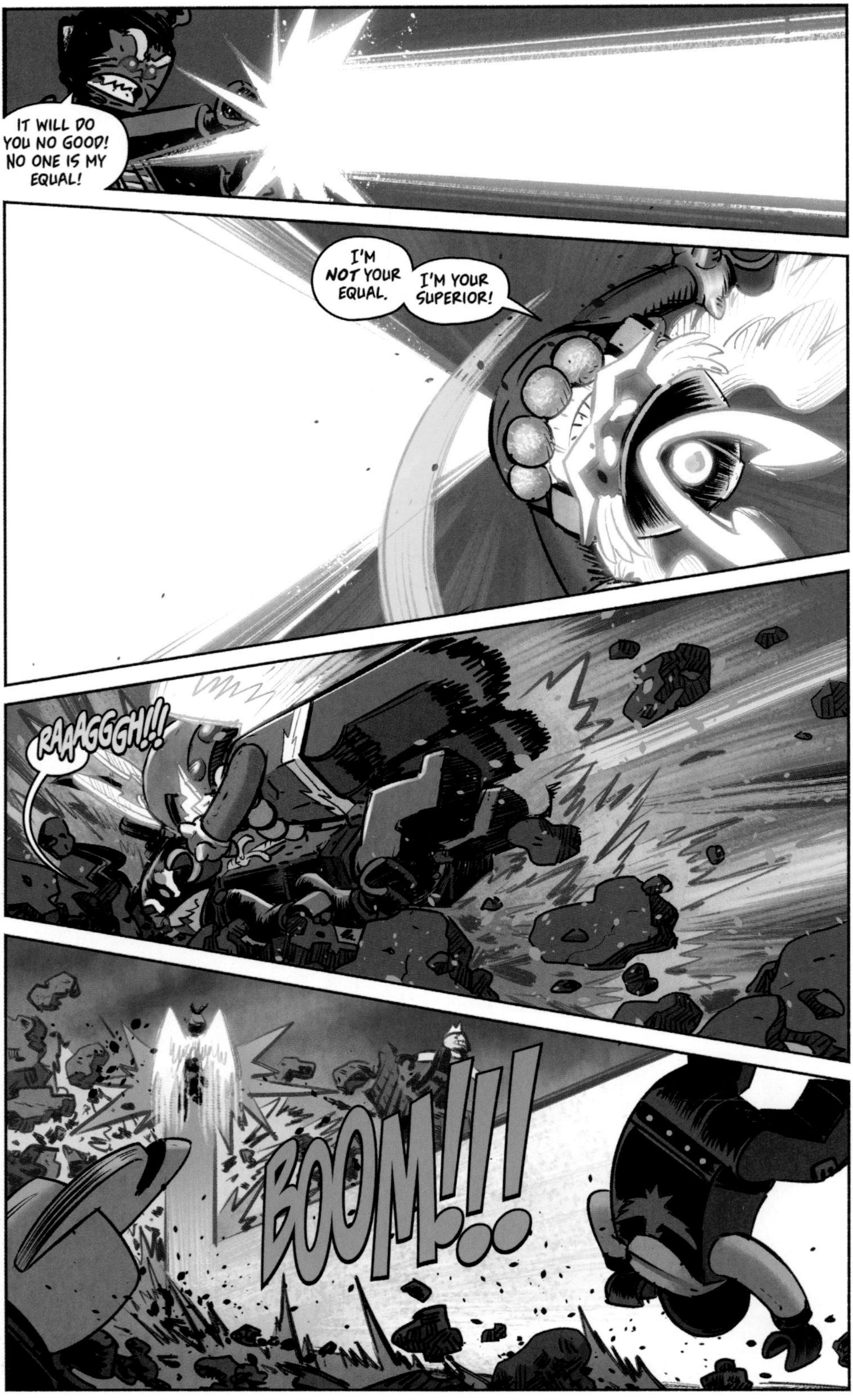
IT WILL DO YOU NO GOOD! NO ONE IS MY EQUAL!
I'M NOT YOUR EQUAL.
I'M YOUR SUPERIOR!
RAAAGGGH!!!
BOOM!!!

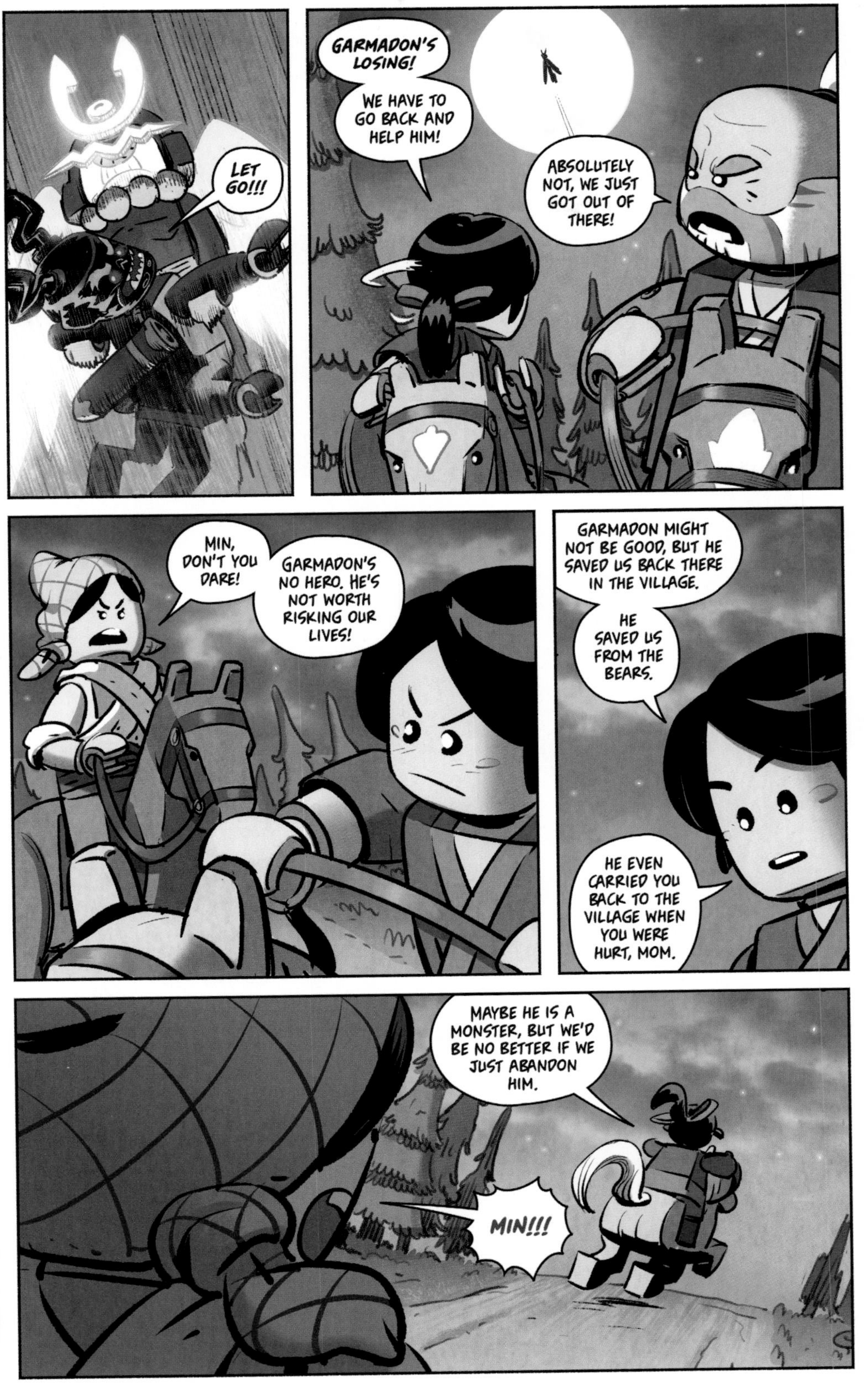
LET GO!!!
GARMADON'S LOSING!
WE HAVE TO GO BACK AND HELP HIM!
ABSOLUTELY NOT, WE JUST GOT OUT OF THERE!
MIN, DON'T YOU DARE!
GARMADON'S NO HERO. HE'S NOT WORTH RISKING OUR LIVES!
GARMADON MIGHT NOT BE GOOD, BUT HE SAVED US BACK THERE IN THE VILLAGE.
HE SAVED US FROM THE BEARS.
HE EVEN CARRIED YOU BACK TO THE VILLAGE WHEN YOU WERE HURT, MOM.
MAYBE HE IS A MONSTER, BUT WE'D BE NO BETTER IF WE JUST ABANDON HIM.
MIN!!!

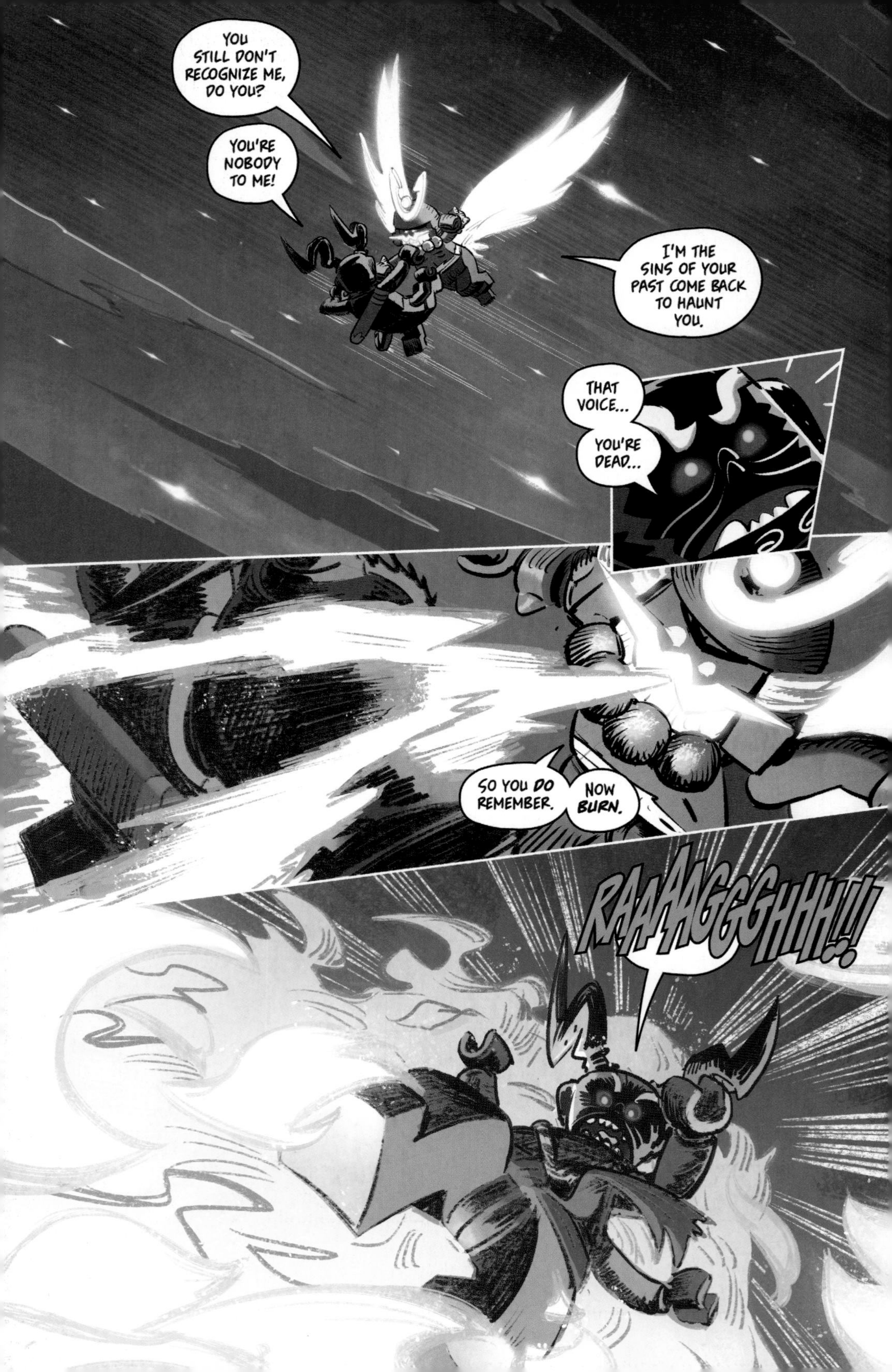
YOU STILL DON'T RECOGNIZE ME, DO YOU?
YOU'RE NOBODY TO ME!
I'M THE SINS OF YOUR PAST COME BACK TO HAUNT YOU.
THAT VOICE...
YOU'RE DEAD...
SO YOU DO REMEMBER.
NOW BURN.
RAAAAGGGHHH!!!

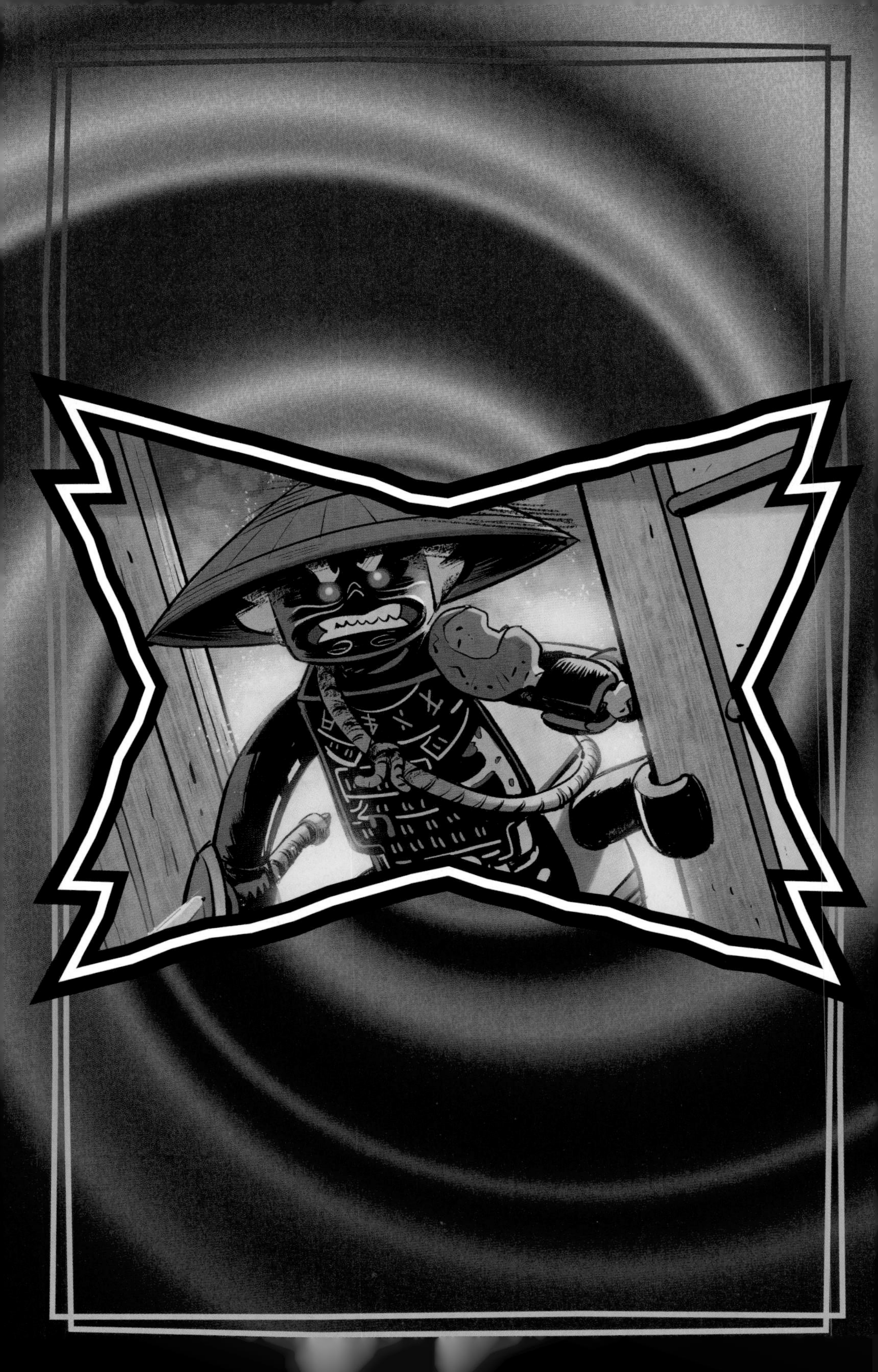

CHAPTER 4
THE SNAKE IN THE GARDEN

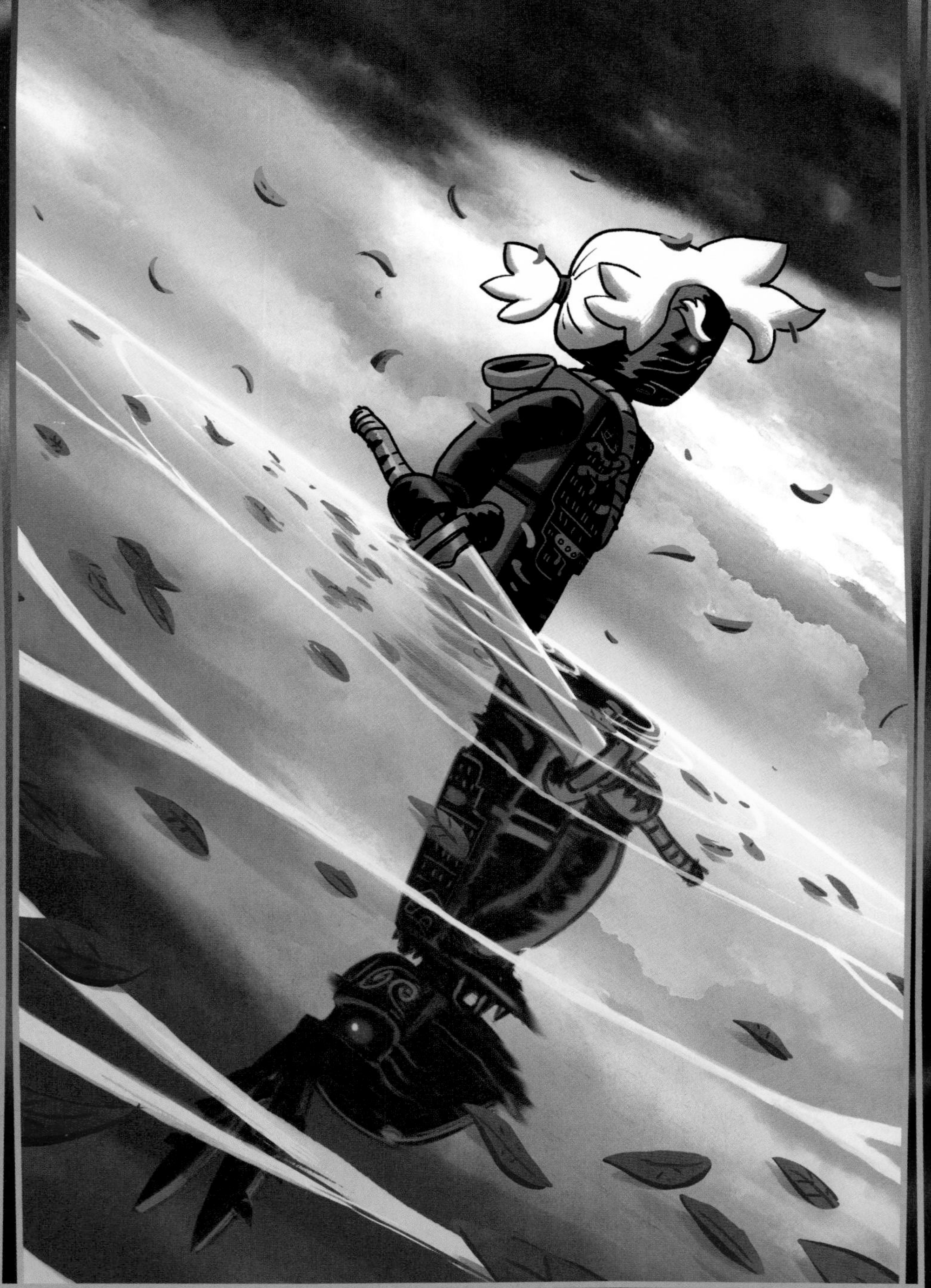

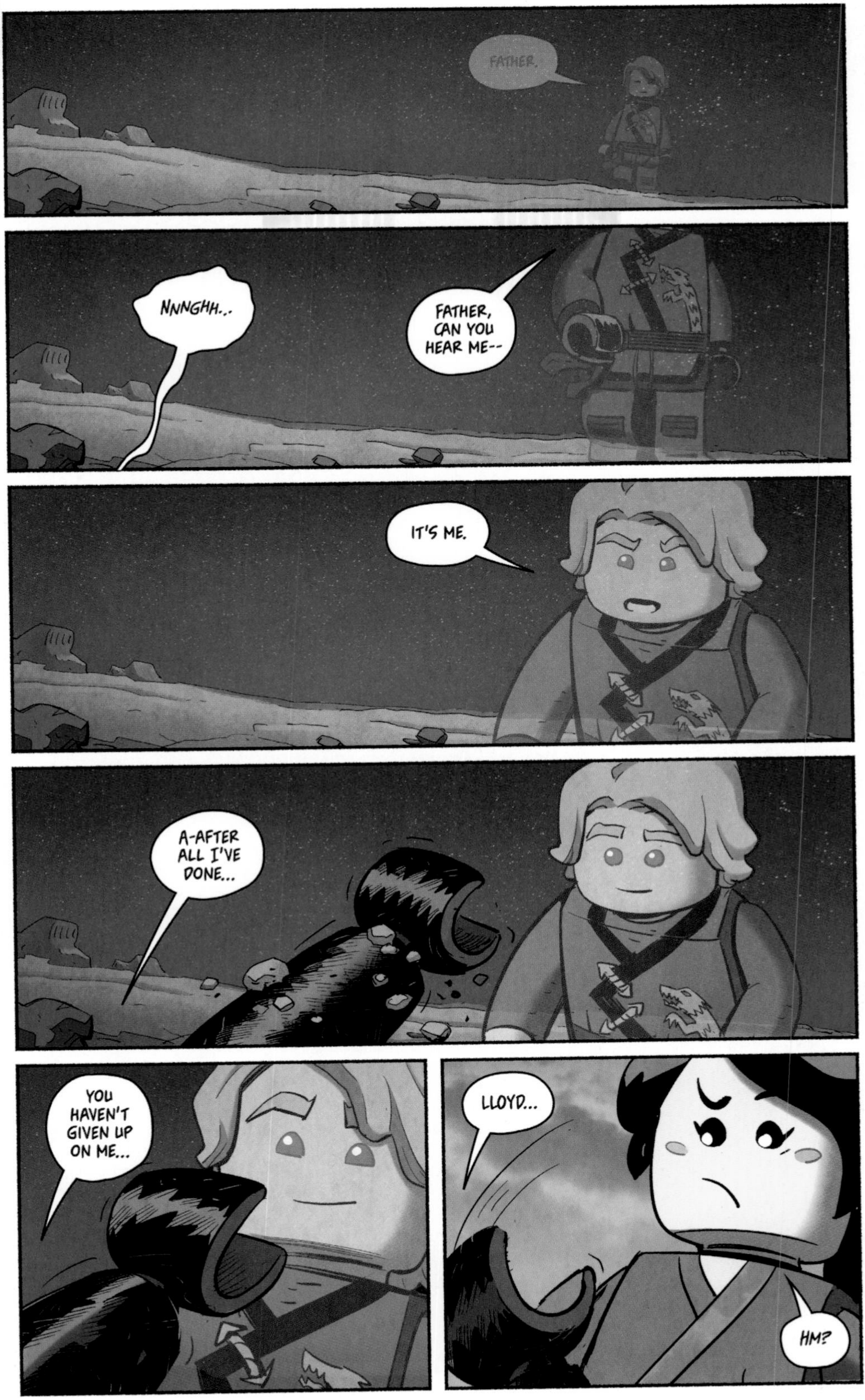
FATHER.
NNNGHH...
FATHER, CAN YOU HEAR ME--
IT'S ME.
A-AFTER ALL I'VE DONE...
YOU HAVEN'T GIVEN UP ON ME...
LLOYD...
HM?

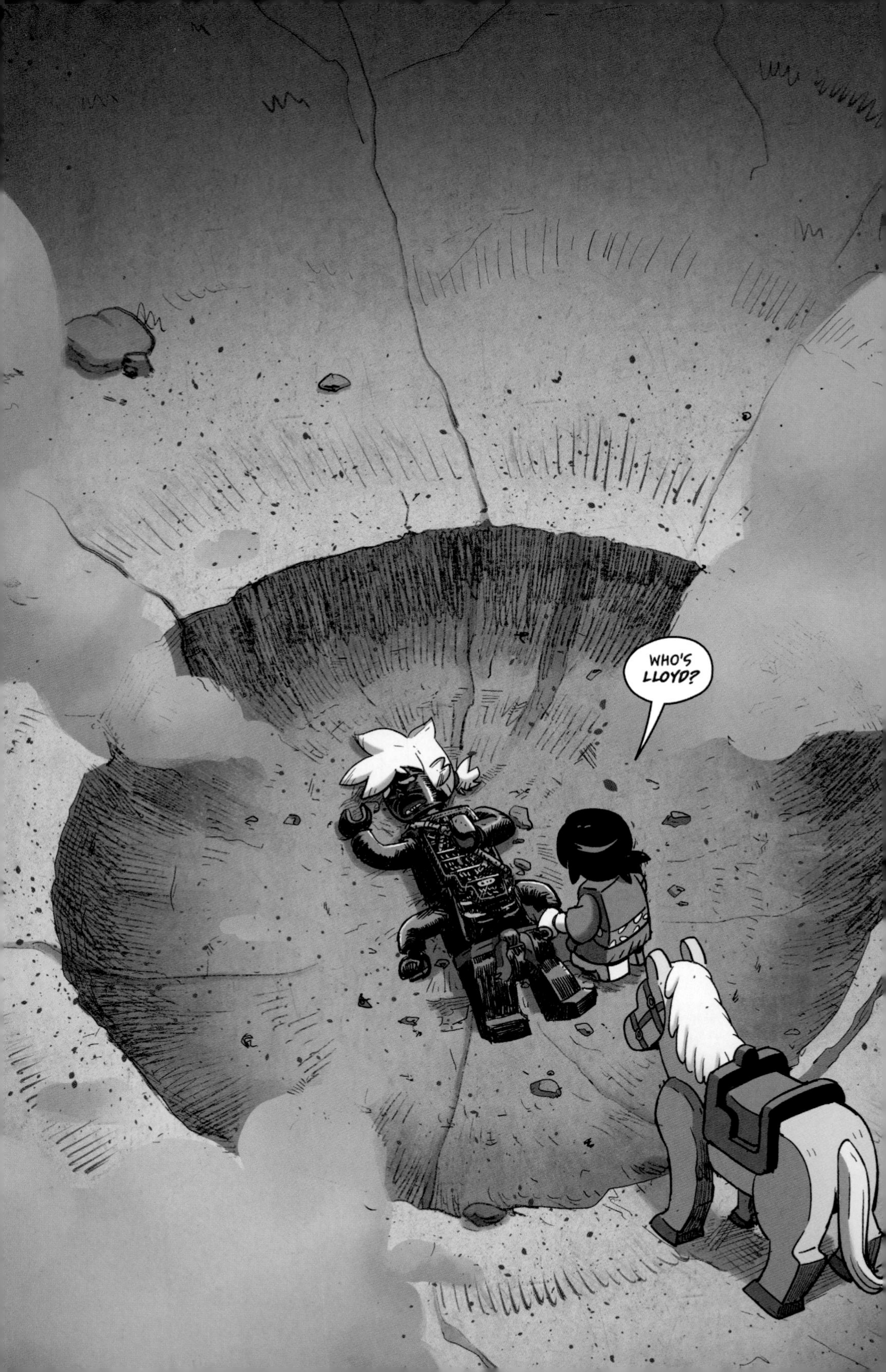
WHO'S LLOYD?

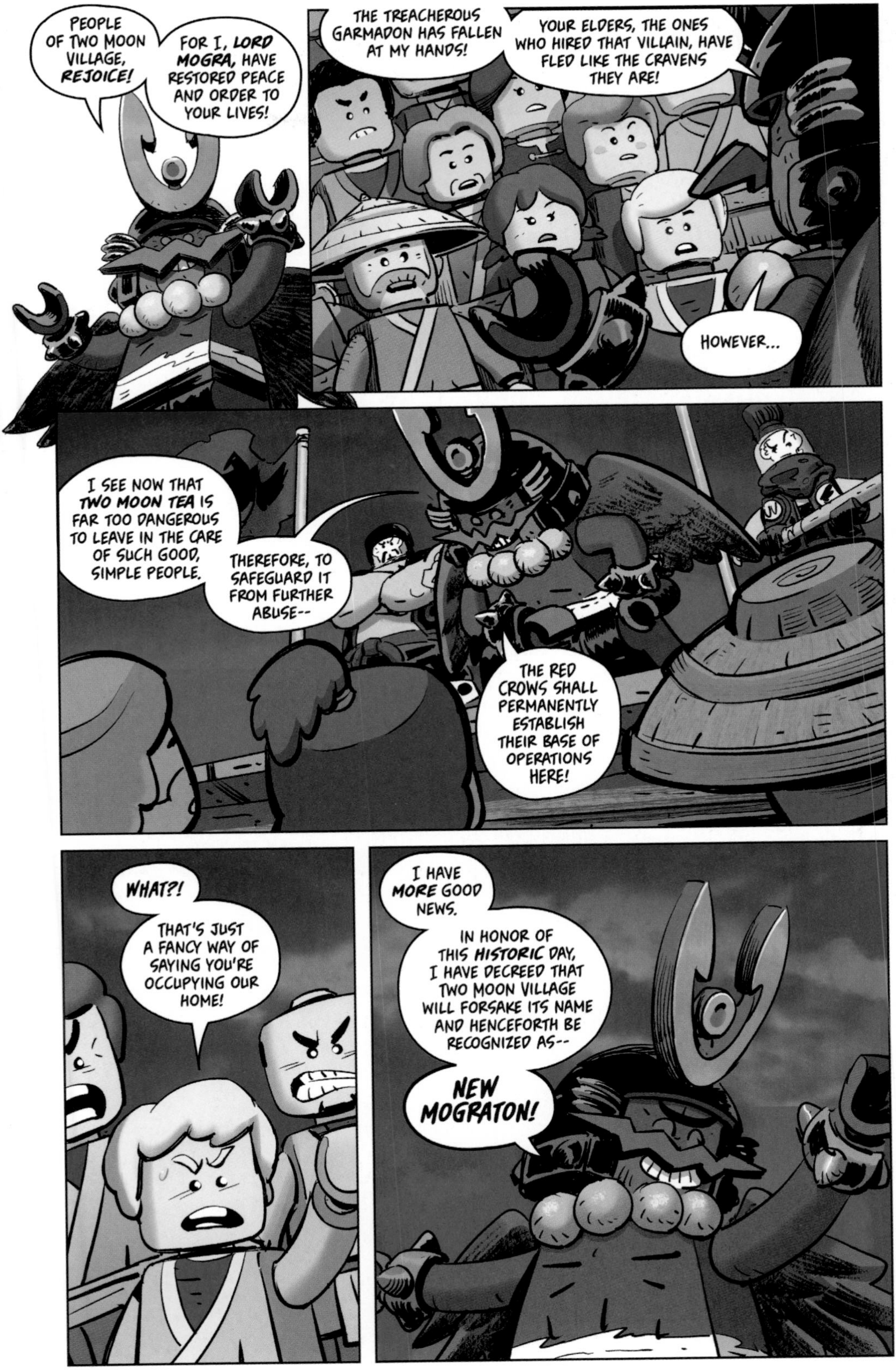
PEOPLE OF TWO MOON VILLAGE, REJOICE!
FOR I, LORD MOGRA, HAVE RESTORED PEACE AND ORDER TO YOUR LIVES!
THE TREACHEROUS GARMADON HAS FALLEN AT MY HANDS!
YOUR ELDERS, THE ONES WHO HIRED THAT VILLAIN, HAVE FLED LIKE THE CRAVENS THEY ARE!
HOWEVER...
I SEE NOW THAT TWO MOON TEA IS FAR TOO DANGEROUS TO LEAVE IN THE CARE OF SUCH GOOD, SIMPLE PEOPLE.
THEREFORE, TO SAFEGUARD IT FROM FURTHER ABUSE--
THE RED CROWS SHALL PERMANENTLY ESTABLISH THEIR BASE OF OPERATIONS HERE!
WHAT?!
THAT'S JUST A FANCY WAY OF SAYING YOU'RE OCCUPYING OUR HOME!
I HAVE MORE GOOD NEWS.
IN HONOR OF THIS HISTORIC DAY, I HAVE DECREED THAT TWO MOON VILLAGE WILL FORSAKE ITS NAME AND HENCEFORTH BE RECOGNIZED AS--
NEW MOGRATON!

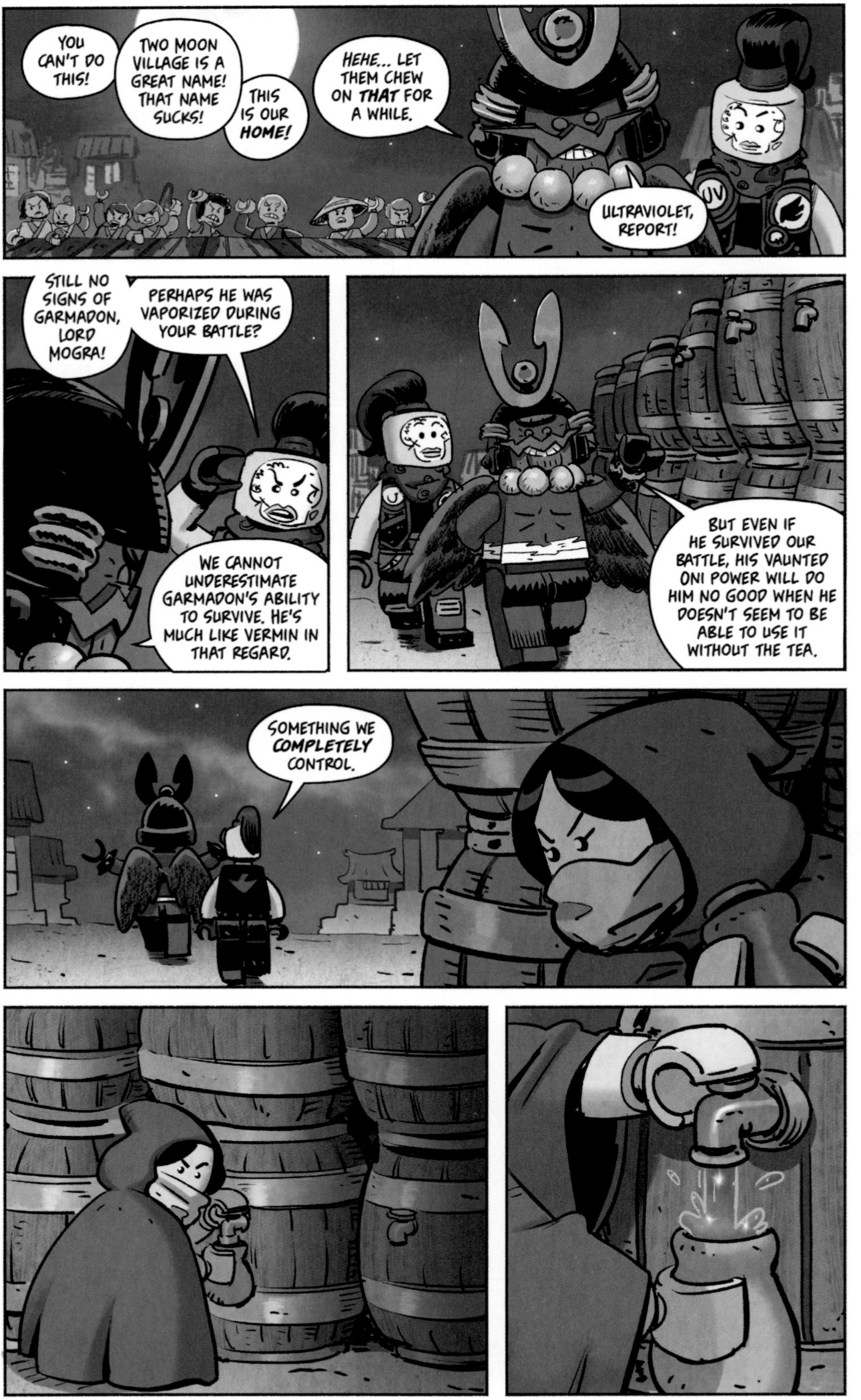
YOU CAN'T DO THIS!
TWO MOON VILLAGE IS A GREAT NAME! THAT NAME SUCKS!
THIS IS OUR HOME!
HEHE... LET THEM CHEW ON THAT FOR A WHILE.
ULTRAVIOLET, REPORT!
STILL NO SIGNS OF GARMADON, LORD MOGRA!
PERHAPS HE WAS VAPORIZED DURING YOUR BATTLE?
WE CANNOT UNDERESTIMATE GARMADON'S ABILITY TO SURVIVE. HE'S MUCH LIKE VERMIN IN THAT REGARD.
BUT EVEN IF HE SURVIVED OUR BATTLE, HIS VAUNTED ONI POWER WILL DO HIM NO GOOD WHEN HE DOESN'T SEEM TO BE ABLE TO USE IT WITHOUT THE TEA.
SOMETHING WE COMPLETELY CONTROL.

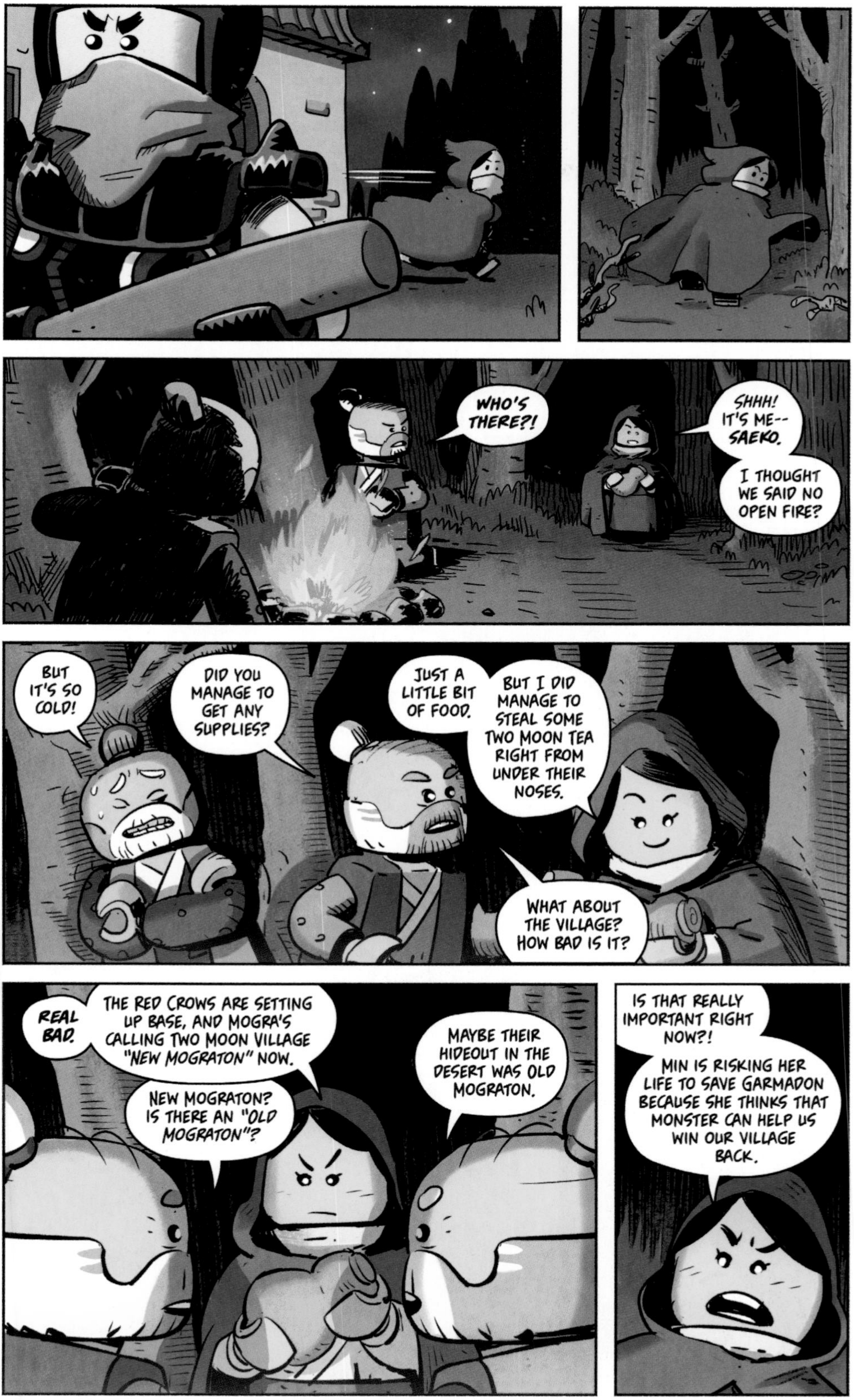
WHO'S THERE?!
SHHH! IT'S ME-- SAEKO.
I THOUGHT WE SAID NO OPEN FIRE?
BUT IT'S SO COLD!
DID YOU MANAGE TO GET ANY SUPPLIES?
JUST A LITTLE BIT OF FOOD.
BUT I DID MANAGE TO STEAL SOME TWO MOON TEA RIGHT FROM UNDER THEIR NOSES.
WHAT ABOUT THE VILLAGE? HOW BAD IS IT?
REAL BAD.
THE RED CROWS ARE SETTING UP BASE, AND MOGRA'S CALLING TWO MOON VILLAGE "NEW MOGRATON" NOW.
NEW MOGRATON? IS THERE AN "OLD MOGRATON"?
MAYBE THEIR HIDEOUT IN THE DESERT WAS OLD MOGRATON.
IS THAT REALLY IMPORTANT RIGHT NOW?!
MIN IS RISKING HER LIFE TO SAVE GARMADON BECAUSE SHE THINKS THAT MONSTER CAN HELP US WIN OUR VILLAGE BACK.

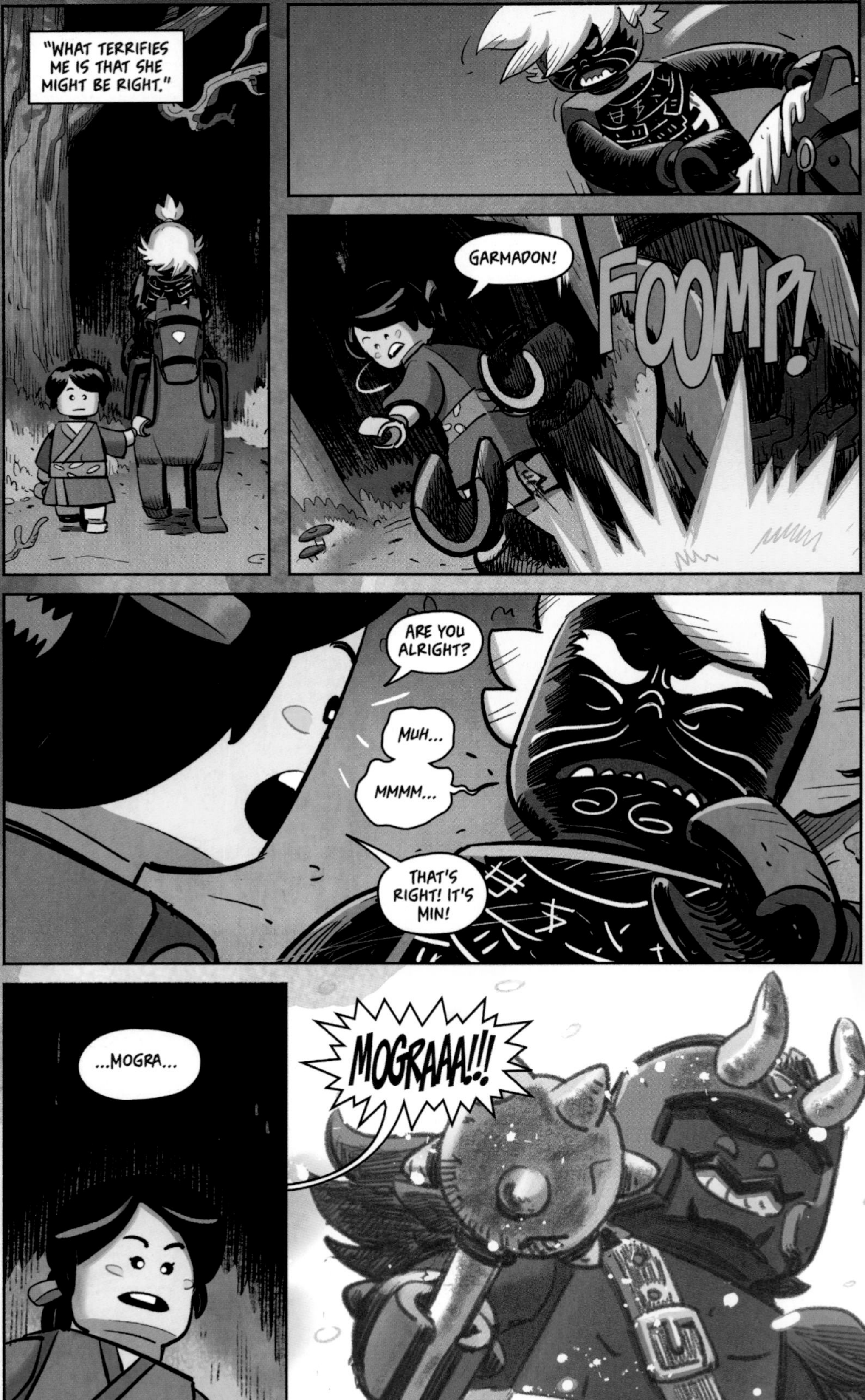

"WHAT TERRIFIES ME IS THAT SHE MIGHT BE RIGHT."
GARMADON!
FOOMP!
ARE YOU ALRIGHT?
MUH...
MMMM...
THAT'S RIGHT! IT'S MIN!
...MOGRA...
MOGRAAA!!!

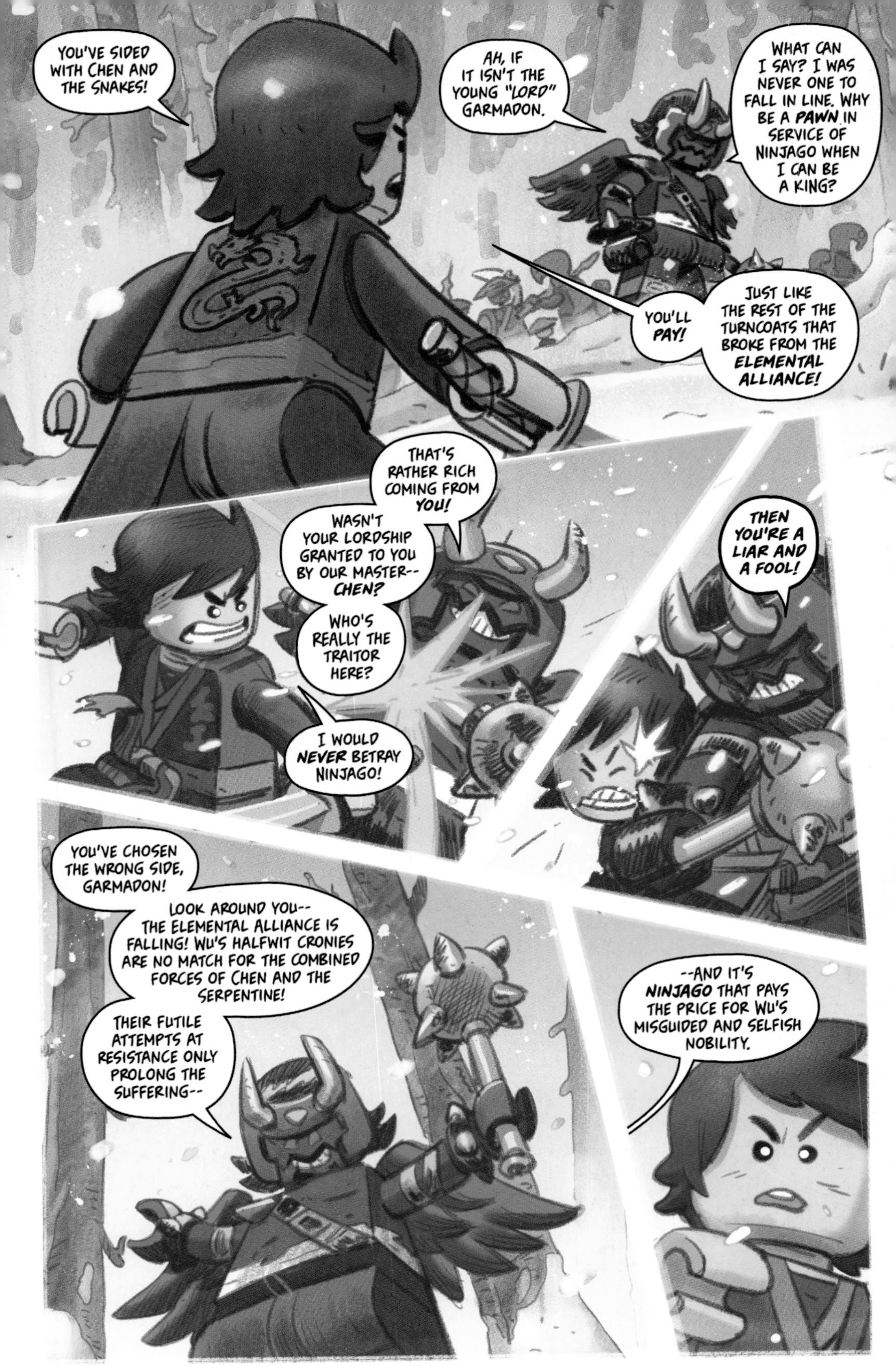
YOU'VE SIDED WITH CHEN AND THE SNAKES!
AH, IF IT ISN'T THE YOUNG "LORD" GARMADON.
WHAT CAN I SAY? I WAS NEVER ONE TO FALL IN LINE. WHY BE A **PAWN** IN SERVICE OF NINJAGO WHEN I CAN BE A KING?
YOU'LL **PAY!**
JUST LIKE THE REST OF THE TURNCOATS THAT BROKE FROM THE **ELEMENTAL ALLIANCE!**
THAT'S RATHER RICH COMING FROM **YOU!**
WASN'T YOUR LORDSHIP GRANTED TO YOU BY OUR MASTER-- **CHEN?**
WHO'S REALLY THE TRAITOR HERE?
I WOULD **NEVER** BETRAY NINJAGO!
THEN YOU'RE A LIAR AND A FOOL!
YOU'VE CHOSEN THE WRONG SIDE, GARMADON!
LOOK AROUND YOU-- THE ELEMENTAL ALLIANCE IS FALLING! WU'S HALFWIT CRONIES ARE NO MATCH FOR THE COMBINED FORCES OF CHEN AND THE SERPENTINE!
THEIR FUTILE ATTEMPTS AT RESISTANCE ONLY PROLONG THE SUFFERING--
--AND IT'S **NINJAGO** THAT PAYS THE PRICE FOR WU'S MISGUIDED AND SELFISH NOBILITY.

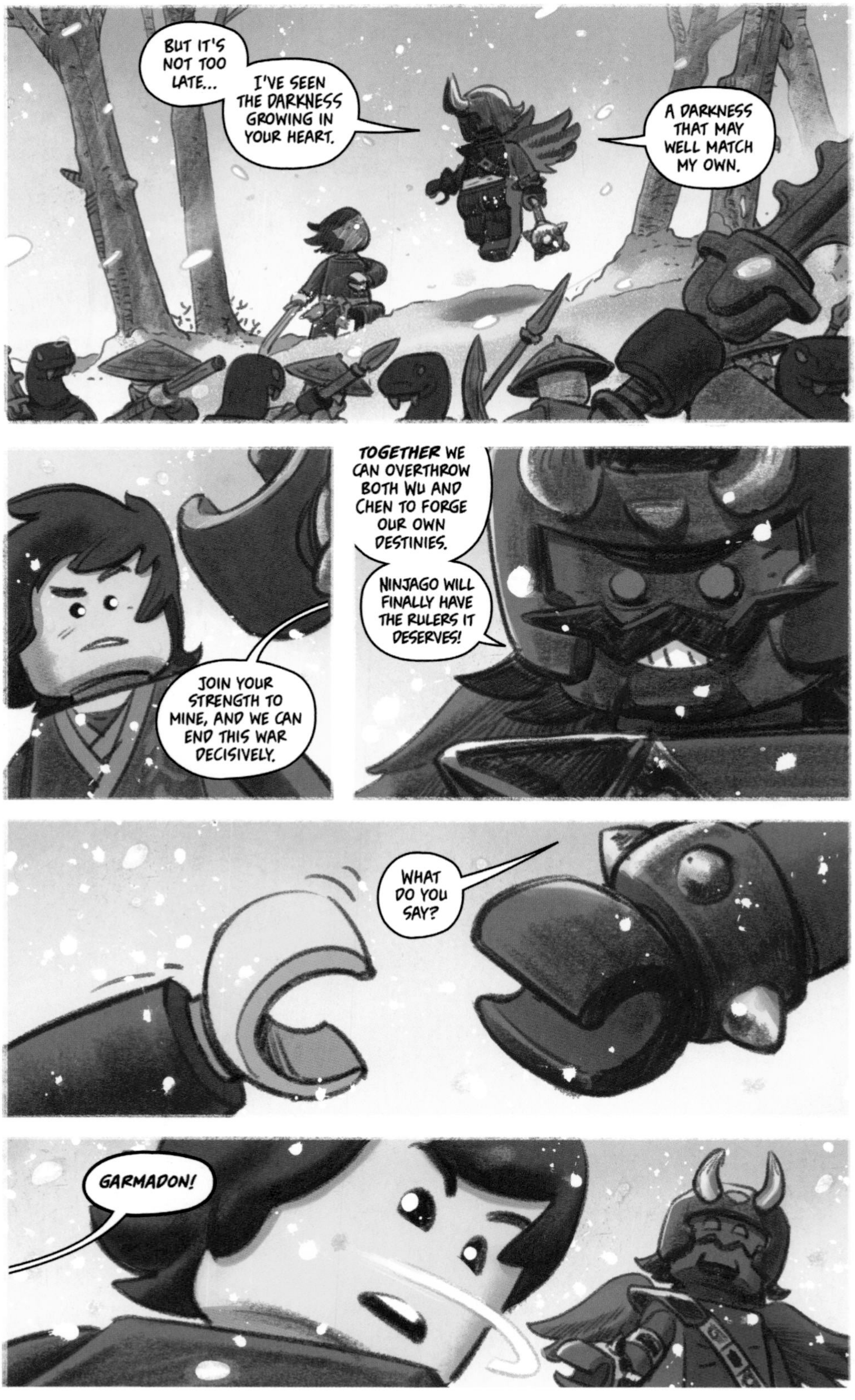
BUT IT'S NOT TOO LATE...
I'VE SEEN THE DARKNESS GROWING IN YOUR HEART.
A DARKNESS THAT MAY WELL MATCH MY OWN.
JOIN YOUR STRENGTH TO MINE, AND WE CAN END THIS WAR DECISIVELY.
TOGETHER WE CAN OVERTHROW BOTH WU AND CHEN TO FORGE OUR OWN DESTINIES.
NINJAGO WILL FINALLY HAVE THE RULERS IT DESERVES!
WHAT DO YOU SAY?
GARMADON!

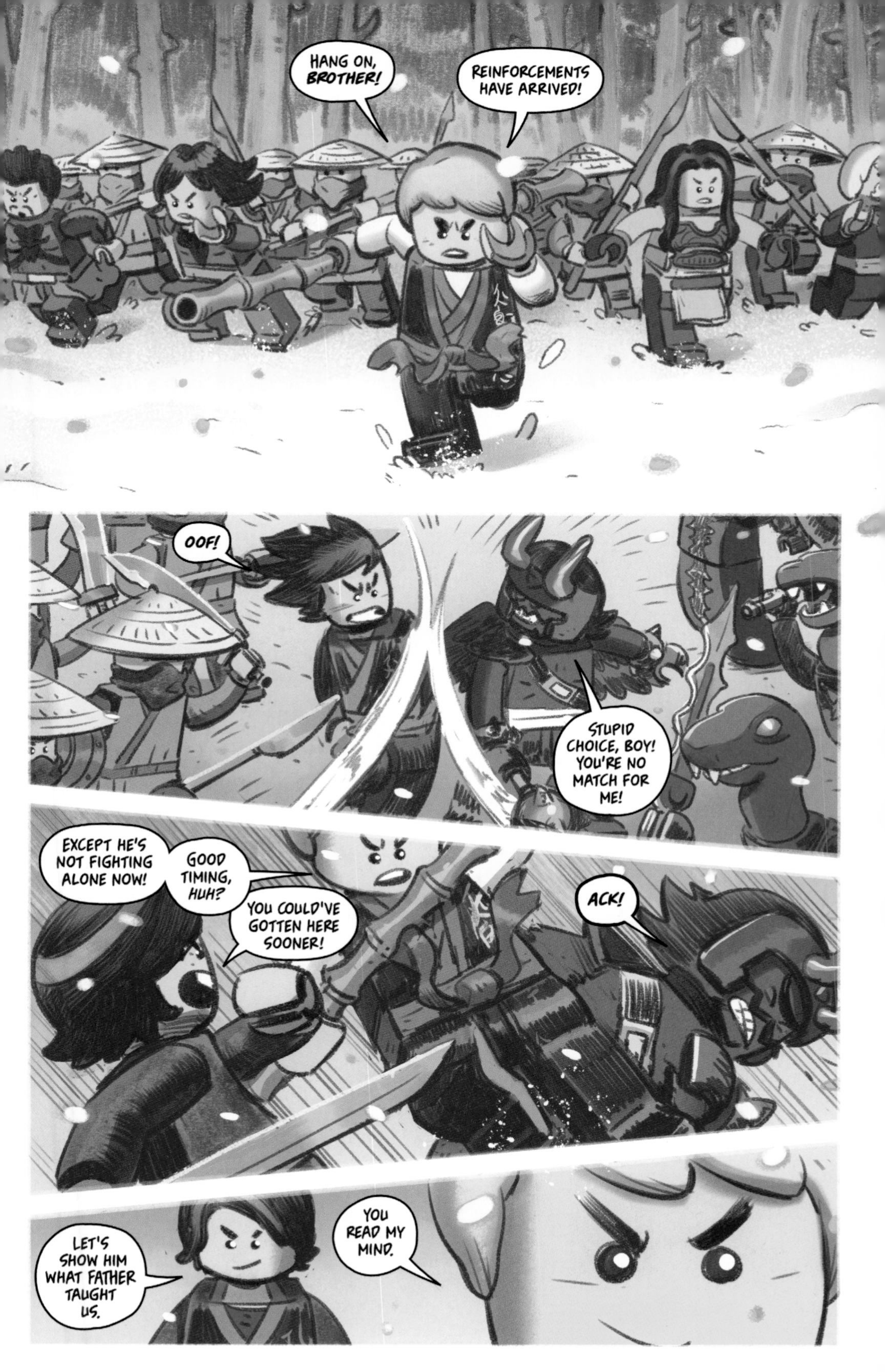
HANG ON, BROTHER!
REINFORCEMENTS HAVE ARRIVED!
OOF!
STUPID CHOICE, BOY! YOU'RE NO MATCH FOR ME!
EXCEPT HE'S NOT FIGHTING ALONE NOW!
GOOD TIMING, HUH?
YOU COULD'VE GOTTEN HERE SOONER!
ACK!
LET'S SHOW HIM WHAT FATHER TAUGHT US.
YOU READ MY MIND.

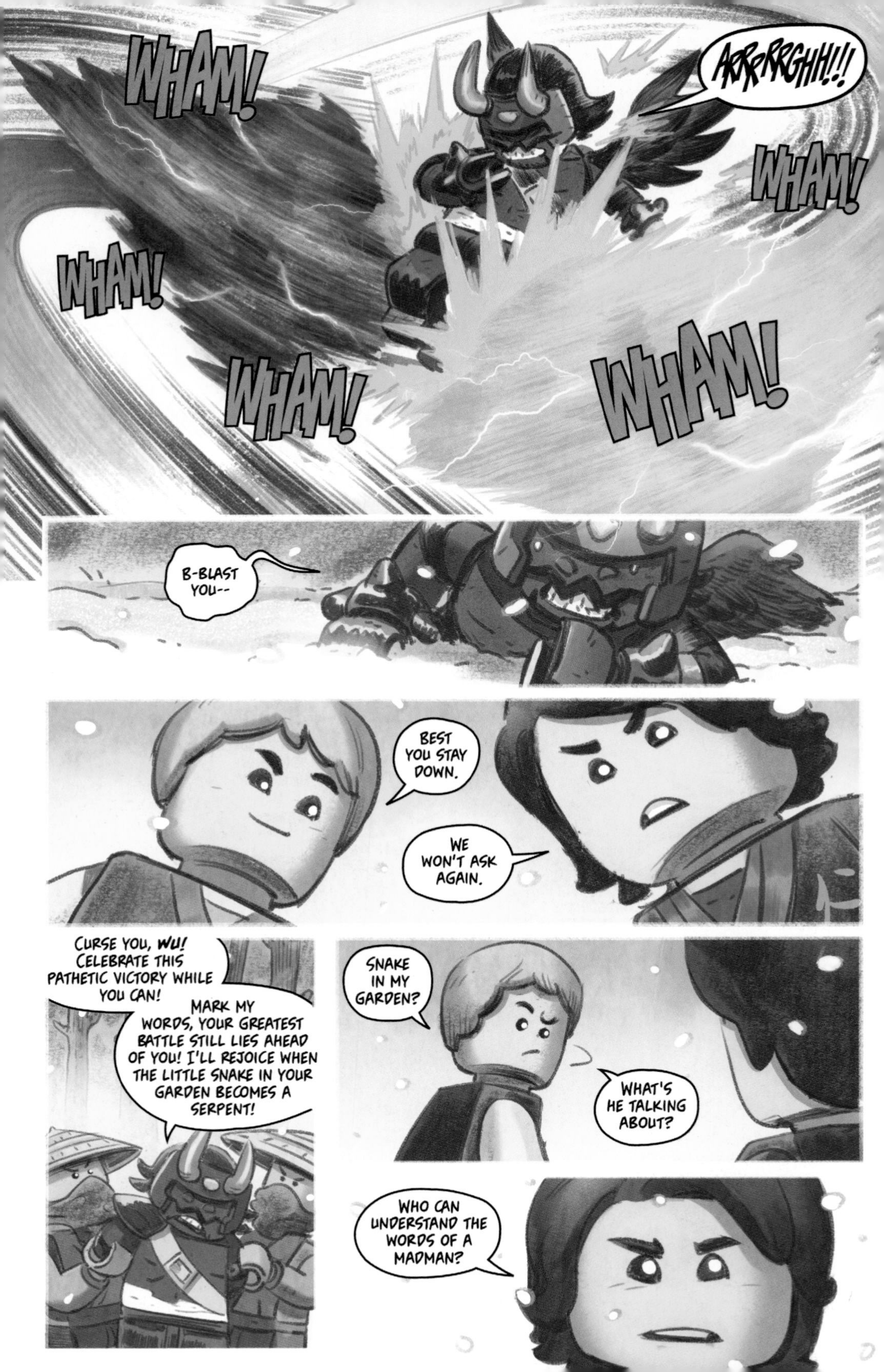
WHAM!
ARRRRRGHH!!!
WHAM!
WHAM!
WHAM!
WHAM!
B-BLAST YOU--
BEST YOU STAY DOWN.
WE WON'T ASK AGAIN.
CURSE YOU, WU! CELEBRATE THIS PATHETIC VICTORY WHILE YOU CAN!
MARK MY WORDS, YOUR GREATEST BATTLE STILL LIES AHEAD OF YOU! I'LL REJOICE WHEN THE LITTLE SNAKE IN YOUR GARDEN BECOMES A SERPENT!
SNAKE IN MY GARDEN?
WHAT'S HE TALKING ABOUT?
WHO CAN UNDERSTAND THE WORDS OF A MADMAN?

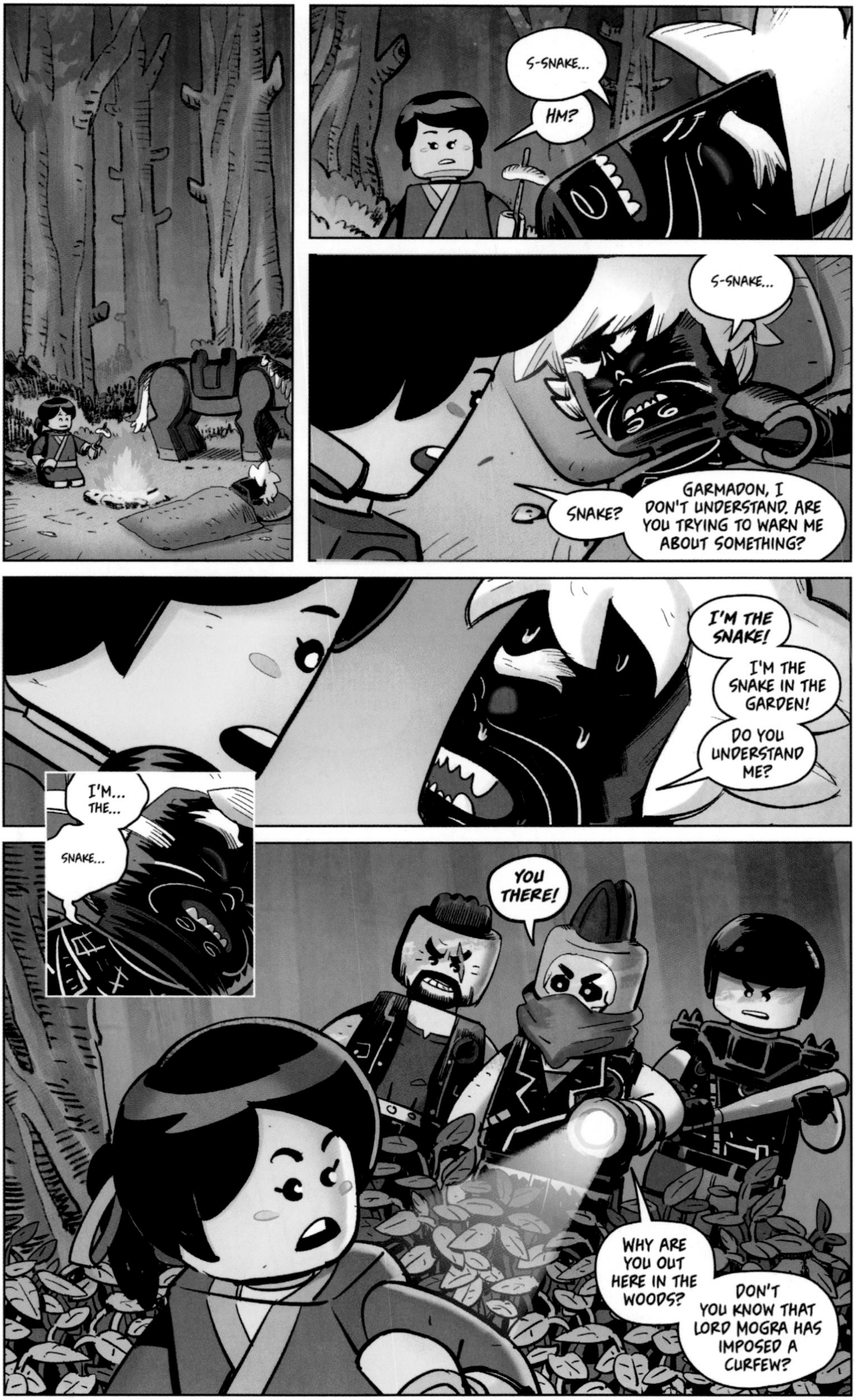
S-SNAKE...
HM?
S-SNAKE...
SNAKE?
GARMADON, I DON'T UNDERSTAND. ARE YOU TRYING TO WARN ME ABOUT SOMETHING?
I'M THE SNAKE!
I'M THE SNAKE IN THE GARDEN!
DO YOU UNDERSTAND ME?
I'M... THE...
SNAKE...
YOU THERE!
WHY ARE YOU OUT HERE IN THE WOODS?
DON'T YOU KNOW THAT LORD MOGRA HAS IMPOSED A CURFEW?

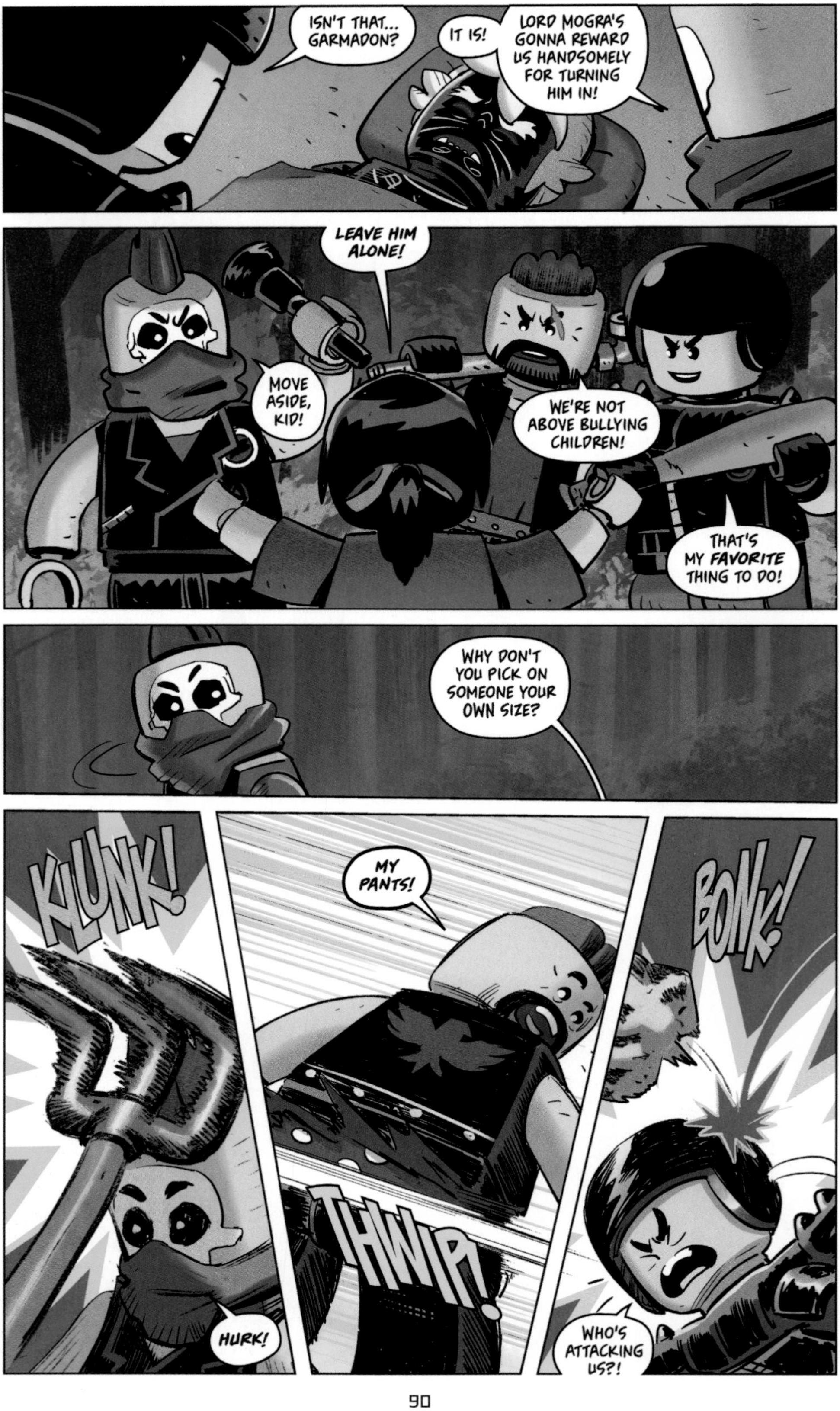
ISN'T THAT... GARMADON?
IT IS!
LORD MOGRA'S GONNA REWARD US HANDSOMELY FOR TURNING HIM IN!
LEAVE HIM ALONE!
MOVE ASIDE, KID!
WE'RE NOT ABOVE BULLYING CHILDREN!
THAT'S MY FAVORITE THING TO DO!
WHY DON'T YOU PICK ON SOMEONE YOUR OWN SIZE?
KLUNK!
HURK!
MY PANTS!
THWIP!
BONK!
WHO'S ATTACKING US?!

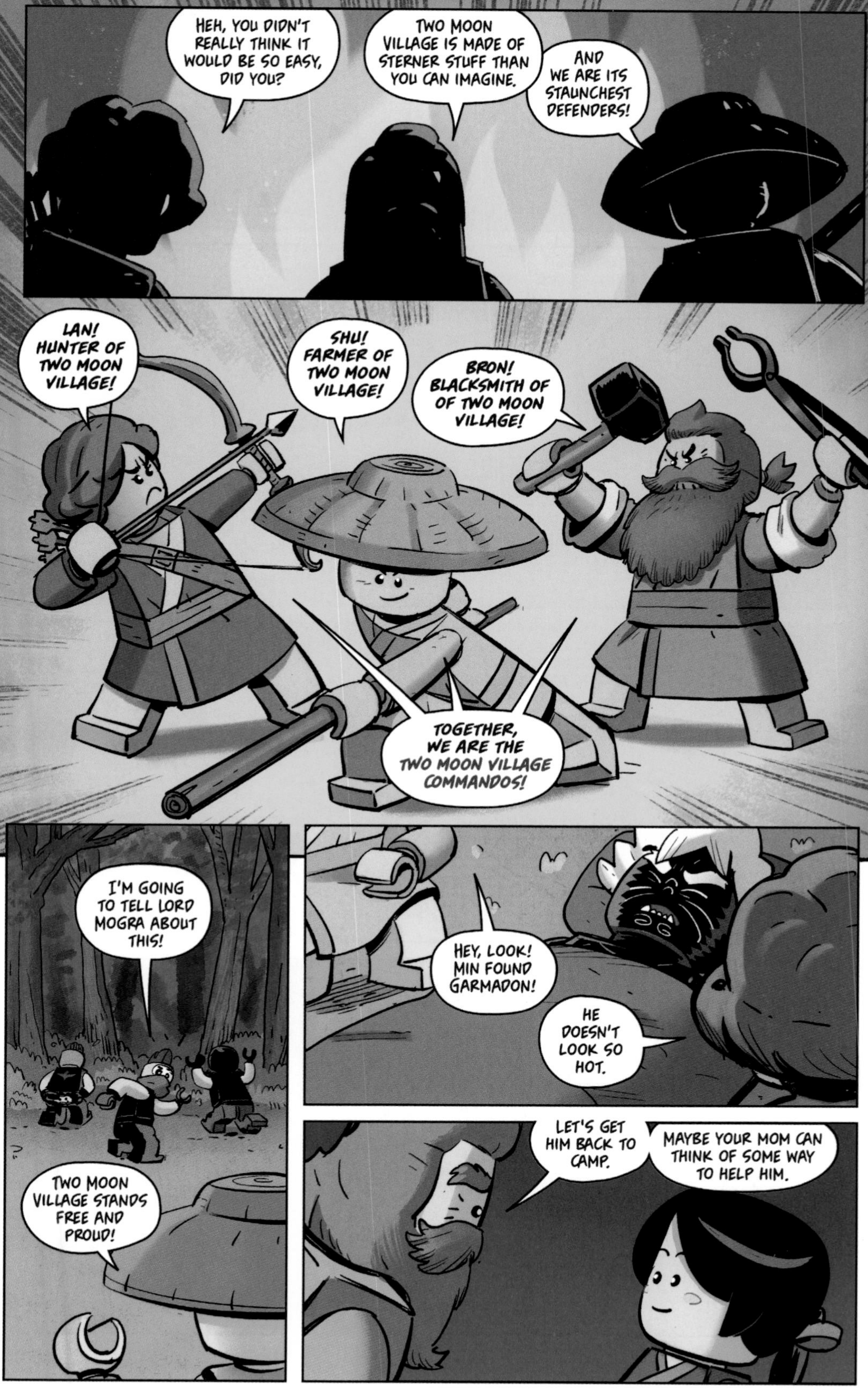
HEH, YOU DIDN'T REALLY THINK IT WOULD BE SO EASY, DID YOU?
TWO MOON VILLAGE IS MADE OF STERNER STUFF THAN YOU CAN IMAGINE.
AND WE ARE ITS STAUNCHEST DEFENDERS!
LAN! HUNTER OF TWO MOON VILLAGE!
SHU! FARMER OF TWO MOON VILLAGE!
BRON! BLACKSMITH OF OF TWO MOON VILLAGE!
TOGETHER, WE ARE THE TWO MOON VILLAGE COMMANDOS!
I'M GOING TO TELL LORD MOGRA ABOUT THIS!
TWO MOON VILLAGE STANDS FREE AND PROUD!
HEY, LOOK! MIN FOUND GARMADON!
HE DOESN'T LOOK SO HOT.
LET'S GET HIM BACK TO CAMP.
MAYBE YOUR MOM CAN THINK OF SOME WAY TO HELP HIM.

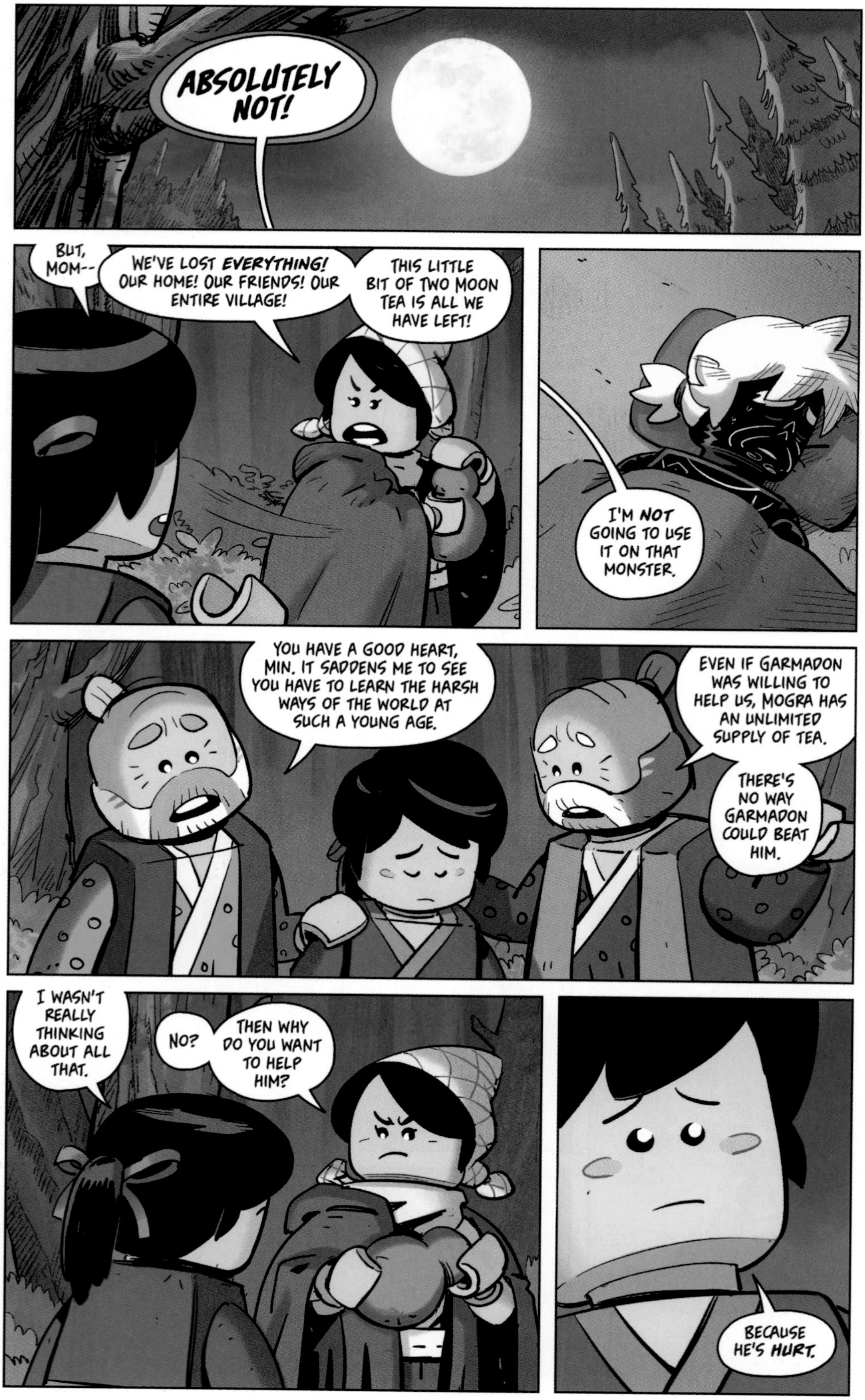
ABSOLUTELY NOT!
BUT, MOM--
WE'VE LOST EVERYTHING! OUR HOME! OUR FRIENDS! OUR ENTIRE VILLAGE!
THIS LITTLE BIT OF TWO MOON TEA IS ALL WE HAVE LEFT!
I'M NOT GOING TO USE IT ON THAT MONSTER.
YOU HAVE A GOOD HEART, MIN. IT SADDENS ME TO SEE YOU HAVE TO LEARN THE HARSH WAYS OF THE WORLD AT SUCH A YOUNG AGE.
EVEN IF GARMADON WAS WILLING TO HELP US, MOGRA HAS AN UNLIMITED SUPPLY OF TEA.
THERE'S NO WAY GARMADON COULD BEAT HIM.
I WASN'T REALLY THINKING ABOUT ALL THAT.
NO?
THEN WHY DO YOU WANT TO HELP HIM?
BECAUSE HE'S HURT.

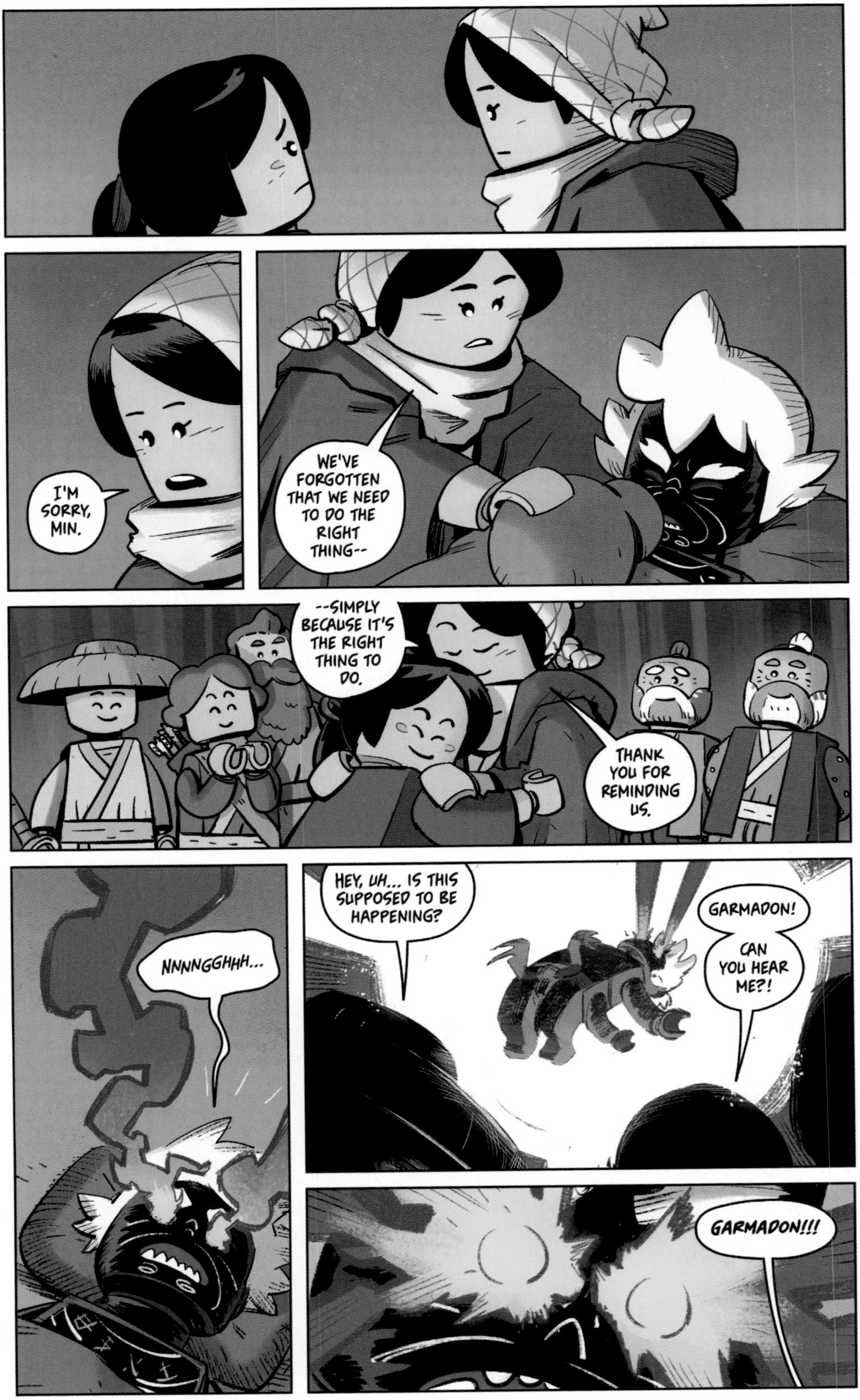
I'M SORRY, MIN.
WE'VE FORGOTTEN THAT WE NEED TO DO THE RIGHT THING--
--SIMPLY BECAUSE IT'S THE RIGHT THING TO DO.
THANK YOU FOR REMINDING US.
NNNNGGHHH...
HEY, UH... IS THIS SUPPOSED TO BE HAPPENING?
GARMADON!
CAN YOU HEAR ME?!
GARMADON!!!

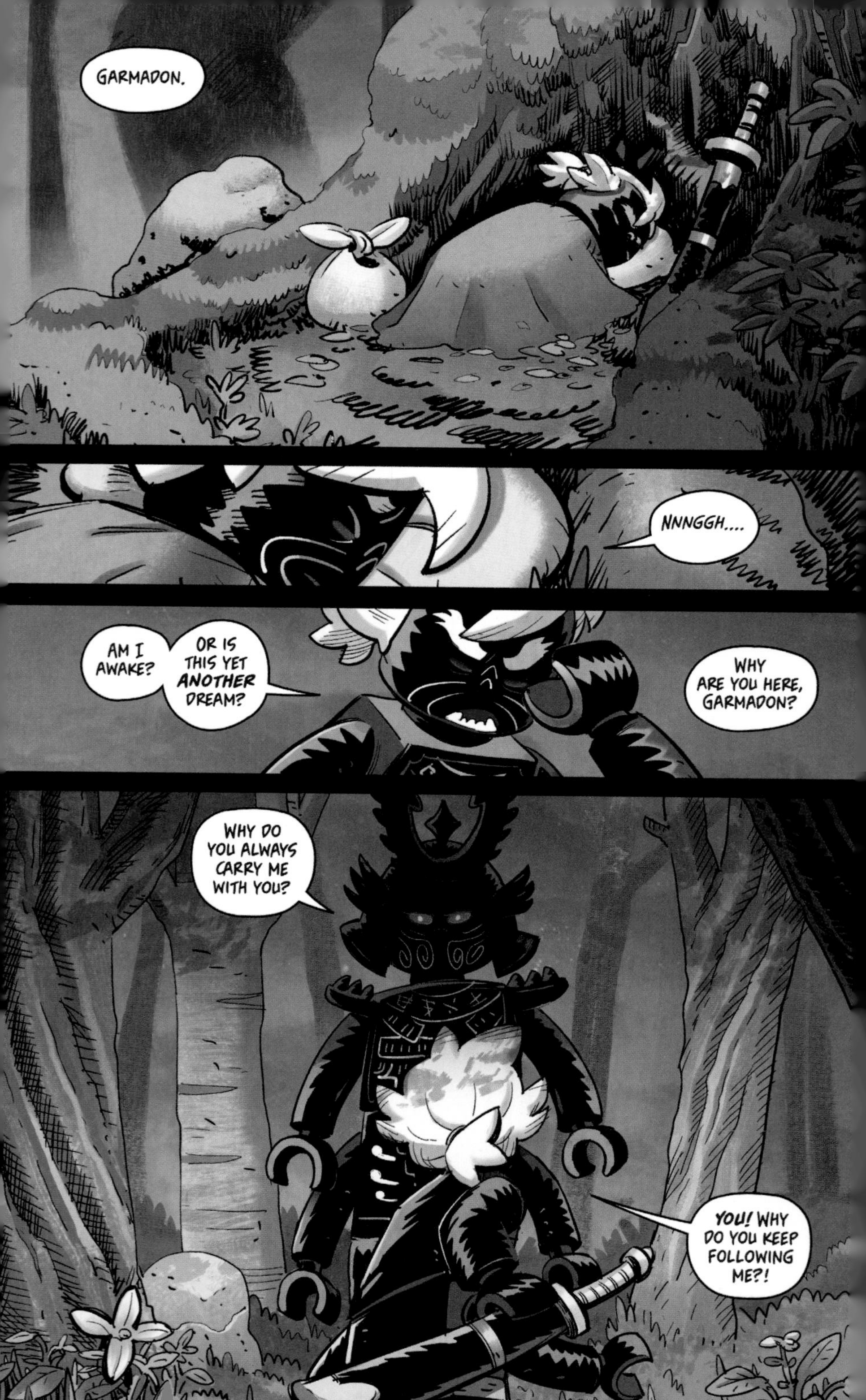
GARMADON.
NNNGGH....
AM I AWAKE?
OR IS THIS YET ANOTHER DREAM?
WHY ARE YOU HERE, GARMADON?
WHY DO YOU ALWAYS CARRY ME WITH YOU?
YOU! WHY DO YOU KEEP FOLLOWING ME?!

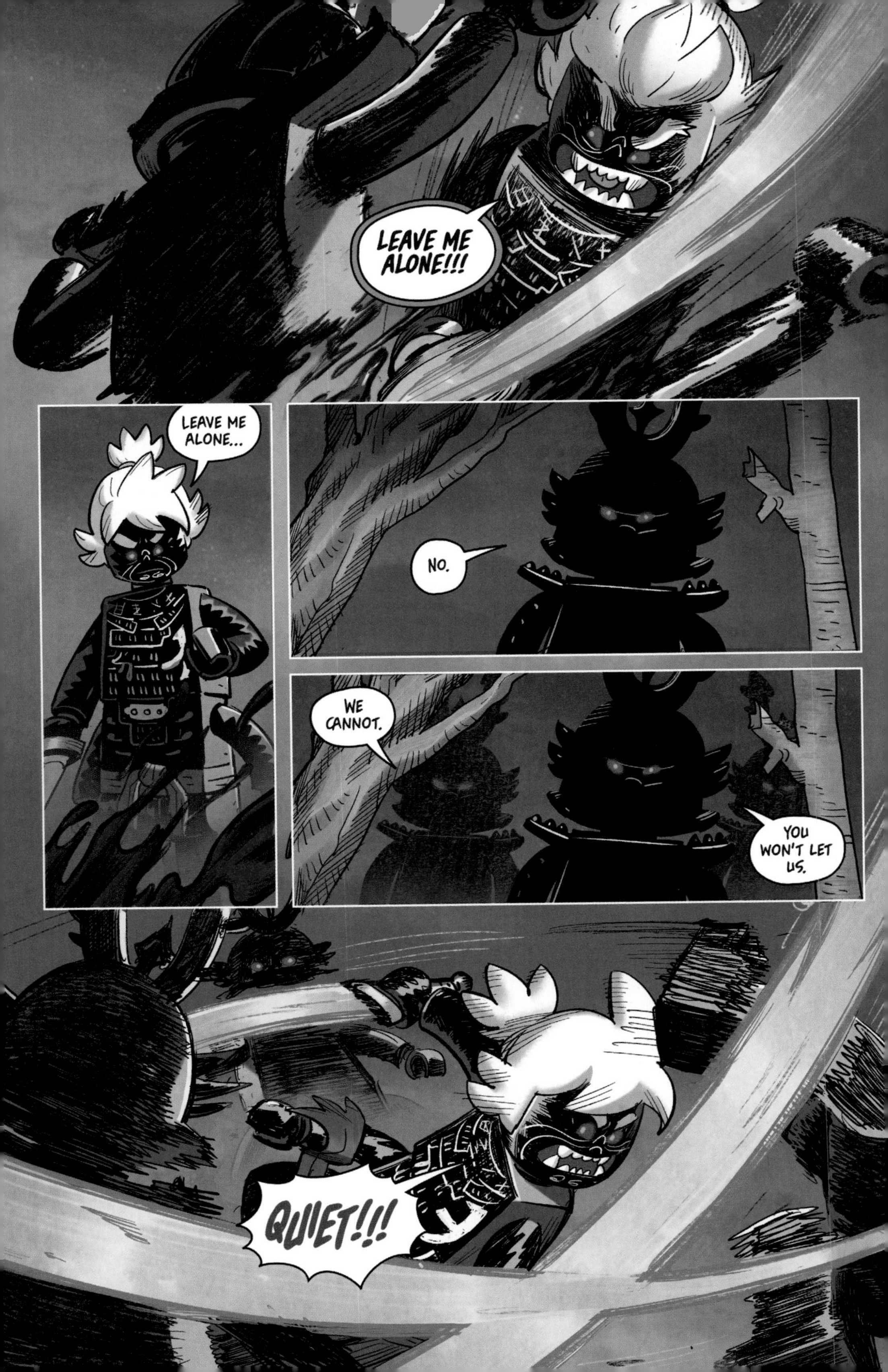
LEAVE ME ALONE!!!
LEAVE ME ALONE...
NO.
WE CANNOT.
YOU WON'T LET US.
QUIET!!!

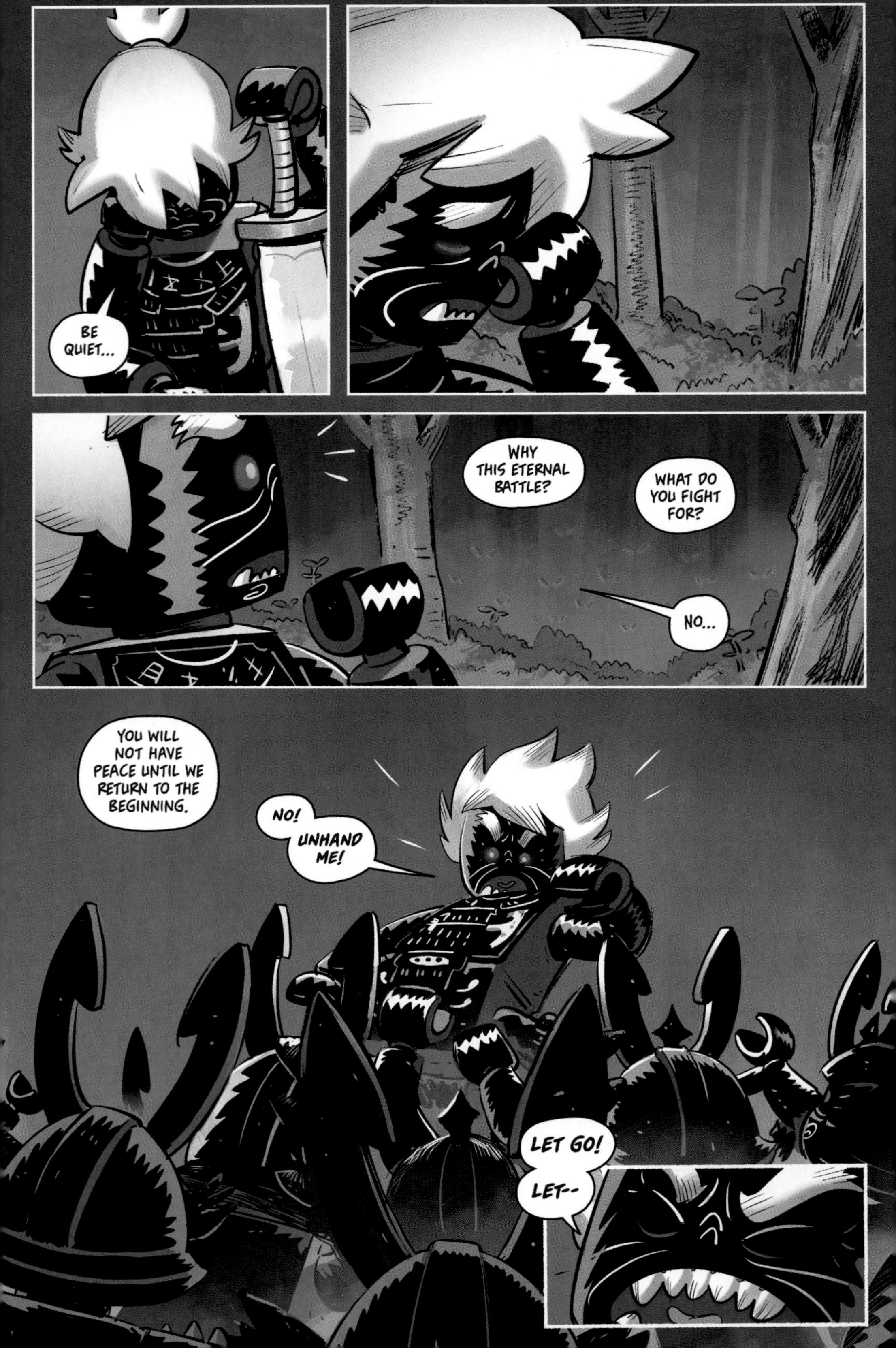
BE QUIET...
WHY THIS ETERNAL BATTLE?
WHAT DO YOU FIGHT FOR?
NO...
YOU WILL NOT HAVE PEACE UNTIL WE RETURN TO THE BEGINNING.
NO! UNHAND ME!
LET GO!
LET--

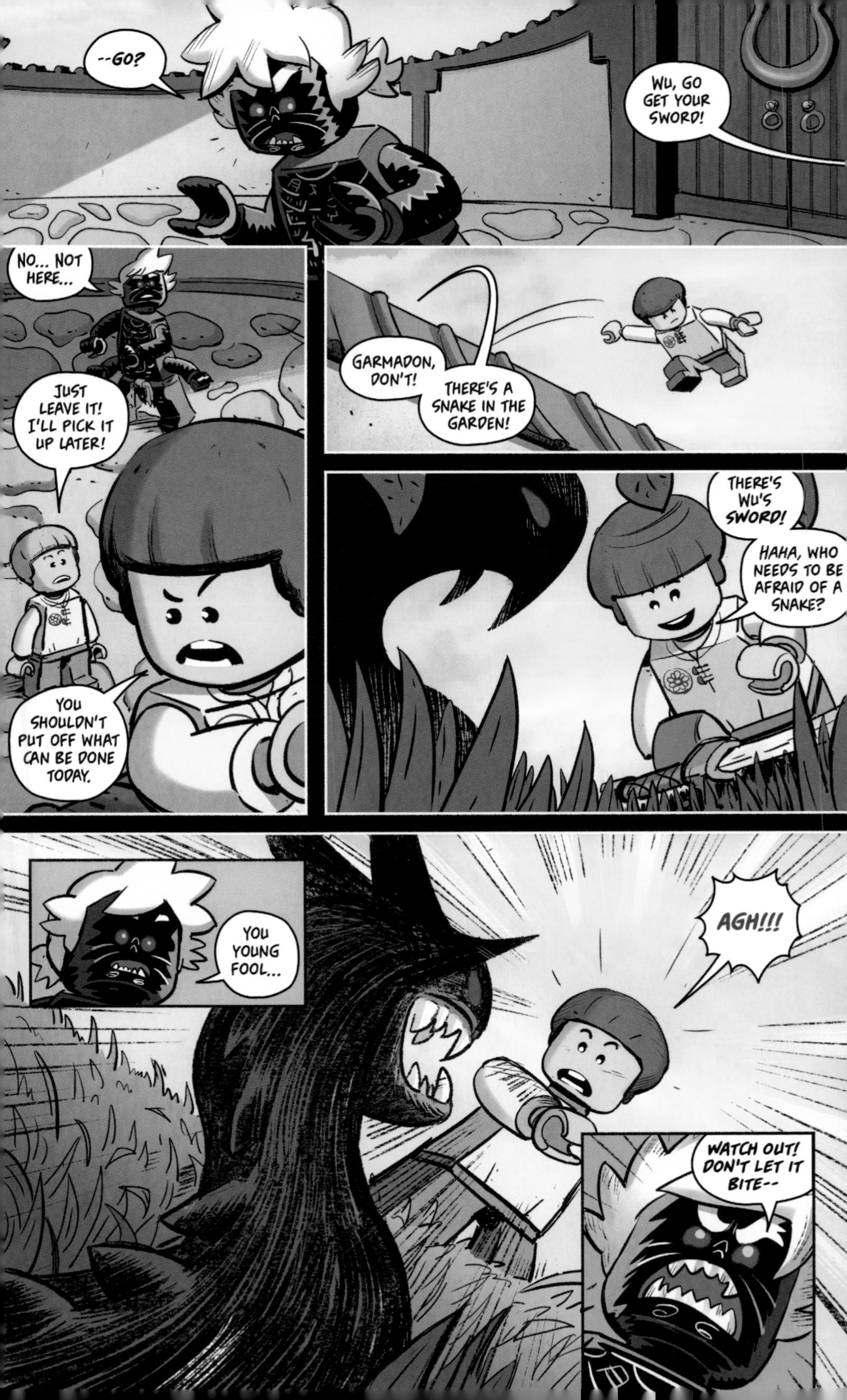
--GO?
WU, GO GET YOUR SWORD!
NO... NOT HERE...
JUST LEAVE IT! I'LL PICK IT UP LATER!
YOU SHOULDN'T PUT OFF WHAT CAN BE DONE TODAY.
GARMADON, DON'T!
THERE'S A SNAKE IN THE GARDEN!
THERE'S WU'S SWORD!
HAHA, WHO NEEDS TO BE AFRAID OF A SNAKE?
YOU YOUNG FOOL...
AGH!!!
WATCH OUT! DON'T LET IT BITE--

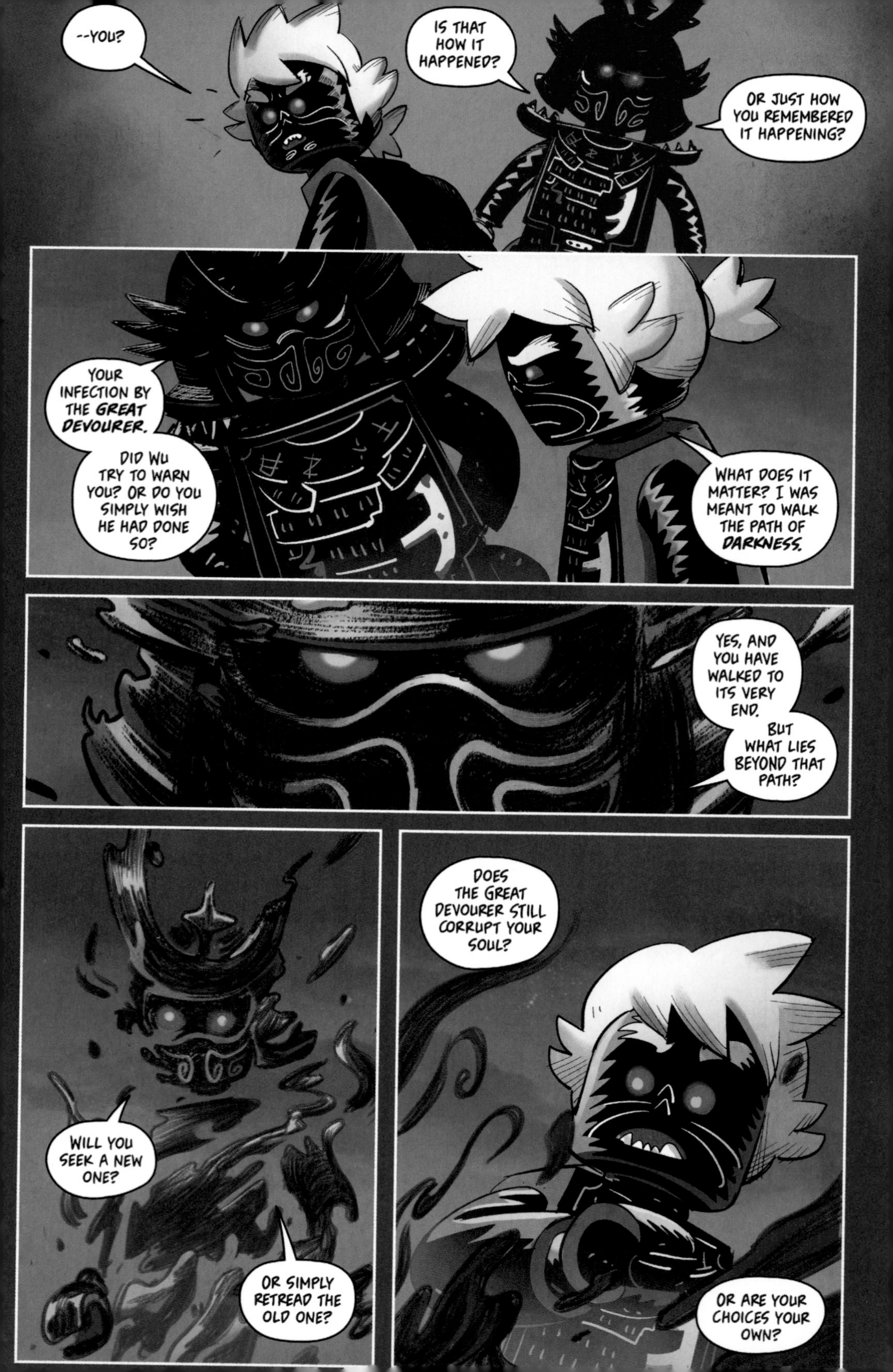
--YOU?
IS THAT HOW IT HAPPENED?
OR JUST HOW YOU REMEMBERED IT HAPPENING?
YOUR INFECTION BY THE GREAT DEVOURER.
DID WU TRY TO WARN YOU? OR DO YOU SIMPLY WISH HE HAD DONE SO?
WHAT DOES IT MATTER? I WAS MEANT TO WALK THE PATH OF DARKNESS.
YES, AND YOU HAVE WALKED TO ITS VERY END.
BUT WHAT LIES BEYOND THAT PATH?
WILL YOU SEEK A NEW ONE?
OR SIMPLY RETREAD THE OLD ONE?
DOES THE GREAT DEVOURER STILL CORRUPT YOUR SOUL?
OR ARE YOUR CHOICES YOUR OWN?

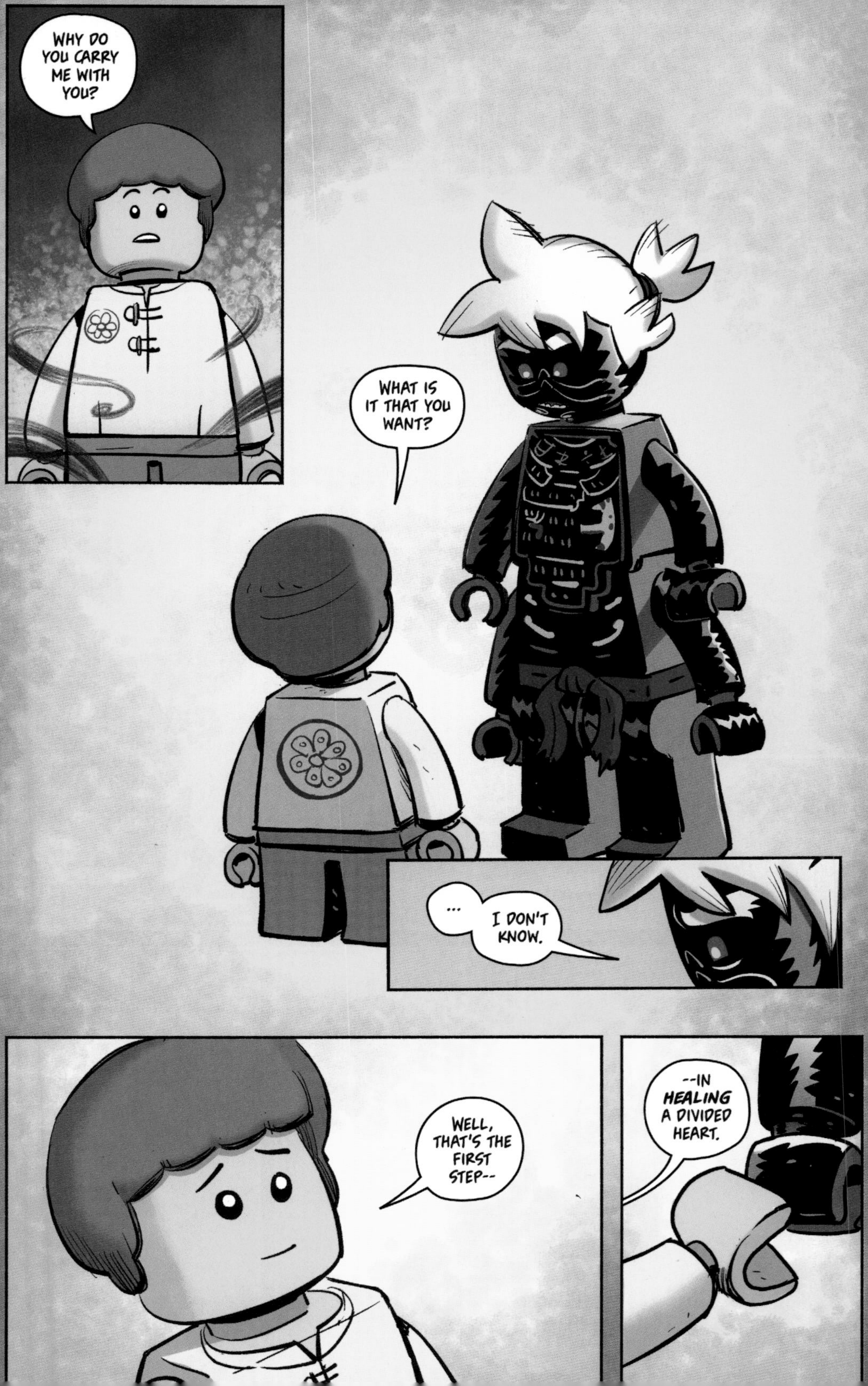
WHY DO YOU CARRY ME WITH YOU?
WHAT IS IT THAT YOU WANT?
...
I DON'T KNOW.
WELL, THAT'S THE FIRST STEP--
--IN **HEALING** A DIVIDED HEART.

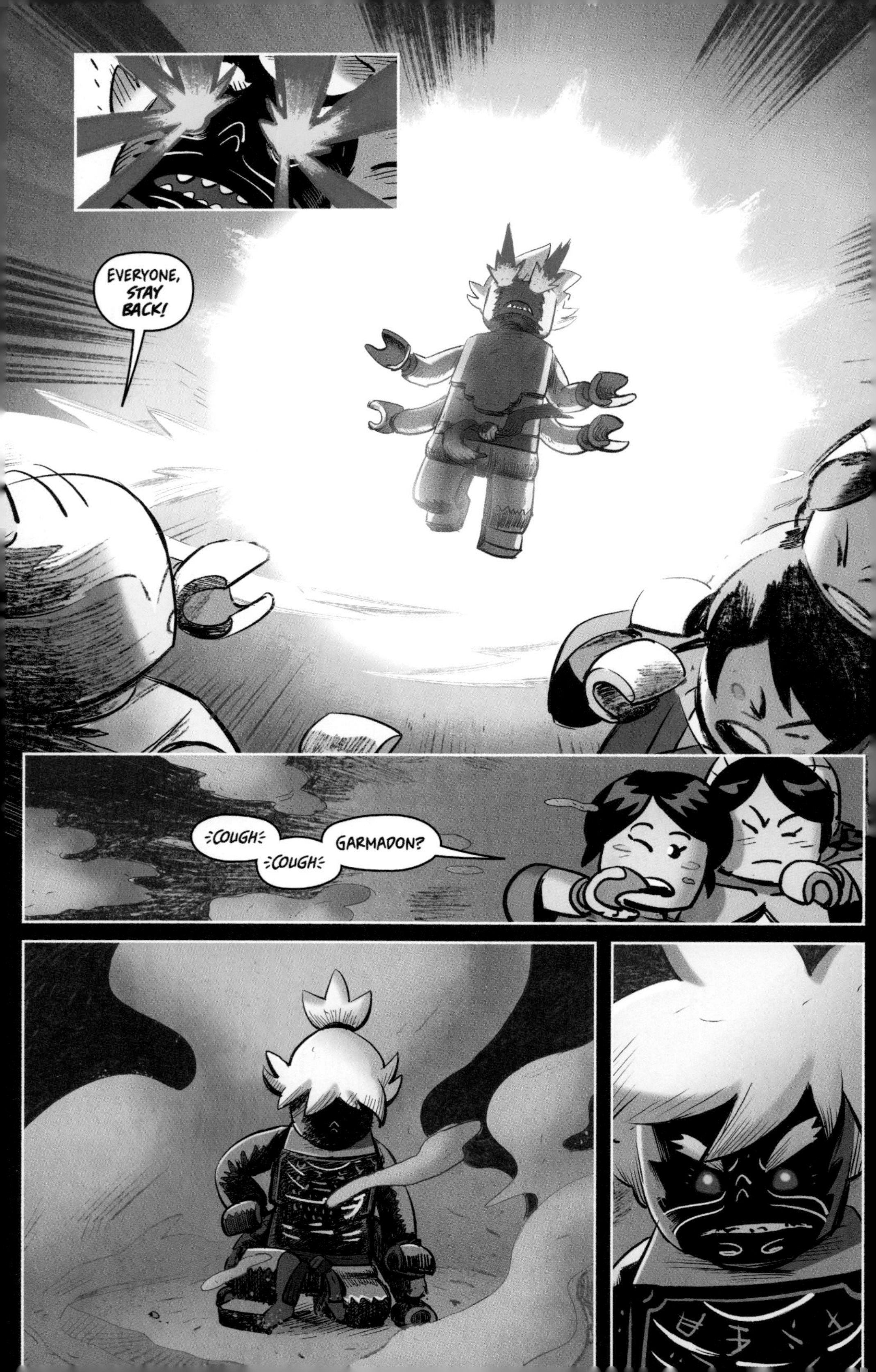

EVERYONE, STAY BACK!
COUGH
COUGH
GARMADON?

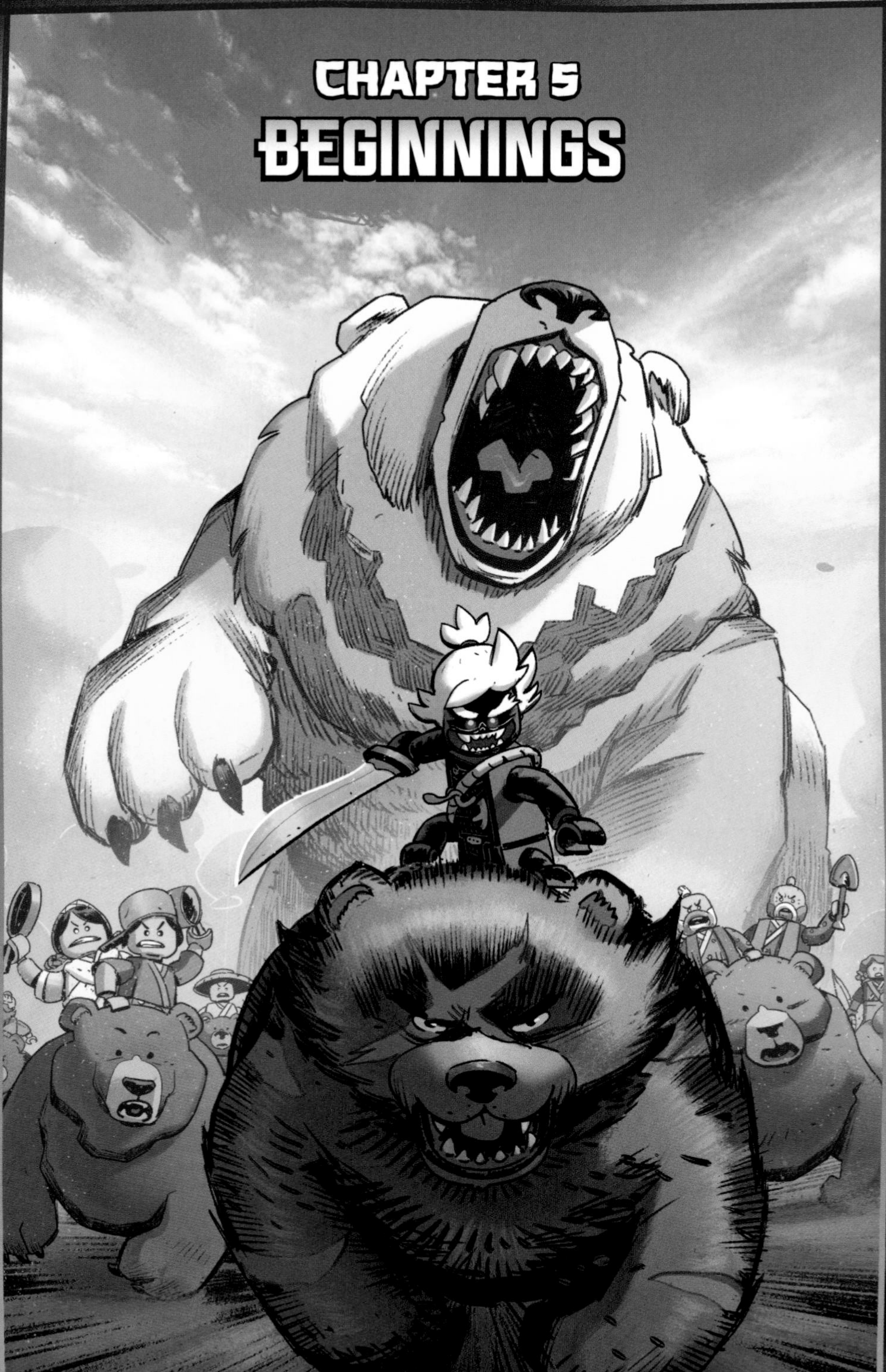
CHAPTER 5
BEGINNINGS

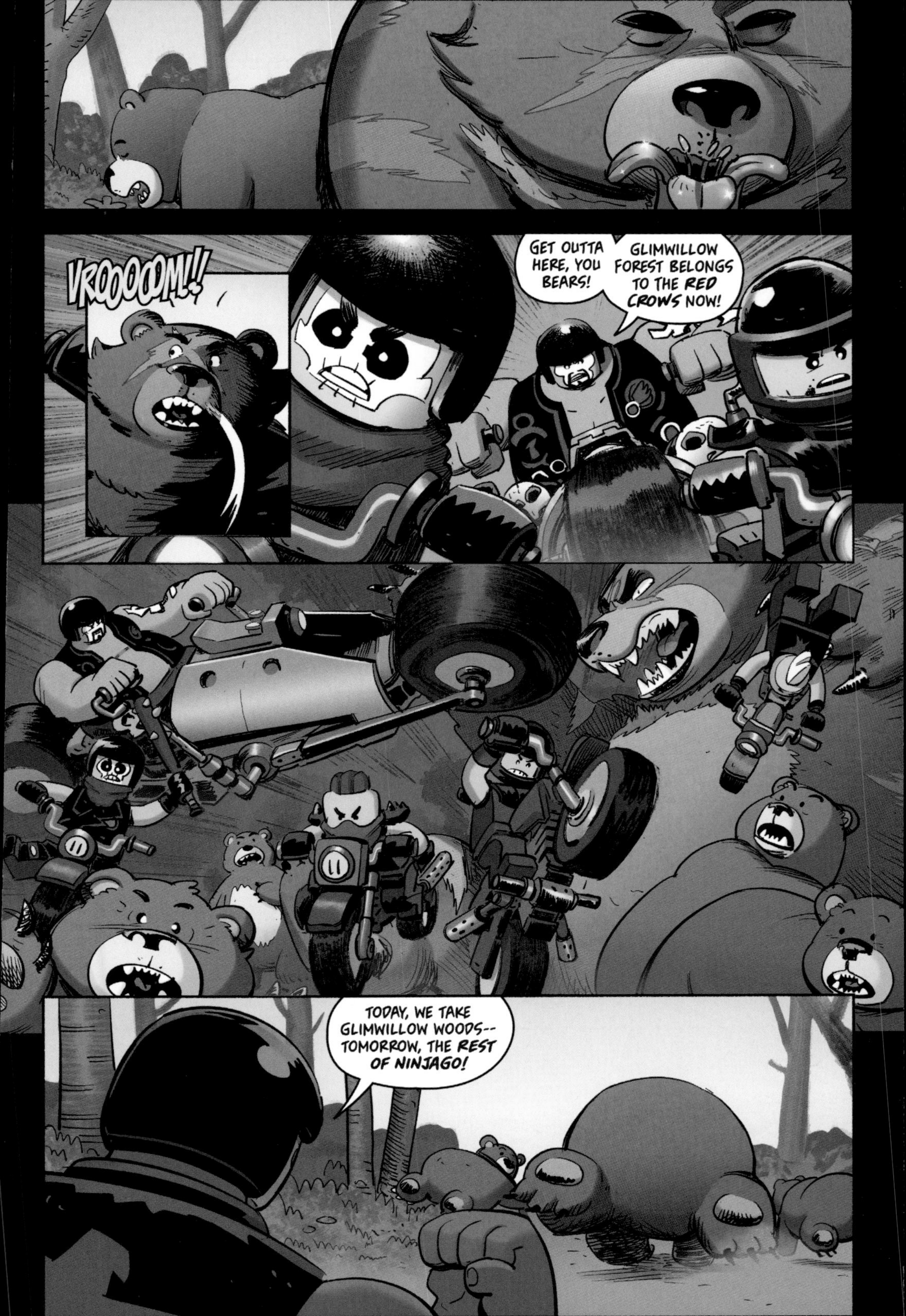
VROOOOOM!!
GET OUTTA HERE, YOU BEARS!
GLIMWILLOW FOREST BELONGS TO THE RED CROWS NOW!
TODAY, WE TAKE GLIMWILLOW WOODS--TOMORROW, THE REST OF NINJAGO!

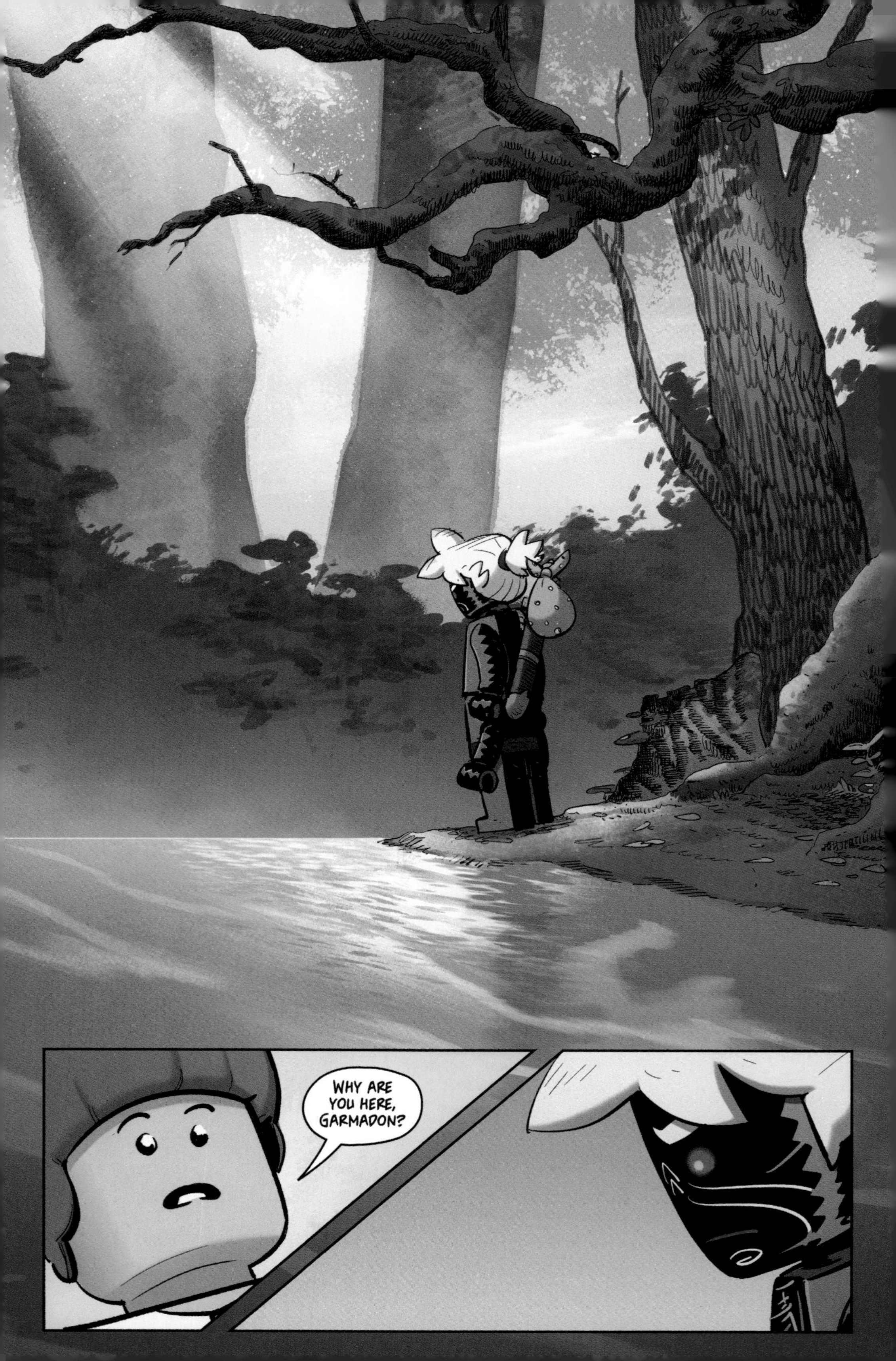
WHY ARE YOU HERE, GARMADON?

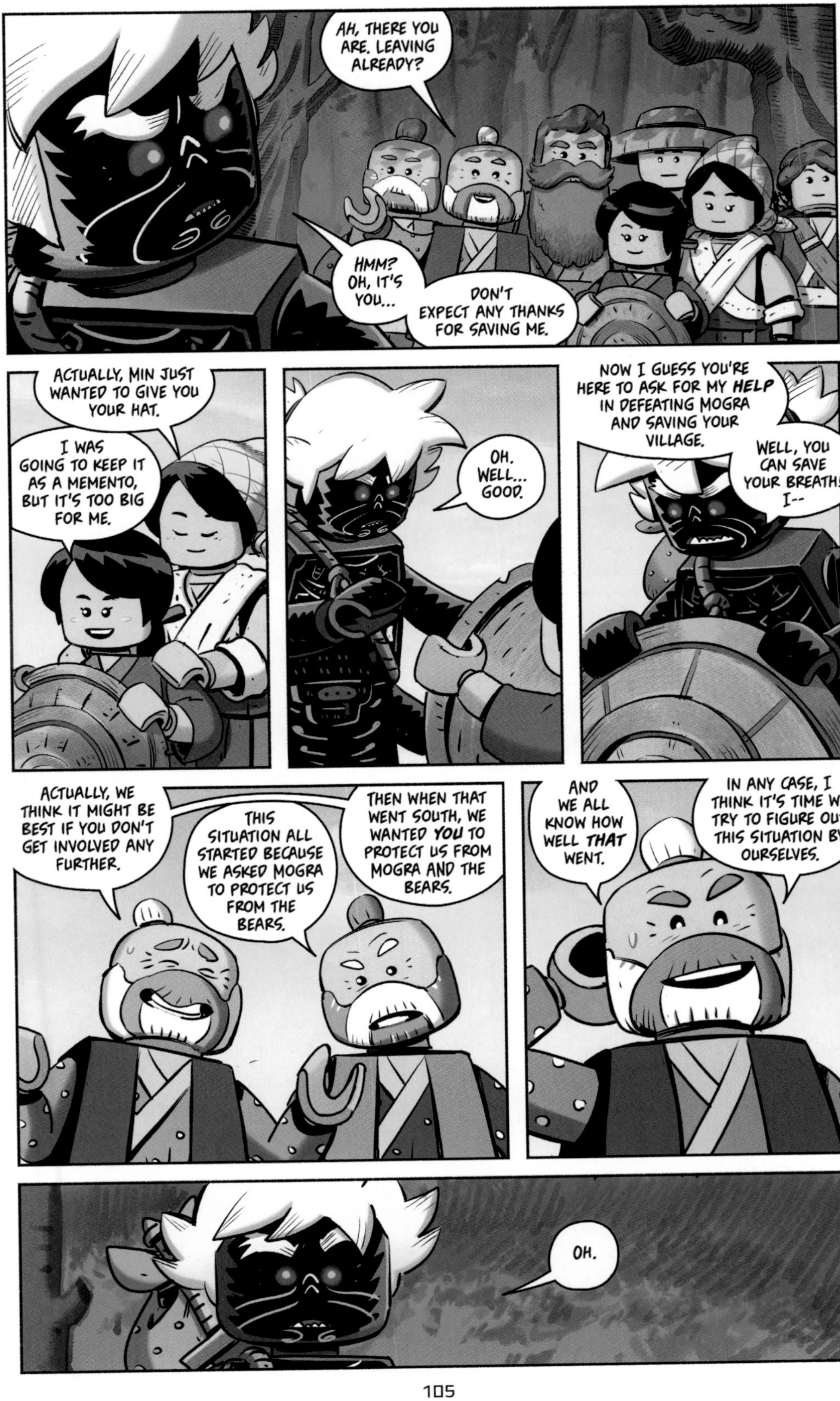
AH, THERE YOU ARE. LEAVING ALREADY?
HMM? OH, IT'S YOU...
DON'T EXPECT ANY THANKS FOR SAVING ME.
ACTUALLY, MIN JUST WANTED TO GIVE YOU YOUR HAT.
I WAS GOING TO KEEP IT AS A MEMENTO, BUT IT'S TOO BIG FOR ME.
OH. WELL... GOOD.
NOW I GUESS YOU'RE HERE TO ASK FOR MY HELP IN DEFEATING MOGRA AND SAVING YOUR VILLAGE.
WELL, YOU CAN SAVE YOUR BREATH! I--
ACTUALLY, WE THINK IT MIGHT BE BEST IF YOU DON'T GET INVOLVED ANY FURTHER.
THIS SITUATION ALL STARTED BECAUSE WE ASKED MOGRA TO PROTECT US FROM THE BEARS.
THEN WHEN THAT WENT SOUTH, WE WANTED YOU TO PROTECT US FROM MOGRA AND THE BEARS.
AND WE ALL KNOW HOW WELL THAT WENT.
IN ANY CASE, I THINK IT'S TIME WE TRY TO FIGURE OUT THIS SITUATION BY OURSELVES.
OH.

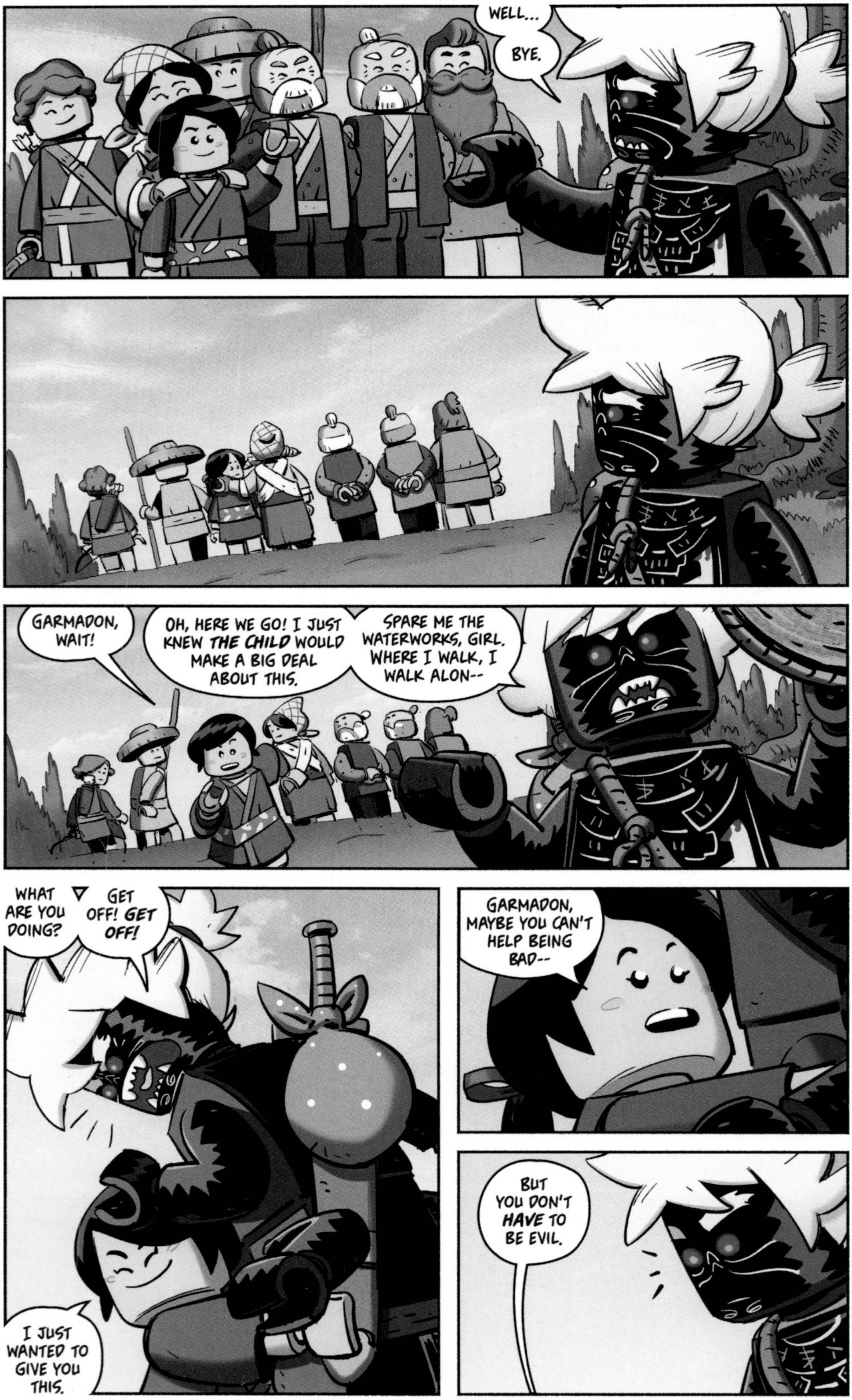
WELL...
BYE.
GARMADON, WAIT!
OH, HERE WE GO! I JUST KNEW THE CHILD WOULD MAKE A BIG DEAL ABOUT THIS.
SPARE ME THE WATERWORKS, GIRL. WHERE I WALK, I WALK ALON--
WHAT ARE YOU DOING?
GET OFF! GET OFF!
I JUST WANTED TO GIVE YOU THIS.
GARMADON, MAYBE YOU CAN'T HELP BEING BAD--
BUT YOU DON'T HAVE TO BE EVIL.

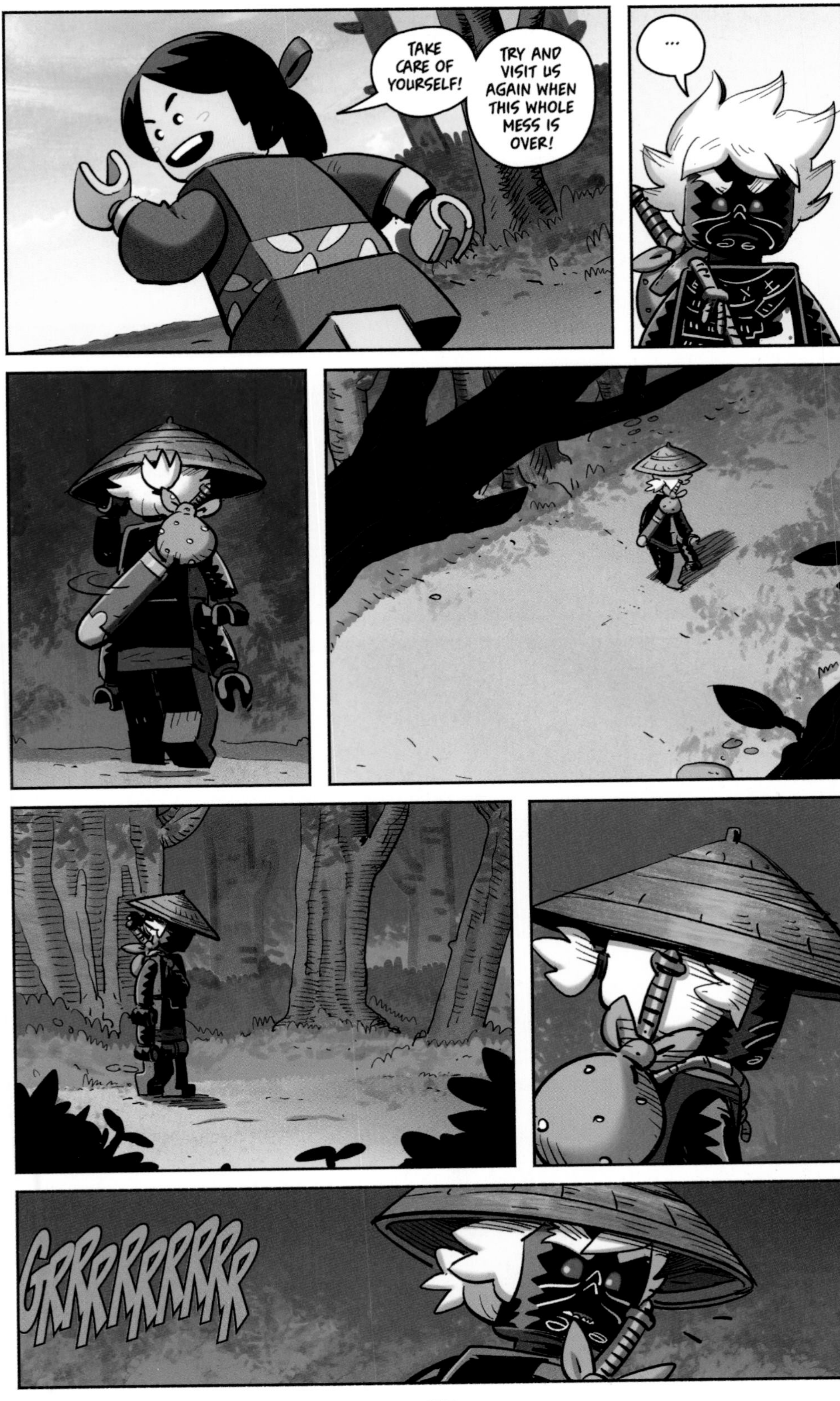
TAKE CARE OF YOURSELF!
TRY AND VISIT US AGAIN WHEN THIS WHOLE MESS IS OVER!
...
GRRRRRRRR

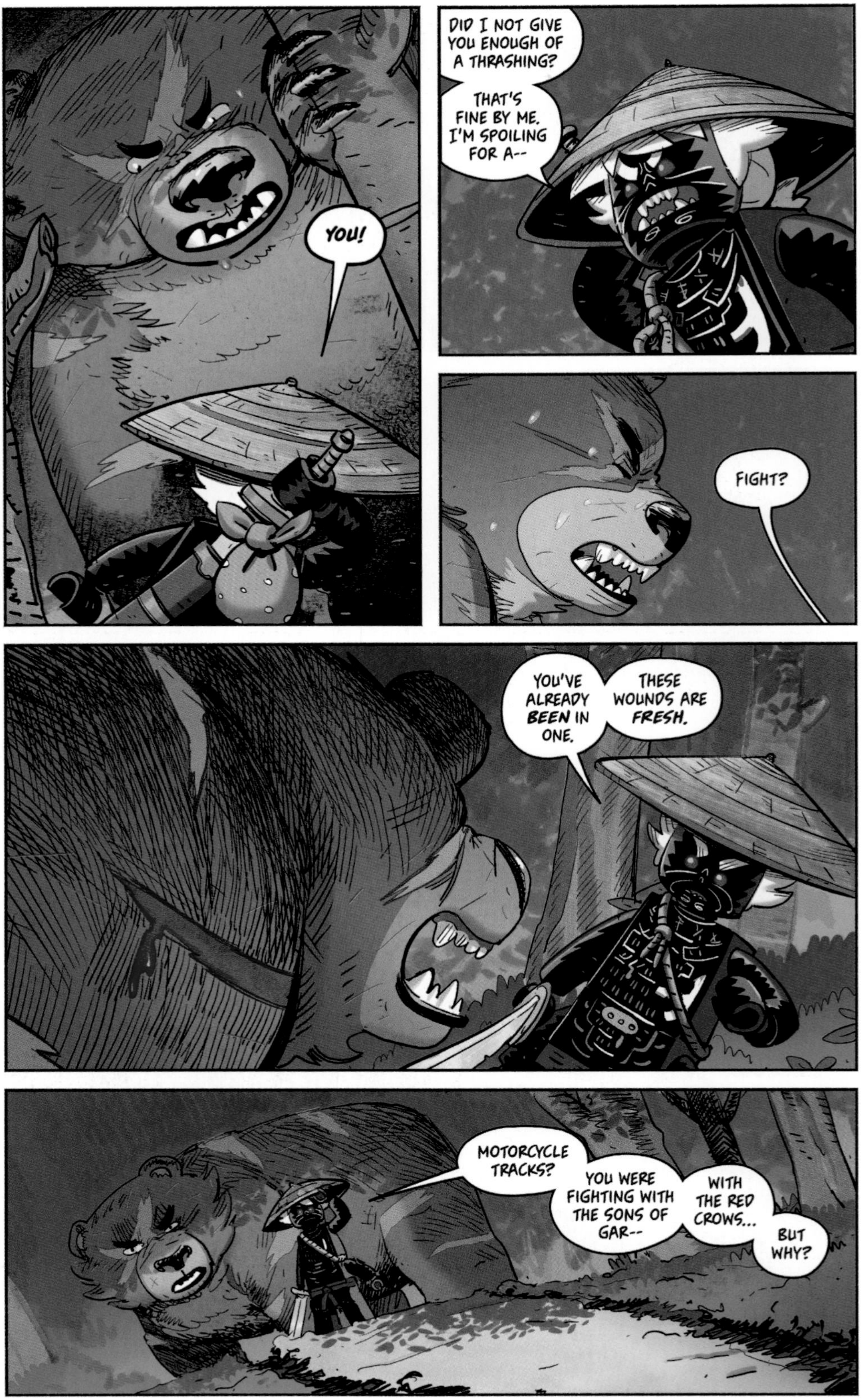
YOU!
DID I NOT GIVE YOU ENOUGH OF A THRASHING?
THAT'S FINE BY ME. I'M SPOILING FOR A--
FIGHT?
THESE WOUNDS ARE FRESH.
YOU'VE ALREADY BEEN IN ONE.
MOTORCYCLE TRACKS?
YOU WERE FIGHTING WITH THE SONS OF GAR--
WITH THE RED CROWS...
BUT WHY?

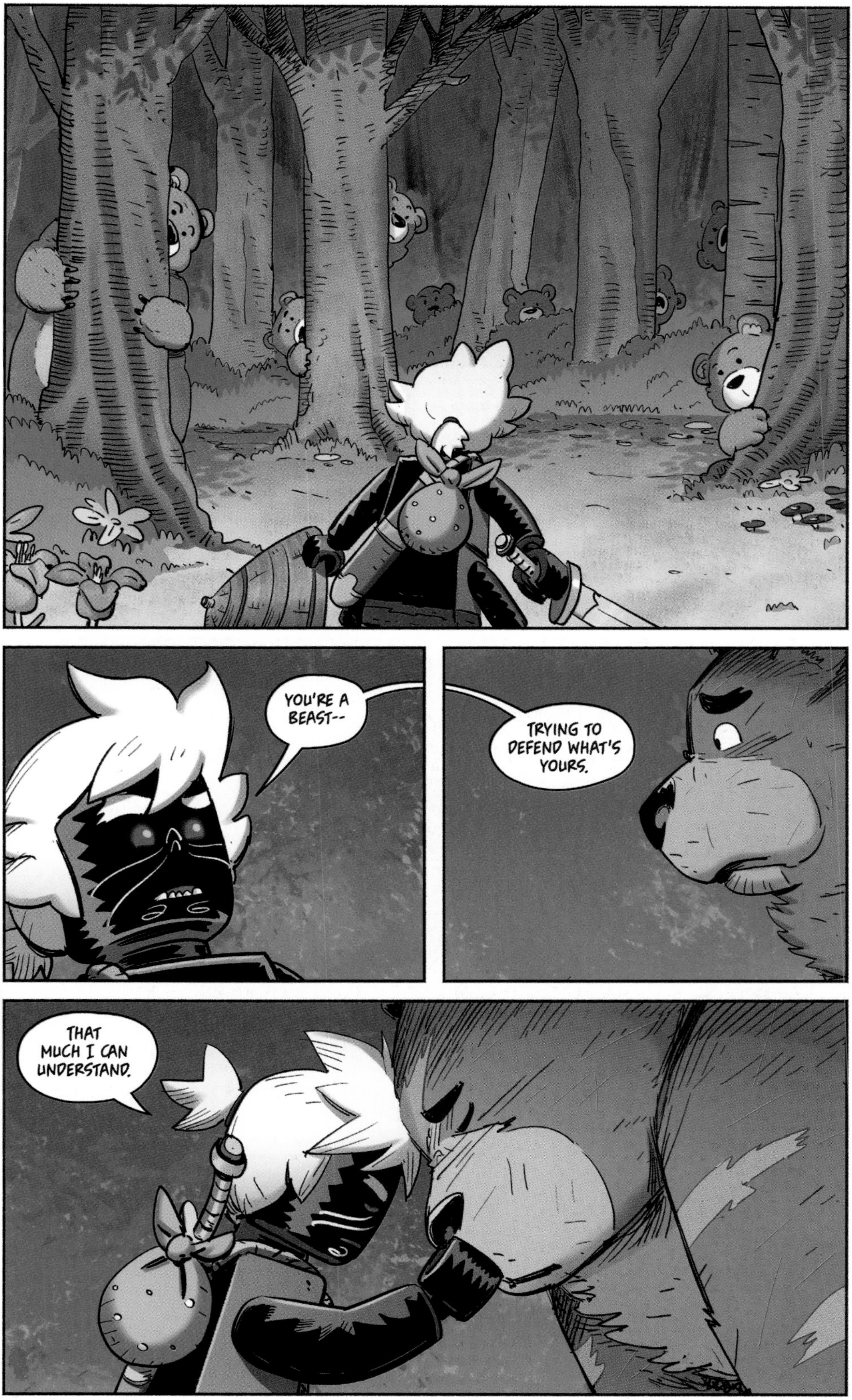
YOU'RE A BEAST--
TRYING TO DEFEND WHAT'S YOURS.
THAT MUCH I CAN UNDERSTAND.

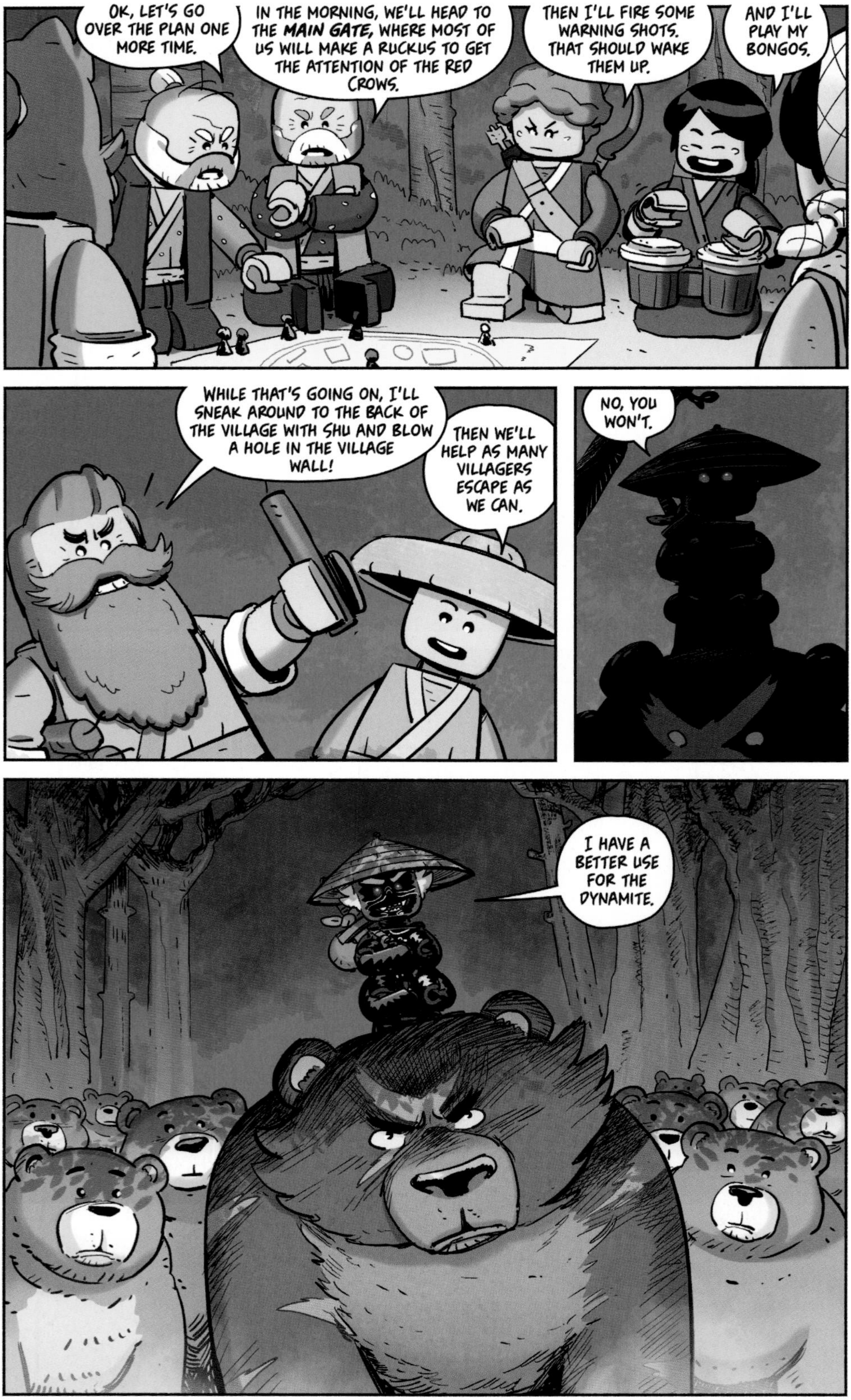
OK, LET'S GO OVER THE PLAN ONE MORE TIME.
IN THE MORNING, WE'LL HEAD TO THE MAIN GATE, WHERE MOST OF US WILL MAKE A RUCKUS TO GET THE ATTENTION OF THE RED CROWS.
THEN I'LL FIRE SOME WARNING SHOTS. THAT SHOULD WAKE THEM UP.
AND I'LL PLAY MY BONGOS.
WHILE THAT'S GOING ON, I'LL SNEAK AROUND TO THE BACK OF THE VILLAGE WITH SHU AND BLOW A HOLE IN THE VILLAGE WALL!
THEN WE'LL HELP AS MANY VILLAGERS ESCAPE AS WE CAN.
NO, YOU WON'T.
I HAVE A BETTER USE FOR THE DYNAMITE.

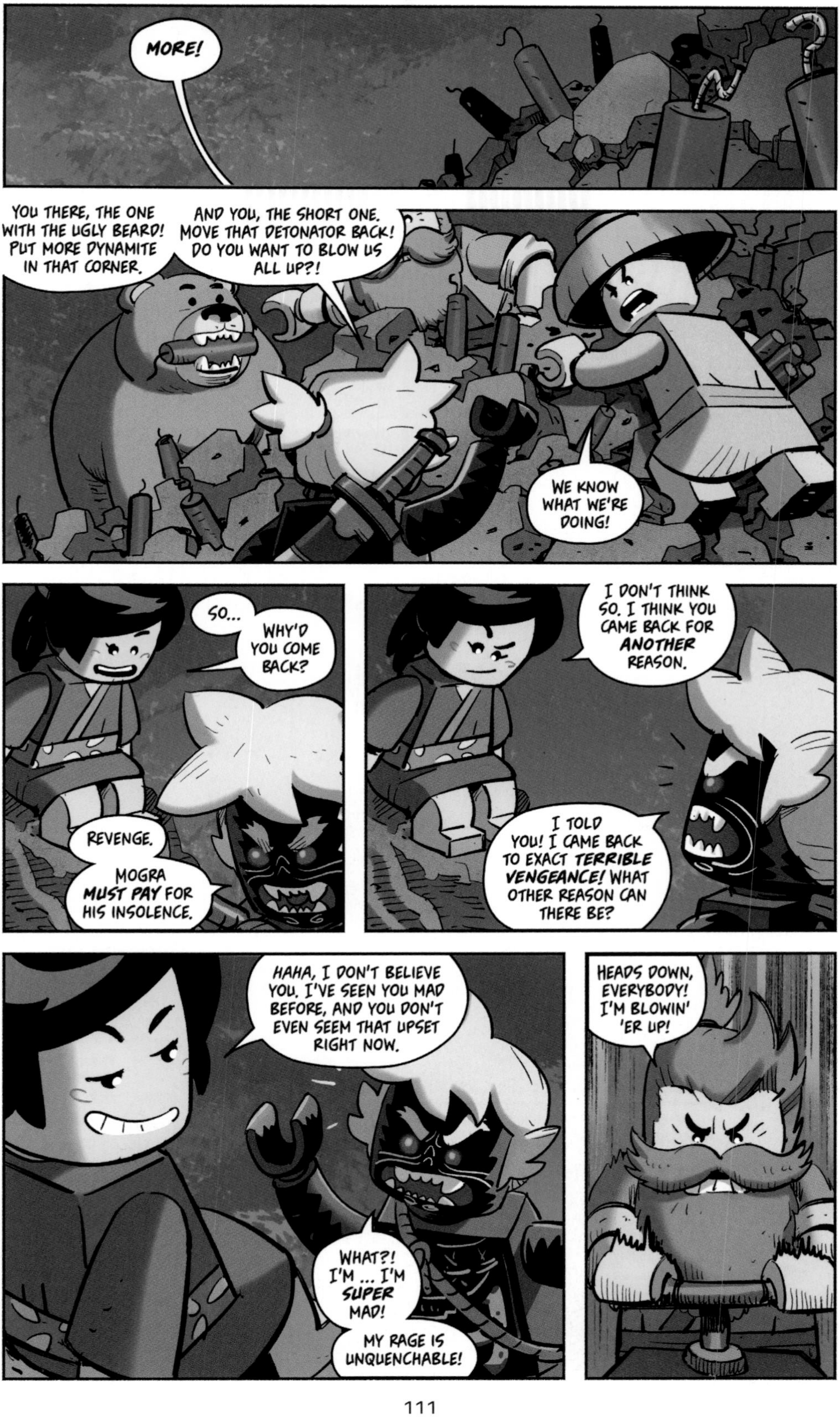
MORE!
YOU THERE, THE ONE WITH THE UGLY BEARD! PUT MORE DYNAMITE IN THAT CORNER.
AND YOU, THE SHORT ONE. MOVE THAT DETONATOR BACK! DO YOU WANT TO BLOW US ALL UP?!
WE KNOW WHAT WE'RE DOING!
SO...
WHY'D YOU COME BACK?
REVENGE.
MOGRA **MUST PAY** FOR HIS INSOLENCE.
I DON'T THINK SO. I THINK YOU CAME BACK FOR **ANOTHER** REASON.
I TOLD YOU! I CAME BACK TO EXACT ***TERRIBLE VENGEANCE!*** WHAT OTHER REASON CAN THERE BE?
HAHA, I DON'T BELIEVE YOU. I'VE SEEN YOU MAD BEFORE, AND YOU DON'T EVEN SEEM THAT UPSET RIGHT NOW.
WHAT?! I'M ... I'M ***SUPER*** MAD!
MY RAGE IS UNQUENCHABLE!
HEADS DOWN, EVERYBODY! I'M BLOWIN' 'ER UP!

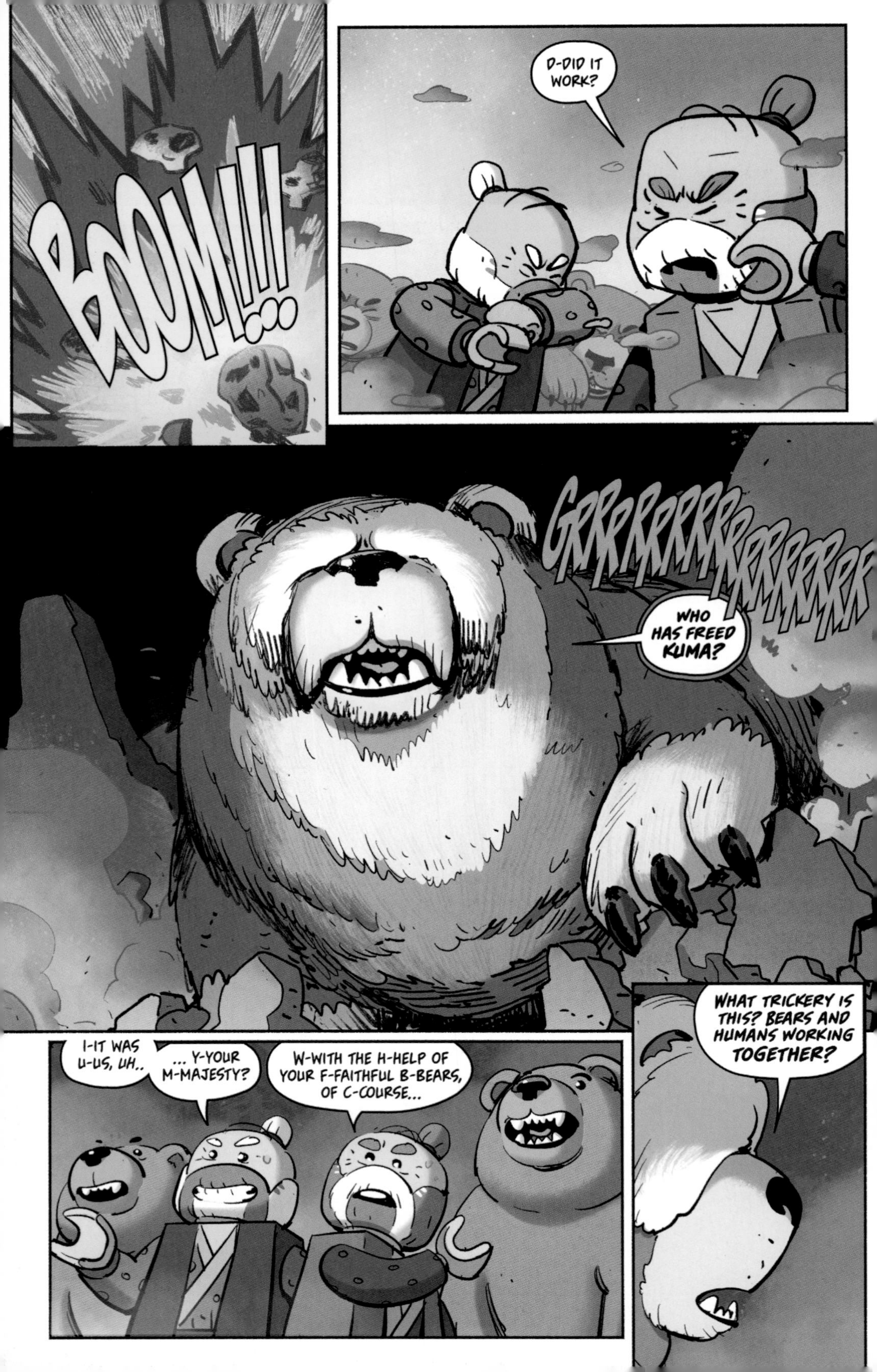
BOOM!!!...
D-DID IT WORK?
GRRRRRRRRRRRRRRRRR
WHO HAS FREED KUMA?
I-IT WAS U-US, UH..
... Y-YOUR M-MAJESTY?
W-WITH THE H-HELP OF YOUR F-FAITHFUL B-BEARS, OF C-COURSE...
WHAT TRICKERY IS THIS? BEARS AND HUMANS WORKING TOGETHER?

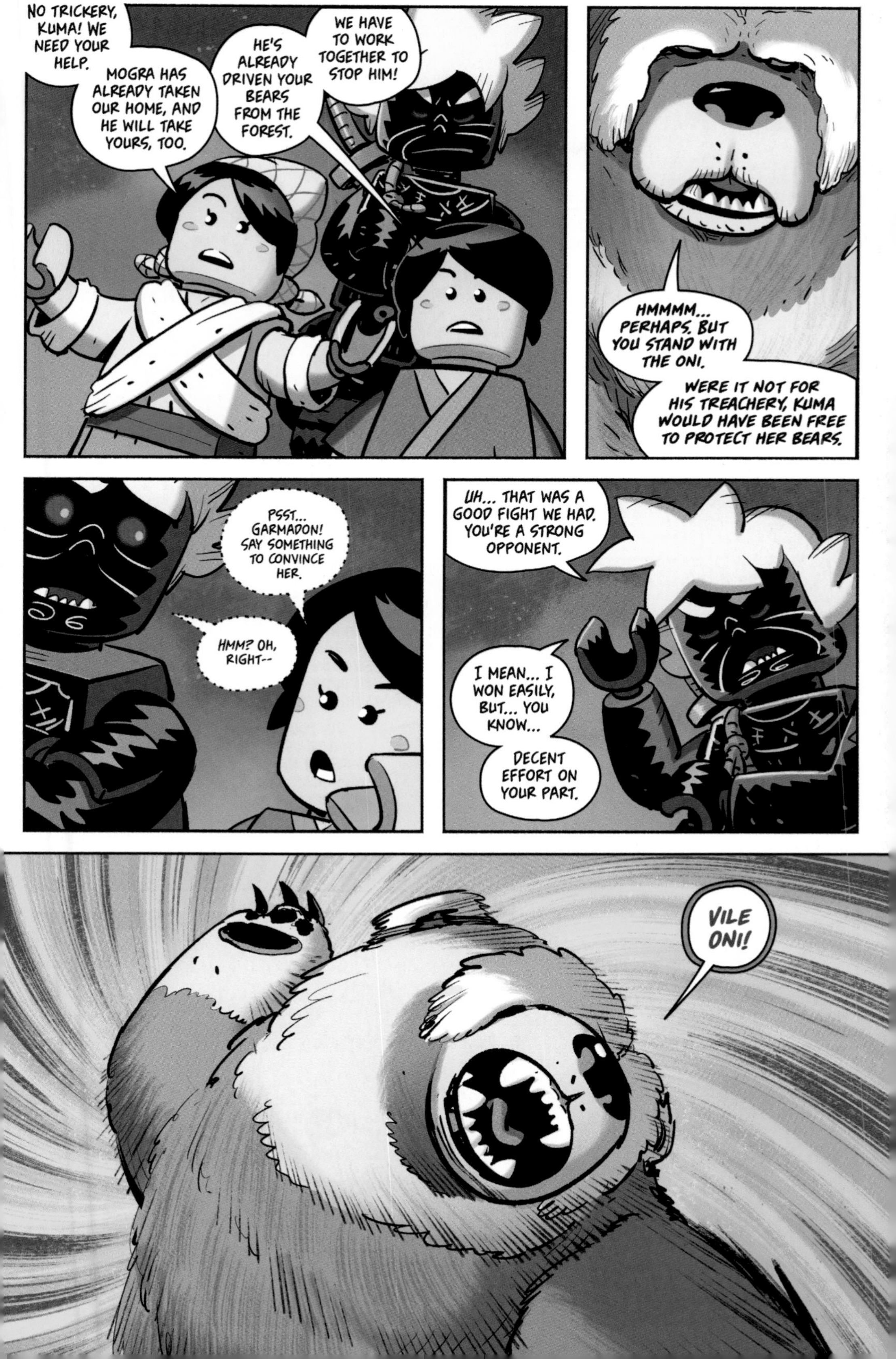
NO TRICKERY, KUMA! WE NEED YOUR HELP.
MOGRA HAS ALREADY TAKEN OUR HOME, AND HE WILL TAKE YOURS, TOO.
HE'S ALREADY DRIVEN YOUR BEARS FROM THE FOREST.
WE HAVE TO WORK TOGETHER TO STOP HIM!
HMMMM... PERHAPS. BUT YOU STAND WITH THE ONI.
WERE IT NOT FOR HIS TREACHERY, KUMA WOULD HAVE BEEN FREE TO PROTECT HER BEARS.
PSST... GARMADON! SAY SOMETHING TO CONVINCE HER.
HMM? OH, RIGHT--
UH... THAT WAS A GOOD FIGHT WE HAD. YOU'RE A STRONG OPPONENT.
I MEAN... I WON EASILY, BUT... YOU KNOW...
DECENT EFFORT ON YOUR PART.
VILE ONI!

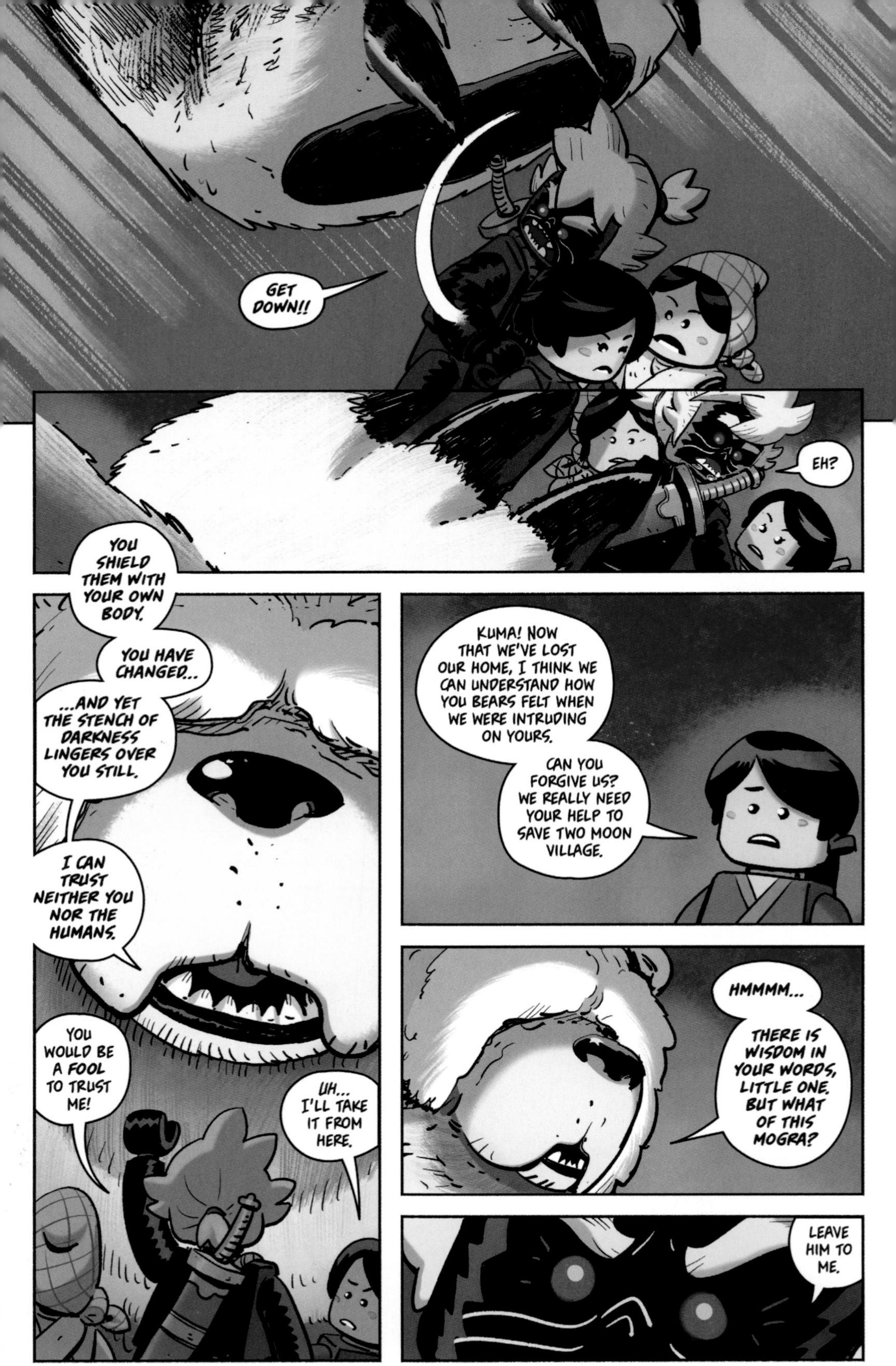
GET DOWN!!
EH?
YOU SHIELD THEM WITH YOUR OWN BODY.
YOU HAVE CHANGED...
...AND YET THE STENCH OF DARKNESS LINGERS OVER YOU STILL.
I CAN TRUST NEITHER YOU NOR THE HUMANS.
KUMA! NOW THAT WE'VE LOST OUR HOME, I THINK WE CAN UNDERSTAND HOW YOU BEARS FELT WHEN WE WERE INTRUDING ON YOURS.
CAN YOU FORGIVE US? WE REALLY NEED YOUR HELP TO SAVE TWO MOON VILLAGE.
YOU WOULD BE A FOOL TO TRUST ME!
UH... I'LL TAKE IT FROM HERE.
HMMMM...
THERE IS WISDOM IN YOUR WORDS, LITTLE ONE. BUT WHAT OF THIS MOGRA?
LEAVE HIM TO ME.

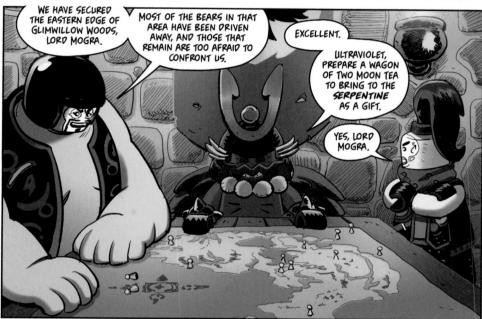

WE HAVE SECURED THE EASTERN EDGE OF GLIMWILLOW WOODS, LORD MOGRA.

MOST OF THE BEARS IN THAT AREA HAVE BEEN DRIVEN AWAY, AND THOSE THAT REMAIN ARE TOO AFRAID TO CONFRONT US.

EXCELLENT.

ULTRAVIOLET, PREPARE A WAGON OF TWO MOON TEA TO BRING TO THE SERPENTINE AS A GIFT.

YES, LORD MOGRA.

THEY HAVE US SURROUNDED!

HE'S ALIVE?

HOW MANY?!

LET'S SEE IF WE CAN COAX THEM OUT OF THIS PACIFIST BENT THEY CURRENTLY SEEM TO BE--

WHAT'S THAT RACKET?!

I'M TRYING TO PLOT MY DOMINATION OF NINJAGO HERE!

Y-YOU BETTER SEE FOR YOURSELF, LORD MOGRA!

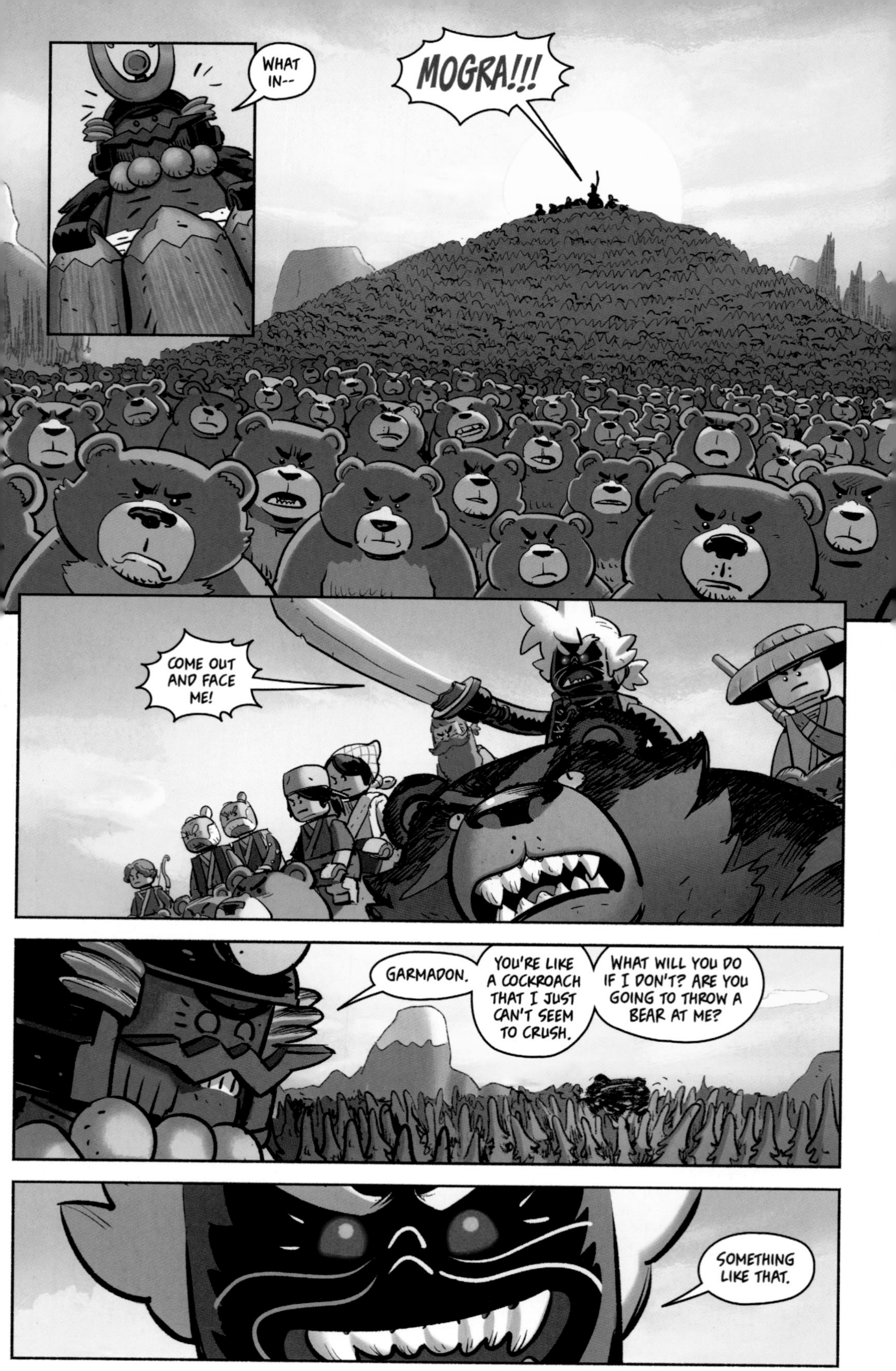
WHAT IN--
MOGRA!!!
COME OUT AND FACE ME!
GARMADON.
YOU'RE LIKE A COCKROACH THAT I JUST CAN'T SEEM TO CRUSH.
WHAT WILL YOU DO IF I DON'T? ARE YOU GOING TO THROW A BEAR AT ME?
SOMETHING LIKE THAT.

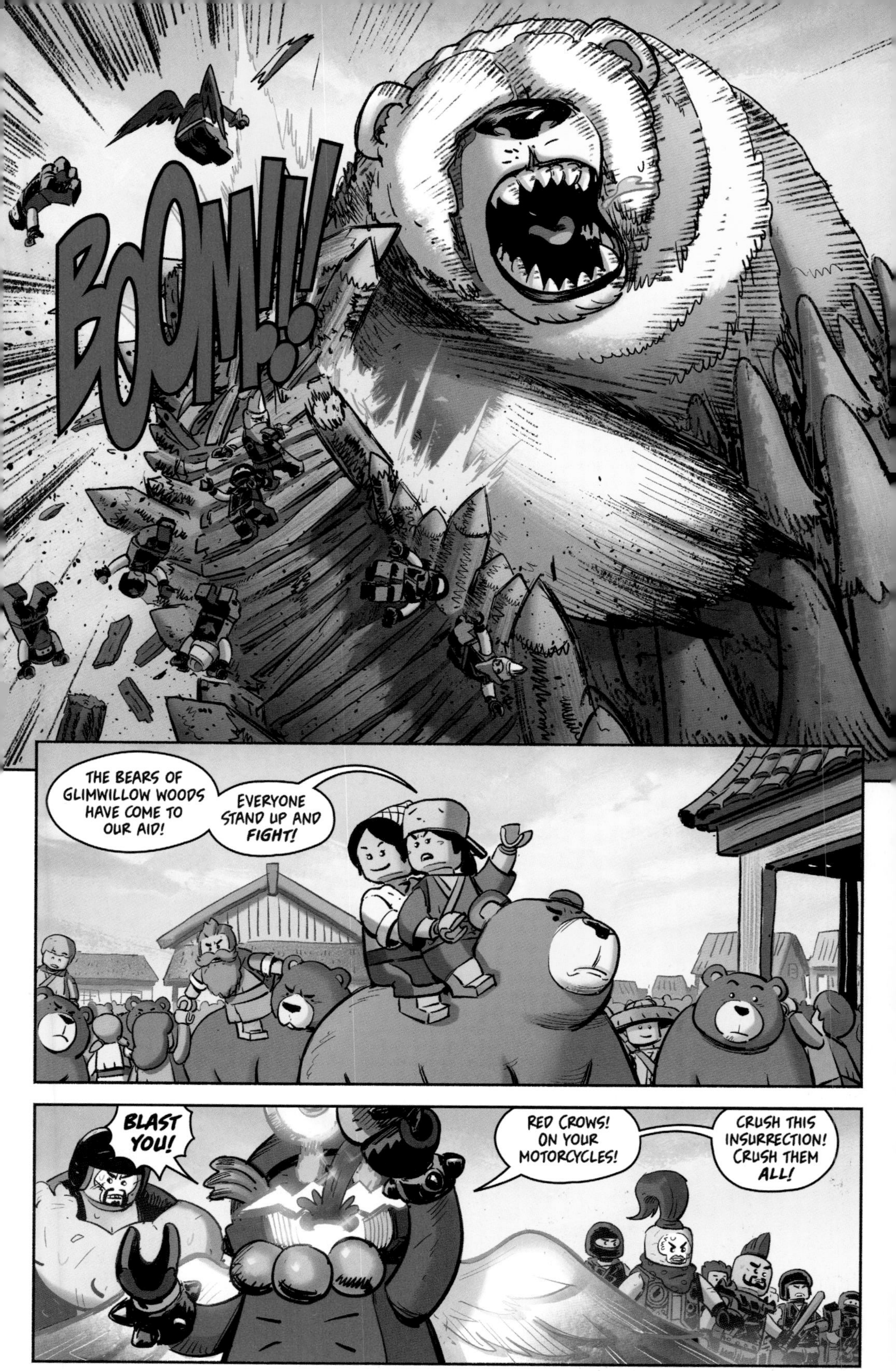
BOOM!!!
THE BEARS OF GLIMWILLOW WOODS HAVE COME TO OUR AID!
EVERYONE STAND UP AND FIGHT!
BLAST YOU!
RED CROWS! ON YOUR MOTORCYCLES!
CRUSH THIS INSURRECTION! CRUSH THEM ALL!

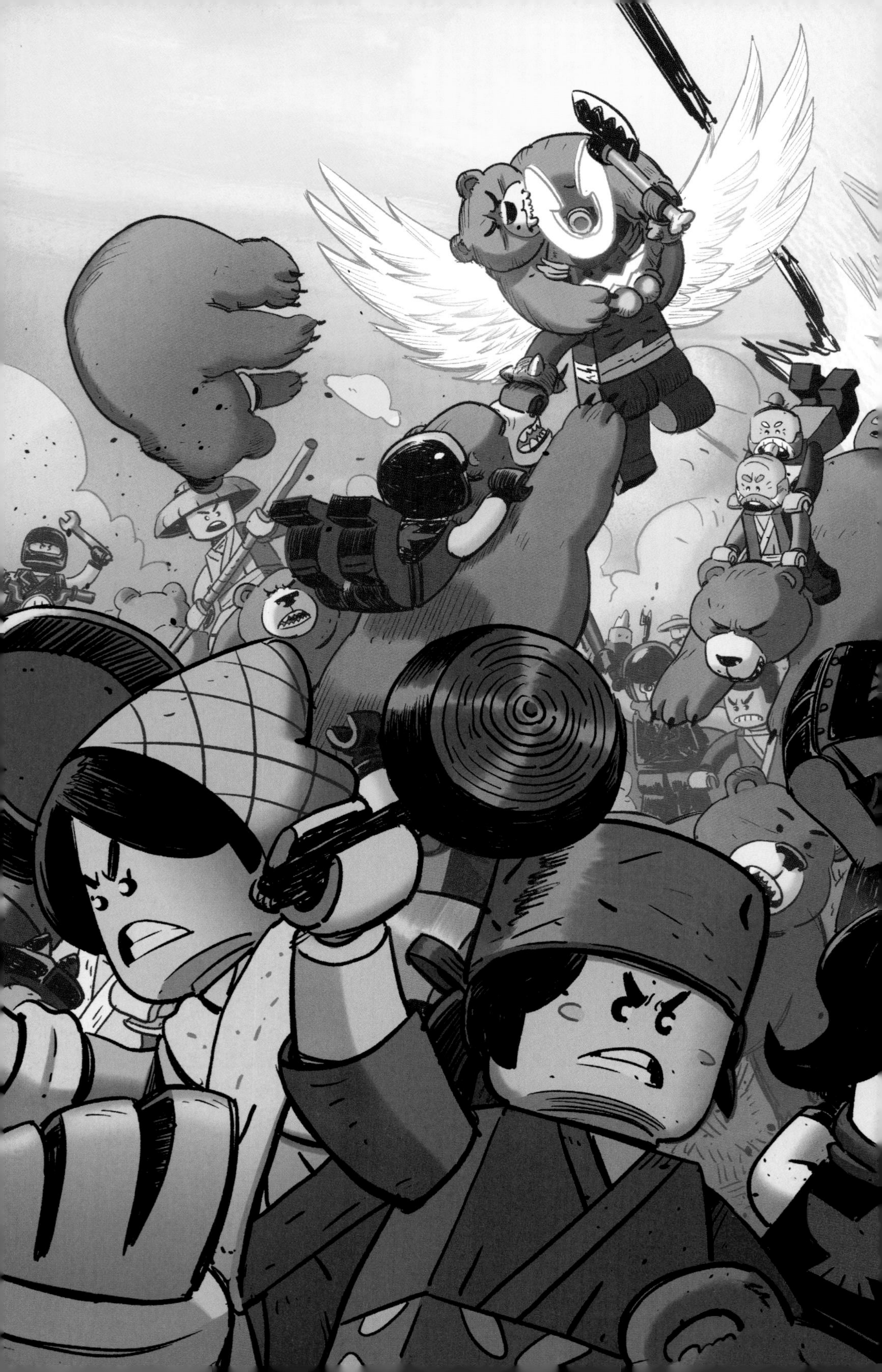

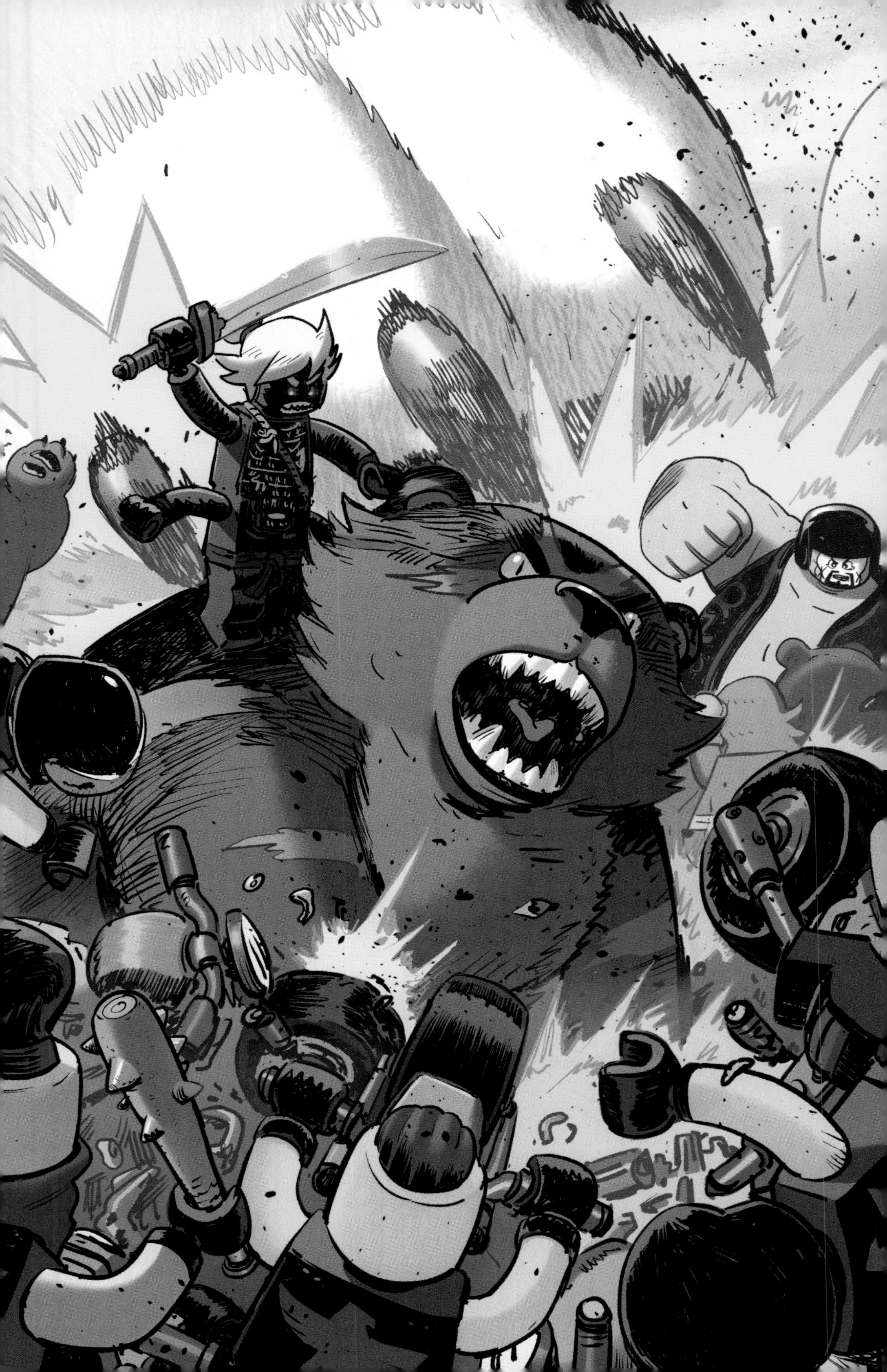

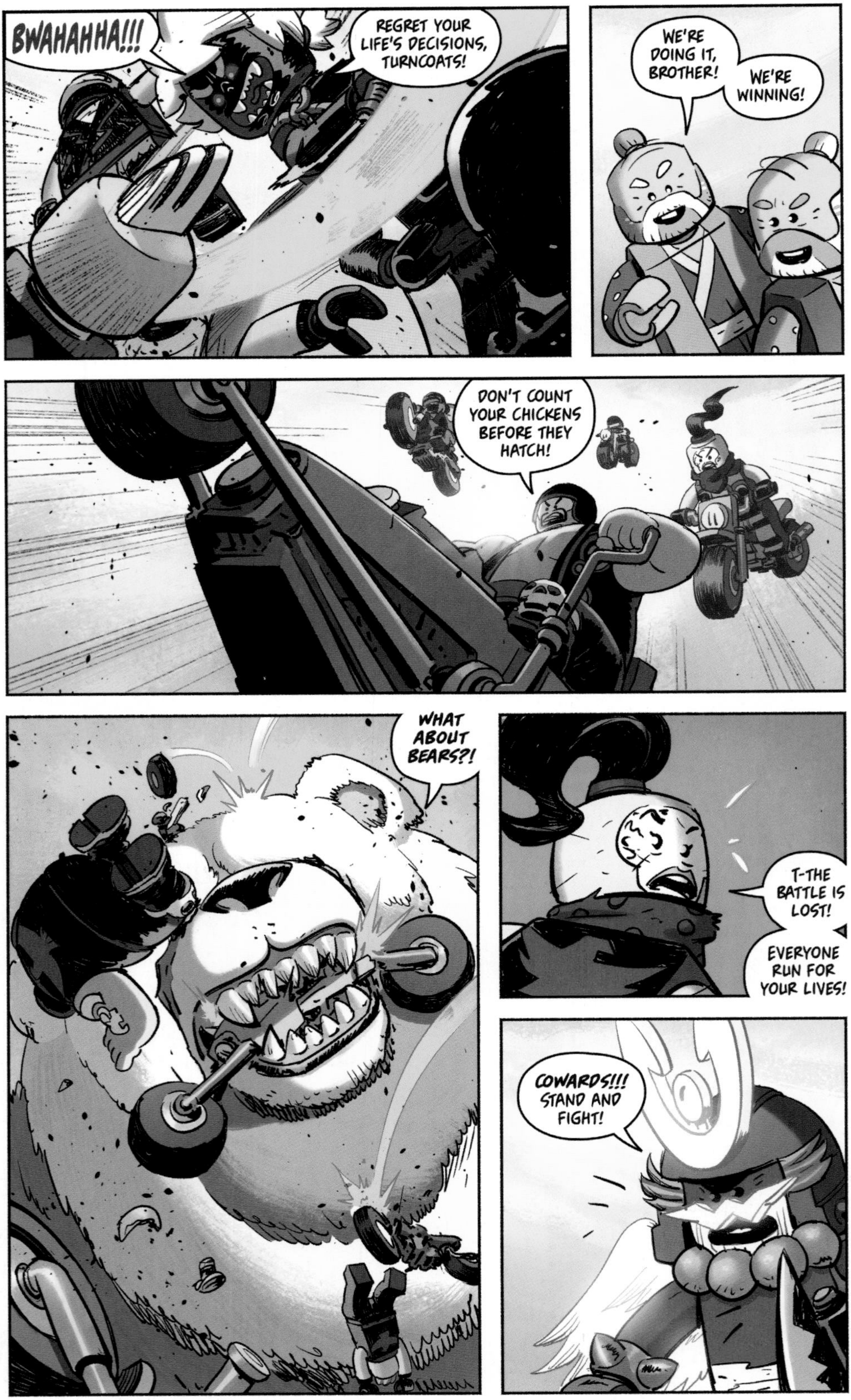
BWAHAHHA!!!
REGRET YOUR LIFE'S DECISIONS, TURNCOATS!
WE'RE DOING IT, BROTHER!
WE'RE WINNING!
DON'T COUNT YOUR CHICKENS BEFORE THEY HATCH!
WHAT ABOUT BEARS?!
T-THE BATTLE IS LOST!
EVERYONE RUN FOR YOUR LIVES!
COWARDS!!! STAND AND FIGHT!

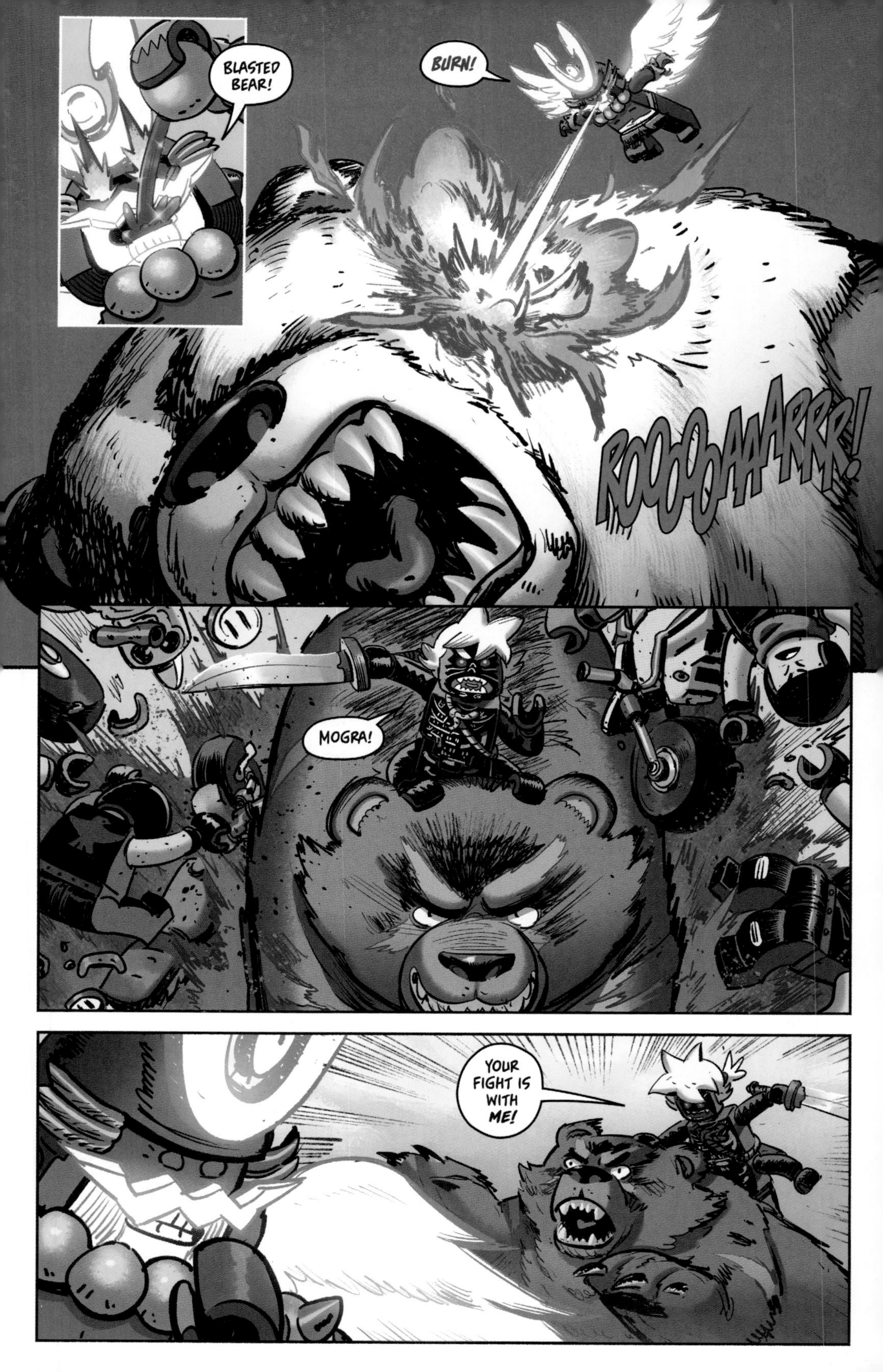
BLASTED BEAR!
BURN!
ROOOOOAAARRR!
MOGRA!
YOUR FIGHT IS WITH ME!

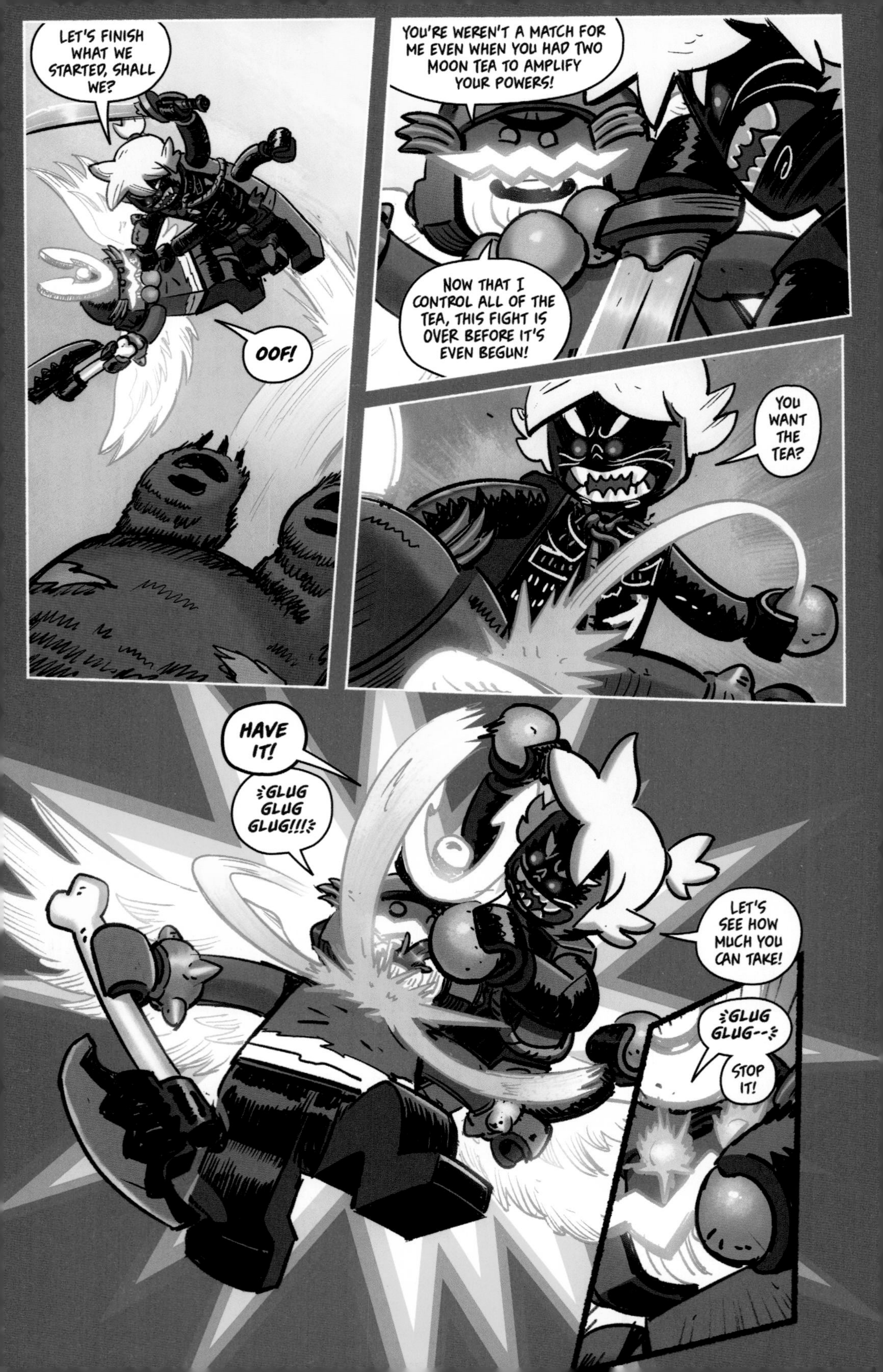
LET'S FINISH WHAT WE STARTED, SHALL WE?
OOF!
YOU'RE WEREN'T A MATCH FOR ME EVEN WHEN YOU HAD TWO MOON TEA TO AMPLIFY YOUR POWERS!
NOW THAT I CONTROL ALL OF THE TEA, THIS FIGHT IS OVER BEFORE IT'S EVEN BEGUN!
YOU WANT THE TEA?
HAVE IT!
GLUG GLUG GLUG!!!
LET'S SEE HOW MUCH YOU CAN TAKE!
GLUG GLUG--
STOP IT!

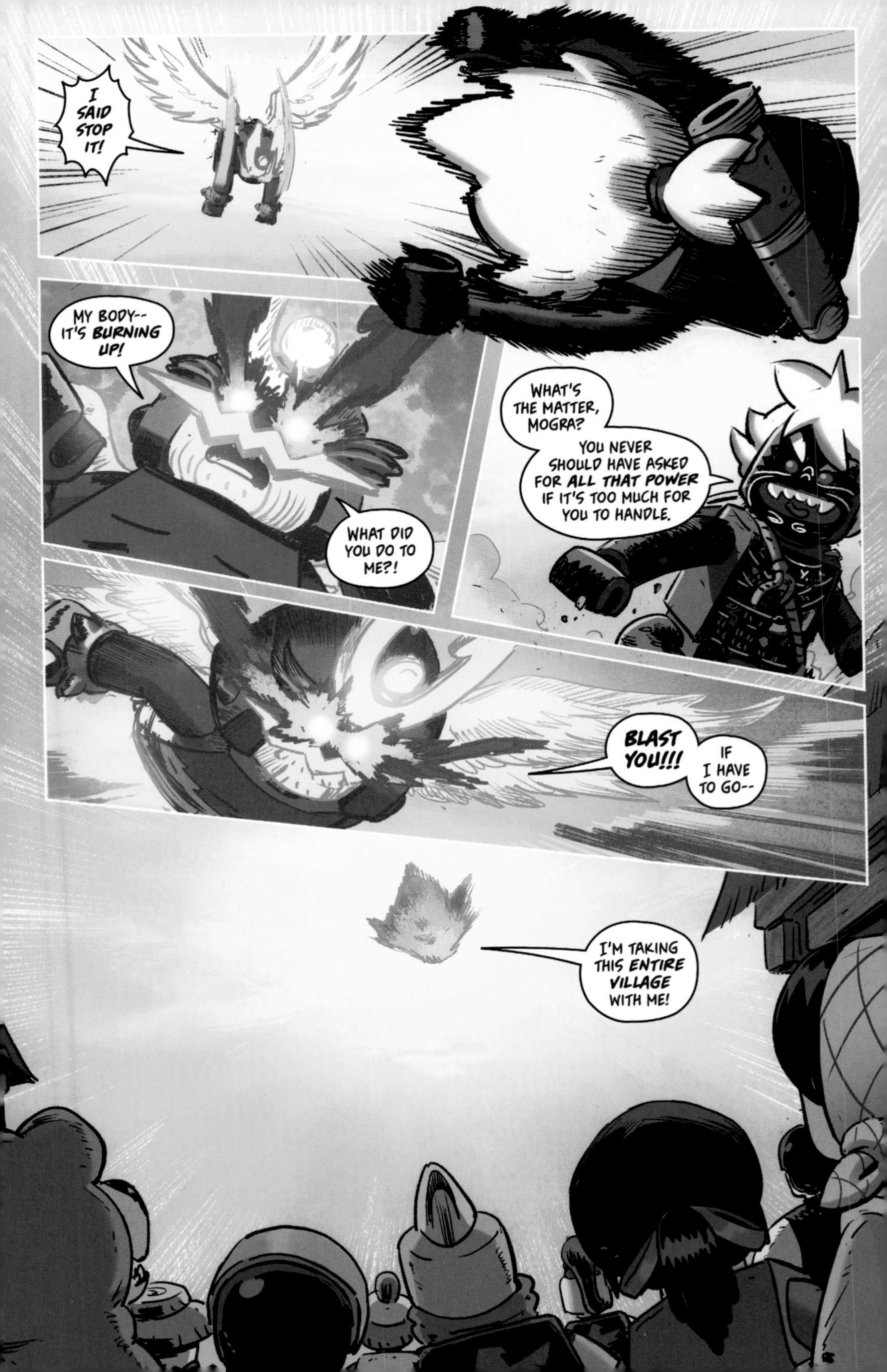
I SAID STOP IT!
MY BODY-- IT'S BURNING UP!
WHAT DID YOU DO TO ME?!
WHAT'S THE MATTER, MOGRA?
YOU NEVER SHOULD HAVE ASKED FOR ALL THAT POWER IF IT'S TOO MUCH FOR YOU TO HANDLE.
BLAST YOU!!!
IF I HAVE TO GO--
I'M TAKING THIS ENTIRE VILLAGE WITH ME!

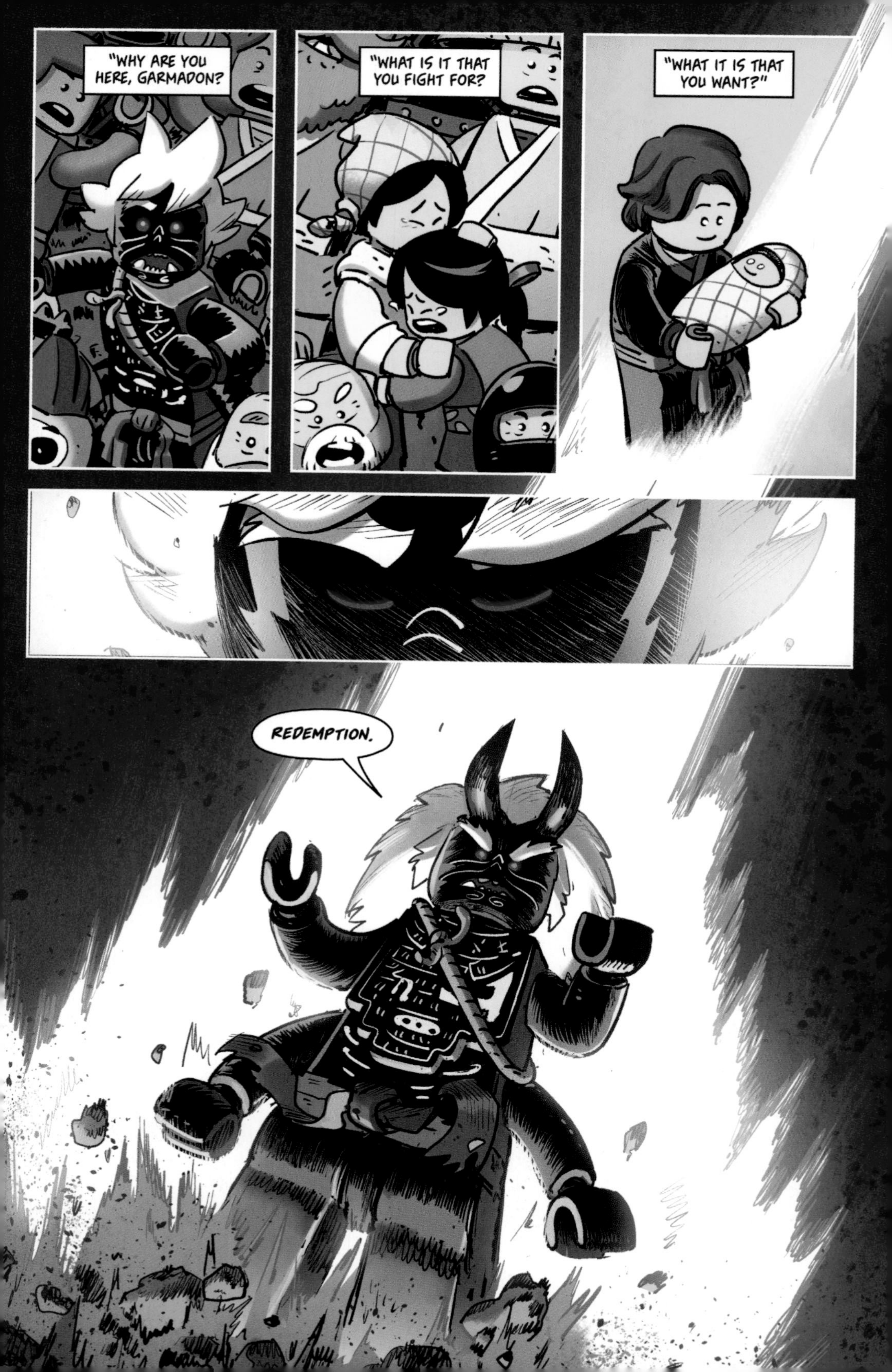
"WHY ARE YOU HERE, GARMADON?
"WHAT IS IT THAT YOU FIGHT FOR?
"WHAT IT IS THAT YOU WANT?"
REDEMPTION.

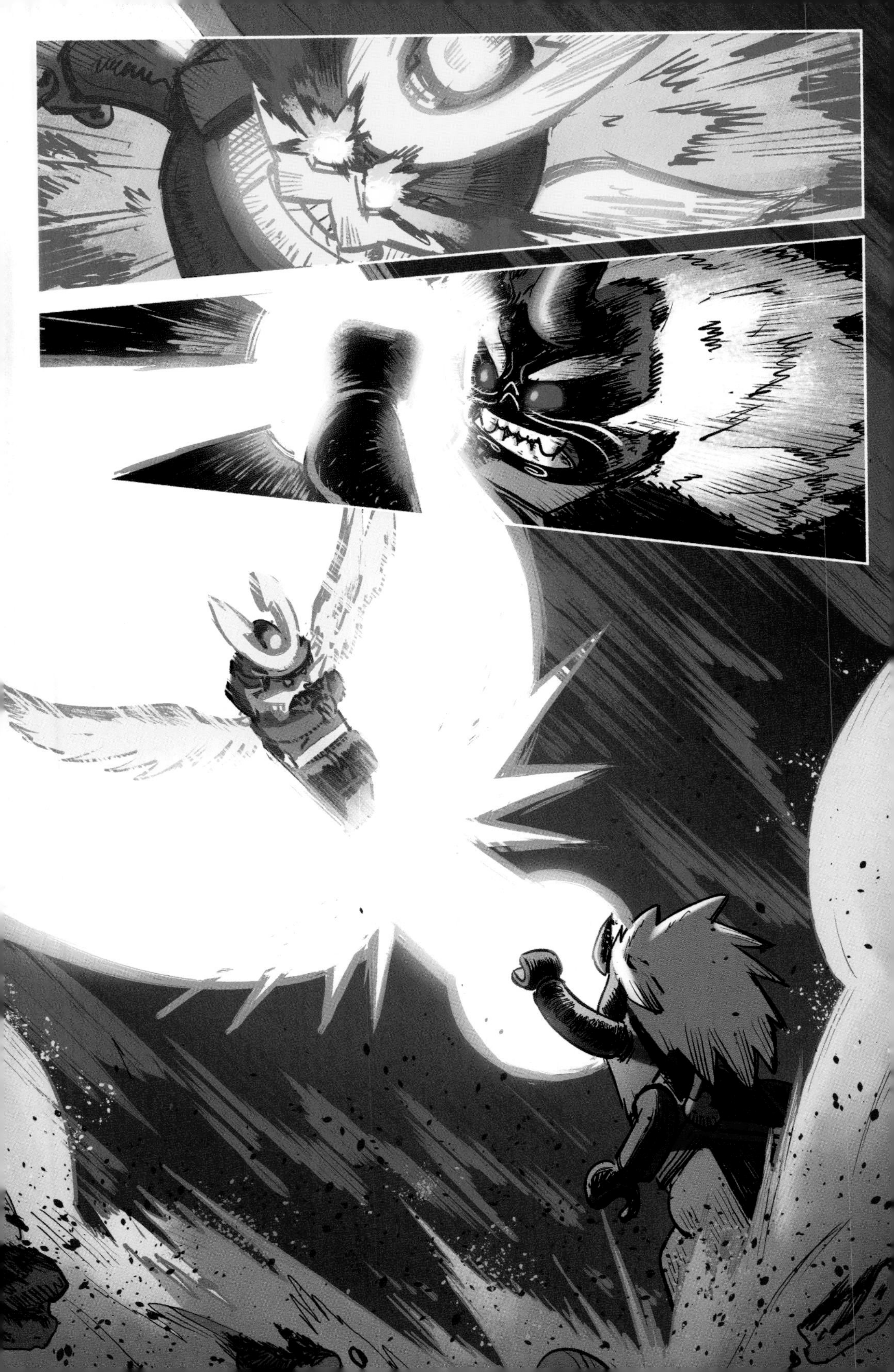

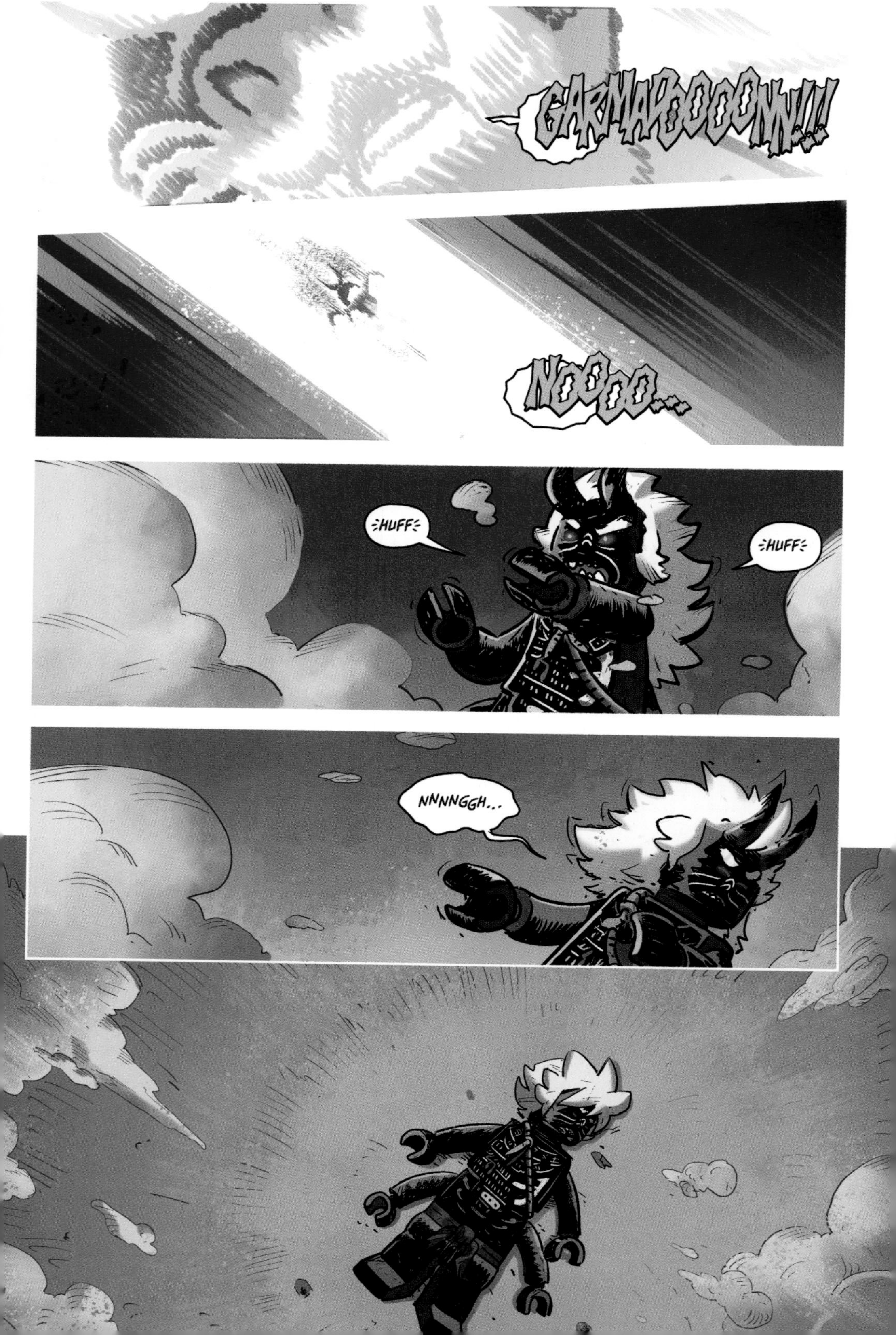
GARMADOOONN!!!
NOOOO...
HUFF
HUFF
NNNNGGH...

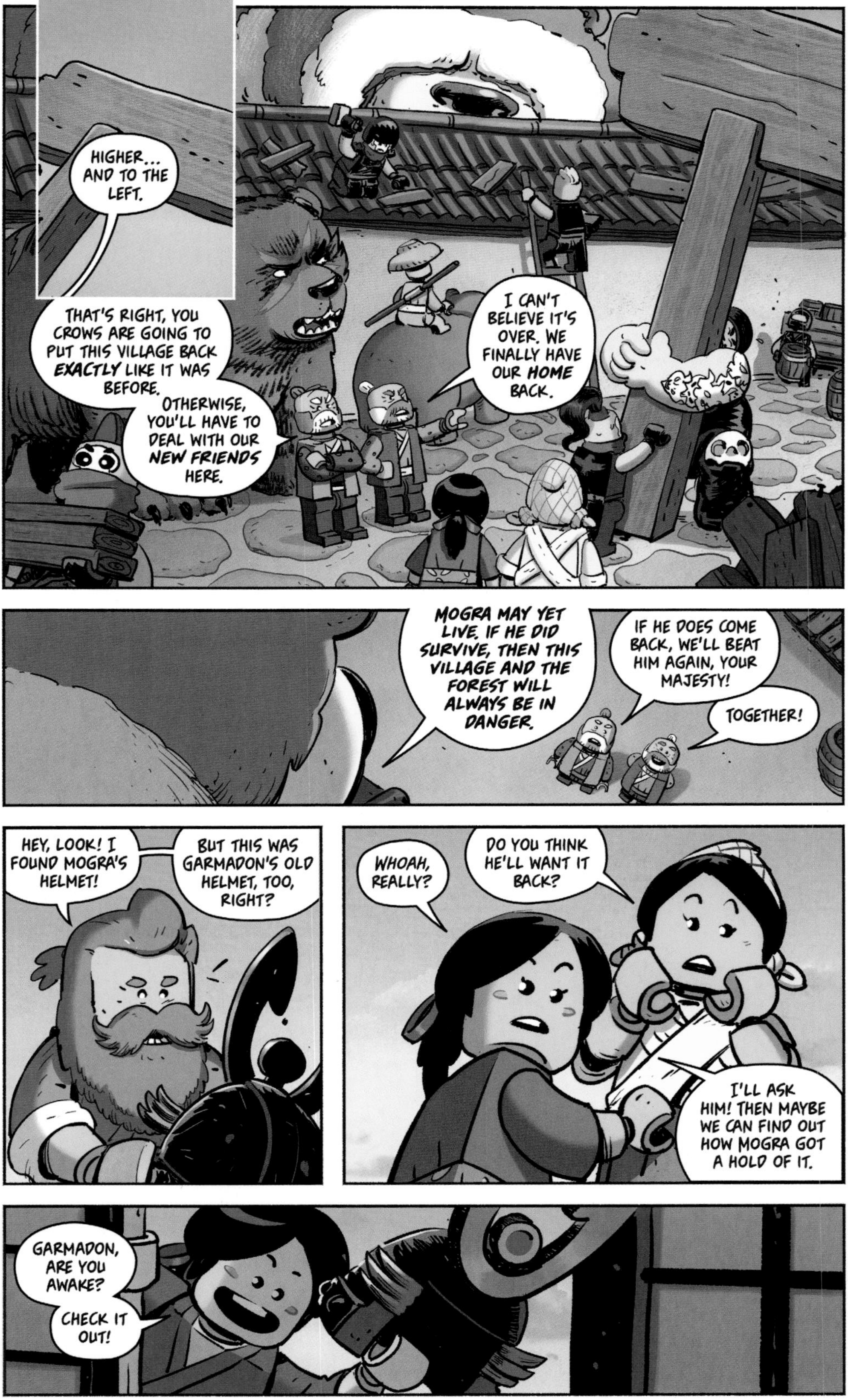
HIGHER... AND TO THE LEFT.
THAT'S RIGHT, YOU CROWS ARE GOING TO PUT THIS VILLAGE BACK EXACTLY LIKE IT WAS BEFORE.
OTHERWISE, YOU'LL HAVE TO DEAL WITH OUR NEW FRIENDS HERE.
I CAN'T BELIEVE IT'S OVER. WE FINALLY HAVE OUR HOME BACK.
MOGRA MAY YET LIVE. IF HE DID SURVIVE, THEN THIS VILLAGE AND THE FOREST WILL ALWAYS BE IN DANGER.
IF HE DOES COME BACK, WE'LL BEAT HIM AGAIN, YOUR MAJESTY!
TOGETHER!
HEY, LOOK! I FOUND MOGRA'S HELMET!
BUT THIS WAS GARMADON'S OLD HELMET, TOO, RIGHT?
WHOAH, REALLY?
DO YOU THINK HE'LL WANT IT BACK?
I'LL ASK HIM! THEN MAYBE WE CAN FIND OUT HOW MOGRA GOT A HOLD OF IT.
GARMADON, ARE YOU AWAKE?
CHECK IT OUT!

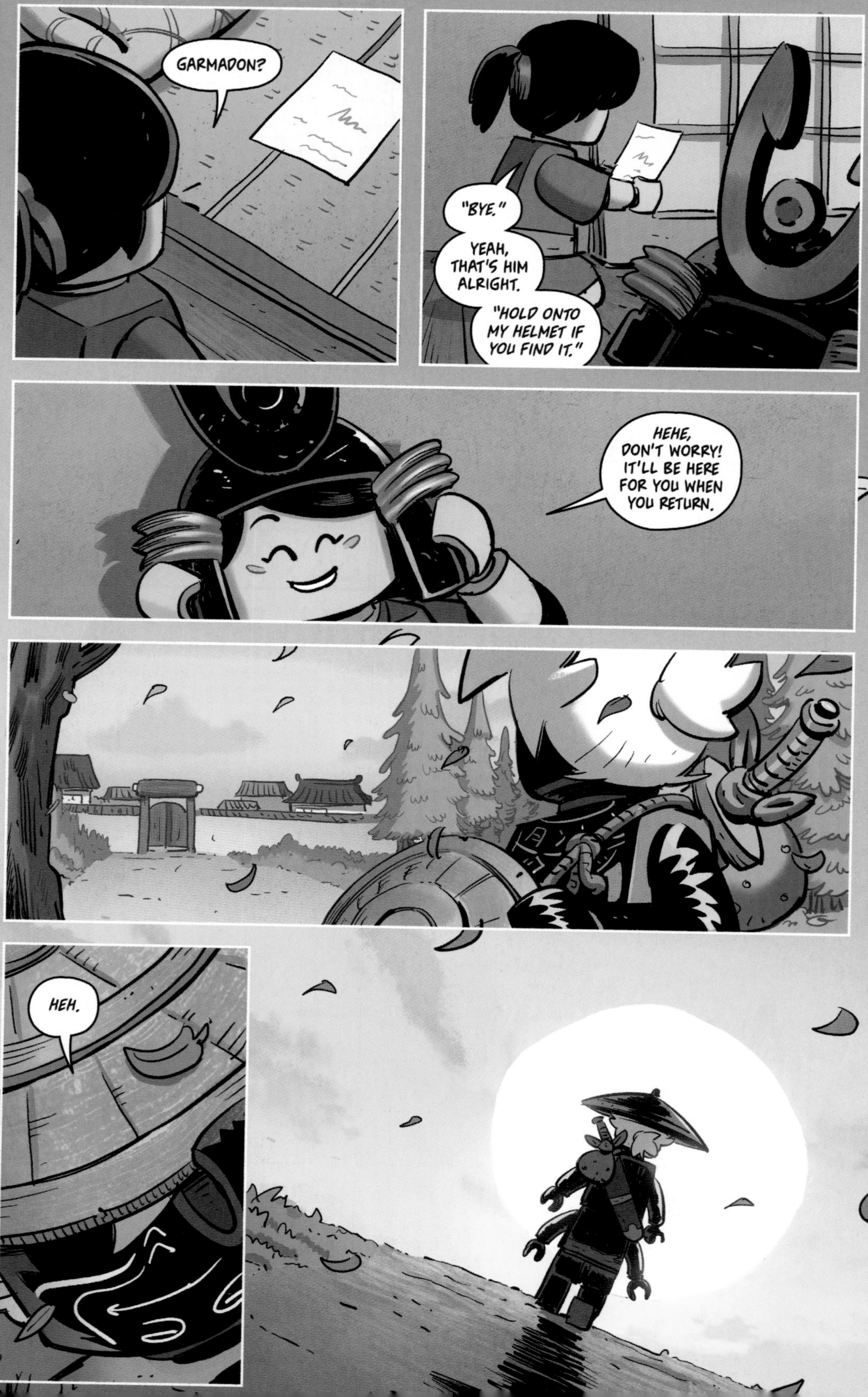
GARMADON?
"BYE."
YEAH, THAT'S HIM ALRIGHT.
"HOLD ONTO MY HELMET IF YOU FIND IT."
HEHE, DON'T WORRY! IT'LL BE HERE FOR YOU WHEN YOU RETURN.
HEH.

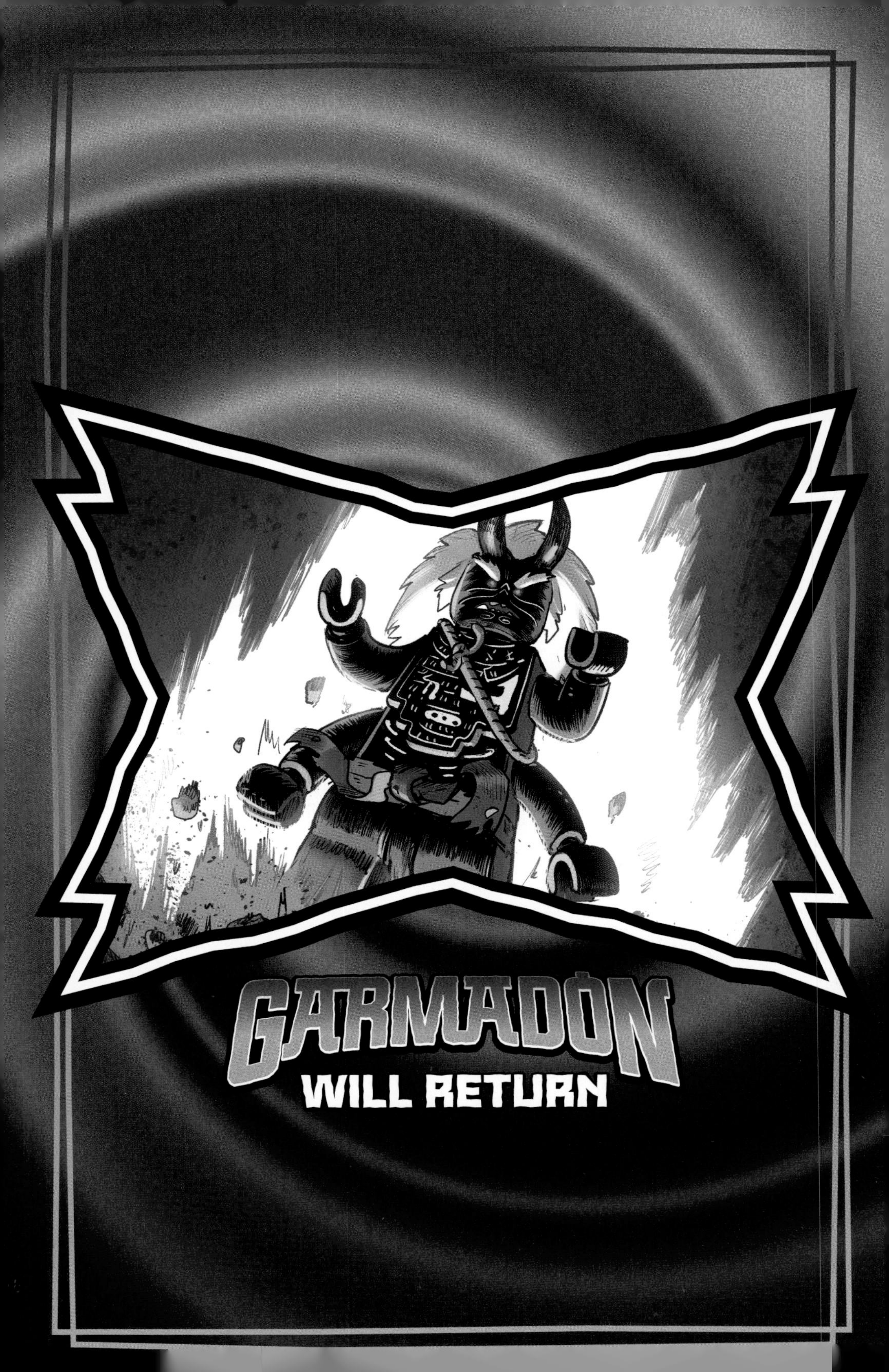
GARMADON
WILL RETURN

LEGO® NINJAGO®: GARMADON VOLUME 1
TRI VUONG WRITER, ARTIST
ANNALISA LEONI COLORIST
RUS WOOTON LETTERER
TRI VUONG COVER
TAKESHI MIYAZAWA & IAN HERRING LEGO IDEAS COVER
TRI VUONG & ANNALISA LEONI SCHOLASTIC COVER
SEAN MACKIEWICZ EDITOR
ANDRES JUAREZ GARMADON LOGO & COLLECTION DESIGN

SPECIAL THANKS TO AMEET'S PAWEL GRZEGORCZYK, MAGDALENA CZYZEWSKA, ERIC HUANG, ALISON LINDSAY, CINDY LOH, JAKUB NIEDZIELSKI, ALEKSANDRA MICHALAK, PIOTR PACZKOWSKI, ULRICH SCHROEDER, AND DAN SHEPHERD, AND LEGO GROUP'S HELLE REIMERS HOLM-JØRGENSEN, TOMMY KALMAR AND MARTIN LEIGHTON LINDHARDT FOR THEIR INVALUABLE ASSISTANCE.

TEACHING GUIDE BY CREATORS, ASSEMBLE INC.

SKYBOUND ENTERTAINMENT
ROBERT KIRKMAN: CHAIRMAN
DAVID ALPERT: CEO
SEAN MACKIEWICZ: SVP, PUBLISHER
SHAWN KIRKHAM: SVP, BUSINESS DEVELOPMENT
ANDRES JUAREZ: ART DIRECTOR
ARUNE SINGH: DIRECTOR OF BRAND, EDITORIAL
SHANNON MEEHAN: PUBLIC RELATIONS MANAGER

ALEX ANTONE: EDITORIAL DIRECTOR
AMANDA LAFRANCO: EDITOR
JILLIAN CRAB: GRAPHIC DESIGNER
MORGAN PERRY: BRAND MANAGER, EDITORIAL
SARAH CLEMENTS: BRAND COORDINATOR, EDITORIAL
DAN PETERSEN: SR. DIRECTOR, OPERATIONS & EVENTS
FOREIGN RIGHTS & LICENSING INQUIRIES: CONTACT@SKYBOUND.COM
SKYBOUND.COM

IMAGE COMICS, INC.
ROBERT KIRKMAN: CHIEF OPERATING OFFICER
ERIK LARSEN: CHIEF FINANCIAL OFFICER
TODD MCFARLANE: PRESIDENT
MARC SILVESTRI: CHIEF EXECUTIVE OFFICER
JIM VALENTINO: VICE PRESIDENT
ERIC STEPHENSON: PUBLISHER / CHIEF CREATIVE OFFICER
NICOLE LAPALME: VICE PRESIDENT OF FINANCE
LEANNA CAUNTER: ACCOUNTING ANALYST
SUE KORPELA: ACCOUNTING & HR MANAGER
MATT PARKINSON: VICE PRESIDENT OF SALES & PUBLISHING
LORELEI BUNJES: VICE PRESIDENT OF DIGITAL STRATEGY
DIRK WOOD: DIRECTOR OF INTERNATIONAL SALES & LICENSING
RYAN BREWER: INTERNATIONAL SALES & LICENSING MANAGER
ALEX COX: DIRECTOR OF DIRECT MARKET SALES

CHLOE RAMOS: BOOK MARKET & LIBRARY SALES MANAGER
EMILIO BAUTISTA: DIGITAL SALES COORDINATOR
JON SCHLAFFMAN: SPECIALTY SALES COORDINATOR
KAT SALAZAR: VICE PRESIDENT OF PR & MARKETING
DEANNA PHELPS: MARKETING DESIGN MANAGER
DREW FITZGERALD: MARKETING CONTENT ASSOCIATE
HEATHER DOORNINK: VICE PRESIDENT OF PRODUCTION
DREW GILL: ART DIRECTOR
HILARY DILORETO: PRINT MANAGER
TRICIA RAMOS: TRAFFIC MANAGER
MELISSA GIFFORD: CONTENT MANAGER
ERIKA SCHNATZ: SENIOR PRODUCTION ARTIST
WESLEY GRIFFITH: PRODUCTION ARTIST
IMAGECOMICS.COM

LEGO BOOKS

Manufactured under license granted to AMEET Sp. z o.o. by the LEGO Group.

AMEET Sp. z o.o.
Nowe Sady 6, 94–102 Łódź – Poland
ameet@ameet.eu
www.ameet.eu

www.LEGO.com

Tri Vuong is a comic artist and writer based out of Toronto, Canada. He is the creator of the popular comic *The Strange Tales of Oscar Zahn* on Line Webtoon and the co-creator/writer/artist of EVERYDAY HERO MACHINE BOY graphic novel from Skybound Entertainment. He is a veteran of the video game and animation industry whose list of clients include Ubisoft, Corus Entertainment, C.O.R.E Digital Pictures, Koei, and Capybara Games. His work on *Bubble Guppies* and *Clash of Heroes* has won multiple awards.

Annalisa Leoni studied at the comic school Scuola Romana dei Fumetti and started her career working for Italian animation and video games studios. She illustrated *Frankenstein: The Modern Prometheus* for La Spiga and colored comic books for Pixar, Disney, Panini Comics, Glénat, and other companies. Most notably, she colored OBLIVION SONG and LEGO® NINJAGO®: GARMADON for Skybound, *Orfani* and *Dylan Dog* for Sergio Bonelli Editore, and *Star Wars: The High Republic* for Marvel.

Rus Wooton is an Eisner-nominated comic book letterer best known for his work on books like THE WALKING DEAD, FIRE POWER, KROMA, *Fantastic Four*, *X-Men*, and many more. An artist, designer, writer, and filmmaker, Rus has been lettering full-time since 2003, drawing for as long as he can remember, and reading comics since before he could read.

READING GUIDE

IMPORTANT SETTINGS

- Ninjago
- Glimwillow Woods
- Two Moon Village

NOTABLE CHARACTERS

- Lord Garmadon: Master of Spinjitzu, former defender of Ninjago. Corrupted by the Great Devourer and became an undead Oni nemesis of the ninja.
- Wu: Lord Garmadon's brother.
- Misako: Lord Garmadon's wife.
- Lloyd: Garmadon's son.
- Min: Child of Saeko, one of the inhabitants of Two Moon Village.
- Saeko: Mother to Min, inhabitant of Two Moon Village.
- Renzo: Villager in Two Moon Village. In charge of producing Two Moon Tea, along with his brother Kenzo.
- Kenzo: Villager in Two Moon Village. Along with his brother Renzo, in charge of producing Two Moon Tea.
- Kuma: Guardian of the Bears. Large and in charge.
- Lord Mogra: Leader of the Red Crows.
- Ultra Violet: Former member of the Sons of Garmadon. Now a member of the Red Crows.
- Killow: Former member of the

Sons of Garmadon. Now a member of the Red Crows.

- Lan: Hunter. Member of the Two Moon Village Commandos.
- Shu: Farmer. Member of the Two Moon Village Commandos.
- Bron: Blacksmith. Member of the Two Moon Village Commandos.

KEY THEMES

- Doing the "right thing"
- Making choices
- Memories
- Family
- Loyalty

DISCUSSION QUESTIONS

1. Is Lord Garmadon a good guy or a bad guy? Or is he something in-between?

2. Why does Lord Garmadon agree to help the villagers of Two Moon Village?

3. What do you think "Shadow Garmadon" wants? Is he real, or just a dream of Garmadon's?

4. In the sequence with Shadow Garmadon, how does the art help you understand their confrontation?

5. Two Moon Tea makes you "more of what you are." For the villagers, it heals their

wounds more quickly; for Garmadon, it increases his powers. What do you think it would do for you?

6. Why do you think Wu throws away Garmadon's helmet? Is it really "just a hat"? Does it tell you anything about Garmadon that afterwards he continues to wear his brother's hat? Do you think it is significant that Lord Mogra wears Garmadon's helmet? Why do you think he leaves it behind in Two Moon Village at the end of the story?

7. What is your favorite panel in the series? How does that art add to your enjoyment of the book?

8. Why do the former Sons of Garmadon join Lord Mogra to become the Red Crows? Do you think that their decision to do so is justified?

9. The artist uses facial expressions of characters (human and animal) to help the reader understand the emotions tied to their words and actions. Pick two panels where the facial expressions helped you understand or enjoy a part of the book. Briefly explain why you picked those panels.

10. Why does Min go back to the village to help Lord Garmadon?

Do you think you would do the same in that situation?

11. What is the history between Lord Garmadon and Lord Mogra? Do you think Garmadon was tempted by Mogra's offer to join him?

12. Several times throughout the series Gamadon has dreams, visions, or flashbacks. Give two examples of ways the author is able to show readers it is a dream through their art.

13. Do you think Lord Garmadon was really "meant to walk the path of darkness"? Are his actions because of his destiny, or his choices?

14. In the beginning, the villagers want to defeat the bears in Glimwillow Woods to collect all of the lilies for themselves. In the end, they partner with the bears to drive Lord Mogra and the Red Crows from their village. What have the villagers learned? Do you think their alliance with the bears will last?

15. Lord Garmadon insists that he return to aid the villagers of Two Moon Village for "revenge". Min says, "I don't think so. I think you came back for another reason." What reason is that? Who do you think is correct?

16. In the end, Lord Garmadon says he wants "redemption". Do you think he is redeemed by his actions in Two Moon Village? Why or why not?

ACTIVITY IDEAS

1. Illustrators practice using the right facial gestures to convey emotions. Try drawing a LEGO minifigure face that is happy, sad, angry, scared, surprised, and excited.

2. A lot of this story is conveyed through action rather than dialogue. How would you go about telling a story without any words? Try drawing a one or two-page comic that tells a brief story entirely through pictures. (If you don't like to draw, write out brief descriptions of what happens.)

3. Costumes and character design tell you a lot about these characters before they do anything: Garmadon's all-black outfit, the red costumes of the Red Crows, and the simple and comfortable clothes of the villagers. Do you think how you dress and present yourself tells a story about you? Design a costume that you think reflects your personality.

4. The Great Devourer biting and corrupting Garmadon begins his turn to darkness--his "origin story". What do you think is the most significant event in your life so far? How has it changed you? Write a one or two-page story or comic telling this story.

5. One great thing about LEGO bricks is you can use them to build your own creations and tell your own stories. Build a scene with LEGO bricks to tell either a story from the book or your own story. You can also build a short comic using photos taken of your LEGO minifigures.

SKETCHBOOK

A

ODACHI
(Great Sword)

Travelling
Pack

B

Knot to
tie up sleeves

HAKAMA

C

UMBRELLA
- super heavy
- only he can lift
- uses as club
and shield

**Garmadon and proposed
alternate looks.**

GARMADON   REGULAR BEAR

**A size comparison between Garmadon, an average brown
bear, and the almighty Kuma of Glimwillow Woods.**

The banner of the Red Crows and Mogra's final form.

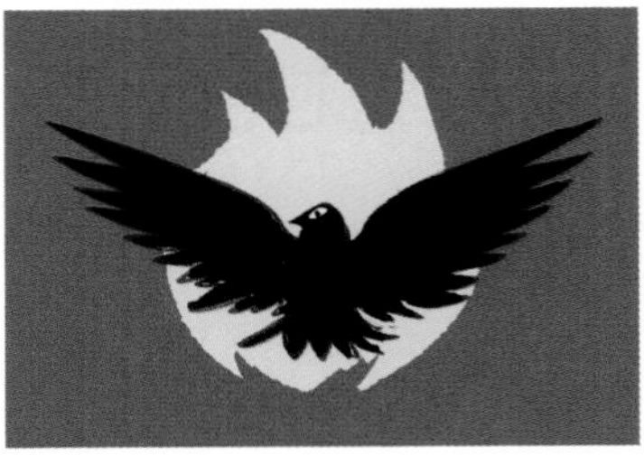

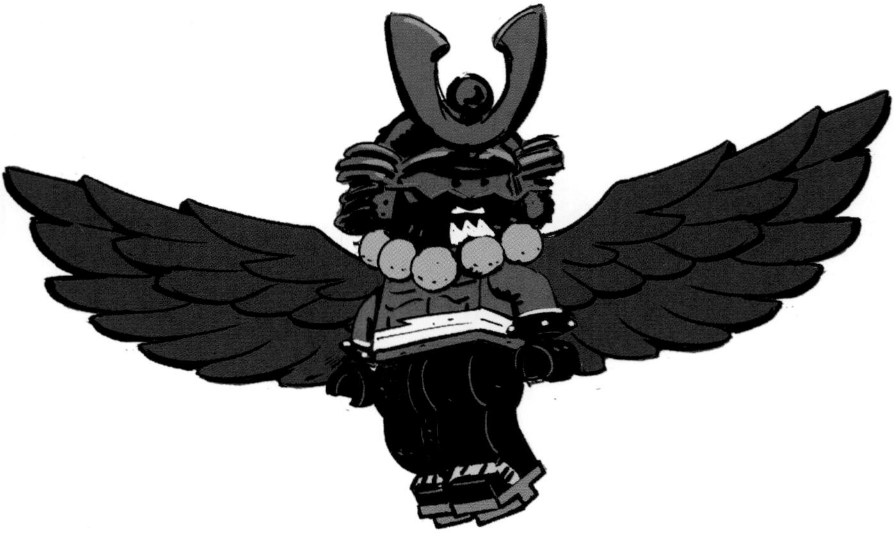

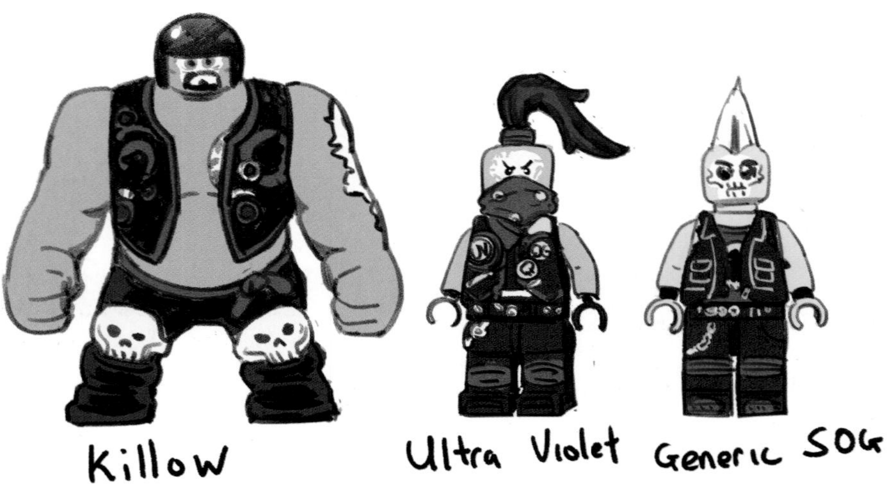
Killow
Ultra Violet
Generic SOG

The former Sons of Garmadon's designs are almost the same, but were revised to include their new logo and red trim.

TWO MOON VILLAGE

Water Mill

The design of humble Two Moon village incorporated design elements from the animated series and was also inspired by real life architecture such as the Fujian water mill in China.

Main Gate

As an Easter egg, Tri used the language of Ninjago to spell "store" on the boarded-up building seen in the Town Square image.

Town Square